BURNING MOUNTAIN

BURNING MOUNTAIN

DARCY TINDALE

PENGUIN BOOKS

UK | USA | Canada | Ireland | Australia
India | New Zealand | South Africa | China

Penguin Books is part of the Penguin Random House group of companies
whose addresses can be found at global.penguinrandomhouse.com

First published by Penguin Books in 2025

Cover images: photograph of rural landscape by Getty Images;
photograph of horses by Irina Mos/Shutterstock
Cover design by Christabella Designs © Penguin Random House Australia Pty Ltd
Typeset in 11/17 pt Sabon LT Pro by Midland Typesetters, Australia

Printed and bound in Australia by Griffin Press, an accredited
ISO AS/NZS 14001 Environmental Management Systems printer

A catalogue record for this
book is available from the
National Library of Australia

ISBN 978 1 76104 977 4

penguin.com.au

MIX
Paper | Supporting
responsible forestry
FSC® C018684

We at Penguin Random House Australia acknowledge that Aboriginal and Torres Strait
Islander peoples are the Traditional Custodians and the first storytellers of the lands on
which we live and work. We honour Aboriginal and Torres Strait Islander peoples'
continuous connection to Country, waters, skies and communities. We celebrate
Aboriginal and Torres Strait Islander stories, traditions and living cultures;
and we pay our respects to Elders past and present.

To Mum: who constantly asked for a happy ending.
So, they quaffed endless flutes of Veuve Clicquot,
rode Vespas into the sunset,
and all lived happily ever after.

To the reader: you already know this novel
isn't going to end well. Enjoy x.

A bush walker, with his dog in tow, steps off the main hiking track deciding to forge through the thick scrub of the National Park. He has no idea this seemingly insignificant decision to comb for wild-flowers will not only alter his day, but turn a town on its head.

He is a little more than forty kilometres from Muswellbrook, off the New England Highway and up Petwyn Vale Road, close to the Maiden Jewel Camping grounds. On a hunch, he takes a shortcut hoping to reach the cliff face along the mountain range, where he'll hunt for native flora.

He is only a few minutes into the bush, searching for rare orchids under the canopy of the tall ironbark trees, when the blue kelpie picks up a scent amongst the clump of scrub. The dog's paws trot along with pace, until it darts off along the dirt trail, faster, *faster*, tracking the smell through the dense bush, disappearing into the thick foliage.

The dog momentarily hesitates as its master calls for it to return, but the scent calls stronger.

It pants. Its muzzle drools. Eventually the kelpie stops with its nose to a dirt crater, and there it begins to dig in a flurry. The animal picks up the find and, buoyant, trots back with it towards its owner.

'Watcha got there, yah dopey bastard?'

The hiker wrestles the object from the animal's fangs. A second later he drops it to the ground.

'Fuck me dead! What in the name of, geez, crikey . . . stuff me!'

He swiftly nudges the animal away with his boot, wipes his hand – repeatedly – down his thigh and thinks he's going into cardiac arrest. The whole time he's still cursing, until he runs out of expletives.

The dog, stirred, confused and overexcited, barks and growls at the item. It takes more than a minute for the man to compose himself, then he snatches the dog by the collar and yanks it away. He gags at the thought of that *thing* being in his dog's mouth and knows, when he gets home, he'll be scrubbing its teeth with a bloody toothbrush.

As the bushwalker charges out of the scrub, dragging his dog through the undergrowth, a kookaburra begins to call. Its low hiccupping chuckle quickly turns into a raucous laugh, and it feels and sounds strange and oddly inappropriate. He presses on, only slowing to look back over his shoulder for a landmark, and sees a termite nest, a clump of Coolatai grass, and a patch of softly textured silvery-green leaves and bright yellow flowers – yellow buttons. He knows he'll remember the spot (how can he bloody forget it?), but it's the landmark of yellow flowers that he'll tell the cops to look for when they arrive.

Oblivious to the dog that has just altered his days to come, Bob Bradbury – Robert only to his late father – sits perched high on the scaffolding, docile and unaware of his impending undoing. He pulls a Winfield from his pack, settles his bum comfortably into the grooves of stacked bricks and lights his smoke. His back aches from another day of loading bricks, and a fresh blister, small and bubbly, red and raw – all thanks to the wobbly wheelbarrow – has swelled in the centre of his palm.

He looks at the bubble. Pinches the soft skin between his nails and makes a small hole at the edge of the blister, then gently squeezes out the clear fluid. He knows he should wash his hand, or swab the area with iodine, but he can't be bothered climbing down the scaffolding to get to the water tap or first-aid kit. Instead, he wipes his palm on his shorts, sits back in the shade and sucks on his smoke.

He scowls as he rolls out the aches in his neck and shoulders. The day's heat has made him lethargic, and with only half an hour before knocking off, instead of finishing the job he figures he'll kill the time hiding from the late-afternoon sun (and his boss).

At the top of the building, Bob looks out over Muswellbrook. The town is sliced in the middle by the main road, Muscle Creek, train line and golf course. Residential homes are divided by the A15, some boozy, poorly played rounds of golf, the noisy pond of frogs, and endless train carriages carrying coal.

Fucking coal.

Coal dust gets into everything in town. It darkens the sandstone, people's driveways, dirties windows and sours the mood of homeowners trying to keep their patios and poolside paving nice.

To Bob's far right, the tallest building is the Anglican Church with its soaring steeple and bell tower. To his left is his favourite pub. The Royal Hotel. Not as fancy as Eaton's, but its chicken parmigiana is bonza.

For once, it isn't the town's pub that holds Bob's attention. No, this other shop has prospects. This other shop has the potential to solve Bob's financial woes. The answer to his fuckonomics is in a simple shop that sells, of all things, fish.

Bob squirms his backside into the contours of the bricks like putty, draws back on his smoke and watches the seafood shop across the road.

It was a laugh when the town saw the sign go up. A little over a hundred kilometres from the nearest ocean, and some stupid bastard moves to town and decides to sell fresh seafood. It was the main topic for weeks down at the pub. Then sure enough, a month later the town had a fishmonger.

A few days after opening, curiosity got the better of them, and people started popping their head in, buying a snapper or some dory, half-kilo of prawns, and since no-one ended up in the local hospital, word got around town quick that this guy's fish was alright.

'Hard working,' they'd say.

'Bloody oath.'

'Is it fresh?'

'Must be. Hasn't killed me yet.'

Three days a week, in the early hours of the morning, the owner drives to Newcastle. Down the Golden Highway, flicking off onto the New England Highway, then landing in Wickham at the fishermen's co-op.

'Struth, you'd have to be keen.'

And he is.

The fishmonger is there and back, and within half an hour of returning, his ice display is layered with the next fresh instalment.

'Gets there first so he can select the best.'

'Nice piece of fish, if I say so myself.'

Everyone in town reckons that if the owner is willing to make the four-hour round trip to Newcastle and back, they're willing to buy.

A year after opening, the fishmonger and his wife have built up a roaring trade.

For three weeks Bob has been working on the building site labouring away, and for three weeks he's watched the little man go about his business in the shop across the road.

During the lunchtime rush there have been the stay-at-home mums buying chips for the kiddies to nibble on while they play in the park. Suits from the real estate, banks and council chambers buying grilled salmon and salad; the law firms going for chilli crab and fresh prawns, with black opal eyes and the odd spike that nicks fingers and stings like a paper cut; fat bastards ordering everything deep fried, and tradies walking out with Chiko Rolls and bottles of fizzy sugar drink, enough energy to kick in and see them through until knock-off time.

The only afternoon when the routine is altered is on a Wednesday.

Every Wednesday right on three, the little bloke kisses his wife goodbye, steps out the front door, lights up a smoke, slides it into the gap where he once had a tooth, and puffs on it like a steam train. He scuttles down the road, then down the side alleyway with two garbage bags, one in each hand. One bag, full of prawn shells, fish guts and other discarded oceanic crap, he tosses into the pale blue 'Cleanaway' dumpster. With the other garbage bag, fat and bursting with the week's cash takings, he hobbles across the road and disappears into the bank. Bob has watched that too. A week's worth of notes, silver and gold dough, all shoved in a bloody black garbage bag. Who would've guessed?

A fucking week's worth.

Bob smiles and thinks, *Someone oughta rob that guy*, then extinguishes his smoke against a brick, *and I reckon that someone oughta be me.* As he flicks the cigarette butt up into the air, he grins with confidence. *Easy as. What could possibly go wrong?*

Joe Thicket – also unaware that a dog has exposed an event that took place before he was even born – drags his feet, as he moves slowly down the footpath. In the days to come, for reasons he will never truly understand, this discovery will too weave across his path.

Unknowingly, he shuffles along; his schoolbag is heavy, and his mouth is dry. He can feel the warmth of the afternoon sun on his shoulders. The thin cotton school shirt is no shield against the relentless heat. The tips of his ears burn, but he doesn't hurry.

He idly kicks the long strips of stringybark that litter the footpath. He likes the leaf-stained patterns on the concrete. The swirls, the impressions the bark and leaves have left, are like fossils, marking time and place. Joe kicks at the bark like a lazy soccer player and scuffs the toe of his school shoe in the process.

Bugger.

There is no shoe polish at home, yet he knows that spit fixes everything. Spit to a child is like a measuring tape to a carpenter – the first tool to reach for. He crouches on the footpath and wets his index finger. It's warm and frothy, and he rubs the tip of his shoe. The saliva soaks into the synthetic leather and the scuff mark dissolves, disappearing almost like a magic trick.

Beside the boy's feet there is a frenzy of black ants busy racing about in unpatterned lines. There is a sense of urgency in their movement, and Joe feels annoyed, confused at why the ants need to rush, especially in the heat. He stands and places his foot above them, hovers a moment and then, in one stomp, he grinds the ants into the concrete.

Fossils, he thinks. *They are ant fossils now.*

Joe wipes the sole of his shoe on the gutter, scraping it clean, clearing his conscience along with the evidence. The air smells of lemony vinegar. The smell of dead ants.

Head down he moves along with haste, weaving between shadows and sunlight, between dogs barking behind gates and local newspapers rolled up and yellowing beside letterboxes, between weeds and patches of flowering groundsel, dodging cars parked in driveways, and garbage bins left on footpaths.

At last, he's home.

While his legs are thin, pale and gangly, they feel heavy as he steps up onto the patio of number thirteen Swiftlet Street. It's an unlucky number for a house. It's unlucky that it's his house. He stands at the front door and, in his haste to insert the key, scratches the wood. He licks his thumb and wipes away the crumbling paint.

He tries not to make a sound. It's late. Late. The school day ended long ago. He has wasted too much time dawdling, stalling to come home.

There is a soft click of the lock turning behind the wood, and he wants to say, *Shhh, shhh, door*. The door swings open without a sound, and he steps quietly into the darkness of the hallway.

Joe peers into the lounge-room. The blob in the armchair, with one stout leg hanging over the armrest, is his father, Trent Thicket, wreathed in a cloud of cigarette smoke. The smell irritates the boy's nose and stings his eyes. The haze is illuminated by the television. The ceiling is dull and stained like a prison cell. It is the colour of burned toast, chalking up the number of smokes it's absorbed.

Joe pauses.

He listens.

The old man is still breathing. Still got air in his lungs to suck back another smoke. To live another day. Still alive to fill the boy's days and nights with fear.

He squints, looking at the back of his father's shaved head. At the dips and bumps, searching for the indent. The bad depression. The dent that makes his father *snap*.

The boy runs his fingers through his own hair, feeling the shape of his skull, small and lumpy. He wonders which bump or dent in his head is the bad depression, the one that will make him *snap*, just like his father.

DAY 1

ONE

Rebecca Giles grabbed a bottle of beer from the fridge and flicked the top off with a spoon. The metal lid flipped in the air then hit the kitchen floor with a ting, before rolling under the fridge.

Ah, bugger.

It wouldn't be the only bottle top under there.

She leaned back against the kitchen bench and poured the golden liquid from the bottle into a tall weizen glass. But she was too quick, too greedy. The beer frothed and spilt over the side, dripping onto the floor tiles. With her foot, she mopped over the spill, using her sock to soak up the mess.

She had just returned from an afternoon run and was now pink-faced and thirsty; only instead of grabbing a bottle of water to quench her thirst, she had decided on a beer. As she raised the glass to her lips, her other hand lifted her long dark ponytail in the air and off her back. She could feel the sweat in her scalp, dripping down her neck and back, under her breasts. She contemplated whether she should hit the shower or finish the rest of her beer and help herself to a second. Mid-thought, she felt her mobile buzz against her thigh. She dropped her ponytail, fished around in the pocket of her tracksuit pants and looked grim-faced at the screen when she saw Detective Sergeant Bray's name. It was her last rostered day off. She wasn't due back at the station until morning.

She tapped the screen and Bray's voice barked, 'Where are you?' Bray had a habit of skipping greetings.

'Just back from a jog.'

'Where'd you run?'

'Outta town. Down along Kayuga Road.'

'Fair trek. Keepin' fit?'

'Uh-huh.' The beer was already back at her lips and her answer echoed inside the glass.

Bray was stalling, and he wasn't good at small talk.

'Whatcha doing right now?'

Here it comes.

Giles sculled until the glass was empty before answering. She held back a burp and looked down at her feet, squeezing her toes in her wet socks. Finally, she replied, 'Just doing my housework. Mopping the floor.'

'Yeah, well, it can wait.'

'You know it's my last day off, Bray.'

'Welcome back. I'll pick you up in ten.'

'What's happened?'

'Some mongrel mutt has found a bone out near Mount Wingen.'

'Huh! Lucky dog. Beats a Schmackos or a bully stick then. What kind of bone?'

'Skull.'

'What?'

'*Cranium.*'

'Human?'

'Presumed so. Ten minutes,' said Bray.

'Fifteen. I need a shower. Can't turn up in trackie daks and a sweatshirt.'

'The skull doesn't have eyes, Giles. It can't see what you're bloody wearing.'

'Bit unprofessional, don't you think, Sarge?' Giles tried to hide the smile in her voice.

'Ten,' repeated Bray. 'It can't smell either. Skip the shower, toss on a suit.'

And the phone went dead.

TWO

When Amy Thicket heard the front door unlock, she had tucked away the car registration papers in her hand and turned to greet her son, noting she had stood in the same spot for so long that her bare feet had almost glued to the sticky kitchen floor.

She had watched the boy walk into the kitchen, waited until he dropped his schoolbag to the floor and kicked off his shoes, before kissing the top of his head, smelling his hair, and feeling the day's heat that had cooked into his scalp. Now, as he sat at the kitchen bench, his arms folded, head resting on his forearms, she poured a glass of watery green cordial, then opened a packet of brand-name biscuits. The elastic band that had held the morning's local newspaper was now wound around a ponytail at the nape of her neck; strands of grey and chocolate-brown hair fell into her eyes. She puffed at them with good humour.

'Hot?' she asked.

The boy nodded.

'Missed you heaps today.'

'Really?'

'Bloody oath.'

'You always say that.' Joe rolled his face deeper into the crook of his arm.

Amy cocked her head. 'Yeah, I do, don't I?' She grinned, scrunching up her cheek. 'Because it's true. Missed you every second of my day. Now, pull your readers out of your schoolbag. You can read to me while I peel some veggies.'

As Joe slid off the stool to collect his homework, Amy asked, 'Do anything interesting today?'

'Nuh.' Joe shrugged. He dumped his books on the bench, then moved the packet of biscuits closer to his seat. 'What did you do?'

She sighed. 'Just my mornin' shift. Then . . . home.' She didn't tell her son that, after collecting the mail, she had stood by the kitchen bench for the rest of the afternoon staring at the car's green-slip notice and registration papers. That she'd been looking at them for so long the account balance was a blur. Or that the car had only two weeks of registration left before it was illegal to drive, before she'd get slapped with a fine or risk the cops seizing the vehicle. She had no idea where she'd get the money to pay the bills or any necessary repairs – and considering it was an old heap of shit, repairs were a definite possibility.

No, she couldn't explain any of it to her son. So, when she had heard the key in the front door, she had hidden the rego papers and green-slip notice behind the kettle and put a smile on her face.

'Anythin' else happen today, Mum?'

Finally, she answered, 'Hmm . . . nope. Other than work, nothin' much, really.'

Joe was quiet. She saw him look over her face. Then at her arms. She had a rosy welt on her forearm, beginning to yellow. It looked sore and inflamed. She'd forgotten to cover up. She had a thin cotton weave cardigan for moments like these. *Too bloody late now, he's seen it.*

Joe swallowed before asking, 'Was Dad okay today?'

Amy ruffled her son's hair in affection. She knew he was asking questions because he needed to know the mood of the evening. To put him at ease, she reassured him, 'Yeah. Yeah, course. He had a good day.'

Her eyes fleetingly sparkled.

Amy Thicket's face was surprisingly soft for a woman whose husband often behaved like a raging bull.

THREE

It was a little over a forty-minute drive from Muswellbrook to Mount Wingen. A straight run up the A15 on the New England Highway, only slowing down to pass through the towns of Aberdeen and Scone.

Detective Sergeant Bray was behind the wheel of the Sonata, while Giles sat in the passenger seat and watched the farms, horse studs and distant mountains flick by from the side window. Before Bray arrived to collect her, Giles made time for a quick shower and was now dressed in a black tailored suit and a white cotton blouse. Her long dark hair was twisted up in a clumsy French roll and her lips were glossed in a dewy plum. Her calf muscles still burned from her earlier run, and the quick beer and hot shower made her feel more like taking a nanny nap than investigating the possible discovery of human remains.

Giles adjusted the vents in the car, felt the cold air hit her arms and face like a slap. She needed to freshen up, wake up, focus. As a bug splattered the front windscreen, leaving a luminous yellow and gooey streak, she asked, 'You sure it's a human skull?'

Bray shrugged. His dark brows furrowed. 'That's what I've been told. Scone station got the call-out first, then called us in. Said they needed a couple of homicide detectives. So, I'm thinking they either believe the skull is real, or it's partial bone and they can't determine if it's animal or human, or it's someone's discarded Halloween decoration.'

Giles felt her arms tingle. 'If it is human, got any idea who it could be?'

'Nup. But if it *is* real, then on the bright side, we might be able to bring closure to a family. That could be someone's loved one out there in the bush.'

Giles knew of the heartache families endured when the whereabouts of a missing relative remained unknown. Without a body, there was no true sense of closure, only futile hope. She swallowed, sat back, and stared at the bug splatter on the front window.

Bray flicked the indicator and veered off the New England onto Petwyn Vale Road.

He asked, 'How polished is your knowledge of osteology?'

'Os-what?'

'That answers that, then,' Bray grunted. 'Inspector Falkov said if we're unsure of what we've found, we can send a photo to the forensic anthropologist.'

'Yeah, well, photos I can do.'

Ahead was a beat-up old ute and a police paddy wagon parked beside it. Bray pulled up alongside a scribbly gum for shade and killed the Sonata's engine. Giles checked the time and temperature on the dashboard, noted it in her pocketbook, then rummaged through her backpack for a pair of latex gloves and shoe covers. She shoved them in her pocket. Her loose bun was falling out, and wisps of dark hair brushed her cheeks. She tucked them behind her ear and said, 'Try not to look so grim when you talk to the bushwalking explorer – his afternoon has already turned to shit.'

Bray lifted his head; a forced smile flicked across his face then dropped just as quickly. Giles knew they both needed to work on their soft skills. Neither projected an air of approachability. In fact, Bray and Giles had earned a joint nickname, 'The Grim Reaper's cleaners', because of their dark hair and eyes, Bray's heavy brows – which looked like two furry frowning caterpillars – and Giles's normally icy carapace. It didn't help that they both preferred to wear black business suits to work either. Whenever they were assigned together, the other officers thought it was funny to hum Chopin's funeral march as they exited the station – even if it was just to pick up a sandwich for lunch.

Giles rubbed her cheeks in her palms, trying to soften and relax her face. She could feel the tension in her forehead already.

The clock on the dashboard now read four-twenty. She jotted down their exact GPS location in her notebook and then clicked her seatbelt; as it retracted, she felt like she had more space to breathe again.

'You happy to talk to the uniforms and witness?' Giles didn't wait for Bray to reply.

The moment she opened the car door, the heat smacked her in the face and the taste of dust was on her tongue. Two uniforms from Scone Police Station shook Bray's hand and led him to a man sitting in the open on a fallen log. He was dressed in shorts, t-shirt, hiking boots, thick woollen socks covered in spiky burrs, and no hat. Both he and his panting kelpie looked overheated.

'Took your bloody time.' The bloke sucked back on a rolled smoke and squinted into the sun as they approached him.

'Detective Sergeant Bray, and this is Detective Senior Constable Giles.' Bray shook the man's hand. 'Muswellbrook Police Station's a little more than fifty clicks, you know.'

The dog looked thirsty, and the bloke was sunburned on his nose, dry-lipped, and edgy.

'You out of water?' asked Giles.

'Yup,' replied the hiker.

'Didn't get an offer of a drink?' Giles's question was directed more to the young constables than the hiker.

'Nup.' The bloke scowled, scratching at his bare arms, leaving white streaks and flaky skin. His forehead shone pink.

'Let me get you both some water.' Giles turned and headed back to the Sonata for bottles. The dog needed a drink, and the guy needed a distraction – and some bloody shade. On her return, she tossed one bottle to the man, and twisted the lid off the other, slowly tipping the water into her cupped palm. The dog lapped it up.

'When you're ready, let's go stand in the shade,' said Bray. 'I'll need to get a few details.' He stood patiently, hands on his hips. His suit jacket had fallen open and as he leaned back into a stance it pulled his business shirt tight across his chest, showing off his solid torso and the span of his shoulders. Bray was an absolute unit.

The poor sorry bastard on the log had sensed Bray would be his only form of support. He'd already looked Giles over, and the way the corner of his lip twitched, then dropped when he met her eye, she knew he'd guessed she wasn't the type to tolerate banter about being a female cop at a crime scene.

'Where's the remains?' she asked one of the uniforms.

'Back there. In the bush. Down the track a bit.'

'You left it unattended?'

'Eh?'

'One animal's already picked it up and run off with it today.'

The uniform stuttered, 'I-I just thought –'

Giles cut the officer off and asked the bushwalker, 'Where exactly?'

The hiker thumbed over his shoulder. 'Down that way. Near a patch of yellow buttons and a termite nest. Can't miss it – the yellow buttons – I dropped the skull along the track.' He mumbled, 'Probably can't miss that either.'

Giles nodded, flashed him a comforting smile. *Poor bloke looks bloody shaken.* She stepped away and headed off down the trail, leaving Bray to interview the hiker and handle the uniforms and dog.

The area was cooler, shaded by the tall gum trees, and the ground was thick with clumps of grass, dried leaves, twigs, and fallen branches. Giles had walked for about five minutes, picking her way through the trail, and was deep into the scrubland when she spotted the tall, wedge-shaped termite mud mound and a cluster of yellow florets. She scanned the field of yellow buttons, before moving on further, where she pulled up abruptly and the bush seemed to go silent.

Jesus.

She crouched down and rummaged in her jacket pocket for a pen. By her feet, the skull lay turned up. Its lower jaw was missing. The bone was shades of brown and grey and green, stained over the years by soil and tree roots, before it was disturbed and pulled to the surface by either the dog or another animal first.

Giles didn't need to take a photo for verification. It was obvious it wasn't made of plastic, or tossed in the bush as a hoax. With the tip of her pen, she nudged the item and rolled it over. Dark soil was caked in the skull's eye sockets and nose. A clump of red clay clung to a cheekbone. It was like the skull was looking back at her, and Giles sighed, *Well, hello. Who might you be?* She took note of the size, the exposed coronial where the sutures connected, and the coloured staining of the bone. *How did you get out here?*

'Giles?'

'Up here,' she called back.

She listened to Bray crunching through the bush as he made his way down the grass-flattened track. At her side, he leaned over to take a closer look for himself. 'Shit. That's real.'

The moment of silence dissolved, and slowly the sounds of the bush seemed to return. Chirps, buzzing, trills, all pulsating and throbbing in her ears louder than before.

'What do you think? Child? Teen?' asked Bray.

'Not an adult.'

'Not an infant.'

'Juvenile, perhaps? Teenager?'

'At a guess, how old?'

'Dunno. Twelve, fourteen? No idea.' She pointed to where the sutures joined the bone around the top of the skull. 'Not fully formed or connected. Definitely not an adult.'

Bray stood up and stretched. He wiped the sweat from the back of his neck and winced. 'I was kinda hoping it was a prank. Dumb kids giving cops a wind-up.'

Giles also stood, tucking her pen back in her pocket and pulling out her phone. She took a couple of photos and sent them on to Inspector Falkov. Her text message was one word: *real*. As she waited for a reply, she asked Bray, 'What was that bloke doing out here, anyway?'

'Black-eyed Susans.'

'Huh?'

'Pinching pink bells and orchids. He's a native gardener. Cheaper to collect saplings from the bush than from the nursery. But native-plant theft isn't our priority, Giles. That is.' Bray pointed down at the skull and then surveyed the area around them. 'Where do you think the rest of it is?'

Giles shrugged. 'Not sure if a wild animal dragged this from another place and then the dog found it, or the rest of the skeleton is close by. Who knows how big the search scale could be?'

'I'll get Turner to start looking into missing persons. Bloody media is going to jump all over this. The moment they report we've found what we believe to be human bones off the side of the road, we'll have the press, the locals, and the Missing Persons Unit on our backs.'

'What are we gonna tell them?'

'Nothing yet. Just that we're waiting for forensic investigators to examine the scene and for the results of forensic testing to confirm.'

'Nah, we'll come across as dickheads.' Giles laughed. 'Seriously, anyone could confirm just by looking at it.'

'Then we'll make sure no-one else *can* look. Let's clear the zone and seal it. This area is now a crime scene. I'll put one of the uniforms out here to keep an eye on this.' Bray flicked his hand at the skull. 'I wanna try and keep the buzz of this discovery down to a simmer. I'd like to know what we're dealing with first, before giving too much away.'

FOUR

Bob Bradbury picked at the fresh blister. It was sore and tender, but he wasn't in any real pain. He thought of his father. His dad was a brickie, whose hands were like bricks themselves. Great mass of callus chunks, they were. When he was a boy, his old man never gave him the strap, just the hand.

Tha-woomp.

It stung like buggery. Across his thighs, in his guts and would burn his eyes.

Bob sneered at the memory. He spat white foam onto the blister and rubbed in the saliva. The wet and the wind cooled the now pink and heated area, and he felt a moment of relief overtake the bitterness.

His face was angular, jaw and cheekbones defined. Brown eyes, large and lined with dark lashes. When he was out in public, his face made women take a second look; only Bob was forever staring at his feet, and the world around him was merely a blur of colour, noise and movement. Was it lack of confidence, or lack of interest?

The building supervisor looked up and saw Bob sitting on the brick pile. He cleared his throat and hollered, 'What's up with you?'

'Huh?'

'Fair dinkum, Bob, you ain't even packed up and it's gone five already. Overtime's bloody over.'

'Five, hey?'

'Yup. Five-o-two, to be exact. You lookin' for brownie points or is your watch slow? Go on, piss off and get outta here. It's quittin' time.'

Bob pulled himself out of the brick pile. His thighs felt numb and tingled from the short spell. He called back down to the supervisor, 'Shit hey, must have been daydreamin'. Thanks, boss.'

The supervisor didn't answer. Instead, he mumbled to the ground, 'Daydreamin'. Is that what you call it? I'd say it was just plain slackin' off. Bloody overtime for staring at your navel.' He continued muttering to himself all the way back to the small demountable office.

Bob was normally packed up and ready to shoot through ten minutes before the boss had called it quits. But he'd lost track of time, preoccupied thinking about the fishmonger. It didn't take him long to climb down the scaffolding, collect his stuff and wash his face and hands under the tap. He swung his work bag up over his shoulder. Gave the building supervisor a nod through the window as he stepped over broken bricks, bits of lumber and offcuts and made his way towards his car.

Bob smiled sincerely for the first time all day as he jumped into his Torana and smelled the Armor All that had been cooking into the dash. He patted the steering wheel affectionately – and burned his hand.

'Shit!'

He'd forgotten to put the sun shield across the windscreen in the morning; now he could hardly grasp the steering wheel, it was so bloody hot. Inside the cabin, it felt like a hundred degrees. He cranked the window and turned over the engine. The SLR 5000 rumbled. The engine had a slight misfire, but nothing that a tune-up couldn't fix – once he had some spare cash.

He flicked his better half a text, telling her, 'leaving work – home soon – stopping at pub for a quick frothy.' Then he filled the next two lines with 'x's. The text sent, within a few minutes the Torana rumbled down the main road. The only thing that had improved the value and appearance of the car since the day it had been purchased was a wash. When he first bought the car, which had spent years rusting away in a farm shed neglected, his head was full of 'round-to-its' and 'gonna-do's'. The old cockie wanted the space and the car gone, so Bob paid a tuppence to clear it out of his shed. There was so much dirt in the boot he wondered if he could grow wheat in it. But the car polished up nice and the credit card paid for a tow and a new set of tyres. It had potential. He had big dreams for it, and he was proud of it.

Bob was all smiles as he thought, *A little bit of cash. And I might give the car a tune-up, and finally get that ring on the hand.*

At last, he felt like his life was getting on track.

. . . A ring. That's it. I'm doin' it. I'm popping the question. Both brows raised at the thought. *Bloody hell!*

It was something he felt he could finally achieve. A purpose and a direction. *A fucking goal.* Something that a garbage bag full of cash could help make happen.

The houses were set back on large blocks, concealed by the streetscape of trees. Oaks, wattles and jacarandas obscured the view from the residents' windows.

Bob had no intention of stopping at the pub. That was a lie – but the kisses were honest. Instead, he parked his noisy car at the end of the road under a jacaranda. The trees were in full bloom, and bursts of purple dotted the township and fragranced the air.

The blue-purple tubular flowers had littered lawns, footpaths and –
after a few gusts of wind – Bob's car roof and bonnet.

The town loved their jacaranda trees, apart from the council street
sweeper, who constantly called the local radio station to complain
that the litter of buds made the roads and footpaths dangerously
slippery when wet. *You'll be chopping the bastard things down the
moment someone has a bloomin' accident!* But the trees still stood
and merrily painted the town in shades of violet and blue.

Bob figured that the canopy of the tree, with its cluster of flowers,
was a reasonable spot to hide his Torana. And from the back end of
the alleyway, it would be easy to make a quick return to the vehicle.

On foot, Bob ambled down the path towards the laneway
between the fish shop and the library, to see if his idea was plausible. He wanted to step it out. A walk-through of his plan. Count
the steps from the dumpster in the laneway back to the car. Maybe
even run and time it.

His vision was simple. Snatch. Run. Drive.

Can't be that easy? Can it?

Bob shook his hand, shaking off the dull throb in his palm,
annoyed by the distraction. He needed to think through his scheme.
Perhaps enact how his plan would play out.

At the dumpster, he raised the lid and peered inside, his stomach
jolting from the smell. The lid felt greasy and slippery in his hand.
He let it go and listened to it clang shut and echo. Then he sniffed his
palm, balked at the stench, and wiped it across his chest. Bob turned
and looked for places to hide, then walked back down the laneway.

*Snatch and run. Just grab the bag. And don't look the fishmonger
in the eyes. That's all you've gotta do.*

He lifted his wrist, tapped the starter button on his cheap
digital watch to count the seconds, then ran as fast as he could
back towards his car.

FIVE

Bray tapped his phone, ending the call with Inspector Falkov, as Giles slinked under the police tape. 'Forensic anthropologist and a forensic archaeologist are being sent. They're on their way up from Sydney. ETA is anyone's guess. I wouldn't expect them to land here for at least another couple of hours.'

'Two?'

Bray shrugged. 'Anthropologist for the body, archaeologist for the excavation.'

'We don't have a body, just a skull.'

'That's why they're coming.'

The gravity of what had been found was starting to sink in. A discomfort had settled over them, the pending wretchedness ahead of the investigation. If it wasn't death by misadventure, it was the burden of unravelling the wickedness that would have taken place, uncovering the events that had cost a life and left a skull behind for a dog to find.

Giles shuffled her feet, nudged the tufts of grass with the tip of her boot. The only thing that brought her comfort was that somewhere a family member or friend might finally be able to lay a loved one to rest. Giles sniffed and could feel the dust up her nose.

'Do you want to call in the local patrols or the State Emergency Service volunteers to search the area? See if we can find anything?'

'Nah,' said Bray. 'I want to keep it contained for the moment, undisturbed until our experts arrive. I'd rather give them a clean slate to work with, not one we've trampled all over thinking we could be helpful, but instead made their job harder. They'll know what they're looking for. Then, if they need the troops, we'll call them in.'

'Hmm. Do you know them, the forensic team?'

'Nup. This is the first time I've come across a skeleton, Giles. You?'

Giles shook her head. 'Decayed bodies, yes, skeleton, nah.'

'Most deceased I've dealt with have been in the early stages,' said Bray. 'With that pink-white appearance, skin slippage and some hair loss. A couple of times advanced decomposition. You know, purging of decompositional fluids out of their eyes, ears, nose and mouth.' Oblivious to Giles's discomfort, he elaborated, 'Bloating, skin leathery and dark. Still smell the scenes when I think of them. Then there was that girl you found in the cattle trough . . .'

'Okay . . . okay!' said Giles.

She winced, rolled out the tension in her shoulders, and pushed away the images of her last case. 'Guess it's a good thing we've got authorities joining our team.' She knew the consequence of incorrect procedures. It could mean not finding justice for the victim, and she felt some assurance knowing experts were on their way.

Bray frowned. 'We haven't met them yet. Let's wait until they arrive and then make up our minds. They'll want to assess the area, then get started first thing in the morning.'

Giles looked out across the bushland at the presumed radius of where a gravesite could be. 'It looks so peaceful. Beautiful.'

'Peaceful now, but if they find the site, this area will be a mess once the dig is underway.'

There was a musty tang in the air. Giles breathed in the faint smell of mulched leaves, of dry wood and the earthy soil. She listened to the hum of flies, crickets and other insects she couldn't identify. There was the sound of rustling leaves in the canopy above as the subtle wind drifted through the branches. She noticed the melodic calls of birds. Took note of the bright yellow buttons and the grey twists and ribbons of fallen bark, accepting that it would all look, smell and sound different within a day.

'I've placed the uniforms to secure the site until our forensic experts arrive. Don't want another animal picking up the skull. Detective Callahan is about ten minutes away – he'll keep the media calm if any turn up. Personally, I'd like to get a headstart before the technicians. A jump.' Bray finally smiled. 'You hungry?'

'A bit.'

'If I don't take the opportunity to grab a bite to eat now, I have a feeling it'll be hours before I get another chance. Callahan can tag in while we grab a meal, keep the site secure until the team from Sydney arrives. Let's go out to Denman and have a steak.'

'Denman? Long way for a steak.'

'Turner can pick me up from there later, bring me back.'

'I'm not coming back to the scene?'

'Nup.' Bray's smile fell. 'Come back in the morning. After dinner, you can visit your father.'

'You want me to ask him for help?'

'No.' Bray poked his finger into Giles's shoulder. '*You* want to ask him for help.'

Aside from the odd Thai takeaway and visit to the drive-thru bottle-o, Giles hadn't ventured out much since moving to Muswellbrook more than a year ago. She had kept to herself, socialising mostly with her team; and even then, that was sporadic.

The pull to return to Sydney still felt strong. She had fought against feeling settled in the country town, not wanting to get too acquainted and comfortable in its surroundings. She didn't want to start calling Muswellbrook home. She had returned only to spend time with her father – the change of pace and outlook was a bonus, but it wasn't a lifestyle change. Not a permanent change. As pitiful as it felt, she knew she would only be in the Hunter Valley for the length of time it took for her father to succumb to his illness.

Still, Giles missed her city life. Late nights jogging over the Harbour Bridge. She loved the subtle tremor and vibrations under her feet as the bridge rattled from trains and eight lanes of cars. The bridge she now jogged across after dark was one lane over the Hunter River. Bondi Beach was replaced with the Hunter Beach, sandstone blocks instead of sand dunes down by the meandering stream. Country kids didn't look out for rips or dumping waves, but turtles and snakes. And replacing the brilliant city nightscape, she had the open-cut mine, its twinkling lights and moving beams from the front-end loaders and excavators that loaded up coal twenty-four-seven to be transported and processed.

After Bray had talked her into a steak – *A girl's gotta eat* – she entered the pub in Denman with a feeling of trepidation. It was another place she'd tried to avoid, to stop herself sinking deeper into country life and a return to her roots.

Bray paused and said, 'Now, Giles, you might think it's the chicken parmigiana or the rack of ribs you should go for, but I'm telling you, steak. It's perfectly chargrilled over hot coals and full of iron. It'll help build up those muscles of yours. This is my treat – you just pick your choice of gravy, and I'll sort the rest.'

'Mushroom.'

Bray gave her a look of scorn. He loosened his tie, undoing the top button and said, 'Peppercorn's better.'

'No, it isn't. I'll grab the beers.'

Bray made a beeline for the back of the pub where the bistro was situated. Giles headed towards the bar, quickly swallowed up in the muffled chatter and bursts of laughter bouncing off the rustic brick walls and wooden floor. She weaved her way through the pool tables where a couple of tradies were playing a robust game of pool. Balls clicked, and cheers were followed with dirty banter and backslaps.

The two types of men in the pub were obvious. Fluoro sticks and jackaroos. The reflective strips on the tradies' and miners' work shirts weren't needed. Giles had already spotted them, and the farm boys' R.M. Williams boots and belts were what separated them. Giles took note of the pocketknives in leather pouches that sat on the farm boys' hips, worn like a badge: stock knives with blades for hoof paring and another to castrate cows, or gut rabbits from rib cage to pelvis.

The tradies' arms were honey sun-kissed in colour, where the farm boys' were butter pecan and brown sugar. Giles liked their bare arms and calf muscles; maybe she should visit the pub more often.

Keep your toes in your shoes and socks, girl, she told herself, then dropped her head and grinned at the floor.

At the other end of the pub, she stood at the bar, hot and thirsty, and could almost taste the schooner of beer before she had it in her hand.

Behind the wooden benchtop, the barmaid looked Giles up and down. There was a hint of recognition on both faces. A sense of familiarity. Flashes of forgotten memories.

Giles was the first to acknowledge it. 'Hey, Carol.'

'Geez, well, I'll be stuffed! It's Benjamin Giles's kid, right? Rebecca? Is that you? All grown up?'

Giles smiled. 'Yeah, it's me.'

'Well, give us a twirl. Let me see how much you've grown.'

Giles stepped away from the counter and did a fancy princess spin, a half-curtsey, head cocked to the side. All she could think was, *Carol. Bloody Carol. All these years and she's still pulling beers for the boys.*

She remembered Carol Raleigh from when she was a kid, sitting in the Ford, waiting for her father to finish a few beers inside the pub; slumped in the back seat sweating, thirsty. She'd be thinking, *Dad'll bring me a lemonade soon, surely. He's been in the pub forever. It's hot out here. Come on, just a lemonade, Dad, please, please.*

Then good old Carol would spot Giles in the car and yell to her old man, 'Either go home or give that kid a bloody drink, you lousy bastard!'

Giles would get a glass of cold lemonade, and her father would get another hour in the pub.

Yep, good old Carol. Her cheeks were now round and rippled like two fat mandarins. She'd changed – her hair was greyer, and she was a little plumper – but her smile was the same.

'God damn, kid, I think it's been almost twenty years since I last saw you.'

'Yeah, about that.'

'Where have you been?'

Giles felt herself shrink a little. After her six senior years of private boarding school in Sydney, she'd obtained her UCWE at uni, entered Goulburn academy, graduated, and spent the last ten years policing in the city.

She cleared her throat. 'Sydney. Put in for a transfer and came back home a little over a year ago. I'm at Muswellbrook Police Station now.'

'Yep, knew that. Followed your last case. Was in all the news-papers.'

Giles was aware of the reputation she'd gained from that case. Did Carol think she was a reckless cop who pulled her gun and just kept shooting until the job was done, or the hero who caught a killer?

'Yeah . . . well . . . here I am.' Giles slapped her palms on the bar top.

'The bush will always pull you back, honey. You might have changed your leaves, sprouted fresh blossoms, but your roots are still here.'

Giles only grinned. She didn't have the heart to tell Carol she hadn't returned to her roots by desire. But Carol was still looking her over, and Giles shifted a little, uncomfortable at the stare.

'Damn me.' Carol smiled. 'You're the spitting image of your mother.'

The grin on Giles's face froze. *Shit. Of course Carol would have known her mother. Carol was born in Denman, never left. Still owned and ran the pub.*

Carol, catching the flash of pain in Giles's eyes, said, 'Sorry, love. Thirty years feels like yesterday to an old chook like me.' Then she switched topic. 'How's your father?'

'Good, still in Merton Court, because of his . . . you know.'

'Yep, I know.' Carol picked up an empty schooner glass – it was chilled and frosted. 'What will it be?'

'Surprise me. Make it two. My partner's ordering some meals.'

'Take a seat. I'll bring it over. On the house, as a welcome home gift.'

Nodding gratefully, Giles stepped away from the bar and found a quiet table for two in the corner by the window. She took a seat with her back to the rest of the establishment.

As she waited for Bray to return, she looked at her reflection in the large window. She recalled her mother's features from the few old photographs she had stared at a million times. Giles had her mouth, heart-shaped, full and round with a cupid's-bow top lip. She also had her mother's thick dark hair and dark brown eyes. She was only a few months old when her mother died, and she had no real idea what sort of person her mum had been, aside from the much-loved wife of Superintendent Benjamin Giles.

And while the loss of her mother had left a feeling of emptiness, it was the thought of losing her father that now sat heavy in her stomach.

It was a little after six and the pub was starting to fill with miners and contractors looking for a meal. It had been almost three hours since the skull had been found and while the uniforms and Detective Senior Constable Callahan were keeping the scene secure until the forensic anthropologist and archaeologist arrived, Giles knew it would be days of collecting evidence for the team to analyse; weeks, possibly months before there would be a positive identification of the skeletal remains. So a steak at the pub didn't seem like such a bad idea. She and Bray could use the time to debrief and agree on what steps they'd need to take next.

Bray returned to the table, his hands full. He dropped a set of forks and steak knives with a clank, along with a scrunched-up bunch of serviettes and salt and pepper shakers.

Giles immediately began to rearrange the utensils and condiments neatly. As she refolded the napkins, she asked, 'So, what have we got?'

'T-bone.'

'No, the case.'

'Oh, Turner's at the station running missing persons – going back the last twenty to thirty years around the area.'

'The skull still had its top teeth.'

Giles knew that different teeth formed at various points during childhood, and certain bones in the skeleton remodelled at different rates, but that was the extent of her knowledge, and she wasn't sure if any of it was useful. They desperately needed the forensic team from Sydney to match the teeth with dental records to help determine the age, and possibly the identity.

'So, you agree that the skull is a youth?'

'Yeah, I do.' Giles nodded. 'Early teens.'

'I think it's a fair guess it's an adolescent, however I told Turner to start his search from aged eight up. Don't want to miss anything.'

'There was a crack in the skull, close to the eye socket.'

'Skull could have been damaged by a wild animal, resulted from scavenging, or cracked from a tree root while in the ground?'

'Or the cause of death?'

'Forensic team can confirm that. Let's wait until Turner finishes consolidating the list of missing persons. I'd say the victim was buried more than ten years ago. Otherwise, it would ring a bell. Since I've been at the station, I've not known of any missing kids. Falkov recalls an incident almost twenty years ago. Didn't say much, said he'd pull the file.'

'From the area? The Upper Hunter?'

'Yeah. Strange how it hasn't become an urban legend. You know, a bogeyman story of a real missing kid that parents can tell, to stop their child from nickin' off or hitchhiking.'

'Maybe people have forgotten.'

'In this town? Nah. They have long, long memories.'

'Yeah, I just witnessed that at the bar.' She glanced over her shoulder. Carol was loading beers on a tray, and Giles knew if she needed someone with a long memory, a good memory, and perhaps even an unbiased memory, Carol would be the first on her list to interview.

'Our unidentified person could be a child from the city,' added Bray. 'Interstate. And Mount Wingen was just the dumping ground.'

'Do you think it was an abduction and dumping?'

Bray lugged his big shoulders up and down in an effort to shrug. 'Hmm, hard to imagine a kid delirious and lost in the bush with heatstroke. Not with so many farms nearby, campers and hikers, plus with the highway a little more than a half-hour walk. Not really in the middle of nowhere, is it?'

'Nup,' agreed Giles. 'Only after all these years on the job, I've learnt sometimes the strangest shit that makes no sense at all can still happen.'

'Then let's keep open to all possibilities,' he grinned, as Carol arrived at the table with two schooners.

'Thanks, Carol. You didn't have to.'

'Nah, it's nice to see you back home.' The pub owner tipped her head. 'Tell your dad I'm still waitin' for him to pop into my watering hole for a beer.'

Giles scrunched up her nose. 'You know the doctors have told him not to drink anymore?'

'Yeah, well then, tell him he's *not* bloody welcome here. Christ, I'll lose my business and my reputation if I start serving water. I've already got enough tourists and hippies drinkin' mocktails and bloomin' expresso martinis. This is a pub – give me back the good old days of real beer-drinking men. Nowadays they waltz into the bar askin' for lolly-flavoured alcohol with ridiculous bloody names. If you want butterscotch or cotton candy, go to the sweet store. I ask myself sometimes, is this a pub or a confectionery shop?' She tipped her head towards the beers on the table and, in a rubbish attempt at an Italian accent, said, 'Well, *salute!*' before the Aussie twang crept back. 'Enjoy the beer.'

'*Cin cin*,' said Giles, as she raised her glass up at Carol, who flashed a smile and patted her shoulder, then headed back to the bar.

Giles lifted her beer higher in the air. Bray met it with a chink of his glass and they gulped, thirsty from the hot day. Both were secretly pleased they had a beer in their hand and not a cocktail.

Giles wiped the white foam from her lips. 'Carol hasn't changed a bit in twenty years.'

'Nah, you're wrong. Carol has changed *a lot* in the last two decades. Just like the pub, she's been revamped and remanaged by two different husbands.'

'Really?' Giles laughed.

'Yeah, now eat.'

The waiter from the bistro had arrived with two plates loaded with fries, salad and a whopping steak drowning in peppercorn gravy.

'Peppercorn? I asked for –'

'Kitchen ran out of mushrooms,' Bray smirked. Giles watched him cut a great chunk from his T-bone. With a mouth full, he asked, 'Aside from the obvious, what questions have you got for the great Superintendent Benjamin Giles?'

Giles looked down at her meal, steaming on the table. While her father had left the force almost two years earlier because of his illness, the crimes team still spoke of him in the present. She picked up her knife, stabbed the steak, and said, 'It's not the questions. I'm worried he might not have the answers.'

SIX

Belinda Marrone – Bell to her friends – stood at the laundry basin. She dabbed cotton balls in rubbing alcohol and scrubbed at her skin and nails. The pastel acrylic paint seemed more stubborn than usual. She had spent the afternoon painting birdfeeders that she sold on weekends at market stalls. The feeders were artistic – circus and high-tea themed. When she painted, it wasn't the person who purchased them, but the birds themselves that she created the intricate designs for. She marvelled at the hierarchy in the bird world. Once the feeder was filled with seed, the pecking order ran in size. The bigger species bullied the smaller species off the feeder plate, winning prime position and first choice of grain. The sulphur-crested cockatoos were at the top of the pecking order. Bell loved the cockatoos, but she also thought they were nasty, selfish pricks so she would tint her yellow paint, dulling its brightness. Her way of putting the bullying birds back in their place.

As she dried her hands on an old rag, she heard the hum of an engine. She knew that sound. The sound of her man coming home. She swayed to the noise of the car changing gears. Her floral boho dress twirled, the flowy fabric wrapping around her thighs.

Bell dumped the rag and left the laundry as the car pulled into the driveway. Out at the kitchen bench she stuffed a powdery marshmallow in her mouth to sweeten her breath. She combed her frizzy hair, the colour of a muddy puddle, with her fingers, untangling the knots at the ends and twisting the tips into loose curls. She shook the thin straps off her shoulders, tugged down the dress, lowering the neckline, showing more skin, then elegantly propped herself against the kitchen bench.

The front door swung open, and Bob stood in the doorframe looking like he had put in more than a day's work. Dirt in the smile lines of his eyes, dust drawing the edges of his nostrils, stain of sweat under his armpits and prickly hair around his chin. Bell loved a man with a bit of gruff on his face. She watched him look her over, his grin at her poised stature, then she ran towards him, and Bob dropped his tool bag to the floor just in time to catch her jumping into his arms. She wrapped her thighs around his waist.

'Give us a kiss,' said Bell, linking her fingers behind his neck.

Bell knew she was heavy, but Bob held her up with his hands under her bottom. He took her kiss until he couldn't hold her any longer, then gently let her go and she slid to the ground.

'Hungry?'

'Starvin'. What's for dinner?'

Bell cocked her head. 'Pumpkin soup.'

'Nice.'

'Soup's from a tin.'

'I'm sure it'll be great.'

She smiled, spun on her heels. As she skipped back into the kitchen, she called over her shoulder, 'Got some fresh bread rolls too.'

'Nice.'

Bob dropped his head. Rubbed at the swelling in his palm. He hated tinned soup. But he loved Bell.

SEVEN

'Well, stiffen the wombats, what are you doing here, love?'

Visiting hours at Merton Court were long over, but the nurses at the age-care facility had let Giles sneak in. It was one of the perks of being a cop.

Giles had found Benjamin sitting in a comfy recliner in the corner of the communal lounge-room. A woollen crochet blanket of patch-work squares in gaudy, clashing colours was draped over his legs. It made Giles wonder if the maker of the blanket was colourblind – or were they the only balls of wool they could find?

'See you've come empty-handed. Lucky the staff take care of me.' Benjamin had a plastic mug of milky tea in one hand and cake crumbs were sprinkled down the front of his shirt.

'Might have a dried-out mint in the car console. You want that?'

Benjamin licked his finger and dabbed at the icing sugar sprinkled on his blanket. 'Nah, I'll stick with titbits and woolly fuzz, ta, love.'

'No worries.' Giles bent down and kissed the top of her father's head, which he brushed at like he was swatting away a fly. She grinned, then plonked down in the recliner beside him, leaned back and stretched out her long legs, hooking her ankles together. They both faced the large bay window that looked out onto a rockery lit with dim garden lights.

'What are you drinking?' asked Giles.

'Old ale. Would prefer a Guinness.' Benjamin winked, raising his plastic mug of tea in the air. 'Been sitting here drinking with the flies. Can I offer you the last slice of sponge cake?' His shaky hand reached out and lifted the plate from the coffee table, the cake almost sliding off.

Giles grabbed the plate from her father and put it back down.

She and Benjamin never talked much of his declining health, even though it had been two long years since he was first diagnosed with Amyotrophic Lateral Sclerosis. She had watched his deterioration with despair. His twitching, his cramping muscles and his struggle to walk were rarely discussed between them. ALS would eventually affect Benjamin's speech, swallowing and breathing, and although he had some difficult days, he could still breathe without assistance and talk coherently. His mind was razor sharp. There was no putting Benjamin back in the knife drawer, and that kept Giles's spirits up.

'Nah, I just ate a whopping steak at the pub.'

'Steak, hey? Why didn't you come and pick me up? Take me with you?'

'What? To eat a steak?'

They both knew there were limitations to what Benjamin could consume.

'I could have watched you eat the steak! It would've been just as enjoyable.'

'No, it wouldn't. Not for me.' Giles scrunched her face.

'Not all about you, love.'

'Hmm.' Giles frowned, gave him a fake disapproving stare, then changed the subject. 'Guess who I bumped into?'

Benjamin gave a small shrug. 'Wouldn't have the foggiest.'

'Carol Raleigh. I can't believe she remembered me.'

'Just because you left the Hunter Valley doesn't mean I stopped talking about you, Rebecca. Course she'd know you – I bragged about you enough to wet her ear.'

Giles couldn't hide her smile. 'Gee, it took me back. And you know what, it reminded me of when I was a kid, and you'd leave me in the car to have a beer at the pub. Back in the days when you *could* leave kids unattended in vehicles.'

'You were ten, not a bloody baby, plus the windows were down. I wasn't baking you in the bloomin' car – you could've got out and sat under a tree.'

As a single father, Benjamin Giles had struggled at times between parenting, policing and the pub. Actually, he'd struggled with lots of things: housework, washing, making proper meals. He didn't have many relatives' or friends' homes to visit, so she didn't have much to compare their lifestyle with. She thought the bottles that stacked up on the kitchen bench, the unmade beds, her crooked ponytails that he grappled to tie and would yank out strands of her hair every time he tried – as well as the regular visits to the pub – were all part of a normal childhood.

'I liked her back then,' Giles said. 'I reckon she'd make a good friend. God knows I don't have many in this town.'

'You can like the people in this town, Rebecca, but you can't get close to them. Not when you're a cop.'

Giles succumbed to the sugar temptation, peeling the top layer from the slice of cake and popping it in her mouth. As she chewed, she switched topic; her dad was sounding a little irritable. 'Got any plans tomorrow afternoon?'

'Thought I'd saddle up the emu and go for a ride downtown in the morning, but I've got the afternoon free.'

Giles smiled. She deserved that crack. 'I was thinking of taking you for an outing, if I manage to get a break. Check you out of Merton Court for an hour or two – change up the scenery a bit.'

And she'd know more about the case by the morning. Detective Turner would have an update from Missing Persons, and the two forensic officers might have a clearer idea on the age of the skull. She could pop in for another visit and update him. Benjamin Giles's forty years on the police force were always a valuable resource, plus his knowledge of the town's history kept her looking at cases from all angles. ALS might have made Benjamin retire from the force, but Giles still valued his knowledge. In many ways, she considered him a silent partner of the Crimes Unit Team.

Benjamin was one step ahead of her. He wiggled his index finger towards her face. 'You've got a fresh case.'

'Yup.'

'And you need your old man.'

'I always need you, Dad. You know that.'

'Well? Go on. Spill the tea.'

'Falkov's called in a forensic anthropologist and archaeologist.'

Benjamin tried a low whistle, only it was light and airy, more like an out-of-breath exhalation. 'Found yourself some skeletal remains, huh?'

Giles nodded.

'You know who they're sending out?'

'Not yet.'

'Where?'

'Out near Mount Wingen. Well . . . a dog found them. Ran off into the bush, came back with a skull.'

'Wingen? Geez, bloody Wingen, hey? Hope someone gave that dog a treat.'

'It got a pat and a drink of water.'

Benjamin huffed. 'Quite the find. Did you see the skull?'

'Not official, but Bray and I were thinking maybe a teenager, early teens. The sutures on the top of the skull where the flat bones interlocked at the edges still had gaps, not completely closed, so younger than thirty.' That was where her expertise ended. 'The skull has been there a long time, Dad, so now we're pulling up files on missing persons from twenty to thirty years.'

'Huh.'

'You got any thoughts?'

'A few.' Benjamin went quiet. He looked out over the dimly lit garden bed and brushed the last of the crumbs off the blanket. 'Any trauma to the skull bone?'

'Yeah, but no idea if it's related to a potential assailant, or from the environment.'

Benjamin nodded, taking a moment to mull over the discovery. Eventually, he turned back to Giles and said, 'A kid went missing out that way, almost twenty years ago.'

'From Mount Wingen?'

'Nah. From Burning Mountain, close enough to Mount Wingen.'

Giles felt hopeful. She might just have herself a name. An identity. She breathed in deep, then asked, 'Who?'

'Oliver. Oliver Lavine.'

Giles sat quiet for a moment. It was as though the child's name was sinking into all the corners of the room, seeping into the furniture. She repeated his name in a whisper. 'Oliver.'

'Yeah,' murmured Benjamin. 'Christ, it was a difficult time. The kid's mother, Janet Lavine, she just wouldn't give up on her son. She either came into the station, rang, or cornered officers whenever she saw them in town to ask what progress had been made. She stuck up posters, ran an ad in the newspaper on the anniversary of him missing, even saw a few clairvoyants. But after nearly four years, with nothing new to tell her, she realised the case had gone cold. She gave up on us – and let us bloody know it too! Then she sold up and left the pain and memories behind. Moved to Crookwell, I think.'

'Did you give up?'

'Never. But hope is a strange thing, love.'

Since her father's illness, hope was something both Giles and Benjamin clung to. Only she knew too well that hope waned and faded, it stretched and shrank. It changed into something else. Desolation.

'How old was the kid?'

'Almost fifteen,' said Benjamin. 'Ninth grade in high school.'

Giles did the maths. Oliver Lavine was the same age as her, only she was at boarding school in Sydney. The name didn't ring a bell, nor did the story of his disappearance. But she'd been engrossed in her new school, her friends, school activities. She swallowed down the taste of raspberry and cream that still lingered in her mouth. 'How did he go missing?'

'It was the start of the school holidays. Around the first weekend in April 2006. Oliver and four friends went for a hike up Burning Mountain, followed the trail to the lookout. Five went up the mountain, four came back.'

'So there were witnesses when he went missing? Or suspects?'

'Not really. At the top of the mountain, they parted ways. The group got into an argument of sorts, didn't all come back down the mountain together. Somewhere along the way, Oliver Lavine disappeared.'

Giles was confused, but cautious not to undermine her father. 'And the mountain was searched?' she asked lightly.

'Thoroughly.'

Giles bit her lip.

'From Wingen to Murulla,' added Benjamin.

'Were the friends ever suspects?'

'Nuh. They were kids. After the argument, Oliver took off, and when they got to the bottom of the mountain, he was gone. Vanished. Completely bloody disappeared. Look, Rebecca, a full search party was all over that mountain. Cops, dogs, horses, volunteers, you bloody name it. We didn't have bloomin' drones back in those days, just rows of vehicles, animals and people all looking for him. It was concluded that when he reached the bottom of the mountain, he must have got into a car, because we couldn't find a trace of him. It was the only reasonable conclusion.'

'Yeah, but we found the skull on the other side of the road, Dad. Not on Burning Mountain. Deep in the bushland further on near the cliff range and creek of Mount Wingen. Do you think this could be Oliver?'

'Maybe? I mean, we never found him. Never got a single call saying someone had sighted him in another town. Sure, people called in with tips over the years, but all were a waste of time. We ran it in the papers as well, stuck up police posters. Mrs Lavine stuck up her own. Got zip, nothing, for the effort. Case was never closed.'

Giles reached for the bottom layer of cake. The raspberry was sticky, and the icing sugar dusted her hand. 'The friends, did they tell you what the argument was about?'

'There were four boys, and a girl. They got into an argument apparently about her. Teenage stuff, you know, young crush, calf love. It'll be in the report. My report.'

'Was this your case?'

'The whole station worked on the case. Everyone in the Hunter wanted to find the boy. I was the lead detective. It was my crime scene. Except I didn't really have one.' Benjamin shuffled in his seat. 'Wowee, if it is young Oliver, it'll be good to take another crack at it. Closure's always good for the soul.'

Giles also shuffled in her seat. 'So, did you have a theory? A suspect?'

'Yeah, that spiderly tingly feeling, the gut instinct. The hunch. But you know better than anyone that you can't press charges because of the hairs on the back of your neck. We almost came close to solving it. Just didn't have enough to stick.'

After a long pause, Giles prodded. 'Want to share it with me?'

Benjamin looked down into the cooling tea in his shaky hand resting on his thigh. He frowned. 'I couldn't find a reason why anyone would want to hurt the boy, see the boy dead. It seemed more plausible that someone saw him alone, took the opportunity. A sinister opportunity.'

Giles leaned forward, lobbed the last bite of sponge cake back onto the plate and wiped her hands, urging her father to continue.

'I had a fair idea at the time. Couldn't get it over the line. Insufficient evidence.' Benjamin brushed off the crumbs down his shirt, avoiding Giles's eye and said, 'You might want to take a look at Bernard Nestor.'

Giles tilted her head. 'Why does that name ring a bell?'

'Because he was our next-door neighbour.'

EIGHT

Joe Thicket lay in bed waiting for his mother to come and wish him goodnight. He scratched at the edges of the horse stickers that decorated his bedhead. Traced his finger around the smaller image of a baby foal.

His mother appeared at the door. 'Night, Joe.'

Joe rolled over. Smiled. 'Nigh-night.'

She tipped her head. Flicked off the light. As she was about to leave, Joe called out, 'Mum?'

'Hmm?'

'Do you think I could get new shoes for school?' he asked, shrinking under the blanket.

When his mother didn't answer immediately, he knew she wouldn't make a promise she couldn't keep. Promises were made in the sunshine but expected to be delivered under storm clouds, and now she was probably adding *new shoes* to her list of troubles.

She mumbled, 'We'll see.' But the words didn't fall from her mouth out of habit. Joe knew everything she said and did around the house was carefully thought through. They both lived and spoke with caution.

~

Before turning off the kitchen light and heading for bed, Amy Thicket retrieved the registration papers from behind the kettle and stared at them. *That bloody car.* She knew the brake pads were worn. She could hear them squealing for attention when she stopped at the traffic lights. Plus, the tyres were almost bald. The car pulled to the right every time she braked; the wheels were unbalanced. Like her life. Pulling her, pulling and pulling.

She couldn't share her woes with her husband either. He'd been out of work for almost a year, and her casual job at the supermarket hardly covered the rent, the electricity, the groceries, the necessities. Yet Amy felt she was a resourceful woman, a survivor of sorts. She could make a pasta meal with a few grams of mince, stretch a loaf of bread into a week, cut back, scrimp, save, leave milk out of her coffee, wash her hair with soap.

But the car was a problem. Too hard to sell. No-one would buy it, and if they did she wouldn't get much for it. And she'd not replaced the faulty airbags.

She could do an insurance job, maybe. She had no claim history. It would be believable enough. Run it into a tree, perhaps? But how could she stage an accident when the airbags would likely let fly lethal pieces of metal? She had spent the afternoon googling images of faulty airbag accidents, of casualties who ignored the recall. And when she had looked at the pictures of the fatalities, she had thought, *Stuff me. It's bloody steak-knife Tuesday, hosted by Sweeney Todd and fricken Freddy Krueger.*

She sighed, then tucked the rego and green-slip papers deep into the bottom of the garbage bin. It stopped her from thinking about the due date and motivated her to get rid of the car. She knew she could catch the bus to work. It would only add an extra twenty minutes to her commute.

With her worries literally in the trash, she questioned whether she was capable of writing off a car. How fast would she need to be going before turning the vehicle towards a tree? She doubted she was quick enough to shield her face from the impact.

Amy sat down in one of the kitchen chairs and practised the collision. She pressed her right foot flat and firm on the linoleum floor, an imaginary accelerator, trying to position her arms to shield her throat, her eyes, her face, her brain from an exploding airbag. Forearms across her throat, wrists over her eyes and palms up to protect her brain. She mulled over how best to survive the crash. Pondered how much pain it would cause.

At the sink, she grabbed a filleting knife from the top drawer and without thinking she thrust the tip of the steel blade into her forearm. She winced but didn't yelp. Blood trickled as she removed the knife from her skin. She was surprised there wasn't more blood.

She rinsed the knife and left it in the sink. Then found a band-aid from the cupboard and covered her injury. Before going to bed she poured two fingers of Vat 69 into a glass from a bottle she hid from her husband behind the brand-name cereal boxes and filled it with equal parts water. She drank it quickly with two aspirins and then headed for bed.

Under fetid sheets, her husband was naked, waiting for her. He slid his palm under her knee and pulled her towards him. She watched his nostrils flare as his hands clumsily pawed at her. His breath hot as he grunted. His rough fingers on her breasts, calluses massaging her nipples. There was nothing erotic or passionate about their 'lovemaking'. Although she did fantasise – but not about things that were amatory or stimulated arousal. Instead, she visualised an airbag exploding in her husband's face.

~

In the main bedroom of the neighbouring house, their light-cotton bedsheet was also damp with sex and sweat. Bell was a starfish. Her legs and arms took up most of the bed. If it wasn't for the slow rise of her chest, she'd look dead.

Above the bed, the fan blades spun at a slight angle, threatening to whirl down at any moment and sever a limb. Bob rubbed his eyes with his knuckles, blinked, and stared up past the spinning blades. He couldn't sleep. His stomach felt empty, but he wasn't hungry. He swallowed and felt the saliva make a tight ball in his throat and get stuck in his chest.

The room seemed empty. A bed. Two mismatched side tables. One table with an alarm clock, the other with an ugly copper touch lamp and fake leadlight. Bob frowned, twitched his nose, and thought of money. The problem lay in how to get the garbage bag out of the little fishmonger's hand. *Spook him, and then snatch it? Like a jump scare? Spring out from behind the dumpster?*

Bob rolled onto his side, tried to play it out in his mind, move by move. His vision looked ridiculous. *What are you thinking?* He had an *idea*, but he didn't have much of a plan. He hadn't thought it through. Would he need a gun? *Fuck sake!* Or maybe one with no bullets? *Just for a warning.* He wouldn't use it.

Bob mumbled out loud, 'And I need a disguise.'

Bell rolled over. 'Ha? Bob?'

'Yeah?'

'What?'

'Nothing. Go to sleep, Bell.'

Bell flopped back on her back. Arms flung above her head, outstretched.

Bob pulled the cotton sheet over her, only his hand was shaking. The thought of a gun scared him. *Call it off, you dickhead.*

He jumped out of bed, stumbled through the door and down the hall into the bathroom. He lifted the toilet seat and emptied his guts into the bowl. His nose stung and the smell lingered even after he flushed.

It's the beer, he told himself. *Too many beers. And the shite tinned soup.*

Only his hands still shook, and his arm tingled. He felt overheated and panicked. The bravado was fading and the coward in him rising – right from his stomach to his mouth. Bob wiped his bottom lip with the back of his hand and wondered if he should dump the whole idea. And yet it felt like it was too late to stop. The momentum of the scheme was pulling at him.

Fuck sake, relax. You won't get caught.

Bob knew no-one would notice him in the laneway. He was used to people seeing straight through him. Ignoring his presence. He'd learned from an early age how to sense a person's rejection before they'd even made up their mind to leave him behind. Bob thought he'd recently seen a glimmer of 'that look' in Bell's face. Had he imagined it? Or was it there?

The ring. Buy the fucking ring. He didn't want the dream of spending his life with Bell to dissolve.

Without the dream – without Bell as his wife – the abyss that was his life would be darker still.

On the other side of town, Giles kicked off her shoes, slipped out of her work clothes and draped them over the back of the winged chair in the corner of the bedroom.

She flopped down on her bed, rested her hands behind her head and looked up at the ceiling.

Bernard Nestor?

She couldn't remember his face, but the name unsettled her. She could remember the ramshackle house he lived in. The small orchard of fruit trees at the end of his property of just a few acres. The horses he had kept. And the rundown windmill.

As a child, she would constantly creep away to play around the well on his farm. She remembered Benjamin's stern warnings to stay away, but she was drawn to the place. When home alone – which was more often than they both wanted to admit – she'd sneak away and play, hidden amongst the weeds.

She would be watchful of thistles and stinging nettles, as she stretched out on her stomach amongst the peaches that had fallen from the nearby trees. The place had smelled of horse dung, rotting fruit and stagnant water. In the sun, she would stretch out her hand, span her fingers like a star until they were stiff and sore, as milkweed beetles, tentatively at first, crawled onto her fingertips, then palm, then slowly made their way up her arm.

Milkweeds were strange black and red insects that looked like the ugly ancestor of a ladybug. Soon enough, a little colony would crawl all over her body, tangle themselves in her hair, tickle her neck with their long antennae. She would lie in the warm grass, skin tingling, until she'd hear her neighbour and his dog returning. Then she'd shake the beetles off and scurry through the hole in the ring-lock fence that divided the properties.

Giles opened her eyes. Blinked.

She could remember the peaches, the beetles, the well, but couldn't remember Bernard Nestor; only the feeling of panic when she heard him and his dog returning.

DAY 2

NINE

By the fallen log at the side of the dirt road, two equipment vans, a police vehicle and two Sonatas were parked. Giles added a sixth vehicle to the end of the line.

She grabbed the tray of coffees from the passenger seat and approached Detective Senior Constable Callahan and Detective Sergeant Bray, who were standing at the front of one of the Sonatas.

'Just us?' asked Giles. 'No media?'

'Been and gone,' said Callahan. 'Nothing much for them to see, and only little to tell.'

'Brought you a surprise.' She held out the tray towards them.

Callahan's face lit up and he was quick to reach for a cup. 'Cheers, thanks.'

In the last few months, Callahan had let his short stubble grow into a thicker beard, tamed and trimmed into a ducktail; longer at the chin, shorter at the sides. It was motley coloured, with whiskers of brown, grey and tinges of red. Every time Giles looked at him, it made her jawline feel itchy and she had to resist the urge to reach out and scratch him under his chin.

Callahan peeled back the plastic lid of the coffee, took a large gulp, then scooped the froth from the inside of the paper cup and sucked it off his finger. It was as if Giles had offered him coffee and a meal, and she wondered just how long he'd been on duty.

Both Callahan and Bray had ditched their suit jackets. The sleeves of their business shirts were rolled up, buttons at the neck undone, ties missing. Fatigue already starting to set in. She handed Bray a coffee and he tipped his head for her to look at the map.

On the bonnet of the car, a large topical map was spread out and anchored down with creek stones. The area was zoomed in on where the skull had been found, and Giles noticed hand-drawn gridlines in pencil, the lanes pointing in a north–south direction, and, in the cross-grid, the outline of a body.

'You're shitting me. You found it?'

'Not me,' said Bray. 'Our little forensic team of two are like mini-bloodhounds. I wouldn't play hide and seek with either of them.'

'You're impressed,' smiled Giles.

'Maybe, just a little,' said Bray, then he gulped down his coffee. When the cup was empty, he twisted it back into the cardboard tray. 'The forensic technicians have found what they *believe* to be a cut grave. They haven't begun to dig – no skeleton yet, but looks promising.'

Callahan stepped forward, casting a shadow across the map with his broad shoulders. His finger swirled over the top of the chart. 'We did a sweep of this area; couldn't find any personal effects, weren't expecting to after all this time. Nothing went *beep* on the metal detector or caught our attention.'

'But progress has been made,' said Bray.

Giles raised a brow, gave them both a small shrug. 'So? What are they like?'

'They're not here for a cut lunch,' said Bray. 'I'll walk you down the track and introduce you.'

~

A marquee had been erected just off to the left of the trail. The canopy was set up to cover and protect the area believed to be the gravesite. A mound of topsoil had already been removed and the freshly dug earth smelled of rotten egg. Giles stared at the pile of basalt soil, chunks of red clay, leaf litter and upturned yellow button flowers. Already the scene was a stark contrast from the day before. She stepped under the canvas shelter. Two figures in light-weight breathable coveralls were kneeling over the site of fresh soil, exposing the edges of a cut grave.

Bray took the tray from Giles and began handing out coffee with introductions to the two technicians. 'This is Liam Edison and Kelsey Nichols.'

Giles briefly took them in. From what she could see of Liam, he looked tall and lean, grey flecks mixed in his sandy blond hair. Kelsey seemed much older – hair wiry grey and her face dotted with sunspots. But it was the gravesite that drew Giles's attention. 'You found it.'

'Yeah,' said Edison. His voice was mellow, calm. 'We didn't even rely on geophysics or Google Earth. Not even a drone.'

Giles blinked. Had she and Bray missed the obvious? 'How then?'

'Did a bit of field walking. Is there sugar in this?' Edison lifted the coffee in the air.

Giles looked up at Edison, noticed the hazel flecks in his light brown eyes, three freckles on his cheek. She kept her gaze as she shook her head.

He smiled, continued, 'The vegetation gave it away, and the kelpie. When the body decomposes, the surface level will sink into the grave. Visible as an anomaly.'

Neither she nor Bray could see any anomalies the day before. 'And the kelpie's hand in it?' Giles asked.

'Saw where the dog dug. Kelsey and I decided to scratch around too.'

'Ha! So, the dog found it.' Giles grinned, then noticed she was the only one smiling. Worried that she had already offended the two technicians, she tried to retract her comment. 'I mean, the dog helped point you to the right place to look.' She turned away and grabbed a coffee from the tray Bray was still holding. The brew was steaming, full and frothy, but she almost wished for a Red Bull with a shot of Jägermeister instead.

'Something like that. Guess we had better luck in the second innings.' Kelsey still hadn't cracked a smile since Giles had arrived, not even when Bray had offered her a coffee. Giles figured she probably wouldn't get one now.

'Don't get too excited,' said Edison. 'We haven't found a skeleton. Just what we believe to be a grave. But if there is a skeleton down there, it's been buried in what looks like a deliberately cut grave, and this implies disposal by a third party.'

'If that's the case,' said Callahan, 'I guess that would make it official. If there *is* a skeleton down there, then this is a homicide, and the area here is our crime scene.'

Edison nodded, crouched lower, pointed and traced the original edge of where the grave was cut. 'Here is where the grave starts. It looks and feels slightly different to the surrounding area – the soil filling is a subtle, different colour.'

'Any chance of finding trace evidence after all these years?' asked Bray.

'Maybe,' said Edison. 'Sometimes paint can be transferred from the tool that's used. But the person who dug the grave may not have the tool anymore. There could be footprints preserved beneath the body.'

Giles's face lit up, but Bray added, 'The person who dug the grave may not have the pair of shoes either.'

Or they may now be wearing a different size shoe. Giles thought of the four friends of Oliver Lavine.

'I'd expect that any natural fibres will have gone by now,' Edison went on. 'However, man-made ones, like nylon or zips, would probably have survived. If we find skeletal remains, they'll need to be moved where I can do a more in-depth analysis to establish identity and the potential cause of death. It's going to take time, though. We need to photograph every step, document, and sketch diagrams. We'll work as fast as we can, but with care. It's going to be a slow process. Every step we take is irreversible, unrepeatable.'

The wind had picked up around them, warm and rank with the smell of freshly churned soil. A flock of white cockatoos screeched in the distance, and the monotonous humming of insects made Giles's ears ache. *A long and slow process.* She wanted answers. She wanted to ask, *How slow?* But she didn't want to pressure the team or piss them off any more than she had already. She puffed away a fly and was about to turn and leave when Edison continued, 'What is interesting, this is a full-size grave. Seems as though it'll be deep, and the body laid out, not dumped.'

'Huh?' Giles cupped her hand at the back of her neck, her fingers kneading the muscles and spine. She was trying to follow Edison's logic, work through the scene calmly. 'Laid out? What does that say about the grave?'

'If you were digging a clandestine grave, you'd want to get the job done as quickly as possible – get my drift?'

Giles, Callahan and Bray nodded.

'Normally a grave to dispose of a body is likely to be relatively shallow, maybe even irregular in dimension and depth. Most of the time too small for the body, which then needs to be bent in some way to fit in the grave, sort of shoved in. But this . . .' Edison's hand motioned down the length of the grave, '. . . this has been dug deep, with thought. I guess what I'm trying to say is, if there's a body down there, it was buried respectfully. With dignity. If you can call concealing and disposing of a body a dignified act.'

'Someone who knows the victim?' asked Giles.

'Or guilt,' added Callahan.

Edison shrugged. 'I just study the remains. Profiling the possible predator is your job.'

Giles looked over at Bray, rolled her eyes.

'Fun mob,' she mumbled to Bray and Callahan as they headed back down the track to their vehicles.

'Nah, just focused,' said Callahan. 'They'll eventually loosen up around us.'

As they neared the dirt road, they could hear a steady flow of traffic from the New England Highway in the distance, and the murmuring from the uniforms. Giles wondered if the Police Media Unit had disclosed information to the press. Aside from the discovery, there wasn't a lot to tell the public.

'What has the media been told?'

'They know we found a skull. That's about all.'

'Uh-huh.' She leaned against the driver's door of the car, folded her arms, and waited for Bray's instructions on their next steps.

'You talk to your dad last night?'

'He said a kid went missing from Burning Mountain almost twenty years ago. Name of Oliver Lavine.'

'Turner came up with the same name. Falkov too. They've pulled the file.' Bray flicked his hand in the air, waving off the insects. 'Look, Giles, there's not much you can do here, it's a bit of a waiting game. Go back to the station. Turner will bring you up to speed with the info on file.' He gave her a wink. 'Go easy on him. He's had a long night.'

⁓

As Giles arrived in town, she looped around the back roads, only so she could drive underneath the railway bridge and look at the walls that were artistically lined with a collage of silver metal frogs, platypus, dragonflies, turtles and white cockatoos. She slowed the Sonata to take in the artistry. The dragonflies were her favourite.

A few metres up the road was Muswellbrook Police Station. In front of the building the Buxus had been recently trimmed and was a neat rectangle garden hedge. The lawn had also been freshly mowed. The country-style building with its silver galvanised roof and wrap-around veranda looked welcoming to the passer-by, although behind its exterior sat a modern brick building equipped with a fully functioning gym, dining-room filled with flash furnishings, the latest police technology – and a Nespresso machine.

Giles pulled into the car park at the side of the building. She snatched up her notebook and locked the vehicle. The minute she entered the police station, she was greeted by Constable Griffin manning the front counter.

'Mornin', Detective Giles.'

'Keeping the town in order, Griff?' She flicked her finger against her brow, giving him a quick salute.

No longer a probationary, Constable Griffin was probably wondering why he was still stuck on the front desk.

'Yep, yep, all in good order, ma'am.'

Is it? It was obvious he'd not heard about the recently discovered skull.

She moved on, made a beeline down the corridor towards the kitchen. She needed another shot of caffeine and a moment or two in the air-conditioning to refresh, recentre her thoughts, clear her head before sitting down with Turner.

The image of the cut grave, the skull, and the thought of who could possibly put a child into the earth had unsettled her. She needed a name, or confirmation of the one her father had given. She wanted to bring this child back to life in memory, and hopefully give closure to the family – and to her father.

Giles slipped her chipped white enamel mug under the nozzle of the coffee machine and hit the latte button. The machine gurgled to life.

She had picked up the mug at a marketplace in Sydney years earlier. For twenty bucks she got a zingy drink that tasted like passionfruit and petrol. But it was the cup it came in that she had wanted. It reminded her of a mug she had as a kid. While it was ring-stained inside and the handle was bent out of shape, it evoked memories of early mornings sitting at the woodpile with her father. Cold morning frosts that revealed hundreds of spiderwebs strung between the blades of grass.

Giles could still picture the two of them together when it was quiet, when the dog next door hadn't been let off its chain and still slept in its hollowed log. She couldn't remember Bernard Nestor, but she could remember his dog.

She recalled how she liked the silence before the animal began to bark the neighbourhood awake until it was freed. The mutt would wreak havoc in town, roaming and scaring kids, chasing cats, then either returning home on its own, or by force after complaints to the police. As a child she had feared the beast, and only felt less afraid when her father whispered in her ear one day, 'Don't worry, Rebecca, I'll shoot the bastard thing before it hurts anyone.'

The coffee machine stopped gurgling as Turner entered the kitchen and leaned against the fridge. 'Did you check the use-by date on that milk?'

'Ugh.' Giles sniffed at her mug. 'Didn't look lumpy in the milk tank.'

'Should be safe then.'

She smirked at Turner, admired his buttoned-up, single-breasted suit, and his silk grey Christian Lacroix tie in a full Windsor knot. 'Did I miss the dress-code memo this morning?'

Turner straightened his tie, ran his fingers through his strawberry blond hair and mumbled, 'Nope.' He shrugged. 'Just a suit.'

'Dapper!' She watched his neck go pink, held back her smile and asked, 'Got any bikkies to go with this?' She lifted her mug in the air.

'Yep. Inspector Falkov hid the Tim Tams in the third drawer.'

'Atta, detective.' Giles winked, twitched the side of her cheek and clicked her tongue, then helped herself to a chocolate biscuit. 'Got lots to tell?'

'Missing Persons Unit in Sydney gave a shortlist. Thousands are reported missing every year – most are adults and located within three months to a year. Most missing children are found quickly. The age you and Bray are suggesting is a teen, and the length of time is long. Runaways are mostly teens who take to the city, so this, out at Wingen . . . this is a little different.'

Turner stretched out his hand for a biscuit. Giles pinched another from the packet and dropped one in his palm. 'The *Just vanished from sight* list is short. I mean, there were the Beaumont kids, but they don't fit the age and dates, there's a girl from Oakleigh in Victoria, a twelve-year-old female from South Australia, and in New South Wales a child from Grandville, one from Narooma, and then the case file lodged at our station.'

'Oliver Lavine, right?'

'Yeah. Oliver Lavine.' Turner shoved the whole biscuit in his mouth, continued talking as he chewed. 'Aged fifteen. Disappeared the sixth of April 2006. Last seen at Burning Mountain.' He flipped open his notebook to check his facts. 'Last to see Oliver alive were –'

'Four of his school friends,' interrupted Giles. 'Dad already told me. They hiked up the mountain together. On the way back, Oliver went on ahead. When his friends got to the bottom, he was gone.'

'Vanished.' Turner licked the chocolate from the corner of his lip, then grinned. 'That's what their statements say in the file.'

'But they weren't suspects?'

'Everyone's a suspect, Giles. But none of the evidence, not that there was much to go on, incriminated them. Their stories matched.'

'Rehearsed?'

'They were kids, but not a single one tripped up. All stuck to the same tale – Oliver Lavine went on ahead, and when they got to the bottom of the hiking trail, he was gone.'

'How meaty were their statements?'

Turner paused. Twisted his lip. After a moment he said, 'It wasn't light reading, but not extensively detailed. They were young teenagers, still in shock.'

Giles twitched a shoulder. 'In shock, or hiding something, making them reluctant to give too much detail in case they tripped up?'

'You think they may have omitted part of their story?'

'Dunno. But I'd like to read their statements. You have four different perspectives. I'd like to see if they're told from one viewpoint.'

Turner's neck pinkened again.

Giles went on, 'Dad said they had a bit of a spat, small quarrel, before Oliver took off. Did their statements include what they argued about?'

'Nup.'

'Right there could be the first omission of their story.'

'It could be unrelated to why Oliver took off.'

'Perhaps. But they didn't mention it in their statement.'

Turner was slowly nodding, like he was absorbing the possibility. 'Yeah, I think that would be a good place to start.'

Giles smiled. 'Might be worth chatting to them again. You got names for these four friends?'

Turner looked down and read from his notes. 'Bob Bradbury, Belinda Marrone, Phillip O'Dell and Paul Cooper. They were the last four to see Oliver Lavine alive.'

TEN

Phillip O'Dell – Phil the dill – stared at his reflection in the chipped vanity mirror. His face was pale, almost translucent if it weren't for the clutter of freckles.

His mother called him Ginger Nut. Sometimes he got the nickname Carrot or Blue, because of his bright tangerine hair, or Ug – short for ugly. Dill was a butter-faced melon, hard on the eyes, but no matter what people called him, he would answer.

Dill's fate and reputation in Muswellbrook had been sealed since the third grade. His mother had moved them from the Central Coast after separating from Dill's stepdad, and he'd started his first day at the local public school halfway through the week and school term.

Mrs O'Dell had hurriedly purchased her son's uniform, one size larger so he had room to grow into it. And on Dill's first day, he'd complained that his pants were too big and wouldn't stay up. He had watched his mother huff, torn between her child and a stack of boxes waiting to be unpacked at their new home. Dill knew that the sooner his mother got rid of him, the sooner she'd get on with sorting the new house. He wanted to go home at the end of the school day and find his bed made, and his toys lined up on shelves, but he also needed a belt to hold up his pants.

Outside the classroom door, Dill had complained for the umpteenth time, 'But, Mum, me pants won't stay up.'

'Give us a bloody look.'

Mrs O'Dell had grabbed the top of his trousers, rolled the material over the waistband a few times, then opened the classroom door and pushed him in.

There Dill had stood. Tall and skinny. His face was red and full of freckles, trying to smile with his yellow stubby teeth and mop of orange hair. His pants were rolled up so high that the waistband sat just under his ribs, leaving a two-inch gap between his shoes and shins. His mother had sent him in ripe and ready to be bullied. And considering Bob Bradbury was also on top of that bullying list, it was inevitable they'd end up mates.

On that first day, in the playground, Bob spotted him sitting in the shadow of the bottlebrush tree and sidled up beside him. Dill had felt his face flush, warm and stupid, but relieved he had made a friend. From then on, every day Bob and Dill sat under the bottlebrush. They'd listen to the swarming of bees above their heads collecting nectar and pollen, but neither seemed bothered by the insects busy in the shrub. Instead, the new alliance of theirs made them feel brave. Bold. Whatever the two had in common that had cast them out of the other groups, it seemed to draw them together – bonding them.

Dill was comfortable sitting in silence beside Bob. Bob didn't demand conversation or crave to be entertained. Dill couldn't think of a single story to tell him that would be interesting, and yet Bob seemed to need none. Dill didn't ask questions about his home life, and perhaps that was because he wished not to be asked of his own.

From the third grade, right through primary school, then high school, they had stuck together. Both were occasionally picked on, but gave back as good as they got. It was easier to share the shunning with a mate, and the two became inseparable.

By seventeen, Dill had grown tall and gangling. He was clumsy, and hopeless at remembering stuff because of the amount of weed he smoked. Meanwhile, Bob had sprouted into, well, a hulk. When Bob left school, he got a job as a brickie's labourer, moved out of home and into a rented small weatherboard home with Bell. Dill, on the other hand, still lived with his mother and chose smoking and selling weed over making an honest living.

The building site had quietened. Tools were down. It was midday – time for a smoko break and lunch. Dill idled down the road towards the tuck truck and his mate.

Bob nodded, sweaty, feet cooking in his steel-capped boots, dust up his nose and in the corners of his eyes. Dill returned the nod, fresh and pink-skinned. His faded Linkin Park t-shirt was too big, and his stubbie shorts were too tight and small.

'You look beat,' said Dill.

'Some of us have to work for a fuckin' living, Dill,' Bob answered, but there wasn't a touch of malice in his tone.

'Just mean more than usual, that's all.' Dill swatted at the flies. Puffed them away from the corner of his lip.

'Am a bit.'

'Somethin' wrong?' asked Dill.

'Nah, something right,' Bob answered.

Dill lifted his head, frowned. Not a lot went right for Bob, so it made him instantly curious. 'Like?'

Bob narrowed his eyes into the sun, looked around at the tradies lined up at the tuck truck ordering vanilla slices, meat pies and cartons of flavoured milk. The canteen on wheels was quickly running out of stock, and if Bob didn't jump in the line soon, he'd be stuck with an egg and lettuce sandwich or a salad roll. He joined the back of the line. 'I'll get us a pie each, then I'll tell you.'

The girl who drove the tuck truck was always a little flirty, slow at serving, and scantily dressed. 'How you doing, Bh-ob?' she asked, her voice breathy, almost whispering when she said his name.

Bob grimaced, only giving a sharp nod of reply. He hated the girl's aspirated tone, and couldn't for the life of him work out when he'd given her the impression he was up for a sultry greeting, when the only thing he wanted from her was food.

Every day at morning tea, and again at lunch, she'd be there in her truck selling pies, drinks, cakes and sandwiches in her lowcut top, tight pants and painted face. The blokes on site would suck in their guts as they lined up, grabbing sneak peeks at the outline of her bum. But not Bob. Dill knew his mate was a one-woman man.

'What do you want, Bh-ob?'

'Couple of pies, sauce, and chocolate milks.'

'Banana,' hollered Dill. 'Make mine a banana milk.' His smile looked like an upturned banana itself.

A few minutes later Bob and Dill were sitting in the shade on the scrap pile, out of earshot of the rest of the crew. They peeled back the pastry on their pies to let them cool down.

'Chuck us some dead horse.'

Bob tossed Dill a plastic sachet.

'Thanks, Bh-ob,' mocked Dill.

'Fuck off. It's Bob. One syllable. No sigh in the middle. No pause in the fucking middle either.' Bob wiped away the sweat starting to build up on his top lip. 'Pass back the sauce, prick.'

Dill squirted the red gunk on his pie, then tossed the sachet back at Bob, watching his shaky hand squeeze the rest of the contents over the cooling meat.

He frowned. 'What's up? Why'd you invite me to lunch?'

'Thought I'd buy you a pie.'

'Bullshit.'

Bob grinned, leaned forward, and in a hushed tone told Dill what he'd observed across the road the last few weeks at the seafood shop. He put forward his idea, but there was no concrete vision attached. Just an end goal without a game plan. Dill could tell that Bob hadn't put a great deal of thought into it at all, besides visualising holding a garbage bag of money.

'Struth! Are you flaming nuts?' Dill shoved pastry in his mouth and almost choked on the crust. 'What the fuck, Bob?'

'Shut up. It's no big deal.'

'Sounds like a big fuckin' deal to me.'

'Nah, it's not.' Bob looked annoyed. 'I'm just gonna snatch the bag in the alleyway. It's only one week's takings – the guy will recover. He'll make it all back the next week. I'm not gonna hurt him, wreck his shop or anything. Just get the bag, that's all. If you help, we can go halves.'

'I don't know, Bob. It's a little risky.' Dill tapped his foot. 'Can't you think of another way to get some cash? Hock something?'

'Like? I own shit.'

'Gotta be another way to get extra cash?'

'Like a job? I'm already slaving my arse off, Dill, staying back whenever there's overtime. And I've got stuff all to sell.'

'You've got a penis.' Dill laughed, but Bob didn't find the crack amusing.

'Stop being a prick. Look, I promise, it's a snatch and run, that's all.'

'Sell weed with me, Bob. Just sell a few bags of pot a week – that'll get you on top of things.'

'No. I don't want a criminal record.'

Dill's eyes widened. 'But you want to *mug* someone?'

'I'm not going to get caught.' Bob had lost patience. 'Are you in or not?'

'When?'

'Next Wednesday. We hide in the alleyway, and just before the bloke tosses the garbage in the dumpster, we'll jump him – but not hurt him.'

Dill was still tapping his foot. 'And then what? We just run off with it?'

Bob nodded. 'Run to a parked car.'

'Like a getaway car?'

'Yeah, like fucking Batman.'

'Batman was the one that stopped thieves – he didn't do the robbing.'

Bob looked sullen. 'You know what I mean, Dill.'

'Yeah. But why? Why rob someone? What's got into you?'

Bob looked up at the juiceless sky, as though it might squeeze out a drop just for him. 'I just need the bloody money, Dill.' Bob knew that wasn't reason enough, so he added, 'It's Bell. She's . . . she talks every now and then about starting over. Skipping off to a different town.'

'You can't leave town, mate. What about me?'

'I know. I think she feels unsettled.' Bob took a breath and plunged. 'A ring, Dill. I need to buy a ring. A good one. I'm hoping to pop the question to Bell, and I just need the fucking money to do it.'

Dill smiled, bright and golden. He slapped Bob on the knee. 'Huh! You sneaky little bastard. Mr and Mrs Bradbury, hey?'

'Yeah, sorta think it's time. Next step and all that. Maybe the Torana can be our wedding car.' Bob beamed. 'Don't tell Belinda. I want it to be a surprise. Buy a decent ring. Get hitched. It's just that I can't get ahead, that's all. I can't fuckin' make ends meet. But a garbage bag of cash will make it happen. It's a one-off. Never again. But it would be easy, Dill.' He stressed, 'I reckon we can do this.'

Dill sat in silence. Staring at his pie. His foot no longer tapping.

Bob could see the weight of his request settle on his mate. He swallowed. 'So . . . are you in?'

ELEVEN

Giles followed Detective Turner out of the kitchen and down the corridor to his desk. The two of them had eaten all but the last Tim Tam and decided they'd better get back to work.

Giles was already firing questions at him before they sat down. 'Do you have the full file?'

'Yup. Pulled all the boxes from the archive – blew the dust off.'

'Have you read through it all?'

'Those were heavy boxes, Giles. I've started trawling through. Your dad collected a lot of info.'

Giles kept her face blank, but her eyes were smiling. 'Somewhere in all these notes is our answer; probably even the name of our suspect.'

'There was a long list of names, all crossed off with alibis checked.'

At Turner's desk, they pulled up chairs and sat down.

'And the people that gave those alibis, were they checked?' asked Giles.

Turner fired up his computer, wiggled his mouse, and the screen came to life. 'I haven't got that far yet. Got distracted with the witness statements.'

'The friends?'

Turner nodded, reached inside the box and handed her a folder with the statements. But Giles was thinking ahead, of Burning Mountain and the trek up to the lookout.

'How did those kids get out there? It's fifty kilometres from Muswellbrook.'

'Parents, family members dropped them off, came back a couple of hours later to collect them. Because kids didn't have mobile phones back then, it was the old *Meet you at the picnic bench in three hours.*'

'So how did they get home?'

'Paul Cooper was collected by his older stepbrother. Bob and Belinda got a lift with Phillip and his mother. At the end of the day, they assumed Oliver had already been picked up before they got back down the mountain. Only when Mrs Lavine arrived to collect Oliver, nobody was there. She waited a while, thinking the kids were still coming down the track, then got fed up with waiting and walked the trail herself. The group was already gone.'

Turner scrolled through the National Missing Persons Co-ordination Centre's website. 'This photo was taken three weeks before his disappearance.'

On the monitor, the image was of Oliver Lavine dressed in school uniform, smiling for his portrait. A face that seemed both ordinary and complicated. A youthful boy, dimples, with light blue eyes that looked deep into the camera lens. It was as though he was calling, *Do you see me?* Giles stared for a moment at the screen. She wanted to say, *I see you, Oliver.*

'In the weeks after Oliver vanished, the NMPCC did their best with missing persons posters, and over the years reminded the public of his disappearance at events like International Missing Children's Day and National Missing Persons Week. But for all the effort, none of it gained a single fresh lead.'

Giles shook her head. 'It's like Oliver Lavine has been forgotten. Or the people who do know something have chosen to forget.'

'The search was exhaustive. Volunteers combed the rocky areas, in case Oliver had slipped down between a crack. Nothing. Police divers went into the dam nearby. Again, nothing was found. It was believed he may have walked out of the bush, got into the wrong vehicle, and came to grief.'

'Foul play with the driver?'

'Possibly.'

'That's what Dad thinks. He reckons Oliver got into the wrong car . . . or was he planning to run away?'

Turner sighed. 'A fifteen-year-old? With no spare clothes or money? And a backpack that only had a hat, some lunch, spray to keep the mosquitos away – apparently the kid was allergic to mozzie bites – and a drink bottle.'

'Was the backpack ever found?'

'Nup. From the mother's account in the report, Oliver didn't seem the sort to run away. Timid. Not gutsy. Almost like he'd be too scared to stand on his own feet. Kinda needed his mother, if you know what I mean.' Turner's eyes met hers. Like Oliver's, they were pale blue and soft, yet to be hardened by the job. Giles lifted her fingers to her own face and wondered if she needed to start smiling more.

'What are you thinking?' asked Turner.

'Hmm.' Giles looked away, back at the screen and at Oliver Lavine's eyes squinting in a smile, cheeks bunched up, dimples, mouth closed. *Was he forcing the smile?* 'I'd like to track down the four friends who were there on that day and question them again.'

'Geez, if they didn't give anything up back then –'

'Either they're keeping something back, or maybe they don't know they're holding the key to break open the case.'

'You think they'll remember something new?'

'They were the last to see him. Time and maturity might make them look at the situation again from a fresh perspective.'

'But would their memory be reliable?'

'I guess I'll find out.' Giles knew she was at the mercy of the forensic technicians. Unable to make a strong start until she had more information, confirmation the skeletal remains were in fact Oliver's. Until then, she could use that time to think beyond the forensics, and collect as much information as possible on how Oliver went missing. Science couldn't change the result, but people could change their story. She could spend the next few days interviewing the four, to gain more understanding of who the young boy was, and how and why he was separated from the group.

Giles turned her mug around. The handle sat awkwardly in her left hand, but at least she didn't have to risk cutting her lip on the chipped rim. 'What about Oliver Lavine's father? Most child abductions are the parent, commonly on weekends or holidays. What's on the dad?'

'Not his real dad, but stepfather. Real dad passed away when Oliver was four. Stepfather and mother had already split up and gone their separate ways at the time, stepdad was working, had an alibi – that checked out. No history of violence or substance abuse. No history of mental illness, bipolar, depression or PTS – nothing – and happy to continue helping support the mother, paid child support. When most children are taken by a father, it's a form of power, revenge or control. But Mrs Lavine's ex wasn't a narcissist. Distressed and distraught at his stepson's disappearance, yes; suspect, nope. All he was left with was grief.'

'Stepfather didn't get someone to do the job for him?'

'His bank accounts and phone records were all investigated. House searched and even a surveillance team watched the home. But nothing. Clean.'

Huh! Good job, Dad.

They both stared at Oliver's image on the screen. Giles could hear Turner's light breath, while hers was harsh and sharp. There was the subtle spicy smell of Turner's aftershave, and she knew she probably smelled of soap and coffee. Giles cleared her throat. 'Who else was on the list?'

'People in Oliver's circle. Friends, teachers, sport coaches, few family members.' Turner scratched his head, then added, 'Friends of the mother. All checked out.'

'Dad said there was another person of interest, Bernard Nestor. That's who he had his eye on.'

'Yeah,' Turner nodded, 'that's in the file too. He wasn't in Oliver's circle; however, Bernard Nestor was heading back from Tamworth with a horse float and two horses. Passed by around that time in the afternoon.'

'He was in the area at the time? And that was confirmed?'

'By Nestor himself. Also a few witnesses. He drove straight by around the time those kids descended the mountain. He wasn't just a person of interest, he became the focus. Warrant to search the property. Comprehensive.'

'But no arrest?'

'Nope. No polygraph either. He was a suspect, but no charges were laid. They searched his property top to bottom – even the well on his farm was drained.'

The well. Giles shifted uncomfortably in her chair.

'Obviously nothing relating to Oliver Lavine was found.' Turner pulled up another file onscreen, clicked and a photo appeared. 'There. Bernard Nestor.'

For the second time in two days that sense of familiarity and recognition swept over her. 'Christ, I remember him. "Pockets".' She felt her stomach tilt, could smell the sour and sweetness of her half-drunk coffee. Either the milk was on the turn, or it was the image of Nestor lingering on the screen that was feeding a rush of nausea.

'Pockets? Who the bloody hell is Pockets?'

'Bernard Nestor.' She leaned in closer. Her hand took over the mouse, zooming in on the twenty-year-old photograph. 'I'd forgotten his name, but not his face.'

Nestor's fringe was long and slicked back, greasy from hair oil. A few strands hung over one eye, making him look lopsided. His eyes were saggy, with drooping eyelids. A mouth that twisted in a grimace, not a smile. Something about the man had punched the air around her.

'He was my old neighbour. He would give horse-riding lessons to kids in the area. Not just riding, but skills like manoeuvring through gates, cutting a cow from a herd and holding it.'

'But why Pockets?'

'I called him Pockets, because every time I was around him, he'd have his hands jiggling in his pockets . . . scratching at his hip like you'd scratch an itchy bite –' Giles stopped mid-sentence. Her face ashen.

'Giles?'

Oh, shit. Her stomach lurched once more.

'I've gotta go, Turner.'

'What?'

'I need to do something.' Giles snatched up her car keys and swung out of her chair. 'Back soon!' She was down the hallway in a near sprint, then out the front door.

TWELVE

The old fibro house with its flat tin roof baked in the sun on number thirteen Swiftlet Street. Inside, the air was hotter and more stifling than outside. Trent Thicket sat in sweat and rage. In desperation, he had sent the same text seven times. All were left unanswered.

Surely someone would hear the phone ping. Someone would know the messages needed a response. Eventually Amy would hear it ping and know it required an answer.

Farrrking reply.

He'd been warned: *never* ring while she was at work – text only. Wait. But he was done waiting. He hit the call button and listened until the phone rang out.

He wasn't used to his demands being ignored. In defeat he stomped his foot. The display cabinet rattled. Trent swallowed and reached for his Winfields. The packet was light. He shook it. Flipped the lid and counted.

Two left.

He'd smoke one now, but then he'd be down to his last. Already a great craving for nicotine surged through his veins. The incessant feeling of stress that pulsated made him crave stimulants. His constant need to feel weightless, the yearning for the euphoria, the high he sought that felt like it was never attained. Now the panic of running out of smokes, unable to get a nicotine rush – the thought of that withdrawal made his foot begin to twitch.

He knew his wife would be home in less than half an hour with another carton. His fingers tremored as he lit up, drawing the nicotine deep into his lungs. But with one smoke left, he knew he wasn't going to make it. He couldn't last half an hour on just one. Two ciggies in thirty minutes wasn't enough to keep his body in the chair.

Trent Thicket sat back in the broken recliner. His foot impatiently pawing at the carpet. Sullen, his bony forehead lowered. His nostrils sucked in the humid air. His mind was brooding. The anger, the rage was starting to set in. The aggressive nicotine withdrawal.

He was on the brink of feeling *the snap*.

THIRTEEN

Giles had driven twenty minutes out of Muswellbrook to Denman, to her old childhood house. From the outside, it was hard to imagine it was once the contented home she'd shared with her much-loved father until the age of twelve. As a child, she couldn't see the things that other adults saw. The unpainted eaves, the unattended garden, the junk and rubbish that stood by the forty-four-gallon drum. The trash that never made it into the incinerator and sometimes blew away in the strong winds, left strewn and scattered across the front yard until Benjamin was motivated to pick it up.

Giles remembered how she would lean her rusted pushbike against the side of the house in the drive next to the car. How she would play like a wild child, collecting treasures along the creek bank, bringing them home to share with her father. Feathers that she'd found, strange shaped stones collected along the creek bed, twisted driftwood that looked like dragons or coiling snakes, and native Billy Button flowers that she'd stumbled across in paddocks. She'd pick the golden-yellow globe-shaped blossoms, and frown when her father called them woollyheads. She liked the words Billy Button better.

When Benjamin was admitted to Merton Court, the house had been emptied and boarded up. The front door hammered closed.

It took Giles three hard kicks – and a sore ankle – to break the seal. The door still stubbornly clung to the nails and planks, and Giles had to shoulder it open.

As she rubbed her arm, the light of the day spilled from the front door into the lounge-room. The room looked larger now that it was empty of furniture, although the carpet was still there. Ugly maroon, green and mustard tones, with enormous floral tapestry prints of pink and red roses, and blue flowers that looked like peri-winkles. As a child the carpet had itched the back of her legs and offered little cushioning for her backside.

Giles grinned, moved further through the house and into the kitchen – also empty, except for a small stepladder that had been left behind.

She could see the imprints where the old solid wood dining table once stood. It was on that table that Giles would draw pictures for her father in biro and lead pencils. At the other end of the table, her train set would be permanently set up. They would eat their evening meal there and discuss topics like adults. Benjamin would be sipping beer – or, after a hard day, a whisky – and Giles would have warm Milo in her enamel cup.

The house now felt cold and destitute. The old fuel stove had not been lit in almost two years and was empty of wood or ash. It had cooked its last meal, and the top plate had toasted its last piece of bread. But the memories warmed her, and Giles knew if she looked hard enough, she could fill each room with hundreds of them.

She made her way down the hall to her childhood bedroom, where the only other things that remained were the old solid wood wardrobe and a steel-frame bed. She opened one of the panel doors of the wardrobe, then dragged the bed frame towards it. Stepping up onto the bed's edge, on her tiptoes, she leaned in, and was able to reach into the back corner of the cupboard.

Her hand patted the top shelf, her fingers splayed as she felt along the backboard until they landed on something soft and spongy, a spidery feeling. She flinched at the first touch, then scooped it up in her palm and, without looking at it, tucked it into her pocket.

As promised, Giles picked up her father from Merton Court for a short outing; short, because it was only a five-minute drive from the care home. Giles felt her father needed a change of scenery, and she needed someone who could look at the case and see it through a different lens.

At Two Rivers Winery, they sat outside the cellar door in the courtyard overlooking the vineyard and down to the river. After Giles convinced Benjamin to let her take a photo of him with the cheese and antipasto platter – like a seasoned foodie – they settled in.

The flies tickled Giles's ankle and she kicked her leg to shoo them away, only to connect her foot with the table. The platter, plus the two glasses of Babbling Brook shiraz, rattled. She quickly snatched the wine stems and steadied the glasses. 'Whoops! Almost.'

But Benjamin had paid no attention to the near mishap. He sat soaking up the view of grape trellises, sandstone sculptures and mountains in the far distance. His oversized hat shielded both his face and shoulders from the sun.

She lifted the brim to see her father's expression. 'Where did you get this ridiculous hat from?'

Benjamin smiled back at her. 'You'd rather talk hats than the case you're on?'

Giles dropped the corner and could no longer see her father's eyes. 'Let's talk about you first. What have you been up to?'

Benjamin shrugged. 'Not much. Just robbing people of their hats.'

'Okay, no need to be a smart arse. I'll talk about the case, if you like.'

'Nah, I'd rather talk about mundane, useless, boring shit with you. Falkov can chat with me about the case. At least he rings me.'

'I don't ring you. I *visit* you, in person. Look around! I've even taken you on an outing.'

'Yeah, well, Falkov gives better conversation. He tells me what's happening about the joint.' Benjamin tipped his head back, lifting the rim of the hat so his eyes could settle on her. 'Does your skeleton have a name yet?'

'No. But I think we all know the chances of it being Oliver Lavine are pretty high. They've found a grave; now they need to dig for a skeleton, get it back to the lab. It'll be a while before the bones are placed back together in an anatomical position, plus DNA samples take forever to be returned from forensics. I'm thinking a month, maybe a little longer, before we know for certain.'

'Yet Falkov's happy for you to keep chasing the leads from the old case.'

'It's that spidery, niggling feeling, Dad. The whole station's got it.'

Benjamin reached for his glass. The involuntary rhythmic shaking was more obvious when he tried to steady the ruby liquid swirling in the bottom of the flute. He gulped quickly to avoid spilling the wine down the front of his shirt. 'Bring me a sippy cup next time, sweetheart. I'm not sure I can be trusted with glassware anymore.'

Giles took the wine glass from her father's hand and placed it safely back on the table. 'What do you know about the four kids on Burning Mountain?'

'They were school friends. It was the holidays. They trekked up to Burning Mountain to see the view, watch the smoke.'

'Hmm.'

Giles had visited Burning Mountain once as a child herself. It had taken its name from a smouldering coal seam that ran underground through the sandstone. It had been estimated that the seam had been on fire for more than six thousand years. It was a popular trail with park benches along the way, walking bridges, and, at the peak of the mountain, a built-out lookout that extended over the drop and rocks below. The area was pink and cooked. Sulphur-tinged smoke rose from the ground, and the path of the fire had left the area barren, rocky, with no traces of life. The surrounding trees were dead shells, most had fallen. It was an eerie image – it was like standing on another planet altogether and perhaps that's what drew the friends.

As Benjamin broke off a small piece of cheese and tossed it to a magpie waiting for titbits, Giles took a sneaky photo of the two of them, then tucked her phone away. The bird hopped along the grass, and cocked its head before snatching up the morsel.

'Shouldn't feed cheese to magpies, Dad.'

'Got no more mealworms left in my pocket.' Benjamin winked.

'I've got a theory.' She tilted her head. 'Want to hear it?'

Benjamin emitted a slight chuckle. 'Bloody oath.'

'I think something happened out there, between the friends. Something bad.'

'Nah. It was the holidays. Dumb kids hiking to fill in the day. Better than smoking behind the hay shed or lighting fires.'

'Yeah, but one of them never returned, Dad.'

'Hmm. True. Up the top of the mountain, they had a bit of a niggle with each other, and Oliver walked on alone. Had a sook, that's all. That was the last those kids saw of him.' Benjamin lifted his head and the sun fell across his face. 'You should be looking into Nestor. Those kids had no reason for Oliver to disappear. Nestor, on the other hand, might have had plenty. The *why* always points to the *who*.' Benjamin nodded at the platter for Giles to cut another slice of cheese. From the tip of the knife he took the cheese, then tossed it to the waiting magpie.

'Dad! You're going to give that bird a heart attack.' Giles looked away as Benjamin opened his quivering palms towards her and said flatly, 'I had to follow the lead on Bernard Nestor to the very end, until I was exhausted, until I was sure I'd looked at it from every possible angle. That's why I kept following Bernard Nestor. I didn't want to think, *What if I missed something*, then have it come back to bloody haunt me.'

'Does it haunt you?'

Benjamin shrugged. 'I feel guilty sometimes that the case eluded me. That I wasn't able to solve it. I'd kicked over every stone and turd. Still . . .' Benjamin looked down at the platter, and as Giles went to cut another piece of cheese, he shook his head, fluttered his hand to let her know he didn't want any more. 'I know you'll look at this case with fresh eyes, Rebecca. I'm not worried that you're going through every single scrap of paper, every shred of evidence. You'll find that I did my due diligence. Who knows, you may find something that went past me, may even finish what I started. I just want you to know, whichever lead you choose to follow first, whatever the outcome is, I'm certain you'll make me proud.'

Giles smiled, lifted her face to the breeze. 'Do you think if Mum was still alive, she'd be proud of us?'

'If your mother was still alive, we'd be even better versions of ourselves.' There was a tenderness in his voice. A dreamy *What if*. How their lives would be different if both father and daughter were nurtured by the woman who'd left their lives decades ago. It was perhaps a better response than she'd expected.

They sat in silence for a while, sipping wine and picking at the platter. When Benjamin had enough to eat, he placed his tremoring hand on Giles's knee and said, 'But I am proud of the version you have become, Rebecca.'

'You're not too bad either, Dad. The two of us did okay together. We made it work.'

'That we did. I've got fond memories of you growing up, sweetheart.'

'Before shipping me off to boarding school?'

The quip was one Benjamin had heard a million times. He only smiled. Giles knew her dig no longer got a rise out of him. However, she could never really understand why her father sent her off to the school, when they only had each other.

Benjamin repeated, perhaps to keep the mood of the outing cordial, 'Like I said, I have fond memories, Rebecca.'

'Your best memory?'

Benjamin exhaled. It was somewhere between a groan and a laugh. 'Hmm, let's see. Your God-awful dance recitals I had to sit through. Making crap book-parade costumes out of cereal boxes and bloody rubbish bags. And your shite scrambled eggs loaded with parsley and cracked pepper.'

'*Yeah.*' Giles clutched her stomach and laughed. 'I made eggs a lot, before the neighbour's dog got to my hen.'

'Dog? It was a fox.'

'Nah, you said a fox, but I saw blood-sodden feathers scattered and strewn around the doghouse.'

'The doghouse?'

Giles frowned, but she didn't want the conversation to be about them – she had come for answers. She wanted to find a voice for the skeleton, maybe a voice for Oliver. She wanted it to be a good policing day. She took another gulp of wine and said, 'Did you ask any of those kids if they ever took horse-riding lessons from Bernard Nestor?'

From her pocket, she retrieved a small pioneer yarn doll; but instead of being made with strands of twisted and tied wool, the plaything was made of horsehair. As a child, she had hidden it in the back of the old wardrobe and now dropped it on the table. Its head and body were simple weaved loops from a horse's mane or tail, and its arms and legs were stiff from the strands being tightly braided.

'Where the hell did you find that?' Benjamin's eyes were dark and hard. It was the stillest she had ever seen him.

Giles felt a flash of betrayal against her father. 'It was just one of the many little dolls Nestor left for me. Only this one I hid from you. I don't know why, but when you threw the others in the incinerator, I hid this one in the back of my wardrobe.'

'Did you like these little dolls?'

After Nestor had given her the first doll in person, she would find the little horsehair figures left for her in the places she visited and played. Almost like a game of hide and seek. Or was it a way of saying, *I know where you go to play?* The doll on the table she had found strung up and dangling from a tree branch along the river, at a place where she would sit on a boulder and toss pebbles into the creek below. The tiny doll was swaying in the breeze, waiting for her. Others she had found on the seat of her bicycle, or in a nook in the ring-lock fence that separated their properties.

Giles shook her head. 'I don't why I kept it secret from you, Dad. I was just a dumb kid. They were dolls, made just for me.'

'Grooming, Rebecca. You don't see –'

'I do see, Dad. But I was a child at the time, not a cop.'

The moment of tension only lasted a few seconds. The magpie had seen the antipasto platter unguarded and seized the opportunity to swoop down and pinch the last of the brie.

'Ah, geez,' huffed Benjamin. 'Just when you think you've made a friend, you realise you can't bloody trust any bastard.'

Benjamin and Giles watched the magpie tip back its head and gulp down the wedge of cheese.

'Guess not,' mumbled Giles, and when she saw her father's shoulders relax, she asked, 'What else do you have on Bernard that's not in the file?'

Benjamin sighed, tucked his shaky hands between his legs. After a moment he said, 'Jacob Colton.'

'Who's Jacob?'

'A year before Oliver went missing, Jacob Colton was one of the kids who took horse-riding lessons from Nestor. It was Jacob Colton's mother who first came and spoke to me about Nestor. But she wouldn't put in an official complaint.'

'What was the complaint?'

'Look, Rebecca, I didn't home in on Bernard Nestor for no reason. It wasn't just because he was in the area at the time Oliver disappeared – he was already on my radar. Jacob Colton's mother said Nestor's methods of teaching were perhaps inappropriate. Made her son uncomfortable. Jacob ended the lessons, and that was the end of that.'

'Inappropriate?'

'Uncomfortable touching while instructing. A misplace of a hand? It's a murky grey area, you know that. The kid wasn't assaulted. But, as a cop, my intuition after talking with the kid and mother . . . you just know, Rebecca. You know that the inevitable is bubbling under the surface.'

'So, was Nestor ever charged?'

'With what? Being creepy? You think I didn't try to find more on him? I kept my eye on him, that's for sure. Then twelve months later Nestor drives straight past Burning Mountain, and, *poof*, Oliver Lavine vanishes.'

FOURTEEN

When Amy Thicket opened the front door and entered the house, she knew something was wrong. The haze of smoke that usually consumed the lounge-room no longer lingered. The cloud had almost cleared. She could see the ceiling. The colour of overcooked toast.

Oh, shit! She'd forgotten her husband's carton of cigarettes.

Panicked, she stuttered, 'Trent, I-I forgot. We were flat strap at work, slipped my mind. I'll go back. I won't take long.'

It was too late.

Trent Thicket's muscular body twisted as he rose out of his chair, up, up, up. He turned off the telly. The thumping of his feet rattled the glass in the display cabinet. He grabbed Amy by her hair and dragged her towards the door, snatching the car keys from her hand. 'I'm driving,' he spat.

She was not going to argue. She knew she had to go with him. She had stuffed up.

All day thinking about the damn car and new school shoes – it had made her forget her husband's smokes. It was her duty, her job, to ensure his careful handling for everyone's safety.

Now she had gone and let the bull out of the gate.

~

In the middle of the hot bitumen road, young Constable Griffin took off his police cap and wiped his brow. If Inspector Falkov gave out gold stars for immaculate uniforms, Griffin would be the leader on the board. He believed the shinier his shoes, the better the job he'd be allocated. Except the job he had been assigned to now sucked. He'd been standing in the hot sun, redirecting traffic around a fire truck for the last half an hour, desperate for a cool drink and some shade. He was fed up with giving courtesy waves to every damn car that drove past. Now, when he looked down at his polished shoes, it wasn't the feeling of pride that filled him, it was the feeling that he just wanted to kick someone in the nuts and call it a day. He couldn't help wishing Inspector Falkov would send him on a general duty that was more interesting than fucking traffic control. Manning the front desk was better than this.

Three volunteers from the Rural Fire Service had just finished dousing a fire in the kiddies' park. They began rolling up the hoses and loading the truck. Behind the truck, the police patrol car was parked with its red and blue lights flashing, cautioning the oncoming vehicles.

Some silly bugger had dropped a smoke on the grass – not deliberately, just from stupidity. With the long winter months gone with hardly a drop of rain, the dried grass and the light hot breeze, the cigarette had lit the park on fire. Now, every fuckwit within the vicinity that had called emergency services when the sky had filled with thick smoke was standing on the corner, offering him their advice, making sure it was put out.

The group of rubberneckers watched Griffin as he motioned drivers to slow down, drive around, and then waved them on. He felt their eyes upon him, and on Detective MacCrum who looked equally pissed to be at a children's park. MacCrum had been assigned to shadow him through the boring procedure of traffic control.

On the footpath, MacCrum paced, then shouted, 'When you're done, Griff, you better put some tape around that charred swing set. Keep the kids off it until the council can pull it down. Don't want it collapsing on a child.'

Constable Griffin's head dropped. 'Yes, sir.' The heat from the hot tar road was cooking his feet. He wanted crime unit action – *action*. Anyone could hold out their hand and motion for cars to slow down. It was all too easy.

That is, unless Trent Thicket was driving the bloody car.

Griffin recognised the rusty white Honda Civic as it approached. It wasn't dropping back to forty kilometres, so he stepped out in front, held up his hand and hollered, 'Slow down!'

The car came to an abrupt stop beside the constable. The door opened, and the big man started to climb out.

Griffin pushed the door back against him as Detective MacCrum jumped to Griffin's defence and yelled to the driver, 'He said slow down, not stop!' MacCrum pressed his pointer finger hard against the driver's window, at a spot that would have landed right between Trent Thicket's eyes. 'Stay in your car, sir. Keep moving.'

Thicket looked past MacCrum, scowled at the young constable, before driving ten metres up the road, where he pulled up again. His huge bulk emerged from the car, and he headed back towards Griffin on foot.

The three volunteer firemen, grotty with soot-smeared faces, looked at each other, silent, unmoving.

Griffin's mouth was dry. He quickly noted that Trent Thicket was in shorts and thongs with a bare chest. There was nothing to grab onto, nothing to hold him down with. No fire hose at the ready to force him back.

Then, the man began to charge. Head down. Eyes on the lanky young cop.

'Allegedly, *allegedly*. Careful with your words, detective.'

Giles gave a nod. 'Sir.'

Falkov's look of scorn faded and he continued, 'Your father did his best, but without enough strong solid evidence the case didn't get off the ground. He laid out fact after fact, but it was still circumstantial, implied. The report states the police prosecutor wasn't convinced he had enough to build a solid case out of the complaint, and the two versions of events – one from the child, Jacob Colton, and the other from Mr Nestor – a jury could go either way, and we would lose the opportunity for charging him altogether.'

The doll seemed to catch both their eyes. 'But the doll, sir?'

'So? Nestor made you and some other kids a toy.' Falkov pinched the bridge of his nose and ran his fingers down it. 'Look, Bernard Nestor gave horse-riding lessons, helped kids up on horses. Touching would be involved – a slip of a hand, accidental. Lifting a child up to a saddle and holding them by the thigh, not the foot, could have been an oversight, not an incident.'

'Repeatedly? So that his hand bumped the victim's groin *every* time?'

Falkov shrugged. 'Hard to prove. No witnesses, just the child's confession to his mother, and she reported it to your father.'

'Did Bernard Nestor give these dolls to his prey? Because he gave them to me. I remember him, sir. I remember him offering riding lessons. Eventually I showed Dad these dolls and asked if I could take up horse riding. I thought he'd be delighted; instead, he lost it with me, took the dolls, and burned them all. But he didn't know about this one.' Giles pointed to the small pocket-size doll on the desk. Its looped body, plaited legs and arms in black and chestnut horsehair looked ominous. 'I could have added weight to this case if he hadn't shipped me off to boarding school.'

'Giles, you were young. Your father didn't want you in town living next door to a neighbour he was trying to collect evidence on and prosecute for possible . . . it was a possible paedophilia case, Giles. *Christ*, why would Benjamin want his daughter around that? Sending you off to Sydney may have been his way of keeping you out of harm's way. He certainly didn't need you living next door to it, let alone being a part of it.'

'I went to the neighbour's property a lot, sir. I played by his well, ate peaches from his tree. I saw things. Things I didn't understand. I could have been a witness. Substantiated the claim.' She pressed her index finger down hard on the files on Falkov's desk. 'I could have helped get this case over the line.'

Falkov's face paled. 'Are you saying you were a victim?'

'I'm *saying* I could have added something to the case.' Giles knew there was no way, as a child, her father would have allowed her to be caught up in a grubby crime. But she wasn't a child anymore, she was a cop. 'Just ten minutes with Bernard Nestor, sir. Please? Let me see if I can dig up something new. Then if you think I'm personally involved, I'll hand it over. But I have to find something solid first, and I feel I'm the one who can get it.'

'He's slippery, Giles. He has never been charged with a child sex offence. Nor has a complaint been lodged since. Not in the last twenty years. If we start poking around now, it'll come across as a witch-hunt, harassment.' Falkov flicked his hand towards the table. 'This doll isn't enough.'

'Just because he hasn't acted on the idea doesn't mean he doesn't think about it. He possibly has other means to satisfy these thoughts.'

'He doesn't mix in circles, socialise with other offenders, has no online interaction. He's a solo predator . . . *if* he is a predator. One that your father couldn't pin anything concrete on. Concerns and a complaint twenty years ago, yes; evidence, no.'

'If you *had* been able to convict him, then he would have been locked away long before he was driving down the highway with his horse float. He wouldn't have been in the area the day Oliver Lavine went missing.'

It was a low blow. No cop wanted to be told that a lack of conviction meant a perpetrator was able to offend again.

'You don't know if that's the case. Nestor is still innocent until proven guilty, detective.' Falkov's face had turned ruddy. She had stepped over the line.

'Yes, sir.'

'Facts and hard evidence. Do I make myself clear?'

'Yes, sir. But we know that he drove back from Tamworth and passed Burning Mountain around the time Oliver went missing. And that's a fact. If I had a chat with him, sir, I could lay down the next piece. Just a friendly knock on the door.' Giles watched to see if the colour would fade from Inspector Falkov's cheeks. When she thought he looked slightly calmer, she pressed, 'Sir?'

Falkov leaned back in his chair, resting his hands behind his head. 'Years ago, detective, I was fortunate enough to be introduced to a military officer who dealt in explosives . . .'

Giles clamped her lips. She knew if she didn't pick up the moral of Falkov's story, he wouldn't agree to her request. She gave him her full attention.

'. . . he later became a training officer in this field. Interesting thing he said: when blowing up things, it's not about creating a whopping bang, an overkill on the C4, it's about using just enough explosives to do the job. No more. He said he taught soldiers how to blow a dewdrop off a clover leaf – not a tank a few metres off the ground.'

'Sir, I promise, I'll hardly shake the earth . . . as light and gentle as a mouse. Let me see if I can breathe some life back into the file.

I'll talk to him as the kid he used to live next door to years ago, not a cop digging around.'

Falkov scratched the back of his head, like a dog with a flea bite. The harder he rubbed the more Giles felt the urge to scratch her own head. She stared at him, waiting for his answer, wondering if all those years ago she got into boarding school because her dad was a cop, and she was smart. Or did she get a scholarship because of a sob story about living next door to a possible paedophile?

Giles lost patience. 'Is that a yes, sir?'

SIXTEEN

Amy Thicket tossed the change in the car's centre console and the carton of smokes at her husband. The sharp corner hit his cheek before bouncing off and landing on the floor by her feet.

'Pick it up,' he snorted.

Nobody moved.

The veins in Trent's neck and near his temples protruded and pulsated. He dropped his head and slowly shook it. Amy couldn't help seeing the image of an angry bull rubbing his horns on the steering wheel. She thought, *Trent's first attack, way back then, should have been his last. I should have sent him straight to the slaughterhouse.*

She reached for the carton by her feet, praying he would resist the urge to smash her head into the dashboard. She saw him tighten his grip on the steering wheel, before he started up the Honda Civic and pulled out of the supermarket car park.

Trent turned sharp left and the rear wheel clipped the edge of the gutter. He was cutting through the back of the residential area, up a road that was in the opposite direction to their home. At the t-intersection, he turned. They passed the racecourse, the thoroughbred stud farms, the fields of olive trees, picking up speed, when, in the distance, the enormous dirt mounds of spoil piles dumped from the coalmines came into view. As they continued along the winding stretch through the countryside just outside of town, Amy looked in the side mirror and watched the town of Muswellbrook disappear behind her.

Trent Thicket seldom drove. His early-afternoon drinking habit had him constantly over the limit; plus, with his messed-up sleeping cycle, he was forever drowsy, irritable. Amy believed her husband's mental fatigue and sudden bursts of anger would impair his driving. She had worried about Joe getting in the car with his father, and now that she was in the car beside him, she was terrified. She stole a glimpse at him – there was almost a smile on his face. She could sense his excitement. The thrill of being in control again.

'Where are you going?' she whispered.

'I'm taking you on a drive.'

Any other couple would look out the window, gaze at the National Park mountains and farming paddocks, at the clumps of gum trees and small herds of cattle and enjoy the sweeping landscape before them. But the Thickets' relationship was not romantic or nostalgic. They both stared straight ahead at the road before them.

The car leaned into the corners. Trent ignored the 'Reduce Speed' sign as he came over the crest. White posts with cat's eyes that marked the peak of the crest flashed past. The tyres hit loose gravel at the side of the road and kicked up stones that rattled under the vehicle. The Honda bumped over potholes and layers of asphalt that had been repeatedly laid to repair and plug the holes along the road. Amy could feel the rumbling of the uneven surface through her body.

'Open it!' roared Trent.

It wasn't a request, it was an order. Amy ripped the cardboard carton and packets of Winfields fell out onto her lap. She grabbed a pack, peeled back the plastic and foil, and pulled out a smoke.

'Light it up for me.'

Sparking the wheel of the lighter, Amy sucked back on nicotine as the flame flickered at the tip of the cigarette. She felt a wave of calmness.

'I said light it, don't smoke it.'

They came to the end of the next t-intersection, and Amy was afraid Trent would drive the two hundred and fifty kilometres all the way to Sydney. She handed him the smoke and, to entice him to return home, she gently reminded him, 'School's finished for the day. Joe will be home soon.'

'And?'

Amy's mouth opened and then closed. The next time she opened it, the words that tumbled from her mouth came without thought. 'Take me home, Trent.'

She noticed her husband's hands shaking on the steering wheel. His breath becoming rapid. She could hear her words looping in her head: *Don't upset the bull, don't upset the bull.* Troubling images of the later years of their marriage flashed. Still, she pressed, 'Trent, I want to go home.'

Trent Thicket slammed the brakes. The Honda skidded off the road and came to a halt by a paddock where startled cows looked up at the vehicle that was now covered in a swirl of dust.

'Fuck. *Farrrk.*' Trent pounded his forehead on the steering wheel. The horn blaring each time.

Amy sucked in a breath. Had the car pulled up a moment later, they would have driven straight through the fence – or worse, collided with a fencepost. She wanted to scream until her lungs hurt.

Amy swallowed. *It's always going to be like this.* She tried once more, 'Trent. Please.'

He tilted his head towards her. 'Okay, I'll take you home.' Trent's arm moved quick. He snatched her throat, squeezing her

Adam's apple between his thumb and finger, twisting the skin like a screw. 'Let's go home and be a family, Amy.' Then he shifted the car into reverse gear.

Trent accelerated back towards town. The Honda took the corners fast, pulling to the side. As they approached the floodway, the vehicle hit a dip in the road and scraped the undercarriage, then bounced like it was on a rollercoaster. Amy knew if they didn't slow down the bald tyres on loose gravel would fail to grip. She also knew her son had no idea that he should be ready to run the moment his father walked through the front door.

Amy grabbed the edge of her seat, then slid her hand further down between her legs and manually lifted the lever, adjusting the seat, pushing the base a few more centimetres away from the dash with her legs.

As they sped up the hill towards the next crescent, the car took the next bend in the road. Still blurry eyed and light-headed, she reached out and yanked the steering wheel, forcing the car to leave the road and veer between two white bollards.

The Honda Civic soared over the edge towards a ditch and a cluster of scrub and trees.

In mid-air, both Amy and Trent snapped their heads, stared, silent and bewildered into each other's eyes. For the first time in sixteen years, they didn't have a word left to say to each other.

The boy was in a hurry. In his haste to insert the key, he scratched another paint chip from the front door. Once again, he licked his thumb and wiped away the crumbling paint, knowing his father would eventually spot the nicks and scratches.

Be more careful, Joe scolded himself. Then he opened the door, stepping into the darkness. As he moved quietly down the hallway, he noticed that while the house was hot and stuffy, the air was clear. He looked into the lounge-room, expecting to see his father in front of the TV. Instead, the television was off, and both the smoke haze and the man were gone.

Mum? he whispered, but only in his head. He wanted to scream, *The bull is out.*

Joe crept slowly through the rooms of the house, lingered in the doorways. He had long ago learned the signs that things had turned bad. His mother, who would spend the night sucking in her bottom lip to hide the swelling. Masking where her lip had split by pretending to hook a stray hair from her mouth with her fingernail when she spoke. The sparce kitchen bench where preparations of the evening meal had not begun. Then, his father's fleeting remorse by barking, 'Did you learn something today?' And Joe in the middle, feeling the pull to choose sides.

Joe tiptoed down the hallway. It was not until he had peered into every room that he was certain nobody was home. This, he had never experienced before. An empty house.

In the kitchen, Joe climbed up onto a stool at the bench and waited for his parents to return. Nervous, he picked at an old scab on his knee, watched the dark crust flake away and fresh blood bubble up under his skin. He wondered if he should wait for his parents in the kitchen, or if he should be hiding under his mother's bed.

SEVENTEEN

Giles sat under the shade of a Japanese maple on the wooden bench seat in the backyard of her home. The tree stood like an imposter amongst the camellias and neighbouring gum trees. As though it had snuck away, hiding in her yard, looking for a kinder, quieter place to settle and grow.

Her home was a neat, wood-clad cottage, with a garden of camellias, roses and the Japanese maple. She liked the vegetable garden in the backyard. It was filled mostly with herbs and was too often neglected. When she'd left Sydney and taken a transfer to the Hunter Valley, Benjamin had offered her the family home, but she couldn't bring herself to move in, so she opted to find a place of her own. This had hurt her father's feelings; not that he said anything, but she saw it in his face. This meant the windows of the old place were covered up and the front door hammered shut. The two never spoke of what to do with the family home, so it had sat for the last two years empty and crumbling away.

The sky was now turning pinkie orange with the last rays of light. Giles needed a moment to breathe, to empty her mind of horsehair dolls and of her ailing father. She sucked in the air, thirsty for it. It was as though she had tumbled down Nestor's well, or was falling from one of his peach trees, and was mentally trying to cling to something solid and safe.

On the way home, she had picked up her usual six-pack from the bottle shop. Now, outside in the shade, in the open, she had space and time to think. She needed to relax, and the alcohol helped her to get there quicker.

Somewhere nearby, paper wasps had built a nest and were the first to discover her under the canopy of the maple tree before the flies. Giles stuck her thumb down the neck of the bottle; she didn't want the wasps looting her beer.

Her mind kept flooding with all the tiny things of her childhood. Her home, where, at the back of the house, the land had slanted down to the meandering river that cut through the fields as it made its way from Denman to Muswellbrook and beyond. It was there that Bernard Nestor gave Giles her first doll.

He had stepped out from behind a willow tree, warmly nodded a hello. They had not spoken to each other before then. She had not been that close to him. His face and cheeks drooped like a bloodhound. The skin on his neck looked like cracked cement. She watched his fingers, raw and red, slip into his pocket and he pulled out a small doll made of horsehair. She had never seen a doll like it before and was inquisitive about the braids that looped together, the plaited arms and legs, an entwining body of hay and horsehair. Through the long strands of hair that were balled up to make the head of the doll, she could see tucked inside a seed from a peach.

Her stomach had tightened at the thought of the seed once being in Bernard Nestor's mouth, before it was turned into the toy's head.

Nestor had stretched out his hand, offering her the dolly. His voice was soft and friendly, like a man who would cause her no harm. 'I've made you a little girl. A friend.' He nodded towards the doll lying in his flattened palm. Giles had hesitated, not wanting her fingers to touch his skin if she took the doll. 'Go on,' Nestor had urged. As she reached out and pinched the head with her fingertips to lift the doll up from his palm, she feared he'd close his fist, like a trick; or worse, snatch her by the wrist.

Neither happened, and she took the doll, remembered her manners and thanked him, and as she turned away, she felt him watching her. The hairs on the back of her neck stiffened, and her heart quickened. After that, she no longer did roly-polys down the slope to the creek, and when she saw him in the orchard she stayed inside. But when she thought she was safe and alone, she would sneak away to the well and milkweed beetles.

Giles sucked in a full breath, held onto it for as long as she could. Her chest tightened and sweat began to build up on her top lip. She felt raw and dizzy and ill. She tipped back her head, gulped at the air, then guzzled down the rest of her beer. It quenched her thirst and cooled her throat. She emptied the frothy dregs at the bottom of the bottle over the wilting parsley in the drying veggie patch, as two white butterflies fluttered around the dampened leaves.

As the wind picked up, her hip vibrated, and it took a moment to register the phone call before fumbling in her pocket. She wanted to yell, *What?* But her mood quickly shifted when she saw Bray's name pop up on the screen.

'Whatcha doin'?' he asked.

'Hmm . . .' She looked at the beer froth dripping off the parsley leaves, and answered, 'Watering the garden.'

'Falkov wants the team to focus on just the four friends.'

So Falkov had overruled her father, denied her interview request. 'Is it Oliver Lavine?' Her voice sounded wobbly.

'It's starting to stack up that way. And if it is Oliver, we need to go back to the beginning. Follow the timeline from the start.'

'Okay.'

'And it begins with his friends out on the mountain. If we just keep collecting information and documenting it, the picture of what happened will begin to emerge. Track back Oliver's last few weeks, his final days, then narrow down to what happened in the gap from when he separated from his friends to when he was alone and possibly ended up in that grave.'

'Final *days*? That means starting with his mother?'

'Yep,' Bray agreed. 'Starting with his mother.'

Giles looked at the empty bottle in her hand. The names – Janet Lavine, Bob Bradbury, Belinda Marrone, Phillip O'Dell and Paul Cooper – rolled around in her head. 'Righto.' She tapped the phone screen and decided her next drink needed to be something stronger.

Liam Edison pushed his fringe back from his face. He had been watching a worm dug out from the grave writhing on the pile of dry soil, and bull ants periodically returning to the worm, contemplating their next meal to drag back to their nest. He stepped cautiously to the side. The ants were aggressive, and a bite would sting. Kelsey, on the other hand, kneeled on the ground, either unperturbed by the ants or distracted.

'Ants don't bother you?' Edison asked.

'Nope.'

She reached for a smaller trowel and continued slowly grating back the soil. It was easy to damage a skeleton in the excavation process, and Liam watched as she made sure her body didn't lean on top of the area where they expected the skeleton to rest under the soil. Kelsey was meticulous in her movements.

'Snakes do,' she smirked.

Liam's eyes scanned the area at the thought. Shivered a little. The sun was beginning to set, and he moved to switch on one of the High CRI LED lights by the grave. The area became bright and luminous, and Kelsey's lips pursed like she was about to whistle.

'Ooh. That's the trick.'

She snatched up a brush, flicked it gently over the soil, then looked up at Edison.

'We just found our first bone.'

Liam stepped forward, and down on his knees beside Kelsey, he took a closer look. There was a small crack along the bone where the soft collagen inside had long ago deteriorated.

'Looks brittle.'

'Then I'll have to be careful,' said Kelsey.

'I'll call the detectives. Give them the good news.'

'Which one?' asked Kelsey. 'The boofy one, or the pretty one?'

DAY 3

EIGHTEEN

At the Maiden Jewel Camping grounds, the first light of the morning had only just touched the tip of the cliff face. The stone range along the edge of the National Park glowed a vibrant orange. Giles, Bray and Edison had decided to meet early. Giles and Bray wanted to see the discovery of bones for themselves, and then, making the most of the cooler temperature before the day started to heat up, head on over to Burning Mountain and walk the trek to the top.

It was Giles's idea to try to re-enact the tragic jaunt of the five friends. She wanted to see if the timings correlated with the statements, and if what they could or couldn't see matched the group's original descriptions. Mostly it was to get an idea of just how long Oliver had to potentially hike back down the mountain and climb into another vehicle. The timing felt tight. Edison had decided to tag along to collect soil and rock samples and to scratch his itch of curiosity and explore the territory.

On the fallen log where the bushwalker had previously waited for them on the first day they'd arrived, Giles and Bray now sat lacing up their hiking boots. They were both dressed in navy blue and khaki hiking gear. By Giles's feet was a backpack filled with water bottles, a first-aid kit, stopwatch, camera, pens, biohazard bags and maps of the area.

Liam Edison had also arrived dressed for the bush, and Giles knew he was watching her and Bray fumble with their laces, struggling to loop the speed-hooks at the top of their boots. She thought, *If he asks me if I need help, I'll kick him.* At last, she double knotted the laces that seemed too long for her boots. Beside her, Bray wiped his thumb across his brow and started massaging his temple like he was pushing away a headache. She pursed her lips, almost wanting to laugh. They hadn't even begun the hike and they both looked out of their comfort zone.

'You good?' asked Bray.

Giles wriggled her toes inside her shoes, sucked in the morning air and smirked as she replied, 'Only when I'm on duty.' Truth was, she was beginning to crave a shot of caffeine; or perhaps something stronger and harsher tasting to glug down. 'Are you all good?' she returned the question.

'Yeah,' replied Bray. 'I guess.'

Yeah, thought Giles, *as happy as a tin of worms going fishing.*

Edison, however, had been patient. When he felt he had their attention, he said, 'Now that we've unearthed bone, it's the pelvis that we need intact. It's the more accurate measurement to determine the sex of a skeleton. Kelsey's doing a good job at carefully removing each section. It can be easy to miss a bone when they take on the stained colour of the soil, but they've survived quite well in the ground.

'It will take time, and I still need to get it all to the lab, but from the skull I'd say male. The sloping forehead and square eye sockets are common in males. Female eye sockets are more round. The brow ridges on this skull are also more pronounced. The skull isn't fully developed, but those indicators point to male.'

Bray nodded, looked down at his boots deciding to double knot the laces the same as Giles. He huffed, and when he was done, stretched out his legs and looked at his feet, grinning.

Edison had offered to drive them over to Burning Mountain in his van. Most of his equipment was in it, should he need it. His focus was looking at the terrain, landscape and soil. Collect samples. Botany was always a good source of evidence to help secure a conviction. As he fished around in his own pack, he looked almost apologetic.

'Like I said the other day, the body has been buried in a deliberately cut grave, so that indicates disposal by another person. I guess that's your first indicator and proof of criminal activity. A soil sample from the scene could have a similar chemical profile to that taken from the suspect.'

'We don't have a suspect,' grumbled Bray. 'We don't even have a formal identity yet for our victim. And we're almost twenty years behind on the Oliver Lavine case as it is, so you think the soil would still be on the offender after all these years?'

'Not the suspect,' said Edison. 'But the tool used to dig the grave, perhaps.'

'Lot of people own shovels,' said Bray.

'The marks in the soil suggest a flat blade shovel head,' said Edison. 'Something with a kick plate.'

'Common shovel,' said Bray. 'In most garden sheds.'

'Yeah,' said Edison. 'But when was the last time you upgraded your shovel?'

Giles smirked. She grabbed a bottle of water from her backpack, pondering, 'Where would four children get a shovel?'

Bray shrugged. 'They could have returned with a shovel.'

'How? Pushbike?'

'Paul Cooper's stepbrother dropped and picked him up,' said Bray. 'Phillip O'Dell's mother drove her son, Bob Bradbury, and

Belinda Marrone. Those kids could have spun any number of bullshit stories of why they needed to return with a shovel.'

'I suppose.' Giles clicked her tongue, retracting the idea. 'But they would have needed to hide the body in the interim. And Dad had a whole army out looking for Oliver by then.'

'I guess that theory has holes too.' Bray dropped his head.

They were still stuck in the early investigation process; evidence gathering and information analysis. Every time they jumped to theory development, there were gaping holes in their suggestions and nothing rang true. *Bugger me, every idea is just a bum steer to a dead end.* Giles felt they were miles away from homing in on a suspect, let alone making an arrest or charging anyone. The lack of progress irritated her.

'Either those four were in cahoots and are sticking to their stories, or Oliver Lavine hitched a ride and climbed in the wrong vehicle . . . and that possibly points back to Bernard Nestor.' Giles caught the look on Bray's face when she mentioned Nestor's name. She twisted the lid off the water bottle, pointed it towards him like an extension of her finger and pushed on.

'Dad took photos of what was inside all four backpacks. They ate their sandwiches, drank half their water, but they never got to the snacks. So, what happened on that mountain that made them not open their treats?'

'Something disrupted them?'

'Was Oliver the disruption?'

'Then the idea of eating snacks was overridden by the idea of . . .' Bray shrugged. 'What to do about Oliver? Christ, Giles, that's a big stretch. And if something happened, how did they get Oliver from Burning Mountain down to here? It's about ten kilometres.'

'There were four of them,' said Giles. 'One on each arm and leg?'

The three officers didn't move. It was as if the image had stilled them. Giles almost wanted to apologise for her suggestion. Plus, when she thought about it, it also wasn't plausible. The group would have had to carry Oliver through the town of Wingen.

Edison cleared his throat, swallowed. 'Maybe Oliver didn't come to grief up there; maybe it was closer to the bottom of the mountain? Or even where the skull was found.' He went silent again. 'It's neat. The grave, I mean. If I gave four kids a shovel and told them to dig, I'm not sure it would look that neat and deep. However, I've never come across a grave dug by children before.'

Bray chimed in, 'When I was a kid, my mother said I always made the perfect cup of coffee. I thought it was a science. The level of instant coffee was the same measurement every time on the teaspoon, the boiling water filled to the same level, and the exact amount of milk in every cup. I watched her make a cup and repeated exactly what I saw. It wasn't until I started drinking the stuff myself that I realised it didn't matter.' Bray looked at Giles. 'What I'm saying is, maybe these kids didn't know any different. A grave in their minds had to be exactly that, a perfect cut grave. It's all they knew. And there were four of them. They had time to rest, break, motivate each other to keep digging.'

'Hmm.' Giles pushed back with her father's theory. 'Then there was Bernard Nestor on his way home from Tamworth. Could have had a shovel in his horse float, used to scrape out manure ... or dig a hole in the ground.'

'Think he'd put in the effort to dig something precise like that?'

'Dunno. But I reckon his mind is wired differently. I think he'd be capable of anything.'

'Even if the child's death was by misfortune, whoever dug the grave failed to report it,' Edison added.

'So, whoever dug the grave must have had a good reason not to report it,' said Bray.

Edison nodded. 'Trauma fracture on the skull is possibly your best reason.'

'Was the trauma inflicted – which could point to Nestor? Or an accident, which could point back to the four friends?' Bray continued. 'And are we calling the gravesite the crime scene, or do we now think it's just one location in the sequence, and Burning Mountain is where it started?'

Giles's feet were already starting to ache. She took a long drink from the bottled water, then exhaled. 'I'm not sure if the crime took place here, but I think we can be pretty sure this is where it ended.'

NINETEEN

As the sun rose and the light of a new day spilled into the kitchen, Joe Thicket felt sure that neither of his parents would return. He dreaded what his father may have done to his mother, though somehow he'd always had a hunch this day would come.

Joe slid off the bench stool. His back sore and stiff. Not once during the night had he whimpered or cried and was surprised at his resilience.

In the bathroom, he peed, brushed his hair and teeth, then, back in the kitchen, he made a sandwich, inspecting the slices of bread for mould before adding lots of butter and a smidge of Vegemite. Still dressed in the school uniform from the day before, only now crumpled and smelling musty, he grabbed his backpack, put his lunch inside with the homework that was never attempted, and zipped it up.

Before leaving for school, he stood at the entry of the lounge-room. His finger lifted in the air, Joe began to trace the shape of where his father should be. His pointer finger drawing the shoulders, beefy arms, chest, thick legs, neck and head. He even added two curved horns. The outline of a bull. The outline of a Minotaur that should be sitting in the faded chintz recliner chair, smoking and watching the television.

He mouthed wordlessly to the empty room, *Goodbye, Dad.*

Joe had no intention of calling the police to find his parents. The police had been called to the house many times before. The boy had watched them come and go. He had cowered under his parents' bed, silently begging the officers to help, only to hear them on the doorstep speak to his mother and then for her to close the door. The police would always leave them to fend for themselves.

Joe tucked the house key into his pocket, dropped his head and closed the front door behind him. He had decided to tell no-one his parents were missing.

TWENTY

Paul Cooper – Coops for short, Cunt when he was out of earshot – looked at his watch and smirked. It was the end of a roster, his twelve-hour nightshift was over, and he eagerly anticipated the next few days off.

The mine ran on a four-on, four-off roster. Enough time off to wind down and get the body clock into a new rhythm.

In the muster room, the miners met and briefed with the handover shift. They updated on what was advanced, what was left undone, but their minds were already on the breakfast brew, the *beerfast* that would be waiting for them down at the pub.

In the showers, they stripped naked. A quick scrub down. No-one wanted to spend any more time than they had to at work. The general chatter was charged with noise, laughter and relief for the four-day break ahead. The team soaped up, scrubbed dirt out of their nails, navels and armpits. They blew it out of their nostrils and hoped no stupid bastard would piss on their leg for fun.

Paul liked this end-of-shift ritual. He'd let the soap suds glide down his body and feel pleasure at his team's insecurities. He used his physique like a weapon, a form of torment. He relished the feeling of contempt towards his leanness, watching from the corner of his eye as the older bastards sucked in their beer guts, and the younger ones shuffled, enviously, away from his side.

The team took turns reaching for the shampoo, suds quickly foamed in their hair. Some tested the shampoo bottles first, making sure they hadn't been filled with flocculant. Drillers' floc, or flocculant, was a goopy substance. When added to water it created a sticky slimy solution that stone chips clung to. Some of the crew stuck it in the shampoo bottles for fun – then watched as it mixed with water and became sticky. Flocculant was a bugger to get out of your hair. Any poor bastard that left a shift with sticky globs in their hair couldn't say anything except *Floc you!*

They swung their bags filled with empty lunchboxes and water bottles over their shoulders and headed out towards the car park, where 4x4s sat caked in mud and dust. Utes with toolboxes and chrome gun racks cooked in the heat. Next sat some badly tuned V8s. The younger boys had lined up their WRXs under the only shady trees, and Paul Cooper's recently restored SS Torana, in glossy Contessa gold paint, took prime position under the largest and bushiest eucalyptus. The sight of his car made his chest lift, and he walked with a swagger towards it. All that money working in the mine, and without a girlfriend to drain his finances: what else was there for a bloke to spend his money on?

Inside the car, Paul kicked over the engine, gave it a few revs for good measure. The song on the radio faded out and a quick update on the day's weather followed with the top news stories. Paul swallowed, turned up the dial, caught the end of the news report.

... after the grim discovery of skeletal remains in bushlands near Mount Wingen ...

Paul suddenly felt like he needed to piss. Nauseated, he struggled to focus.

. . . currently being exhumed for forensic testing, believed to be of a youth . . .

A horn blared. Paul jerked in his seat. One of the shift crew was leaving the car park, his hand out the window in a wave. Paul didn't have the strength to wave back, only managing a nod. The news story was over, the radio now playing an ad for discounted whitegoods. He'd missed the details of the breaking story but had heard enough to catch on.

'Fuck . . . *fuck.*'

He snapped his head towards the empty passenger seat, almost as if he'd find Oliver Lavine sitting there by his side.

TWENTY-ONE

They had driven from Mount Wingen to Burning Mountain, and now followed the track leading to the top. It would take them a little under an hour to complete the hike. The path was well maintained, with a few steps cut into the trail and metal bridges along the way. In some areas along the trail, it was steep; other sections were an idyllic stroll under the canopy and welcome shade of the gum trees.

Giles was surprised how she, Edison and Bray had already broken out into a sweat. Puffing kept the conversation to a minimum. A few places along the trek, they passed wooden benches for hikers to catch their breath, or to take in the sweeping view of the valley below, yet none of them asked for a rest stop.

To one side, the bushland was lush, green and inviting. To the other, the trees were dead, stumps, or fallen; the ground sparse, empty and lifeless. The trail of the coal seam underground had cooked tree roots, turning the clay to hard brick, killing off the ability for vegetation to grow.

Giles kept looking down at the stopwatch each time they passed a significant landmark and recorded the time on the map. Timing their return had them troubled. Did Oliver run some of the way?

How far would he need to go before the others lost sight of him, and would sound travel back to them? The sound of an approaching car on the road? A scream? A door slam? Yet none of the witness statements mentioned hearing such a thing.

At the top, the mountain smouldered. Smoke rose from chimney cracks in the ground, and the heat from the coal seam created a shimmering haze over the area. A few kangaroos, attracted by the warmth, had come to bask in the sun and lie on the warm rock. They took off to the scrub when the three officers appeared at the top of the viewing platform.

'*Christ!* To be fifteen again,' said Bray, rolling his shoulders and arching his back.

'No thanks,' said Giles. She turned to Edison. 'You?'

'Nup.'

Bray huffed, blowing air out of his nose. 'A few more years, and you'll be wishing for the agility of a fifteen-year-old.'

'Agility, yes. Middle adolescence, nah,' said Giles. 'I was a moody fifteen-year-old. It's a tough age.'

'You think Oliver and his friends were finding it tough?'

Giles took a moment to answer. She looked out at the surrounding dirt and rocks that were almost bleached white from the heat, and mumbled, 'I think after that fateful day, they would have found things tough.'

The team went silent and stared down at the vast expanse of white ash and pink stone below the lookout. The clay had cooked and made the area more like a moonscape. But the drop under the viewing platform was hardly treacherous. A few boulders, cooked clay, heat and the smell of sulphur. If Oliver had fallen, he might have cracked a rib at most, been bruised, *but died*?

Around Giles's feet, the baked clay was pink and pretty. She swooped down and picked up a piece of broken rock. It was creamy white, rosy in the centre. When she caught Edison's eye, she asked, 'Was it what you expected?'

'Not at all.' He looked around, then back at Giles, and gave a small smile. 'Better.'

Giles twisted her lips at him. To Bray she said, 'If Oliver Lavine fell from the viewing platform, he'd tumble a few metres. If that. It couldn't have been a fatal fall. There are enough tufts of grass to stop the motion of rolling down the hill. It's not a great height, nor is there a crevice to disappear down. And if he walked away, his friends would have watched him for some time – a lot of the mountain range has been cleared of trees. Unless he walked back the other way and came down the mountain through the dense forest?' She stared at Bray and, when he didn't comment, she tossed the pink rock into the sky as though skimming the stone across the clouds. She watched it sail in the air.

'I think you're right,' Giles said finally. 'I need to go back and reinterview the four friends. Chat with Mum. Start at the beginning.'

'Collect a sample of the mother's DNA,' added Edison. 'We can get it from the teeth found in the skull and the denser bones. Send them off to the lab together, and hopefully your mystery will be answered.'

'A-ha. So, you must almost be done at the site then?'

'Almost there.'

Giles flashed a smile. Liam and Kelsey had moved quicker at the crime scene than she expected. The case was like a jigsaw puzzle, and now Liam Edison had given her a corner piece.

Bray crouched and rummaged in his backpack, then handed a bottle of water each to Edison and Giles. He asked, 'Did you get permission to talk to Nestor?'

'Nope. But maybe if *you* asked Falkov . . .' Giles tried to nudge Bray with her elbow, but he stepped backwards and dodged it.

He twisted the cap off his bottle, and she watched him scull nearly the whole thing. 'Perhaps we widen our net, expand our suspect list,' he added. 'Stay open. Don't fixate on just Nestor and Oliver's friends.'

Giles nodded, disappointed. She turned to face the track they'd walked. 'I don't believe Oliver died up here. I can't imagine four teens getting him back down the mountain, let alone another ten kilometres to Wingen. I think the first sequence of events started at the bottom of the mountain.' She turned to Edison. 'You collect your samples, take your time. Bray and I will meet you down there.' She flicked her hand briefly at the trail, and Edison nodded. Back at Bray, she asked, 'Are you going to time me?'

'Yup. I'll give it fifteen minutes, then I'll follow behind, see if I can spot you through the trees.'

'And if you can spot me, then –'

'Then those four statements, from all those years ago, are a bum steer and full of bullshit.'

'Yeah. And the net's the same size, and the suspect list hasn't changed.'

Giles turned and began to slow jog down the track. Bray hit the starter button on the stopwatch.

TWENTY-TWO

The road had been blocked for over an hour. Drivers were re-directed to take the long detour out to Denman and then back into Muswellbrook. A police officer was stationed at the entry point of the road, stopping vehicles trying to access the route, diverting unhappy drivers, while another uniform helped set up a temporary orange and black detour sign at the t-intersection.

Emergency vehicles called out to the MVA were parked along the shoulder, butted up close to the barbed fence, lights flashing but sirens silent. Edderton Road would be closed for some time, due to the discovery of a rusty white Honda Civic that had left the bitumen and crashed into the trees and scrub below.

It would take time to determine what had occurred. The forensics and photographs collected would help clarify if the accident was a result of negligent or dangerous driving. Considering there were no witnesses, tyre marks, other vehicles involved – along with the dry conditions and a stretch of road easy enough to navigate – the Crash Investigation Unit were left scratching their heads and asking, *Swerved at the last minute to miss a kangaroo? Fell asleep? Speed? Distracted? Drunk?*

A volunteer catering crew from the Rural Fire Service had also arrived. A small, white-haired lady had made coffee in environmentally friendly cups that burned everyone's fingers, brewed so hot it burned everyone's tongues. She offered biscuits to the police and fire brigade, with a promise of sandwiches and zucchini slices to follow.

With coffee and bikkies in hand, Turner and MacCrum both stood tall and lean. In the subtle breeze MacCrum's blond hair blew wayward, while Turner's, slicked back with styling paste, stayed defiantly still. They were both looking over the scene as they blew over the top of their instant coffee in the cheap cardboard cups. The car's registration told them who the victim was. They'd be opening an inquest into the death of Trent Joseph Thicket. Yet still, nobody seemed to move.

The crash scene had been taped off. There had been no talk of vehicle recovery yet, or body removal. Thicket still sat in the driver's seat, blood-splattered, shards of metal protruding from his neck, possibly puncturing the carotid artery. It would be some hours before the investigation unit would be finished with the scene, and until they were done, the body would stay in the car, bloated, foam leaking out of mouth and nose, attracting the flies with the stench of death.

The unit was still spraying yellow paint on the tar, locating the exact point the car had left the road. Turner was also grappling to understand exactly what had happened. The road was reasonably well maintained, but he couldn't say the same about the vehicle. He'd never seen tyres that bald. Why hadn't Thicket been pulled over and slapped with an on-the-spot fine for driving a car in that condition? Why had he ignored the airbag recall? Probably because it was bloody Trent Thicket, that's why.

MacCrum sipped his coffee, then snapped his Monte Carlo in half, dunked and shoved the biscuit in his mouth. He chewed slowly.

After a long pause, he said, 'Saw Trent yesterday. I'm wondering if it was state of mind that led to the incident.'

'I'm thinking state of car.'

'Could have been both. I reckon it was the faulty airbag that killed him, not the drop off the edge of the road.'

Turner dipped his head, agreeing.

'Farmer found him.' MacCrum swallowed the biscuit. 'Scared the crap out of him.'

'Even dead, Trent Thicket can still scare the crap out of someone.'

A young officer from the Crash Investigation Unit approached them, holding a plastic evidence bag up in the air. 'You know this bloke?'

They both nodded.

'Smoker?'

'Most likely,' said MacCrum.

'Smoke packs found scattered all around the cabin.'

'Cigarettes aren't illicit drugs,' said Turner, pointing to the clear bag the officer was holding.

'Still a drug, innit?' the constable snapped.

Turner shrugged. 'If Trent was distracted opening the carton of smokes, then it's no wonder his driving was chaotic.'

'Like his fucking life,' added MacCrum, before sipping on his coffee.

The uniform lowered the bag. 'He wasn't the only one in the car at the time of the crash, though.'

Turner and MacCrum glanced at each other. MacCrum took a step forward. 'What do you mean?'

'Passenger side has blood smeared around the front window. Down the bonnet. Like someone's crawled out of the wreckage.'

'How long are they saying the body's been deceased?' asked MacCrum.

The uniform looked impatient. 'A day. At least.'

MacCrum nodded, flicked his hand at the officer, letting him know he could leave. He looked back at Turner. 'Thicket's wife was sitting in the passenger seat yesterday.'

'Yeah?' said Turner. 'Well, she's not sitting in it today.'

TWENTY-THREE

In the cool shade of the weeping tree, Belinda Marrone sipped on a glass of Coke, no ice. She kept forgetting to fill up the ice tray and the Coke had only been in the fridge for an hour or so. It tasted bitter, and she wished it was refreshing, but it wasn't.

On the hard, makeshift rustic bench, she sat. The timber had once been scraped and smoothed, but over the years, with the changing seasons of sun and rain, the wood had cracked and the splits in the timber now pinched her thighs.

Bell clenched her back teeth, yanked at her tiny denim shorts to stop the wood biting into her skin and brushed away the flies landing on her lashes. She tried to settle in, get comfy so she could flick through her magazine, but she was disturbed again when a vehicle she didn't recognise pulled up in the drive.

Stuff me, bugger off. She frowned at the sedan. *Sales guy? Selling religion or solar panels?* She didn't need either of those things in her life. *Real estate? Not my crappy love-shack to sell – sweet.* She stopped guessing when a woman emerged, tall and beautiful, long dark hair in a ponytail that reached the middle of her back, dressed in an expensive-looking black tailored pants suit.

The sound of the car door slamming scared the birds from the nearby feeder. The corellas took to the sky and Bell suddenly felt alone. She cleared her throat and asked, 'Can I help you?'

'Belinda Marrone?'

'Maybe. Who's asking?'

'I'm Detective Senior Constable Rebecca Giles from Muswellbrook Police Station.' A badge was flashed. It came and disappeared as quickly as the smile. 'I was wondering if you had a moment to talk.'

'About?'

'The department is looking into an old case. I have your name on file, and a witness statement you made.'

Bell yanked at her shorts and covered her legs with the magazine. She had only ever given one witness statement in her lifetime. Still, she asked, 'What case?'

'Oliver Lavine.'

The cop's answer had come too quick, giving Bell no time to wish the visit was related to a different matter. She stuttered, 'Ol-Oliver?'

Christ, she hadn't heard his name in years . . . *years*.

'I just wanted to ask a few questions. We can do it here and you can sign an affidavit, or come down to the station?'

Bell held up her drink, tossed her magazine to the side, and shook her head. She wasn't getting changed or going for a ride with the woman, and she didn't give a shit if the cop pegged her as lazy. It was too hot. Plus, she wanted to distance herself as fast as she could from the events of that day. Bell grumbled, 'Why? What do you want to know?'

'May I sit, Belinda?'

Bell reluctantly nodded, patted down her frizzy hair, wishing she'd made the effort to put on some make-up that morning.

As Giles sat at the end of the bench, Bell looked her over. She had caught a whiff of the clean freshness of the police officer, how someone would smell just after a shower. The musky odour of deodorant, hand cream and perfume.

'Belinda, I was hoping you could –'

'Bell.'

'Pardon?'

'Bell. Nobody calls me Belinda. Just my mum.'

'Okay . . . Bell . . . I was hoping to ask you a few questions about the events on the sixth of April, the day Oliver Lavine disappeared.'

'That was about twenty years ago.'

'Eighteen years.'

Bell swatted away a fly and saw the police officer did the same. 'How am I expected to remember something that happened *almost* twenty years ago?'

'We could try? You never know, Bell, a tiny detail might be helpful.'

'Helpful for what?'

'You haven't heard?'

'Heard what?'

She watched the cop lick her lips, eye her over. 'You've not listened to the news of late?'

'Nup.' Bell shrugged, noticed the detective did the same. It seemed that the officer was trying to match her body behaviour, test her compliance. She leaned forward to confirm her suspicion, tucked her hands between her thighs, and the detective copied. Wary, she asked, 'What's this about?'

'We've found skeleton remains near Mount Wingen.'

'What's that got to do with me?'

'Hopefully nothing.'

The comment sounded slightly abrupt and accusing. Bell's mouth felt dry, and she took a sip of her warm Coke. It had lost its fizz.

The cop continued, 'I just want to know a little more about Oliver. What he was like. His last movements.'

'I already did this, years ago. Eighteen years ago. Read my statement. It's all in there.'

'Okay, then what was the argument over?'

'Argument? Who said we had an argument?'

'It's in the file. The group split up, after having heated words. A disagreement then?'

'It wasn't an *argument* or *disagreement*. We were pranking, daring each other to do dumb shit along the hike. Just being young and dumb, seeing how brave we could be.'

'Pranks? Like?'

'It was *dumb*. We saw a goanna, and Paul was goading Bob to . . .' Bell winced. Sucked in her bottom lip. 'It was nothing, nothing to do with Oliver going missing.'

'What happened with the goanna?'

'*Nothing.*'

The detective twisted her lip and Bell was glad when she let it slide. 'When the four of you arrived at the bottom of the hill –'

'Four?'

Giles flicked through her notebook. 'Four: you, Bob, Paul –'

'Nah, three. Oliver left down the hill first, then Paul followed.' Bell held up a hand showing two fingers. 'Bob, Phil and I . . .' With her other hand she held up three fingers. 'The *three* of us arrived after. The other two were already gone.' She dropped her hands back into her lap.

'How did Paul get home again?'

'Paul got picked up by his stepbrother, and Oliver was supposed to be picked up by his mother, but he wasn't . . . obviously.'

'Huh. Paul's stepbrother, what's his name?'

'Lucas.'

'Surname?'

'Mucus.' Bell grinned. 'Lucas-mucus. Because he was always spitting. It was disgusting. He was a pig.'

'Hmm. Did Oliver and Lucas get on?'

Bell snorted. 'No-one got on with Lucas. He was older than us. We never hung out with him. We were in Year 9, Lucas was in Year 12 – only he never finished high school. Left halfway through the first term.'

'Uh-huh.' There was hardly a breath before the next question. 'How long after Oliver left the group at the top of the mountain did Paul leave?'

'Dunno. Ten, fifteen minutes, I suppose.'

'So not straight away?'

'Nup.'

'And after Paul went down the mountain, how long before you decided to return?'

'Same. Ten, fifteen, I think. It was a long time ago.' Bell looked down into her glass of Coke warming in the sun, contemplated tipping it out on the grass. 'I can't remember exactly.'

A short pause to scribble in a notepad, and then another question. 'Did Oliver have many friends in school?'

'Nup. Not a lot of friends. Just us, really.'

'Was Oliver bullied at school?'

'Eh?' Bell felt light-headed.

'Bullying?'

Bell took a breath. 'I guess. Yeah. Oliver got picked on. So did I. School wasn't all that pleasant for us.'

'Who was your school bully?'

'I didn't have *one*, I had *many* . . . for a while.'

'Who was the worst?'

'Paul Cooper . . . but then they all just stopped.'

'What made them stop?'

'Paul Cooper.'

'I'm not sure I understand. Can you explain that?'

Bell felt a sudden surge of self-distrust. The cop's questions were coming too swiftly. To stop herself from yammering she took a gulp of the warm bitter drink and said, 'Look, I don't want to be rude, but I was just on my way out.' It was a poor lie, an obvious one. 'I just remembered I have to be somewhere. Can we do this another time?'

'Sure.' Giles handed Bell a card. 'Think you could come into the station tomorrow?'

'Hmm. Maybe. Yeah.'

'I'd appreciate it.'

Bell watched the cop stand, could smell the fabric softener in her clothes as the air flowed around them. Detective Giles's dark hair was glossy in the sun, and Bell unconsciously reached up and patted down her frizzy hair again. It felt fluffy and unruly. As she watched the police officer leave, the thought of Paul pulled her back to her joyless schooldays. To the taunts and teasing – before Paul Cooper changed the game.

She was reminded of the afternoons when the bell chimed to end another day of school. How she'd sneak out the gates in a different direction each day with her bag over her shoulder and her head down.

Head down. Head down. Don't make eye contact. Walk faster. Keep going. You might get home before they spot you.

The boys were like foxhounds, and she was the table bird. At fifteen she had matured faster than most girls in her year group, her hips and breasts fuller, her hair wild, and considering she was a loner, it made her an easy target. The boys – bursting with hormones, horny and lacking discipline – would spot Bell easily and the name calling would begin.

'Hey, ding-a-ling. Come play with my thing-a-ling.'

They'd grope themselves and try to hurl spit bombs in her direction. *Boys and their fucking spitting.* She'd take no notice of them.

Keep walking. Walk faster. Head down. Head down. Faster. Faster. Walk a little faster. Don't run. No, don't run.

Bell could ignore the name calling, wash off the spit. After a while, the spitting and teasing weren't enough. The taunting progressed to chunks of clay being collected from the back footy oval, kept in schoolbags during the day, ready to be hurled at her as she made her way home. The clay would hit its target and crumble. Like a dirt explosion. Bell would go home, remove her school uniform, shake the dust out of her hair and bra, and wipe it from the back of her neck.

Only, one afternoon, some cocky bastard confused a rock for a clump of dry clay. He picked up a stone instead, aimed and threw it towards her. It had pelted into the back of her head.

Crack.

'Fuckin' bullseye! Dead bang on!'

Bell tried to walk on ahead, but she felt light, dizzy, and fell forward. The next moment, her face was in the grass. She couldn't see. Her eyes were a fog of tears. Then she felt a hand on her shoulder, and when she looked up it was Paul.

Gorgeous Paul Cooper.

One hand slid under her arm, helping her back to her feet, the other around her waist supporting her weight and taking her to safety.

'Keep walking, Bell, fuck 'em. Up here, just around the corner.'

Bell clung to Paul's arm. They walked until he sat her gently down under a camellia bush out the front of an abandoned house.

'You okay?'

Bell had nodded, her face full of snot and tears. She couldn't talk for the air caught in her throat, so she let it go. Let it all out.

All those afternoons of torment flooding from her. And Paul, now to her rescue, sat down beside her, his arm over her shoulder. She sobbed. Her body shook, and when her body stopped heaving, she rested her head on his shoulder. She felt Paul's hand on top of her head. It smoothed her hair, then pressure, his palm firm on the back of her head, pushing her down. While Paul was comforting her, he had dropped his pants.

The cost – the price she had to pay for protection for the rest of her high school years. Nobody knew of this payment, and in her adult years it hung over her, like a black secret that threatened to be revealed to the whole town. That lingering threat reduced the size of her aspirations and the people she collected around her.

Bell looked down at the card, at the name Detective Senior Constable Rebecca Giles, and wondered, *Are you going to finally tell the truth now, Belinda? For Oliver?*

'Lucas Cooper,' repeated Giles.

There was a hum on the phone line and Giles squeezed her fists tight around the steering wheel of the car, frustrated with the mobile reception. She hadn't expected much from her meeting with Belinda Marrone, but now she was impatient to explain her speculations to Bray. She had found the first inconsistency in the story told almost twenty years ago.

'Lucas Cooper,' she said again, louder. 'The stepbrother. You said to widen the net. *Bray?*'

'Sorry, I'm at the gravesite. Reception's shit. Say that again.'

'Lucas. Cooper.'

'What about him?'

'Oliver was the first to walk down the mountain, but what if at the bottom he bumped into Lucas Cooper? And something

happened between Lucas and Oliver, before Paul arrived, or even
when Paul arrived. Belinda Marrone hinted the group was cagey
around Lucas.'

'What about the other three?'

'That's just the thing – the other three weren't at the bottom of
the mountain yet. Oliver left, *then* Paul, *then* the last three. Four
didn't walk down the mountain together, only three.'

'Ha! That shrinks the window of opportunity.'

'Yeah.' Giles knew she was left with an unexplained fifteen
minutes, from the time Oliver reached the bottom of the mountain,
to when he disappeared. 'When we regroup in the morning, I'll
write the timeline up on the crazy board. Use the maps and calcu-
lations we collected from this morning.' Giles grinned. 'The gap's
getting smaller, Bray.'

'Then we're getting closer.' The phone crackled again, and Giles
only caught the last of Bray's words, but it was enough to make her
smile. '. . . let's see if we can track down Lucas. I think we need to
have a chat with the Cooper boys.'

Giles's fists loosened on the steering wheel. 'Thanks, sir.'

'Just so you know, the media visited the site again. Filmed the
white and blue tape flapping in the breeze, and are keen to let
the public know we've got an ongoing homicide investigation. Police
Media Unit are handling it. Official press release went out a few
hours ago and Falkov gave a statement over the phone. The buzz is
starting to build. Radio stations are already running with the story,
and it'll be on the news by this evening – papers tomorrow.' More
crackle down the phone, and Bray's voice came back louder, clearer.
'. . . not a basement story, so expect a bit of interest.'

'Is that good?'

'Might get a tip-off. Spark a fresh memory. Someone reading
the story might remember something.'

'Or, are now willing to talk.'

'Maybe. But we don't have much to tell the journos yet. In the morning, we can brief with the team, get everyone up to speed. I think we've got enough to give this case legs and have another crack. Good fishing, Giles.'

'Yeah, well, I went to go fishing, not to waste time cutting bait.' The phone dropped out, but Giles was still smiling.

Kneeling at the gravesite, Kelsey Nichols puffed hot air onto the lens of her glasses, then rubbed the moisture off with the cuff of her coveralls. She pushed the glasses back up to the bridge of her nose, before leaning in to take a closer look at the cut edge of the grave.

'You're in my light.' Kelsey glanced up at Bray and frowned.

Bray mumbled an attempt at an apology and shuffled to the side.

By her side were hand-held tools, mattocks, spades, trowels and brushes. She raised her hand in the air and asked, 'Pincers?'

Liam Edison popped open a plastic bag and handed her a pair of sterile disposable tweezers. Kelsey's face was a few inches from the dirt, squinting. She carefully lifted a sliver of red from the ground.

'I think it's paint.'

She dropped the shard into a clear evidence bag and handed it to Edison, who lifted it up to the afternoon light.

'Yeah, that's paint alright.'

Edison walked around the gravesite and handed Bray the bag for him to see for himself. Bray's face softened at the sight of it.

'Might be able to match it through chemical analysis with the spade owned by the suspect,' said Kelsey, then she muttered down to the earth, 'Once you cops have a potential suspect.'

TWENTY-FOUR

At number thirteen Swiftlet Street, Joe shakily inserted the key. He flung open the front door and the lounge-room's air was crisp and clear. In the kitchen, the smell of cooking had long gone and there was no evidence of his parents having returned.

'Mum? *Mum.*'

Confused, Joe slammed shut the front door and crouched down behind his father's empty chair in the lounge-room. He wished the bull was there and its great statue could rise and protect him from the growing darkness outside. No-one would come near him if his father was there.

But it was his mother he wanted more. He wanted to hide behind her skirt, feel her hand run over the top of his head and hush him. Soothe away his angst.

Joe left the lounge-room, and in his parents' room he crouched down, crawled on his knees and hid under their bed. He curled up, knees to chest, head tucked in. Afraid of spending another night alone in a dark house. He closed his eyes, and not long after, he heard knocking on the front door.

Mum?

He froze.

There was another knock. Harder, louder, more urgent.

Dad?

He wouldn't answer. If he stayed hidden under the bed, he would be safe. He had played this game many times before.

He wished to be invisible again.

If Inspector Falkov stood still long enough, he'd blend into the ashy coloured wall of his office and go unnoticed. His suit was a melancholy dull grey, like his face and hair. But Falkov didn't stay still for long, and when his blood pressure was on the rise, his face was a red beacon. His mobile and desk phone had been running hot, and his hands had been flailing in the air between both phones, his computer, and squeezing the bridge of his now red nose.

Turner and MacCrum had found Trent Thicket dead in his car just off Edderton Road, and Callahan, who was out at Swiftlet Street, was unable to track down the next of kin, or possibly the second passenger. No-one had presented themselves at the hospital, but it was a fair guess that the passenger was Amy Thicket. They all knew what Trent could be like. *Geez, has the man done something to his wife and then driven himself off the road?* Falkov swallowed down the idea. He pinched the bridge of his nose again, just as the vibration in his pocket gave him a start. Callahan's name was on the caller ID.

'Yes?' Falkov barked.

'Sir, I've done three outside sweeps of the Thickets' house, and nobody is home. I've knocked, loud, *a lot*. I've looked through the windows. It's empty. Workplace says Amy Thicket didn't show up to her shift today, nor did she answer her phone when they rang to see if she was coming in. I've tried to call her mobile, and it goes straight to voicemail. No landline at the house. No bloody doorbell either.'

'The boy?'

'The boy was at school today,' Callahan continued. 'Last seen leaving by his teacher.'

At least the boy is okay.

Falkov perked up. 'I'll get a text alert out to the public for the child and mother.' Before he tapped the call end button, he added, 'It's the mother I'm concerned about. Callahan, make her your priority.'

Just then, Constable Griffin appeared at Falkov's door, looking wide-eyed and anxious. The young constable had heard the news about the car accident.

'What is it, Constable?' Falkov grunted.

'Detective MacCrum and I saw Mr Thicket, sir, and his wife yesterday, when I was on traffic duty at the park fire. They were in the car together, sir.'

'Mrs Thicket definitely was with him?'

Constable Griffin nodded. 'Yes, sir.' He was unsure if the information was helpful or if he'd added to the mess of the situation.

Falkov tipped his head and jotted in his notes. 'Anything else, Constable?'

Griffin shook his head. 'No, sir.'

Falkov scribbled the words 'Last sighting – park fire' before underlining them. Word around town was that Thicket was a roof tiler with back issues, prescription drug issues and anger issues. His wife was left to hold the family together, emotionally and financially. Perhaps he resented it?

The word *uxoricide* rattled around in Falkov's head.

Callahan knew that most thefts occurred around midnight; drunk and disorderly were normally on a Saturday night. However, Sunday night was called 'domestic violence night'.

Sunday nights were when kids were returned from broken families, and single parents struggled saying goodbye to their children with an empty fortnight ahead of them. Parents felt stressed about returning to work, juggling the demands of school and house-work at the same time.

So when Callahan had looked up Trent and Amy Thicket's history in the police system, he wasn't surprised that most of the call-outs to number thirteen Swiftlet Street were on a Sunday night.

What did surprise him was that no charges were ever laid. Amy Thicket had sent the police officers away insisting they were mis-informed: *neighbours wasting police time; the banging was moving heavy furniture; she bruised herself at work stocking shelves; the screaming came from a movie they were watching* . . .

He knocked again, but still no answer, though he sensed there might be someone inside.

Behind him a neighbour flung open the mailbox of number eleven. It hung by one hinge, rusted and neglected.

He watched as the woman scooped out the pile, clumsily flicking through the envelopes. He could see the collection in her hands easily enough – junk, junk, subscription renewal to *Penthouse* (interesting), water bill, and a letter from Centrelink. The neighbour flipped the lid shut. It groaned for want of oil and maintenance.

Callahan hesitated, then called out as she headed back inside to the cool of the air-conditioning, 'Didn't come out to look at the siren, then?'

'Nup,' answered the woman over her shoulder.

Callahan stood in the Thickets' driveway, reluctant to let the neighbour leave. She only paused when Callahan called out to her again. He could tell that she was hesitant to get involved.

'Do you know the family that lives here?' he asked.

'Nuh-ah.' Her frizzy hair was awry. She looked uncomfortable as she tugged at the pocket lining that poked out from the hem of her denim shorts.

'Never spoken to them?'

The dimple in her cheek deepened, but not from smiling – more from worry. 'Yeah, spoke to them. But don't *know* 'em.' The neighbour fanned herself with the mail, shooing flies and cooling herself down. Callahan could tell she didn't want to get entangled in the issue, but didn't want to piss off a cop either. She elaborated, 'No-one in the street knew much about them. They kept to themselves, kind of isolated really. We waved to the kid.'

'We?'

'My partner. We both say hi to the little bloke, but not the dad. Mean son-of-a-bitch. You lot have been called here numerous times, but the wife never pressed charges, so people stopped calling the cops. If she wasn't going to do anything about it, then what were we to do?'

Callahan shrugged. *Yes, what were they to do?*

TWENTY-FIVE

At home, Giles dumped the maps and notebook, with the timings they had made in the morning, on the kitchen table. First she wanted to clear her head before retracing the new movements down the mountain. In her bedroom she swapped her tailored suit for a ratty pair of grey faded tracksuit pants, hole in one knee, and a sleeveless t-shirt with bleach stains. She slipped on her sneakers and baseball cap, then left for a run.

Within twenty minutes, she had come to the edge of town, turning off the main road and leaving the last of the shopfronts and glare of the streetlights behind her. In front, the paddocks opened before her, and she continued in the growing dark down the sealed road and across the one-lane bridge over the Hunter River, hoping she wouldn't meet a car halfway. When she reached the 'flood warning' sign, she slapped it – because otherwise the run didn't count – and as soon as she heard the clangour of her palm hitting the metal sign, she turned and headed for home.

Aside from her puffing and rhythmic footsteps along the tarred road, all she could hear was the rustling of leaves in the paperbark trees tormented by the cooling winds, and the distant bellowing of cows. She had picked up the pace when her pocket vibrated.

Giles exhaled harder, her jog now almost a sprint. At the overpass bridge, she stopped midway and leaned over the rusty rail to catch her breath.

Her pocket vibrated again. This time she pulled out her phone, tapped the screen. 'Dad?'

'Sorry to bother. Know you're busy.' Benjamin's voice was raspy. 'Neck deep in an investigation and all that.'

'Nah, not really. I'd be more productive if I made origami hats out of the paperwork.'

There was silence on the other end, and Giles thought the line had dropped out when Benjamin's voice croaked, 'You get a chance to reinterview Bernard Nestor?'

Giles let her body flop over the rail of the bridge; her hair hung in her face and her ribs crushed against the metal rail. She stuttered into the phone, 'I-I chatted with Falkov. Showed him the doll.'

'And?'

'The focus is on the four friends.' Giles decided not to mention Lucas Cooper. Not yet, anyway. 'DNA sample is needed from the mother. I can't go at Nestor like a bull at a gate until I've got confirmation we've found the right kid.' Giles held her breath.

'You've dropped the lead of Bernard Nestor?'

'No. Dad, I need solid, undeniable evidence. More than a recounting of events. Proof I can hold in my hand. I can't chase Nestor on hearsay.'

'I know, I know.'

Giles watched the river flow below the bridge and the rising moonlight's reflection twinkling on the water's surface. She relaxed, easing her ribs off the rail. The headlights of a vehicle coming down Kayuga Road caught her eye and she turned and jogged the remainder of the crossing.

'Jacob Colton,' said Benjamin as Giles reached the end of the bridge and waved the driver on. The driver looked surprised, probably cursing her, calling her a bloody idiot for risking a run in the dark along the hazardous overpass – and he was probably right.

'Sorry, Dad, what?'

'Jacob Colton. If you can't speak with Bernard Nestor, then get in touch with him instead.'

'Think he'll talk to me?'

'You won't know unless you give it a burl . . . something worth taking a run at.'

The phone went dead, and Giles looked down at her sneakers and grinned.

The sound of the river below drew her attention. In the moonlight, she cut across the nature strip and picked her way through the tall grass and scrub. At the water's edge, she sat on a sandstone boulder, figuring she'd catch her breath first and then sprint home.

By her feet, the clay edges at the river had cracked into a mosaic pattern, looking oddly beautiful with a miscellany of shapes, colours and sizes. Giles gazed at the water and a memory popped into her head of Bernard Nestor. One afternoon, when she was ten, maybe eleven, she had ventured into his paddock. Nestor had surprised her, like he'd been waiting for her by the peach trees. He offered her one of his chooks.

'Heard you lost your hen.'

'Uh-huh.'

'Come down to the coop and pick one of mine. Have a look and see which one you'd like.' She felt she couldn't be rude to the man who had gifted her small dolls made of horsehair, and the recent loss of her beloved hen still ached in her chest.

At Nestor's chicken coop, through the extended wire, she had looked at the birds nesting in shallow metal drums, in nests made of torn magazines, of clothing catalogues for young children, faded junk mail, images of the innocent in confusing and confronting poses.

Nestor had stood by the door of the chicken enclosure. 'Go on in,' he'd said. 'Pick one. There's nine to choose from. All good stock.'

But a young Giles had stood on the outside, looking at the entrance, knowing that if she stepped inside the chicken coop, she'd have to brush past Nestor first, make contact with him, and was worried her clothes would snag on his big, buckled belt. She worried she'd smell his sweat, be too close that she couldn't block out the sound of his raspy breathing. The coop looked more like a cage, and Nestor stood at the only exit. She politely declined his offer and ran home.

Giles shivered. Sprang to her feet. *Oh, God.* The memory disturbed her. She stepped away from the river's edge and dusted the dirt off her hands. Then she turned and began sprinting back towards home.

TWENTY-SIX

Bob's shirt was half-arsed ironed. The collar didn't sit right and irritated his neck. One sleeve was more wrinkled than the other – it was hardly worth switching on the iron.

At the bar, he sat on the high stool with a goofy grin as the drinks and potato crisps were thumped down on the hardwood in front of him. Salt and vinegar chips, two perfectly poured schooners, and a bourbon and Coke for Bell. Bob measured the frothy head of the beer with his thumb and nodded, then he and Dill snatched up the drinks, chinked glasses and sculled. He was thirsty and now felt bloated as he tried to sneak a burp from the corner of his mouth.

Bell saw it and gave him a gentle slap on the arm. 'Manners.'

'Excuse me.' Bob grinned and rubbed his chest.

Sitting between his best mate and his soul mate, in his favourite establishment, Bob felt like a shift was taking place. As though life was whisking him in a new direction, *whoosh*. Soon enough he'd marry the girl at his side, knot themselves together and make a go of things. Everything felt right. He no longer felt like he was rearranging deckchairs on the fucking *Titanic*. Instead, he was confidently putting all his eggs in one basket, and they all seemed to come out frying sunny side up.

That was until Bell said, 'Couple of cops called around the house today.'

'*What?*' Bob spat out his beer. 'Fuckin' what?'

Bell frowned, failing to understand why Bob and Dill suddenly looked scared. 'Police. Detectives. D's. Dropped by. Today.'

'What for?' The muscles in Bob's arms flexed like he was about to crush the schooner in his hand.

'One was asking about next door. Where the little boy lives.'

'Why?'

'Dunno. The other D was asking about Oliver.'

'Who?'

Bell squeezed out the name through her teeth, 'Oliver . . . Oliver Lavine.'

Bob snatched up a napkin. He could hardly meet Bell's eyes as he wiped beer from his legs. He stuttered, 'What? Oliver? Lavine? Why?'

'Haven't you heard? Apparently it's all over the news, gossip around town. Cops have found human remains. Everyone reckons it's Oliver.'

Dill, slow to catch up, asked, 'Oliver? From school?'

Bob ignored him – he had too many questions. 'Is that what the cop reckons? That it's Oliver Lavine?'

'Dunno.'

'Then what did he say?'

'He? Nah, it was a *she*.'

Bob was losing patience. 'What did *she* say?'

'Not much.' Bell's eyes narrowed on Bob. 'Just asked about the day Oliver went missing. They're looking into the case again.'

'What did you tell them?'

'Nothin'.'

'Geez, Bell. When were you gonna tell me about this?'

A shrug.

'*Bell!*'

'I'm telling you now! Crikey, what's got into you?' Her face darkened. 'They'll probably want to talk to you too.'

'What about?'

Through her teeth she hissed again, '*Oliver.* About the day he went missing. The cop asked if I'd pop into the police station. Maybe to reread my statement. If she's poking around in the case again, she'll probably want to speak to the both of you.'

'What's the neighbour got to do with Oliver?'

'*Nothing.* Two detectives popped around at two different times.'

'Twice in a day?'

'I know. Crazy, huh!'

'Fuck, shit.' Bob avoided looking at Dill. Instead, he busied himself with the napkin and scrubbed at his leg.

Bell glared at the two men. 'You two know nothing. Have the both of you been walking around with your head in the sand? Don't you listen to the radio?'

'Yeah, I heard,' Bob lied. 'I just didn't realise it was Oliver from school.'

'Yeah, well, maybe it is, maybe it isn't. Either way, you better start remembering the story you told them all those years ago. *Okay?*'

'Okay. *Okay!*' Bob slid off the stool. 'Gotta use the loo.' Bob tilted his head for Dill to follow.

In the coolest corner of the pub, where the breeze swirled down the side of the building, sliding through the leaves of the jacaranda tree and making its way through the double hung windows, the miners sat in leather armchairs.

Paul Cooper had gone home and slept a few hours after work, then revisited the pub that evening for a meal and the meat raffle. He returned to the group with a tray and the next round of beers. He slid the tray on the table and plonked in the leather barrel chair, sitting back like he was lying on a banana lounge. His legs outstretched, taking up most of the floor space and obstructing the passageway. Purposeful in his posture. He liked to niggle people and get on their nerves.

His t-shirt was tight and showed his bulky arms. He was the type of bloke you'd never drop your head and run at. He may have used his muscles like a weapon, but he used his skin like a shield. Down the length of both arms were tattooed sleeves. A mix of styles forming intricate black-ink etchings, elaborate dot-work sketches and a Japanese koi fish that looped around one elbow. What money Paul didn't spend on his car, he spent on his arms.

Paul twisted his lip in thought, sat up. 'Gotta take a piss,' he said. He was up and out of the chair before the team replied. The group of men were secretly happy to see him leave. No-one could understand the reason for the excessive hair gel and cologne, just for a beer at the pub with the shift crew.

As Paul ambled past Bell perched up on the bar stool, he kicked the wooden leg, making her swing her head around. He knew she was watching him; he wanted to let her know he was there. She'd be wondering if it was an accident, or if he'd meant to annoy her. The thought of this made him smile.

TWENTY-SEVEN

Amy Thicket had stayed hidden and waited until dark to return home. She was bruised and bloody, her shirt torn from where she had climbed out of the car's shattered front windscreen. The nicks on her fingers stung like she had grabbed a fistful of stinging nettles. She looked as if she'd just survived an accident – which she had.

Yesterday, Amy had sat in the wreckage. Her stomach cramped and she was sure she'd cracked a rib. With every breath, a sharp pain seemed to pinch her hip and spine. Her husband was by her side, pale faced, unconscious. The blood still oozing from his neck with each pulse of his slowing heart. His head cocked, his fat tongue resting on his bottom lip, like he wanted to say something. She didn't try to stop the bleeding or find her phone to call for assistance. She wanted no ambulance, no rescue. Instead, in a daze, she watched as her husband slipped away. She neither cried nor smiled, felt no sorrow or relief. His floppy hand, unresponsive, lay close to her thigh. She lifted it, still warm, and could feel his knuckles roll under his skin. She placed it in his lap. It was hard for her to imagine that the same hand had once . . . Amy let the thought go as fast as it arrived.

When she finally had the strength, she crawled from her seat through the window onto the bonnet, then slid off and away from the car. She had walked as far as she could into the bushlands, and when her legs could carry her no more, and the pain in her side was too strong, she sank to the ground and curled up amongst a clump of tussock, resting her head on the tufts. She had slept in the itchy grass all night, clutching her stomach, hoping the pain was only bruising or a cracked rib, praying it was nothing more serious. Her right ear ached from the explosion of the airbag. It felt wet and sticky inside. The natural sounds of the bush were muffled. She was sure she had perforated her eardrum.

During the day, she had baked in the sun, dry-mouthed and sunburned, until she clambered her way to Quarry Creek. Under the shade of the trees, she had drunk the dank water. Her stomach was sore, but her chest ached more for worry about her son. He had often got himself ready and off to school before. Times when she couldn't leave her bed because her body was still tender from the wallop inflicted during the night. She knew he wouldn't call for help, turn to a neighbour, or a teacher. But she had never left him alone all night . . . so her certainty and confidence that he was okay ebbed as the day wore on. As night began to fall again, she was rested and felt stronger. In the cover of darkness, she had the strength to follow the edge of Edderton Road back out to familiar territory and found her way home.

Amy knocked on her bedroom window. She had no keys to get in and guessed if her son was in the house alone, he would be burrowed deep in the blankets of her bed.

She knocked on the window once more. 'Joe? Are you in there?'

The bedspread fell away, and a head popped up like a rabbit in the dark sensing a predator lurking. His eyes were wide and frightened.

'Joe, it's Mum. Let me in.'

Joe Thicket scrambled to unlock the front door. The moment she was inside, he flung himself at her, his face buried deep into her shirt. She winced but allowed the embrace. She could smell the earth and dried blood in her clothes.

'Shh. There, there.' Amy's bruised hand smoothed the top of his hair. Her voice sounded loud in her head. Her right ear was still ringing. Although having her son in her arms was healing enough. 'I'm home now. I'm going to take a shower and change. Dress my wounds. You sit here on the bed. Dad isn't coming home, son. You'll be okay.'

She let her words sink in. His father wasn't returning home. She wondered if, just like her, he felt nothing. No relief or sorrow. She wanted to explain to him that it was like having a family dog put down after it had bitten. While you wished things were different, what had to be done had to be done. Dogs bite, and parents can hurt.

Her son's reaction wasn't what she expected. Instead, he licked his finger and tried to wipe away the dry blood on her cheek. Amy fought not to fold in on herself as she gently reassured the boy everything would be okay. She whispered words of comfort as she left his side mid-sentence and paced lightly through the house, switching off the lights. When the house was dark, back in the bedroom she left only the side lamp on. The police would come again. Questions would be asked. *What happened in the car? Why did you leave the crash site? Do you know it's against the law to leave a fatal accident?* Amy didn't feel ready to answer any of them.

She needed time to think. Time to get her story straight.

TWENTY-EIGHT

Bob unzipped his pants, then looked down at the infected blister on his hand. He grunted, and the echo bounced off the stainless-steel wall. He struggled to pee, and had to take a few deep breaths to relax, let his bladder release. Finally, he heard the stream hit the silver wall. When he was done at the trough, he stood by the wash basin and glanced at his reflection in the lopsided mirror that was water stained and graffitied in black sharpie pen. For what he could see of himself, he looked rattled. And he bloody was.

'Are you smoking weed in there, Dill?'

'Yup.'

'Give us a hit.' He walked to the end of the row of cubicles, heaved open the warped door straining to hang onto its hinges, and hoped the bastard thing wouldn't come off in his hand.

In the last cubicle, the disabled toilet, Dill had lit up a joint and was blowing the smoke up high so it could escape out of the top window. Dill leaned against the wall and handed the joint to Bob who took it and sucked so hard it burned his lips and made him cough. Bob hadn't smoked weed since he was a teenager, but now he felt like he needed it. He needed to mellow, to calm the fuck down.

'What's this shit about cops and Oliver?' asked Dill.

'Yeah, fuck. I know.'

Dill pulled his phone from his pocket. He tapped and scrolled, his phone almost touching his nose as he scanned the screen. After a moment he shoved the phone in Bob's face. 'It's bloody there. Look.'

Bob waved the phone from his face. 'Cop was only asking about Oliver. Nothing about the fish and chip shop.'

'They're not going to ask Bell, "Hey, is your better half thinking of robbing the fishmonger?", are they? Crikey, Bob. I've got a bad feeling. I don't think we should be doing this. Not with cops sniffing around. Fucking two detectives in one day. When does that ever happen? It's a sign, I'm telling you, a fucking sign.'

'Calm down, Dill.'

'Calm down? *Calm down?* You have no idea how much I've got the jitters now, Bob.'

Bob shrugged, annoyed. 'Nah, come on. It's nothing. We stick to our original story about Oliver, okay.'

Dill put out his hand for Bob to return his joint.

'And don't worry about Oliver,' Bob said, taking one last drag. 'The cops were clueless then, they'll be clueless now.'

Dill twitched. Shook his head. 'What do I tell them?'

'Nothing. You tell them nothing. Say you can't remember. It was almost twenty years ago. Say fucking nothing, you hear me? Zip.'

'Alright, alright.' Dill sucked back on the last of the joint. Tossed the browned end into the toilet bowl and flushed.

Bob waved his hand in the air towards the window, trying to clear the lavatory of smoke. 'Still good?'

'So, we're doing it?'

'Yup.'

'Even with the D's sniffing around, I can't talk you out of it?'

'Nup. Fuck 'em. I need this, Dill.'

'Okay. Got a plan?'

'Yup. I've given it more thought.'

When Paul Cooper walked into the men's bathroom, he'd intended to bail Bob and Dill up about the radio report of the skeleton found at Mount Wingen. He wanted to know if the two dickheads thought it was Oliver Lavine. Or if he was getting antsy about nothing. Yet if it was Oliver, he wanted to make sure they were all still sticking to the same story. Instead, when he entered the room, he found it empty.

He could hear voices carrying down the tiled room and got more than a reassurance that no-one was going to talk about that day on the mountain with Oliver Lavine. In fact, he got even more than he'd hoped for. He'd always thought Bob was a gutless wonder and was impressed by the ballsy idea of mugging the fishmonger. He smiled at the simplicity, but also the brilliance of it. After listening to Bob lay out his plan, Paul quietly stepped away, and slipped out of the restroom. He had heard all of it.

As Paul meandered through patrons lined up at the bar, he was still nodding to himself as he pondered, *If you rob someone, then get robbed yourself, you're not going to go to the police. Nah. That would be dumb. And that would be Bob's problem. And my fuckin' windfall.*

DAY 4

TWENTY-NINE

On her way into Muswellbrook Police Station, Giles had stopped at the home of Phillip O'Dell. She stood at the warping front door and rang the doorbell. Two simple notes: *ding dong*. On the umpteenth ring, when nobody answered, she wasn't surprised. She didn't peg Phillip O'Dell as being particularly productive until midday.

Now at the station, the blinds to the meeting room were drawn – purely by habit to reduce the risk of a suspect, or an acquaintance of a suspect, walking past and seeing the images on the crazy board. Except the crime evidence board in front of Giles paled in comparison to previous homicide investigations. The wall displayed only a few photographs of the gravesite and skull, along with the first of the skeletal remains collected from the crime scene and laid out on a stainless-steel table. There were no pictures of a possible victim or suspect, no murder mapped, and none of the gathered information from the old file had been added either. The crazy board looked sparce and empty.

Giles dropped her head, looked down at the enamel coffee cup resting on her knee and wondered, *Clean slate?*

Just as Bray had asked, on the opposite wall she had hung the map of Burning Mountain that highlighted the route of Oliver's hike.

Underneath were the typed-up details of the timeline collected eighteen years earlier. Giles added her own timings from the previous morning. She had underlined the fifteen minutes from when Oliver supposedly arrived at the bottom, to when Paul emerged to find his brother Lucas waiting for him in his car, and no sign of Oliver. It hadn't escaped her attention that the two walls of information were being kept separate.

At the front of the room, Bray sat slumped on the edge of the table, back to his habit of torturing his temples with his thumbs. His chin and jaw showed the beginnings of stubble, or, in Bray's case, coarse bristle. Clearly, Bray had had a late night and maybe an earlier morning than the rest of the team – with no time to shave in between. Falkov stood off to the side, looking like he was inching closer to a heart attack, his neck pink and his lips thin and white.

Liam Edison had the floor, standing centre, between Falkov and Bray. In contrast, Edison looked fresh and alert in casual pants and a denim chambray shirt. When he caught Giles's eye, he straightened up, tall and lean, and modestly ran his fingers through the flecks of grey in his sandy hair. He was deep into an explanation of what had been discovered. '. . . vertebrae and skull are not fused together, so it's safe to say early teens. However, the skull could be before a growth spurt, or just after, and that can vary the prediction of exact age.' He pointed to an image on the board. 'Note that the bone of the juvenile skeleton is not fused, not fully developed. The long bones come in three parts –'

'Long bone?' interrupted Bray.

'Sorry. Bone from the knee to ankle.' Edison looked back at the board, pointed to another image of bone laid on the stainless-steel table. 'Here the length of the femur, the upper leg bone, is too short for an older male. So, we're guessing, after looking at dental and the long-bone length to help to determine age, perhaps thirteen, maybe fifteen, sixteen years old. Male.'

There was a silence in the room. Turner's fingers clicked away at the keys on his laptop and Callahan scribbled a few notes on a pad. Giles took a sip of coffee.

When no-one spoke, Liam continued, 'A rib did show a previous fracture. However, the skull is where I focused. The most dangerous place to hit your head is on the side, just above the ears. The skull is at its thinnest, and there's an artery that can burst and cause direct bleeding in the brain. If you look at this image' – his hand flicked to another photograph – 'you can see the fracture in the skull, which suggests blunt head trauma. Severe brain injury.'

'Are you saying this was the cause of death?'

Liam nodded at Bray. 'More than likely.' He turned back to the photo of the skull, his finger jabbing at the crack in the bone. 'Head trauma can directly lead to blood vessels within the brain rupturing. With a severe head injury, the brain is surrounded by fluid, and it moves within the skull causing potentially fatal bleeding, compressing the brain.'

Bray stopped torturing his temple and dropped his hand. 'Do we know what inflicted the fracture? Tool? Object?'

A shrug from Edison and a sigh from Bray gave the team the feeling that they were done. The meeting had just about wrapped up.

Falkov stepped forward and tipped his head, looking down his kinked nose at Giles. 'I'm sending you down to Crookwell this afternoon.'

Giles swallowed. As the only woman on the crimes team, she wondered if Falkov was putting her forward for interviewing females. Was it her expertise that granted her a trip to Crookwell, or her gender? Giles nodded with forced confidence, determined to look unperturbed. 'Yes, sir.'

Falkov continued, 'You'll meet with Oliver Lavine's mother in the morning. Gently explain what's been found, make no promises, and collect a DNA sample. While you're there, enquire about Oliver's medical history, previous bone breakages, fractures, past injuries.' Falkov clicked his tongue against his teeth before adding, 'Dr Liam Edison will be accompanying you.'

Giles resisted the urge to look at Edison. 'Yes, sir.'

Falkov turned to the team. 'Okay, that's all. Room dismissed.'

There was a moment's silence before a collective, 'Yes, sir,' and the room began to clear.

As Bray slid off the table and made his way towards the door, he quipped at Giles, 'Hope Edison likes a silent drive. I'll give him the heads-up you're not one for idle chit-chat.'

'Is he tagging along to make sure I ask the right questions?' Giles retorted, unamused.

She was sure she could hear the bones cracking in Bray's neck as he craned his head to look back at her. His eyes dark. 'I told Falkov I wanted you *both* down there. Eighteen years is a big gap. Edison has the answers to the *now*, but you need to find the answers for the *then*.'

'Thank you,' she said with a small grin, before taking a gulp of lukewarm coffee. It was over-sugared, sickly sweet, but she needed the energy.

Bray wasn't done. He stepped back towards her, looming large. 'Callahan and I didn't find anything useful at the gravesite. Any natural fibres have long gone, but man-made ones, like nylon or zips, would have survived. Only our kid wore cotton, no zips. We swept the area and couldn't find any personal effects. No idea where his backpack ended up. Could have been dumped at the local tip or washed down a river. Who knows? And kids that age don't carry around wallets with bank cards and driver's licences.'

'Guess not.' Giles realised the crazy board looked empty because nobody could find anything worth adding.

'Ask the mother about the rib injury. You'll know then if you've got the right kid . . . but there will be no chasing Bernard Nestor until the DNA analysis comes back.'

Giles nodded and watched Bray and the last of the team shuffle out of the room just as Constable Griffin entered, arms raised, inching through the doorway side on. 'Detective Giles, someone's turned up at the front desk to see you. Said you called and asked him to come in.'

'This someone got a name?'

'Paul Cooper. He's waiting in the ERISP room.'

THIRTY

They moved as one through the house. Down the hallway to the bedroom, they glided like fish swimming upstream. When Amy Thicket picked up the pace, so did Joe, and when she stopped – the back of her hair swishing like a fin – he stopped too. He had shadowed her every move all morning, gulping at the air, twisting, and drifting between the furniture. The stillness now frightened him, as though a predator would dart out at them. Swallowing them up.

Amy sensed her son's unease. 'Here, sit. Let me brush your hair.'

Joe sat on the edge of his mother's unmade bed as she reached for the soft bristled brush. Joe thought it was useless and ugly. The brush head was strange in shape, ornate with a confusing floral pattern, and the bristles were so soft they didn't even touch his scalp.

'Can you use the comb?' asked Joe.

Amy laid the brush down gently and reached for the cheap plastic pocket comb. 'I just want you to look nice, that's all.'

Joe was silent as his mother combed his hair.

'I have always said, Joe, if you tell the truth, then no harm can come to you.'

Joe nodded. It was easier than speaking. He had to keep all his words stored up for the police. He didn't want to waste a single one of them. He didn't speak much, so he ran out of words after a while.

'And after we both tell the *truth*, Joe, to the police, we can have a milkshake on the main road. At the café. Sit amongst the buckets of flowers.'

Amy reached into her pocket and pulled out a note showing it to him. Proof she could keep her word. 'And if we have enough, we can share a strawberry bomb.'

Joe's mind filled with milkshake flavours. He settled on caramel. Sweet and buttery. Because he believed it would really happen.

THIRTY-ONE

The small interview room was stark white, a table against the wall, centred, with four cheap padded grey chairs, two each side of the table. Paul Cooper sat in a chair closest to the wall, Giles directly opposite him.

Paul's early-morning visit to the police station was unexpected, and Giles felt sure he would fob off her request to come in, but his promptness to arrive early the next morning had pinged her curiosity. Paul was the type who would only show up if he had something to gain, something that was worth saying, and Giles was more than willing to hear it.

However, they were only a few minutes into the interview when a gut feeling rose in Giles's stomach. Something was amiss with the guy. The interview didn't feel right. It felt like the meeting had turned into a game.

His answers gave her the impression they were more about amusing himself than responding to her questions. As she moved through each query, the more awry the interview seemed.

'I'm taking it that you were the leader of the group. The smart one.' It was a statement, not a question. Giles watched Paul take a moment. His eyes darted around the room – at the table, the chairs, walls, box of tissues – until eventually they landed back at Giles.

'Leader? What do you mean by *leader*?'

'Leader. The one they looked up to.'

Giles could also play games, and at the compliment Paul gave a small smile. So she then turned her next comment into a negative. 'Trust earned? Or perhaps a little forced?' He only shrugged and she wondered if she was dealing with a narcissist. The guy was full of himself.

Paul was focused on Giles, and she on him. Both hardly blinked as they followed each other's questions and answers quietly – listening, observing. She felt each pause almost hum in the room as he took a moment before responding. Giles wasn't sure if she was doing the hunting or if Paul was. She searched for the crack in the calm façade. Couldn't find one. If anything, he seemed more flirty than relaxed. She kept her face blank, and asked, 'Whose idea was it to hike Burning Mountain?'

'Bob's, I think. I tagged along at the last minute.'

'Why?'

'School holidays. Nothing much else to do. Why not?'

'Were you invited? Or did you invite yourself?'

The first small crack fleetingly appeared on Paul's face. *Nobody wants to be an afterthought, do they, Paul?*

Again, a shrug. But the façade of aloofness was starting to slip.

'Can you tell me about the hike? Whatever you may remember. I understand it was a long time ago, but anything you can recall is helpful.'

'Isn't it all in your eighteen-year-old report?'

'Yes. But let's hear it again,' she added so the question felt lighter, chattier, less of an interrogation. 'Anything you can add?'

Paul's memory seemed sharp, though lacking in emotion. While the events took place almost two decades ago, his attention to detail was thorough. The only thing he failed to mention were the childish dares, the challenges along the way. And there was no mention of the fall-out between friends once at the top of the mountain. It was the argument at the lookout, that's what Giles wanted to hear. She wanted to know what made Oliver Lavine stomp off, never to be seen again. But she also wanted to know why Paul broke away from the group. *To follow Oliver? Was Paul the reason Oliver stomped off, so he chased him to apologise? Nah.* Giles couldn't imagine Paul apologising for anything.

She tucked a loose strand of her dark hair behind her ear. Picked up the manila folder on the desk and flicked through the faded printed report sheets, purely because she liked the sound of the pages as they crinkled. There was nothing in the old report of the friends playing dares along the trail. That information had been offered when she visited Belinda Marrone.

Giles decided to play her card. She looked at the pages for a moment, then up at Paul, like she had just remembered he was still in the room. 'Tell me about the goading. The little contests.'

'They weren't contests.'

Giles pushed the question again. 'Dares?'

Paul repeated his answer. 'They weren't contests.'

'Was it an option to partake, or were they pressured into participating?'

'I never forced anyone to do anything, detective.'

Giles's spine was tingling. She wished Turner was by her side, to make sure she wasn't misreading the room. She thought about pulling her phone from her pocket, pretend to read a text, excuse herself from the room, bring Turner in. Or she could just up the ante and start ruffling feathers.

Giles leaned in. 'Who was your bully when you were at school?'

'Eh?'

'Who targeted you?'

Paul exhaled slowly. 'No-one. I never gave someone a hard time because I was letting off steam, or because of my own trauma, if that's what you're getting at.'

Just a born arsehole then?

'I never set out to be a bully when I was in school.' Paul sat back. He seemed comfortable in the interview room. 'I was just taller than most my age. Bigger shoulders. Truth is, I didn't have a lot of friends, detective. I realised it wasn't because the other students didn't want to be my mate – they feared me. My height. Deep voice. Once I realised this, it gave me this strange sense of power. It was bestowed on me – by them. I never asked for it. But I could persuade students to do things.' Paul stopped. There was the long uncomfortable pause again, before he added, 'I didn't *bully* anyone.'

'Never tormented anyone? Ever?'

Paul blinked at her but gave no reply.

She pushed, 'Manipulate?'

Paul shrugged.

'Who started it? The games up the mountain.'

'Belinda.'

This surprised Giles. '*Belinda* suggested the dares?'

'No. But it was because of her. We were blokes, just showing off.'

She could picture it. Four youthful boys on the cusp from boyhood to manhood. All alone on a mountain and nobody to watch them try to impress a girl. That awkward age, Giles remembered it herself. The wanton feeling when hanging out near the boys, hoping for their attention. Giles imagined Paul and Bob, Belinda, Oliver and Phillip all those years ago meeting at the bottom of Burning Mountain. The anticipation of the hike. She knew the competition had already started before the hike even began.

Was it Paul versus Bob, or did Paul feel Bob's attention transfer from him to Bell? Perhaps the status was shifting, and Paul was no longer the centre of attention, losing his hold over the group. With Bell pulling focus, maybe Paul introduced the dares as a way of winning back his position in the pecking order.

'Did Belinda have a crush on anyone?' Giles watched Paul lean back in his seat, scratch at his chest to think – *that uncomfortable pause again.* 'Yeah, maybe. She was a little gooey over Bob. Reaching out her hand for him to pull her along the track, stuff like that.'

Excuses to touch? 'Did that annoy you?'

'Nope.'

Bullshit. 'Did it annoy Oliver or Phil?'

'Nope. Look, I wasn't into Belinda. She was new to our group. It was the first time Bob had been around her out of school, aside from weekends at the footy. He was being a bit of a show-off, that's all. I was just playing – being a prick, maybe. Just wanted Bell to see Bob wasn't all that.'

'So, on the mountain, what did you encourage Bob to do?'

Paul's shoulder twitched. 'Towards the top of the mountain, I spotted a goanna. A big one. It sprinted up a tree. I said to Bob, "You know, if you stand under a goanna up a tree, the thing will freeze with shock. Die right there with its claws hooked into the trunk, and for months you'll be able to come out and watch it decay. Right before your eyes, see it picked white by bull ants and crows until it's nothing but a skeleton hugging the trunk of a tree."' Paul smiled at Giles. 'You ever seen a goanna's skeleton?'

Giles shook her head, but she saw a flash of the skull found at Mount Wingen. 'Nope. Can't say I have.'

'Me either. Seen dead cows. Growing up in the country you learn real quick that with livestock comes deadstock. Be it a cow, goat, sheep, even a rabbit or fox. Never seen a goanna, though. Bob said he hadn't either, so I told him to go stand at the bottom of the tree. Right under it. Bob didn't want to. He'd heard stories, we'd all heard stories, of how the claws of a goanna could rip someone's guts out.'

'Is that true?'

'Dunno. Don't know anyone that it's happened to. Myths were told around the playground when I was young. One was of a bushy who was sleeping under the stars and a goanna just split his stomach open while he slept. Hissing and biting into chunks of flesh, chewing on the innards like a dog.' Paul hesitated. 'Or maybe the bloke was already dead, and the goanna was attracted to the scent of rotting meat?'

'Did you help start any of these stories?'

'Start? Nah. Might have kept them alive.' Paul flashed a row of straight white teeth, two dimples. He gave Giles a wink so fleeting that she wasn't sure if she imagined it. He shrugged, still smiling. 'As a kid, I loved a good gory spook story.'

'So, you urged Bob to stand under the goanna.'

'Yup. Bob looked up at the lizard. Fair dinkum, it was bloody huge. I did wonder what would have happened if it dropped on his head. Bob was scared. Bit of a coward. I yelled, "Go on, I ain't got all day. Go stand at the bottom of the tree, right underneath." Giles sensed Paul was enjoying the telling of the story. 'So, Bob was under the goanna. Looked up to see if he'd scared the massive lizard to a stiff death.'

'He hadn't?'

'Nup. The goanna looked down at him, flicked out its tongue and spewed all over him. That's what they do. Spew! It's their defence. Oh boy, you should have seen Bob at the bottom of the tree! His hair dripping of goanna vomit. I laughed so hard I almost threw up myself.'

Giles kept her reaction to a raised eyebrow. 'Then what?'

'Afternoon went to shit. Bob flopped to the ground. I think he cried a little. His hair was dripping and matted in goanna spew. It fucking stunk.'

'What about the others?'

'Bell, Dill and Oliver went to help him.'

'Dill?'

'Phil . . . nickname's Dill.'

'Did you start that too?'

Paul Cooper's lip curled. 'You think I'm a cunt, don't you, detective.'

'I never said that. I just asked if you had a hand in Phillip O'Dell's nickname.'

'Dill earned his nicknames.'

'What about Oliver Lavine? Did you give him a nickname?'

Paul leaned in, resting his forearms on the table. His eyes hard again. 'Look, detective, I liked Oliver. I really did. I'm not sure looking back now if he was really into girls, or if he just wasn't into Bell. But for years after, I wondered what had happened to him. But that shit up on the hill was just dumb teenage stuff. And I can assure you, it had nothing to do with Oliver disappearing.'

'When Oliver took off down the mountain, you followed. Alone.'

'Yeah. And when I got to the bottom, voilà! Gone!'

Paul rose from his chair, looked towards the door and shrugged.

'I'm not finished,' said Giles.

'I am. This is voluntary. I've got nothing else that I think can help you. I honestly don't know what happened to Oliver Lavine that day.'

Giles stood, trying to block Paul at the door. 'Just a few more questions, if you don't mind.'

'But I *do* mind, detective.'

With no option, Giles opened the door and he exited the room without a word.

She followed him down the corridor and watched him leave out the front doors just as Amy Thicket and her son walked in.

THIRTY-TWO

The radio crackled noise of talkback and ads. Bell was busy sweating over hot plates, frying rashers of bacon and boiling eggs that bounced in a pot of bubbling water.

The toaster was down. The kettle on. Strawberry jam and butter in the centre of the table. She twisted her lip and thought, *What else?*

Bob came into the kitchen from the hallway. He was clean shaven and smelled of lavender soap. Bell's soap. He looked down at Bell's bare feet, then at her breasts wrapped and tucked tightly in her dressing gown. While Bell's face was fixed with concentration, Bob's looked sheepish. 'What's all this?'

'Breakfast.'

'For me?'

'The whole damn lot of it.'

'You think I'm hungry?'

Bell scrunched up her nose, gave a flirty grin. 'Just trying to get to your heart through your stomach.'

'No need. You're already there.'

The flirty grin faded. Bell cocked her head. 'Am I?'

'Bloody oath.' Bob looked at the mess already beginning to accumulate on the bench and in the sink. Congealed bacon fat, slimy and starting to stink in the empty plastic satchel dumped on the lid of the garbage, coffee and sugar granules spilled across the bench, oil spat across the splashback. He knew he'd be left to clean up, but the breakfast smelled good.

He sat down at the laminated table. Under his breath, he muttered, 'Crikey.'

Bell was in a hurry. She had little over an hour left to dress and pack her car, before heading off to the Hunter Markets in Pokolbin to sell her handmade birdfeeders. She scooped the eggs from the pot and dropped them into egg cups, then grabbed a texta, held the eggs still with a tea towel, and drew faces on each.

She plonked the plate in front of Bob and asked, 'Whatcha think?'

Dumbfounded, Bob squinted at the faces drawn on the two eggs. 'What the fuck have you done to me eggs?'

'It's Humpty and his mate.' Bell felt defensive. 'See?'

'Which one's Humpty?'

She picked up a teaspoon and cracked one of the eggs over the head with it. 'That one.'

Bob squirmed in his seat. 'It's frowning at me now. You pushed its fuckin' head in.'

Bell waved the teaspoon in Bob's face. 'You'd look the same if you just fell off a wall.'

Bright yellow yolk started to ooze from the crushed shell. Bob picked up a piece of toast and dunked it. Before the yolk dripped from the bread, he stuffed it into his mouth. He pointed to the second egg sitting in the cup. To lift the mood, jokily he asked, 'Then who's that one?'

Bell leaned over the table and smacked the second egg with the teaspoon. It too oozed yolk from the cracked shell. Then she replied, 'Oliver.'

Bob felt the room peel away from him as he stared at the egg. 'Jesus Christ, Bell!' Bob hacked up egg and toast, spat it out into a napkin. 'What's got into you? What's going on?' The image now resembled a skull, and the fragment of broken shell, bone.

Bell sneered, 'You tell me what's going on.'

'Eh?'

'Don't bloody *eh* me. Are you leaving me?'

'No, Bell. Christ. *No.*' He swallowed down the lumps of egg and dough still stuck to his tongue. 'God, no.'

'No secrets, Bob. We tell each other everything. What's got into you these last few days? It's the cops, isn't it? Sniffing around about Oliver.'

'Aren't you worried?'

'Not if we all stick to the same *fucking* story, Bob. That was the deal.'

'It was the deal twenty-odd years ago, Bell.'

'So, what's changed?'

'Dunno, just doesn't feel right, that's all. Everyone's yacking on about it now at the building site. I don't know if I can trust Dill, or Cooper. And that fucking detective has left three bloody messages on my phone. Wants me to come into the station.'

'Then *go*. It's hiding from them that will make them suspicious. Show them you've got nothing to hide.'

'But we have, Bell.'

'No, we fuckin' haven't.' Bell waved the teaspoon dangerously close to the tip of Bob's nose before tossing it across the bench and into the kitchen sink. It clattered, and, when the room went silent again, Bell asked, 'Is that all that's worrying you, Bob? . . . *Bob?*'

Bob looked down at the shattered eggshell and crushed face. *Tell her the truth. Just tell her the bloody truth.*

'If I tell you, you can't get mad, Bell, because I'm doing this for us.'

Bell flapped the tea towel, swirled the cloth in the air and stood with one hand on her hip. The other held the cloth, ready to whip it in his direction. 'I'm already mad, Bob.'

THIRTY-THREE

'For the purpose of this interview, can you state your full name, please?'

'Amy Louise Thicket.'

Giles stared unblinking at the monitor as Callahan and Bray interviewed Amy in a room down the hall. The woman was recounting her marriage, and the events leading up to the accident. Giles felt her skin prickle and her jaw ache as Amy spoke of her rising fear, worry for her child, the tin in which she'd stashed emergency escape money – not to leave Trent, but to hide from Trent. And last, the car accident on Edderton Road that ended in the death of her husband.

Bray moved a tissue box towards her. Amy wiped away her tears, and said in a whisper, 'Then he tried to kill us both, by driving off the edge of the road.'

THIRTY-FOUR

Bob knew he should have brought a bottle of water with him. It was stifling in the tin shed and the heat of the day hadn't even kicked in. He was already starting to dehydrate. His eyeballs felt hot and dry.

Going back into the house wasn't an option. Bell was busy getting ready to head off to the markets to flog her birdfeeders. Plus, if he went back inside, it would mean he'd have to engage in more mindless conversations with her. She was right to be angry with him, though. She had been keen on his idea, but quick to note he didn't have a plan. Well, he did, but it *wasn't a fucking good one* – as Bell had aptly pointed out.

Bob hadn't told Bell about the idea of a ring. That part he was keeping as a surprise. But now, he knew, when he proposed to her they'd both look at it, knowing where the money came from to purchase it. And what about Dill? How would he react to Bell getting involved?

Bloody hell.

Bob flicked the sweat off his forehead. He wasn't sure if it was the heat inside the shed making him sweat, or the morning's cooked breakfast and narky girlfriend. He kicked the galvanised door open, tossed a brick against it to stop it from slamming shut, and lit up a smoke. As he drew back on the cigarette, he found the heat in the back of his throat soothing.

The plan was to toss out the dried tins of acrylic paint that Bell never put the lids back on, give the cement floor a sweep, knock a few webs down and rip out the creeping vine that hung through the roof. However, the breakfast and morning conversation now sat in his stomach, heavy and uncomfortable. The thought of Oliver, and Bell's lack of faith in him, had soured his mood.

Bob coughed from the smoke, then wiped some wood shavings off the tool bench onto the floor. A redback spider froze, then slinked, its body flat on the bench. Bob looked at it. *Ready to pounce? Ready to run?* His irritation at Bell's response still swelled in his gut. He took a long drag of his cigarette until it burned his lips, then blew the smoke over the spider. It didn't move.

'You can fuck off,' he told it with the conviction and tone he wished he'd used with Bell. The resentment towards her shifted to the spider. 'Fuck you,' Bob said before squashing it with the back of his thumbnail until it oozed yellow fluid.

As he wiped the spider goo from his thumbnail across the back of his shorts, on the top shelf Bob spotted his old football. He reached up, flicked his fingers at the tip of it, knocking it off the shelf and into his arms.

He tipped his nose towards the ball and breathed in the scent of leather, and with it came a flash of memories. Other smells – sock tape, heat rub, dust, mud and sweat. He could almost taste the sports drinks guzzled, the orange quarters sucked, and the cold watermelon offered in bright orange Tupperware containers at the end of the game. There were the chants of victory, the team's song sung so loud, it hurt his throat. Then there was the curly haired girl who sat in the bleachers to watch his games, and his coach, who would single him out for pep talks and strategies. Out on the footy oval, he wasn't

'Bob, friend of Cooper's', he was the kid that the fathers winked at after a game and who made the girl in the bleachers smile.

Bob's tender memory felt as fleeting as his time on the field the moment he recalled how it all came crashing down, ending abruptly the day after Oliver Lavine disappeared.

The gloom swept back over him. As he tossed the footy up on the top shelf, it bounced against the ceiling of the shed and in the nook, then disappeared out of sight.

'Hey, dickhead!' Dill's face appeared around the corner of the shed door, as bright and yellow as the spider gunk on the tool bench and his shorts.

'What do you want?' Bob smirked. As ugly as Dill was, he was a sight for sore eyes.

Dill stepped into the shed and pressed himself up in a corner like he was hiding. 'Fuck, guess what happened this mornin'. I think that chick was at my door.'

'What chick?'

'The D. That detective chick – the hot one Bell was talking about. Flaming hid under my bedsheet until she left. Lucky my mum wasn't home. She would have invited her in, made her a cup of tea. Offered the last lamington in the tin.'

'Huh.' Bob reached up and yanked at the vine hanging from the ceiling. It snapped off and dirt crumbled down with it. 'Yeah, well, she's left a few messages on my phone.'

'Shit, hey. What are we gonna do?'

'Bell reckons we should just go into the station and repeat our old story. Get it over and done with. Get the cops off our backs.'

Dill tilted his head. 'Righto.'

'I'm not calling it off, Dill. I can't.'

'If we go ahead, then I still think we need to show a threat. Let the fishmonger know we mean business.'

'It's two against one,' said Bob. 'I'm a big prick. Look at these guns.' Bob flexed his biceps. 'These are mega-ceps. Fucking Tyrannosaurus-ceps.'

'Okay, fuckwit, but I'm still bringing the shotgun. Unloaded, of course. Just for show.'

The feeling of a stalemate hung in the air. Bob reached for another cigarette, lit up and drew back on the smoke, feeling the heat between his lips. He stayed uncommitted to the idea of a shotgun as he watched Dill stand stoic in the corner. After a moment, Bob said, 'I think armed robbery is worse than just a robbery, Dill.'

'Only if we get caught. Which we're not. I'm taking the shotty, Bob.'

Bob dropped his head. 'Righto. Righto.'

'And I've been thinking about our disguises.' Dill dug deep into his back pocket. 'I got us these.' He held up two empty red mesh polypropylene bags.

'What happened to balaclavas?'

'Who the fuck owns balaclavas?'

'Skiers,' snapped Bob.

'When has it ever snowed in this fuckin' town?'

'Geez, Dill, you haven't thought this through. Your head already looks like a fuckin' orange as it is. We can't pull a bit of red netting over our heads. The guy will think he's being robbed by a giant piece of fruit.'

'Listen, Bob, it's better than a poke in the eye with a burned stick. Look, we don't need to disguise ourselves from the whole town; just the shop owner, so he can't pick us out in a line-up.'

'He won't be picking us out of a police line-up, Dill, he'll be down the fruit and veg shop pointing to an orange and a fucking coconut.' Bob bowed his head. His morning couldn't have gone more arsed up if he had tried.

THIRTY-FIVE

It was almost two in the afternoon by the time Giles and Edison hit the road for Crookwell. At home, Giles had hastily tossed some clothes and toiletries into a gym bag, then driven out to Scone to collect Edison from his motel. His temporary accommodation was in an elegant Victorian-style mansion on Kelly Street, and when he emerged with a brown leather Rodd & Gunn travel bag, looking like he was ready for a spot of clay pigeon shooting or fox hunting, Giles had pressed her chin into her neck to stifle her laugh. Her dad would call him a city boy dressing like a country try-hard-wannabe.

They were now more than three hours into their trip and had long ago moved on from exchanging pleasantries – chatting about the case, the weather – to dead silence. Silence was Giles's go-to when the small talk ran dry; before the idle chatter could turn personal.

'Shall we stop for dinner somewhere?' Edison suggested as they were getting close to Bathurst.

The fast-food shops were whizzing behind them, and, if they didn't take the opportunity to stop now, it would be another hour or so before they'd get the chance to eat again.

'Nah,' said Giles. 'There's a great Greek restaurant in Crookwell. If you can fight the stomach grumble, it's worth the wait.'

Edison tipped his head to the side, and Giles took that as a yes.

She had calculated the drive from Scone to Crookwell would be a little over five hours. They'd land in the small country town and be checking into the motel just after seven and squeezing fresh lemon over souzoukaklia by eight.

Giles squinted, her eyes locked on the road ahead. 'When it comes to red wine, are you a shiraz, merlot or cabernet sauvignon?'

'Sangiovese.'

'Huh!'

'Perfect with dips and pita bread.'

Zing! Giles tried her darndest not to smile. The two of them would be getting along just fine.

As she followed the monotonous winding road ahead, her thoughts shifted to Oliver Lavine. 'Are you sticking with a blow to the head as the cause of death?'

'The perimortem trauma indicates a skull fracture.'

'But you can't determine if it was inflicted or accidental?'

Edison looked out the front windscreen for a moment. 'The skull bone is not damaged by a knife or bullet, if that's what you're asking.' Giles knew he had read between the lines when he finally asked, 'Are you thinking there was some kind of accident, and those kids covered it up?'

'Dunno. I feel like we've not got close to what really took place on that mountain. I think there's a lot more to the story than those four are willing to tell. They're not kids anymore. They can't hide behind shock, or youth, for the gaps in their story. On the other hand, I haven't had a chance to chat with Bernard Nestor either.'

'We still don't know if it *is* Oliver.'

'No. We don't.' Giles flicked her hand out towards the road ahead of them. 'Hence the long drive.'

The town of Bathurst was now behind them, and they'd turned onto Vale Road. With at least another two hours' drive left, Giles supposed they could use the last of the trip to flesh out more of the case. 'My gut's sticking with Oliver. Yours?'

Edison nodded. 'I wish Kelsey and I could have given you more than bones. Problem is, cotton normally decomposes quickly – a few weeks, at most a couple of months. Body fluids and toxins also help speed up the process of breaking down the fibres.'

'Although we got lucky on the remains.'

'Yeah, we did. Got lucky on the remains and the sliver of paint.'

'Which do you think is strongest to seal a conviction?'

'Paint. If you find the tool. Otherwise, it's useless. Then we need to rely on the bones.'

Giles was silent. Edison seemed to feel she needed to reassure her that the bones were still strong enough to convict. 'The depth of the grave and location helped to hinder the chances of animal scavengers over the years. The bone structure was surprisingly well preserved. The red clay acted almost like a coffin shell. It took eighteen years for water erosion to wash away the silty soil, and the run-off from the surrounding gullies to eventually expose the skull.'

'Guess that dog was in the right place at the right time.'

'Yeah.'

Giles could feel Edison look at her; she focused on the road. 'If you were to go on your own gut instinct, what feeling do you get from the bones you've collected? What do you think happened?'

'Hmm.' Edison looked back at the road ahead. 'Sometimes it's not the skeletal bones, but the grave itself that holds more answers.'

'Like?'

'A premeditated murder – the perpetrator sometimes digs the grave in advance. Under the body, there's leaf matter, more than usual, where the wind has blown leaves, or overhanging branches from the surrounding trees have fallen into the hole before it's filled in. Then the body is laid on top, and the hole is covered. It's the foliage under the body that can change a conviction from manslaughter to murder. It can prove premeditation.'

'Did you find debris under our victim? More than normal?'

'Nah.' When Giles looked over at Edison, he flashed her a smirk. 'I'm just saying an offender should bring a shovel *and* a leaf blower to the scene of the crime if they don't want to get caught.'

Giles felt the *zing* return.

Edison went on. 'Don't forget the child had a previous broken rib. Recent fracture. Only just healed before he deceased.'

'Clumsy child?'

'Clumsy, unlucky, adventurous, stupid. All typical reasons for a broken bone in young males.'

The country road straightened and stretched out before Giles. She accelerated, trying to make better time for Crookwell. Her impression of Oliver wasn't of an adventurous kid. After a moment, she said, 'I chatted with Paul Cooper, and I get the feeling that Oliver wasn't a typical teenager.'

'You don't think Oliver was robust?'

'Nah. I don't. I can't help thinking he didn't have a big personality like Paul or Bob, or even Phil or Bell. Sort of a child that's more comfortable sitting in the background.'

'More of an observer than a participator?'

'Something like that. I think he was friends with the group because he had no other choice.'

'That's your department, Detective Giles. I guess those are the questions you need to ask the mother.' After a moment Edison asked, 'What else is bugging you?'

Giles looked over at Edison, and he tipped his head towards her hands on the steering wheel where her thumbs were kneading the wheel.

'It's Cooper. At the end of the interview, he said he'd forever wondered what happened to Oliver, and I kinda believed him.' She quickly added, 'Trust me, he's not a person I'd readily give credence to. But there was a sincerity about it.'

'You think he had nothing to do with Oliver?'

Giles shrugged. 'When I came down the mountain, I could see the park area, before I came out of the tree line. If Oliver saw Lucas Cooper sitting in his car, I wonder if he hid. The kids were all scared of Lucas. I wonder if he was waiting for Lucas to leave, or his mother to arrive, before revealing himself.'

'If he hid and saw Paul come down the trail and hop in the car with his brother, then that means he was still on the mountain. Left with the other three.'

'Yeah.' Giles's thumbs continued to rub the wheel. 'But don't tell Bray I'm starting to rethink those last fifteen minutes. I still need to interview Lucas. Kick over every stone and turd.' She grinned and added, 'That's what my father would advise.'

THIRTY-SIX

The two ex-racehorses were still adjusting to their new paddock and territory.

'Wastage', some people would call them. Only, as the animals stood in the moonlight, it was hard to understand how such noble beasts could be called *wastage*. Beyond their pedigree, the animals were a glossy dark and dapple-grey glory. Magnificent.

The grey horse snorted about the old man who was making doll-delicacies in the dark. Late into the night it stomped its hoofs and swished its tail as the old man poked plaited strands of straw through loops with blunt implements, braiding the hay like woollen yarn.

In the dark and quiet hours, the dapple-grey was drawn to the light of the kerosene lamp. It was inquisitive of the old man working away on the straw effigies that were the likeness of children. The dapple moved forward. The creature's large bold eyes brightened, becoming alert as the old man opened out his palm to offer it a treat. At first, the horse was curious about the little childlike figures. Skittish. If it decided to strike or kick the old man, his bones would crumble and shatter. His thin skin would split and rain tiny wishbones down across the paddock.

The horse snorted at the straw treat offered on an outstretched palm. Its lip nibbled and then scooped up the straw doll. A doll that the old man had named: Joe Thicket.

THIRTY-SEVEN

Liam Edison opened the motel door to room number five. The wavering look on his face amused Giles. It only slackened, relaxing a little, when she held up the dinner feast in one hand, and drinks bag in the other.

Edison stepped to the side and Giles brushed past him as she entered his room. On the small table she dumped the plastic bag of overordered takeaway, then pulled the six-pack of beer and two bottles of Sangiovese from the second bag.

Giles held up one of the bottles to show – as promised – they'd be drinking Edison's choice of muse-juice, then she cracked the seal. 'We can have a beer while the wine has time to breathe. Soften the tannins.' She gave Edison a grin and he looked like he wasn't sure how to respond.

'Did you grab some cutlery while you were there?' asked Edison.

In such proximity, Giles could see the motley colours of green and grey flecks in his eyes. They seemed more piercing up close and made her stare longer than she should have.

'I've dined out in so many motels during my career that I've invested in a Swiss army knife.' She smiled, though she could tell Edison wasn't sure if she was joking – she wasn't. But to put him at ease and stop him thinking they were going to eat with their hands, she pulled a couple of wooden forks from the bag.

Edison sat in the chair at the table. Giles sat, legs crossed, on the end of his bed. They ate mostly in silence, partly because they were famished and partly because the small room made them feel closer to each other than they were comfortable with.

Giles hadn't had a chance to change from her suit pants and jacket, but while she had slipped out to pick up the dinner, she could tell from the steam hovering on the ceiling and smell of deodorant in the room that Liam had managed a quick shower. He had changed into casual pants, a crinkled t-shirt, and sneakers. She wanted to ask him, *Does that feel better?* His attire may have been relaxed, but not his face.

Instead, she asked, 'The rib fracture,' as she ripped open the six-pack and passed him a beer. 'How common is that fracture in boys Oliver's age? I mean, I know kids can be robust and energetic – adventurous.'

'Any broken bone in children shouldn't be considered a common occurrence, but it is. You've got a fifty-fifty chance of breaking something as a kid. For boys it's normal to have multiple fractures.'

Giles flipped open the takeaway box and began squeezing lemon juice over the lamb. From another container she ripped apart some pita bread, smothered it with tzatziki and stuffed it into her mouth. As she chewed, her mouth full, she asked, 'What did you break as a kid?'

'Lots of things.'

Hearts? she wanted to quip. Instead, she went with, 'Was that the beginning of your fascination with bones?'

Edison chuckled. 'Maybe. I did love looking at x-rays as a kid.'

The room now smelled potent of olives, garlic, meat, and only a hint of Edison's deodorant. Giles finished her beer and wondered if she should shift to the wine or stick with the lager. She wanted to relax into the night, before visiting Mrs Lavine. If Bray or Callahan were in the room, they would already be hashing out ideas. Yet, while her conversation with Edison about the case wasn't as spirited, he didn't seem to mind bouncing viewpoints around, so Giles continued, asking questions between bites, and Edison kept replying thoughtfully with mouthfuls of food. In fact, Edison seemed more comfortable with the distraction of conversation than the image of her lolling on his bed.

'Do you think Oliver would have had the confidence to get into a vehicle with a stranger?' asked Edison.

'Dunno. Depends on the circumstances, the context of the moment. But that's the gap I can't seem to fill.'

'Or did he just run away?'

Giles shrugged, popped another olive in her mouth. 'From Mum's account in the report, Oliver Lavine didn't seem the sort of kid to run away. There was no apparent motive for him to take off or disappear, which makes me think that, if it was a crime of opportunity, chance, then it was luck for the perpetrator, unlucky for Oliver. That's why I think some of the officers on the original case were stuck on the name Bernard Nestor. Nestor was around the time Oliver disappeared. He was a person of interest because of a previous incident relating to possible child grooming.'

'Paedophile?'

'Not convicted. Suspected. Well, more implied. Certainly on the police radar.'

'Ever convicted after Oliver disappeared?'

'Hmm, nope.' Giles dropped her head, a little troubled with her answer. Twenty years after Jacob Colton's complaint, and . . . *nothing.* Yet in those twenty years since, Nestor hadn't offered horse-riding lessons either.

From the backpack on the floor, she pulled out a manila folder, clutched the file against her chest while she finished the food in the container, and once done, she thumbed through the reports. With no crime scene eighteen years ago, no body, and no collected evidence, all she had were the statements of the witnesses on that day, and very little else. The only other issue Giles had – there was no motive for someone wanting Oliver to disappear.

Giles looked up from the folder. 'If the answers aren't in Crookwell, they'll be back in Muswellbrook – or even at Burning Mountain itself.'

Edison smiled, agreeing.

'Look, I don't know much about archaeology,' said Giles. 'But my training is to look past the gore and assess a scene analytically, search for valuable evidence. My experience with most homicides is that they're relationship killings, where the victim and suspect are known to each other, even if it's a brief passing or exchange; seldom random, but an opportunity presenting itself. Not always preconception.'

Edison nodded for Giles to continue.

'My scene log, when I arrived on the day the skull was found, doesn't make interesting reading. However, tomorrow my two main questions are, what bones had Oliver previously broken, and did Oliver ever take horse-riding lessons?'

Edison took a swig of his beer, emptying the bottle. He looked over his shoulder at the bottle of red, then asked, 'You're not interested in the friends anymore?'

'Huh? What makes you say that?'

Edison tilted his head back at Giles. 'Those two questions seem to point to either Bernard Nestor, or Oliver's mother.'

'I agree the friends could be hiding something. And maybe they've been protecting each other the last eighteen years,' said Giles.

Friends. Was the group really friends? They certainly all weren't now. Had they considered each other friends at school? Eighteen years was a long time to protect someone who may not have been considered a *real* friend. Unless, somehow, they were connected to the lie, and it was more about saving themselves than the other person.

It was the pubescent age that niggled Giles. The first moment when the body starts changing, and, by twelve and thirteen, kids start to become sexually aware. Giles sensed her father had noticed the change in her as a child, the subtle transitioning from tomboy overalls to wearing her jeans on her hips, stretching her t-shirts around the collar so they'd casually slip off one shoulder. She had started to ignore her train set, and instead listened to music in her room, mimicking dance moves, testing her boundaries.

One afternoon, Benjamin had come home early and discovered her experimenting with her mother's old make-up. He had snatched her wrist, spun her around twisting her hand and arm and yelled, 'Go wash that muck off your face.'

Giles wasn't sure whether it was the make-up or the fact that she had helped herself to her mother's belongings that caused his reaction. Either way, her wrist had crackled in his grip, throbbed with pain. It went limp and swelled. She secretly bandaged it and hid the blackening bruising from the world. It took weeks to heal and for the bruises to fade. At the same time, things changed quickly in the family home. It was soon after that Benjamin sent her off to boarding school.

Perhaps it was to save her from acting out against him in the small country town, or from fear that in a few years she might start acting on her sexual urges, potentially ruining her reputation. Kiss the wrong guy. Get a name for herself by the time she'd finished high school? Maybe Benjamin wasn't saving her from Nestor when he sent her off to boarding school; maybe it was to save her from herself.

'Giles?' Edison gently prodded. 'You okay?'

Giles nodded. 'Yes.' She flicked her hand towards the bottle of red on the bench, indicating for Edison to pour her a drink. 'If a bone was broken by malice or abuse, I doubt there'd be a medical record. It would have come up in the original investigation like a screaming red flag.'

Edison handed Giles her wine poured into a coffee cup. The mug was the closest thing in his reach. 'No medical record could mean the child agreed to help conceal the injury. Do you think that's a possibility?'

'Or the parent didn't know the extent of the injury, and the child never spoke up?'

Edison frowned. 'What child would do that?'

Giles searched for words. She had none.

THIRTY-EIGHT

Outside, the night sky was almost soundless, apart from the rain's gentle, repetitive tapping on the roof tiles – nature's white noise. In the last hours of darkness, the birds and crickets had hushed their incessant warbles and trills, wrapping and tucking themselves inside their wings, having silenced their songs until dawn.

Joe Thicket slid open the bedroom window a tiny crack and the scent of petrichor filled his room. He held out his hand to the rain, breathed in deep the smell of wet grass and soil. He strained to hear a new sound coming from the neighbour's house.

Joe recognised the beat and harmony. While the echo was muffled, it was a rhythm that he knew well. The familiar rise and tension of voices. It was the same song, only different lyrics, that was being sung in the house next door. Joe wondered if Bob was thrashing about like his father had, and if the girl, the one who wore thin waif material that hung in layers and swished at her ankles, would flee to the bathroom, lock and hide behind the door and wait until the sun rose and the birds started singing again before coming out and pretending the events had never happened.

Joe climbed back into bed. He peeled one of his horse stickers from the bedhead and stuck it onto his pillow. He rested his head beside it, and pulled the light cotton sheet to his shoulder and closed his eyes. He listened to the drumming of voices. Followed the cadence flow of the tempo shifting. The beat pulsating. The familiarity of the noise lulled him back to sleep.

Amy Thicket could hear a storm on its way, but it had not yet reached her bedroom window. She lay in the dark on top of the fresh cotton sheet; sprawled out, exposed, soaking in the calm. Her heart rate was slow, her breath pattern light. She ran her fingers gently over her bare stomach, soft strokes over relaxed muscles. Her stomach felt supple and warm and pudgy. She felt serene. No longer needing to be afraid of waking to a nightmare.

Undisturbed, she acknowledged it had been so long . . . *so fucking long* . . . since she'd known the luxury of sleeping uncovered, unguarded, naked and vulnerable in a bed. Never again would she need to shield herself with limbs and twisted blankets for protection.

As her fingers ran along her ribs and rested on her breast, and with the entire bed to herself, she thought how strange it was, now that it was all over, she finally felt she had the courage to leave Trent Thicket.

Her woes were all behind her now – no husband, no car. He would take the fall for all the miseries and evil she and her son had endured. In the morning, it would be a new day. A fresh start.

Amy Thicket opened her arms out to her sides and straightened her legs. It was as though she had shapeshifted into another woman altogether. The old Amy was gone. From now on, she would fiercely ward off harm that came towards her, or her son. At last, Amy had found her courage.

Just you fucking try . . .

Amy closed her eyes, her lips pursed as she exhaled slowly, then her mouth slackened into a smile.

DAY 5

THIRTY-NINE

The muffled ringtone of the mobile woke Giles. Her hips and legs were tangled in the bedsheets, and she struggled to kick herself free. The moment she realised she wasn't home in her own bed, she sat bolt upright. Heart pounding. Eyes on the empty space beside her. Edison wasn't there, but she was in his bed. *Shit, shit!* There was a moment of relief when she realised she was still fully clothed, in her black tailored suit, with just her shoes off. Only then did she feel certain that, after the beers and bottles of red wine, she hadn't done something stupid, like try to stick her tongue in Edison's mouth.

The mobile continued to buzz against her hip. She jostled about in her pocket, not wanting to wake Edison – wherever he was. Giles saw Bray's ID on the screen, cringed and answered it.

'Hello?' she whispered.

Bray's voice overlapped hers, barking the moment she hit the answer button. 'I need you back tonight.'

Shoes . . . shoes? Where are my shoes? And where the fuck is Edison?

Bray again. 'Giles? You hear me? Where are you?'

Giles's head thumped with too many questions, and maybe from a little too much red wine. 'Motel. Just about to leave for Mrs Lavine's home.'

'Why are you whispering?' Bray's voice was loud and booming. Far too intense for the early morning hour.

Giles tucked the phone under her chin, wiggled her toes and looked at her socked feet – her shoes were still missing. Edison must have slipped them off, but where the bloody hell did he put them? She searched the floor. 'Eh? Whispering? Nah, just being respectfully quiet.' She was impressed with her lie as she slid off the bed and found one shoe behind a chair. She slipped it under her arm.

'Hang on . . .' said Bray. 'Give me a sec.'

'Righto.'

There was muffled talk on the phone, urgent talk. Giles scratched her head. It felt like a knotty mess. Standing in the middle of Edison's motel room, lying to Bray didn't sit comfortably with her. Giles collected her other shoe by the front door, stuffed a muesli bar she'd seen on the kitchen bench into her pocket, and, before leaving, found Edison fast asleep on the carpet between the bed and the wall of the adjoining bathroom – a bath towel for a pillow, spare blanket as a mattress, and his jacket draped over his shoulder to keep warm. She winced at the empty beer and wine bottles stacked on the small table, cringed at the frivolity of their all-night conversation that was only intermittently broken by the topping up of wine, then turned away, and quietly left the room to her own next door.

Outside, the balmy morning hinted that the day would get sticky and hot. Giles searched for which pocket held her own room key while she waited for Bray to come back on the line.

Bray again. 'Bob Bradbury has agreed to come into the station for an interview.'

'Brilliant!'

'Tomorrow morning. That's why I need you back here tonight.'

'I can do that.'

'That's not all, Giles. Jacob Colton has also agreed to an interview. Did you reach out to him?'

Giles frowned. *Jacob?* 'Jacob Colton?'

'The kid whose mother put in a complaint about Bernard Nestor. Only he's not a child anymore.'

Shit. Bloody Dad. 'What did Colton say?'

'He'll meet with you. Only not at the station. I'll text the details. Look, Giles, he didn't seem overly willing, so tread carefully when chatting to him. He'll be a reluctant witness by the sounds of it.'

Crikey, how did Dad manage to pull that off?

Giles grinned. 'Reluctant, but still willing,' she said, then ended the call with a satisfying tap of her thumb.

Bob Bradbury was also woken by a muffled ringtone of a mobile phone. Only no-one wanted to speak to him – it was just that his alarm was set on repeat.

By his side, Bell slept with both pillows tucked under her head, leaving him with none. They had gone to bed frosty with each other, but he'd try to make it up to her. And eventually, he knew he'd win her over when she realised he was just a guy doing his best to buy his girl a ring.

Bob rolled onto his side, kinked his arm, and rested his head on his shoulder. He loved Bell. Was grateful that she'd come into his life. The irony of it, though – meeting her because of Paul Cooper. Of all bloody people.

Bob swallowed and thought back to his schooldays. In the Year 9 corridor by the lockers, when Paul Cooper was still his mate. Paul had sat on the edge of a dented galvanised garbage bin and said, 'Why don't we piss that loser off? Three's a crowd and all that.'

'Eh?'

'The ginger. Let's get rid of him. Just you and me. The A-Team.'

Bob had wavered by the locker door, then shook his head. But it wasn't because Dill was his best mate, and he didn't want to do the dirty on him; it was because Bob was terrified of being alone with Paul. Paul had a way of asserting absolute control over him. He could make him do things he was too afraid of saying no to. Dill was a buffer. A lifejacket in the unusual friendship of three. So, Bob had answered, 'Nah. Can't. He's my mate.' Then Bob had mumbled, to push the boundary further between him and Paul, 'Dill's my *best* mate.'

Bob would later realise Dill had overheard the conversation as he was coming out of the classroom and sworn to Bob his returned loyalty and gratitude.

Soon after, Bob and Dill had found their talent. On the footy field. Bob's brawn, and Dill's lanky long legs, made them hotshots on the oval. They spent the school term immersing themselves in weekend footy games and afternoon training, because it was the one place Paul Cooper never showed up at.

Slowly they befriended Oliver Lavine, the kid who had Buckley's chance of getting in a full game. They'd pitied him sitting out the matches on the bench. Recognised themselves in him. Then Oliver introduced them to Bell, and Bob watched his friendship group swell, and the space between him and Paul Cooper widened.

His safety net had grown, and Cooper was losing his footing in the group. Bob realised that the more people he could pull around him, the more he felt protected from Cooper's coaxing him into being an arsehole at school. The stronghold was slowly dissolving. Life was finally taking a turn. The unusual friendship of four had decided that, on the first weekend of the holidays, they'd do a hike up to the top of Burning Mountain. They'd been excited. That was until, at the last minute, word got back to Paul Cooper – and he invited himself to tag along.

FORTY

The early-morning bus ride from Muswellbrook to Denman was less than twenty-five minutes. Amy and Joe had hopped on the single-decker at Brooks Street, both fighting back second thoughts of venturing out. However, Amy straightened her backbone, lifted her chin, and motioned for her son to do the same.

Joe only squirmed a little in the seat. The entire journey he had been mute while watching farmlands whiz by from the side window. He pointed to cattle and horses, silos that stood tall like silver rocket ships, at grape trestles, work utes and quad bikes with cattle dogs riding on the back. Some paddocks they passed had crops of barley that grew thick. He was mesmerised by the fields, which were lush, green and inviting, all watered by an expensive pivot irrigation machine dragged around the paddock by a tractor. His mother had nodded at each discovery, a touch of sadness on her face. Joe Thicket had never ventured far from town before, and by the time the bus arrived at Palace Street in Denman, their nervousness had only inched a little towards excitement.

Amy rummaged through her handbag for a sheet of paper with a name and address scribbled down. A pencilled mud map was drawn beneath. She twisted the page, so her sketch matched the cross-section of the streets, then she pointed down the road and said, 'This way, Joe.'

They walked one behind the other – Amy in front, Joe behind and at half the pace – until they reached the gravel road where the homes looked either rundown or abandoned. At the end of the street, they saw the grey and ugly house with the number that matched the one scribbled on the paper in Amy's hand.

'Do we open the gate?' she asked.

Joe looked up at his mother, frowning into the sun, and shook his head.

'Okay, we'll wait.'

Together, they stood behind the rusty metal gate that cut them off and kept them out of the front yard. Amy eyed a cobweb spun between the railing and corner post of the hardwood fence, which a spider had long ago abandoned. She reached out with a finger and broke through the silk, making sure the critter couldn't return. The mooring threads floated in the air, failing to find an anchor.

You have to start again, little one. We all do.

Amy fought the urge to turn and leave. After she'd decided to give it a few more minutes before heading back, two horses, one dark bay and the other dapple grey, stepped out from behind the rusted corrugated shed, brushed and saddled and ready to be ridden. The horses strolled up to the gate and stood in front of Amy and Joe. The beasts' ears twitched, and they snorted at Joe's outstretched hand, inquisitive. Slowly the horses stepped closer. Skittish to the touch at first, they soon relaxed and allowed Joe to stroke and pat their muzzles.

No longer needing to hoard money for her escape, Amy had decided to spend some of it on riding lessons. After all Joe had been through, she wanted to nurture his love of the animals. Only now, the horses looked huge – and dangerous. She wondered if she should have started with something smaller. Safer.

'I see you've met.'

Joe and Amy looked around for the voice. They stilled the moment they saw Bernard Nestor appear at the entryway of the machinery shed. 'Mrs Thicket?'

Amy watched the man hobble out of the doorway of the galvanised shack. 'Mr Nestor?'

Bernard Nestor nodded and limped towards them. And when he flashed Amy a smile, she couldn't help thinking his teeth resembled those of his retired horses.

Nestor flopped his arms on the railing between them like a wet towel. His shoulders dropped. The skin on his neck was taut, as if there was no longer muscle or bone structure to hold him up. When she searched his face for reassurance, he stretched out his hand over the fence and shook hers.

'You ready for a ride, young man?'

Joe stared at Nestor.

'He's a little shy, but he'll warm up. Once you get him chatting, he won't stop.' Amy looked down at her son. 'Isn't that right, mate?' She ruffled his hair. 'Joe?'

Joe didn't respond.

Bernard Nestor looked the boy up and down, then back at the horses. 'You got a favourite? I'm partial to the dapple. Its name is Iceberg.'

For the first time, Joe's face softened. 'Why?'

'Horse's coat looks like dirty snow. But if you can think of a better name while we ride, I'll listen to it.'

And then Joe Thicket smiled. A horse named Iceberg had broken the ice.

Amy imagined the two of them riding side by side. And fleetingly felt concern for the old man. She was sure if he fell off his horse, his thin-tissue skin would tear, and a bone would drop out of his body like garbage spilling from a ripped bin liner.

'First time you've ridden?'

Joe nodded. 'Yes, sir.'

Nestor unhooked the gate, letting the boy inside the enclosure, and closed it again on Amy. 'Then today will be a day you'll always remember.' To Amy, he said, 'This young man and I will ride up through the creek and along the banks. I'll show the boy where the Hunter and Goulburn rivers meet. Go get yourself a coffee on Ogilvy Street. Come back in an hour.'

Before Amy could reply, Nestor turned his back and asked Joe, 'You decided which one?'

Joe eagerly pointed to the grey horse. 'I like this one. I like its name. Don't change it – it's nice.'

It was the most Amy had ever heard topple from her son's mouth with a stranger. And because he didn't flinch, or hide, or look panicked by stepping out of his comfort zone, she took it as a sign to leave.

'An hour?' asked Amy.

'That's what you're paying for.' Nestor reached into his pocket and handed Joe a small pioneer doll made of straw. 'Feed this to your dapple. Get acquainted.'

Before she turned to leave, Amy watched her son step lightly towards the horse, palm flat, outstretched, the pale straw doll in his hand. The horse sniffed at the offering, then its soft lip twitched, scooping up the treat.

FORTY-ONE

In the main street of Crookwell, while Giles waited for the barista to make coffees and toast banana bread, she poked around in the local arts, wine and craft shops, eyeing off jams and chutneys, knitted scarves and woolly socks. The homemade marmalades reminded her of her childhood. The pantry was always stocked with preserved fruit, jams and pickles.

Benjamin Giles had been handsome in the years before falling ill – perhaps even more handsome when promoted to district super-intendent. But he didn't have the desire, nor the time, to pursue a relationship, and Giles felt it was more because his love for her mother was still strong thirty years after her death. Still, he had his fair share of admirers over the years. Women in town trying to win him over with Tupperware containers of shortbread biscuits, pecan pie, bottled nectarines, pickles and chutneys, and loads of mixed berry jams. As a child, Giles never understood the motive for these women's generosity towards her widowed, single father. But the gifts of food were appreciated. If it wasn't for the offerings, Giles might have gone a little hungrier as a kid.

Edison opened the door of his motel room, squinted into the light, and found Giles standing in the morning sunshine. She had showered and changed. Her long hair was pulled back into a tight braid. Her face was fresh with a touch of make-up, and she wore a tailored suit that, like all the others she owned, spelled boring. Her smile felt more forced than natural.

'Mornin'.' She held out a tray with two coffees, toasted banana bread and a blueberry muffin. Giles had figured that, before the mood between them could shift to awkward apologies, she'd set the tone of the conversation, hoping to skip a discussion of the previous night.

Edison, slightly perplexed, blinked into the light and at the tray held out before him. He looked back up at Giles and at the beanie pulled snug on her head. It was wool, knitted in pinks and blues, with ears and a face crocheted on it.

'What's that?' asked Edison.

'A choice. I popped into town and grabbed us some breakfast. You can have either the banana bread or the muffin.'

'No, *that*. On your head.'

'Oh! They were selling them down in the arts centre in the main street. It's a wombat beanie.'

'It's going to reach thirty degrees today. I don't think you'll be needing a beanie.'

'But it's a *wombat* beanie.' Giles pulled the woollen hat off her head, and held it up towards Edison for him to see the cartoonish face of the animal in bright knitted colours.

'I've never seen a pink and blue wombat before.' Edison grinned. He pulled a coffee from the tray and selected the banana bread. The amity between them was back in balance.

Janet Lavine sipped black tea from a pottery coffee mug glazed in earthy greens and browns. If you could compact all the wretchedness of life into a small box and tie it up with deteriorating string, Janet Lavine would be that box. Her lips were colourless, her skin sallow, like a layer of dust had settled on her and never been polished off. With each sip of her tea, her steel-framed glasses misted and hid her pale blue eyes.

Giles's tea was served in a porcelain cup with cracks in the floral glazing. Every time she took a sip, she feared the handle would snap, or the cup would disintegrate and crumble in her hand.

'I have to admit, I was surprised the case was reopened.' Janet Lavine's voice lacked strength. It was soft and hollow. To Giles, it seemed that although she mightn't have withdrawn all hope of finding her son, it was more that the enthusiasm and optimism had been worn away.

There's always hope, Mrs Lavine. Giles swallowed. *Please, don't ever lose it.*

Although perhaps after eighteen years, Mrs Lavine was reluctant to pin her hopes on an outcome that could be another letdown. She jiggled her teabag, then struggled to swiftly remove it from her mug. It dribbled across the tablecloth leaving behind a trail of brown liquid, before it landed on the side of a bread-and-butter plate.

Giles left her teabag in the mug, afraid of making the same mess. She cleared her throat. 'The case is classified as "long-term missing person". But that doesn't mean the AFP had given up on Oliver. His case file was taken over by the National Missing Persons Coordination Centre. Oliver's profile information still remains on the Australian Public Register, but not once, I assure you, has the police ever forgotten about him.'

Janet only nodded, her eyes on the tea stain across the cloth. After a moment she said, 'What does this mean now?'

Giles had to tread carefully. *No promises. No false hope. The woman has endured enough.* 'Well, nowadays, it's standard police procedure to ask for a forensic sample, DNA from the family. Almost twenty years ago, it wasn't common practice. These days, if the police come across unidentified human remains, the family's DNA is already in the system to be matched with the profiles of the missing person.'

Edison had been quietly sitting at the other end of the table. He had politely declined the offer of tea, and now seemed to feel the need to jump in. 'Mrs Lavine, with your DNA, we can determine if there is a genetic relationship when the profiles are matched. Once we compare the STR markers –'

Mrs Lavine blinked. 'STR?'

'Short tandem repeats. Repetitive sections of DNA. Genetic code.'

Giles gave a quick dismissive glance at Edison, before jumping back in. Liam Edison was a scientist, not a detective, and Janet Lavine needed short, clean answers to her questions. Not scientific ones. 'Mrs Lavine –'

'Janet. Call me Janet.'

Giles placed her teacup gently down on the table. It was too bloody hot to drink tea, and Janet Lavine's house didn't have air-conditioning, only an old electric fan on a pedestal that blasted Giles every few seconds. Giles waited for the next short respite of cool air before speaking. 'Janet, I don't want to instil false hope. What we've found may or may not be Oliver. It is, to be blunt, a process of elimination. We'll be sending samples from the remains to be tested, along with your swab. But I need you to know that DNA doesn't always survive in certain conditions, and can degrade in hot weather and in certain soils over time. We have our fingers crossed, and as soon as I receive any results, I promise you'll be the first person I call.'

Janet didn't respond. Her face didn't carry the same enthusiasm as Giles's or Edison's. Instead, she sipped her tea. After a moment she said, 'I worry that I don't have the strength to get back on that rollercoaster, detective. Torture myself with the belief Oliver will be found. You know, for the first few years after he went missing, I'd return to search for him. Only the landscape looked different each time. The trees seemed taller, undergrowth denser, it was never the same as . . . that day. Then, after ten years, the Missing Persons Unit said they could do a sketch of how Oliver would look at age twenty-five. I said, "If you do, I don't want to see it." I couldn't bring myself to see him in any other way than the one I'd last remembered.'

Giles searched for something to say and was glad when Edison left the table for his medical bag by the door.

'Before we take a swab,' Giles nudged gently, 'could I ask about that day?'

It was already documented in the file. The planned three-and-a-half-kilometre round trip to the top of Burning Mountain and back. From the car park the group would have crossed over the timber bridge, passed a small lagoon, then started up the steps and along the trail that meandered to the peak and lookout.

They had been the only ones on the mountain that day, concealed and unseen by the surrounding native trees of narrow-leaved ironbark, grey box and rough-barked apple. The group had made it to the top. Seen the smoke rise from the cracks in the ground. Stopped to eat lunch – but not the treats.

Hmm. This small piece of information still concerned Giles. Benjamin was right. What kid eats the sandwich, but leaves the goodies and treats untouched? The small tiff on the mountain would have happened before the group got to the candy and snacks. And that would mean Oliver started to descend the mountain a little earlier than planned. He would have arrived at the bottom of the mountain before his mother. Then what? Sat under a tree and waited? Hid from Lucas Cooper? Walked to the road? Hopped in a car? Maybe a car driven by someone he knew. Giles's mind flashed back to Lucas. Had Oliver sat in the air-conditioning of his car while he waited for his mother to arrive?

'Mrs Lavine – Janet – did you see Lucas Cooper's vehicle, a blue Ford Falcon, anywhere near the hiking trail – pass it on the road when you went to pick up Oliver?'

'No. Like I told the police. I didn't pay any attention to the cars I passed. And when I arrived, nobody was there. I waited a while, then hiked up the hill to search for Oliver. All the way to the top and back. Nothing. Everyone was gone. I feel guilty because I turned up late to collect him. If I'd been on time, maybe he'd still be alive today.'

Giles wondered how many times Janet Lavine had reimagined that day, tweaked critical details and pictured an alternate version of events. Rolling around the words, *What if? . . . what if? . . . what if?* Giles felt unsettled knowing that Janet Lavine's counter-factual thinking would have done nothing to ease the guilt, and only burdened her more regarding the mundane decisions she had made in those hours, and how dire the outcome was.

The silence lingered in the room, as the two women pondered the regrets of that long-ago April day.

Giles finally spoke. She had one last question, only she wanted to tease the answer out slowly. No suspicions or reading into its meaning. Giles needed to get to the bottom of Oliver's medical history, or, more importantly, the history of the previous fracture. Instead, she asked, 'Do you still have any personal effects of Oliver's?'

'Yes . . . the cupboard.' Janet looked over her shoulder. 'In the lounge-room. It's, it's not a shrine. Just a cabinet. Displaying a few of Oliver's old school certificates, some photos, his baby shoes.'

Janet stood and made her way into the lounge-room, and Giles followed. The room was neat and tidy, made homely with a vase of fresh flowers from the garden. Bright like a ray of sunshine, perhaps a way for her to bring a sense of happiness into her home.

'I didn't move away to forget Oliver.' Janet Lavine spoke with a hollowed sadness, an emptiness that a vase of flowers could never fill. 'I moved to get away from that day. Back home I kept living it over and over. My family and friends couldn't handle my grief and loss. Here, in Crookwell, I can try to make new days.' Janet pointed to an oak glass cabinet that sat in the corner of the room. 'I don't want to be known as the mother with the missing kid.'

Giles's face was soft. 'A lot of marriages and friendships don't survive the loss of a child under circumstances such as these.'

'Hmm.'

Giles stepped forward and looked at the items on display. Janet opened the door of the cabinet, and then stepped to the side. On one of the shelves, there were photographs of the happy times. A school award for improved writing in the third grade. A snapback cap with a football logo of a blue smiling cat. A Lego space cruiser and a Matchbox car. Baby shoes and a teddy bear. Items small in stature, yet vast in memories.

'Oliver liked to play football?'

'Uh-huh.'

'Did he have other hobbies?' Giles swallowed, then continued. 'Sports, motorbike or horse-riding, perhaps?'

'No. He only played a little football; not every game, though. Oliver was . . . he was a gentle soul. A quiet boy. I encouraged him, but . . .'

'So, not a kid covered in scabs, band-aids or yellow lotion?' Giles said offhandedly.

Janet stood quietly, as though waiting for Giles to elaborate.

'Oliver,' Giles hesitated, 'he never broke a bone or had the opportunity for his classmates to sign a cast then?'

Mrs Lavine turned and closed the door of the display cabinet before answering, 'Scabs, scares and broken bones are all part of a young boy's rite of passage, aren't they?'

'How about a rib bone?'

'My mother once cracked her rib, from a sneeze. But she told her friends she'd cracked it from the weight of her sorrowful life.' She turned to Edison. 'Shall we do that swab?'

Outside on the footpath, the day had already begun to heat up and the Sonata sat cooking in the sun. Edison opened the back door of the vehicle and placed the medical bag with the DNA swab on the seat. Before Giles hopped in, she turned back to look at the home of Janet Lavine. It was small, modest, red bricked, with the familiarity of homes built in the late 1950s. The garden was a mix of flowers, both old fashioned and new. The plants cluttered the beds. A multitude of colours from continual planting with little planning. The English garden and native Australian flowers were all clustered together, fighting for their place.

With the sun beating down on her shoulders and neck, Giles could feel the sweat already building. She waved to Janet, who stood at the front doorway, then climbed into the Sonata. The moment she closed the door she flicked the perspiration from her brow and wiped her neck with the palm of her hand. Edison sat in the passenger seat and was buttoning down his shirt and flapping the collar.

Giles kicked the engine over, cranked the air-con to full blast, and Edison lifted his armpits up to the vents.

'What now?' he asked.

Giles stuck her face towards her own vent and said into the flow of air, 'We play I Spy for the next five hours back to Muswellbrook.'

FORTY-TWO

The smell of trash roasting in the large industrial dumpster was thick in the air. A mix of cabbage and rotten egg. It turned Bob's stomach, soured his mouth, and made him desperate to leave the alleyway.

Before heading off to the markets, Bell had sent Dill home – and him back to the alleyway. *A plan,* she had barked. *A better one. Think it through.*

Her response to his idea had staggered him. Wasn't he thinking – no *wishing* – she would talk him out of it? Instead, Bell had slid onto the kitchen chair beside him, hands cupped on the table, and pressed him for more details. Dumbstruck, his voice had cracked as he spoke. He retold Bell how he'd been watching the seafood shop for the three weeks while working on the building site. *The bloke's like clockwork. Predictable.* Bell's gaze didn't budge at his observation, nor did she crack a smile as he shared his idea of snatching the garbage bag of money, pushing the guy away, and making a run for it.

Is that it? Bell had recoiled. *Is that fucking it? That's not a plan, Bob. That's an idea. Basic at that!*

Now, here he was, standing in the alleyway, looking up and down the corridor, trying to conceive a scheme so grand that it would rival any attempted burglary.

'Fuck. *Fuck.*'

Bob slunk down the wall, pressed his back hard against the rustic bricks and lit a smoke. He bowed his head, deep in thought, and stared at his feet. But he just kept coming up with the same plan.

Above him someone whispered, 'The squall's getting close, Bob.'

A foot stepped on his toes and pressed down hard. Bob snapped his head up, and smoke from his cigarette stung his eye, making it water. He squinted through tears as the weight pressed harder. All he could manage to say back was, 'What do you mean, squall?'

Paul Cooper grinned down at him. 'The storm has always been building, Bob. But it's about to burst right over your fucking head. Erupt, Bob. Fucking erupt.'

Bob blinked. Looked up and down the lane. He was bigger than Paul. He could lash out. Kick Paul right off his feet. Stomp on him while he was sprawled out across the ground. Keep stomping until the fucker was motionless.

'I'm telling you, Bob, that detective is going to come for you next.' Paul hunched over, his mouth moving closer to Bob's ear. 'And you'll need to decide if you're going to tell her what really happened up there.'

'What? You spoke to her?'

'Yup.'

'What did *you* fucking tell her?'

There was nothing for a moment. An inane silence, made more annoying by Paul's eyes locking, unblinking, on him. Bob felt tense. Contemplated how quickly he could get back to his feet. Pondered if on the way up he should swing a right hook, land his fist in Paul's guts. But it wasn't fighting Paul that filled him with fear, it was what Paul had said to the detective – or what Paul *could* say to the detective. Only Paul didn't seem like the type of guy who'd throw himself under a bus, just to see Bob fall.

Bob asked again, '*What* did you tell her?'

'Don't worry, I didn't drop you in the shit.' Paul stepped back, easing his boot off Bob's toes. 'Although I did tell her about the goanna.' He smiled, pleased with himself. 'Yeah, I did tell her about that. But the rest of it, Bob, that's up to you. Either way, you're gonna need to talk to her. And you better do it soon, she's looking for you. And you know what? I think she knows you're the one who can tell her how it all ended right there up on that mountain.'

'I didn't *kill* Oliver.'

'I'm not sure she's going to see it the same way, Bob.'

'Fuck you.'

'No, mate. You're fucked.'

Bob felt the urge to rise and swing punches.

'I'm just keeping you in the loop, letting you know, Bob. Being a mate.'

'You're not my fucking mate.' Bob felt the tightening grip Paul had over him when they were at school together. The all-too-familiar feeling of Paul Cooper's emotional stranglehold. And what connected them – aside from their wretched history of tormented schooldays and loathing of each other.

Bob knew Detective Giles would come after him for the truth. He was the only one who could fill the gaps regarding what had happened to Oliver Lavine before he'd disappeared.

FORTY-THREE

Amy listened to the splashes in the bathtub for a moment, before tapping lightly on the door. 'Can I come in?'

A squeaking sound of skin sliding against fibreglass, then, 'Yeah.'

She opened the door to find her son swallowed up in a mountain of bubbles. It had been years since he had a bubble bath. But today, when she had run the water, she had squeezed dishwashing liquid under the tap, and as the suds formed, Joe's face had lit with delight. Now, he sat amongst the bubbles, his hair coated like a white halo.

'You havin' fun?'

'Uh-huh.'

In the sink, the plastic backing of the adhesive bandages sat crumpled, along with tissue spotted with blood. It prompted Amy to ask, 'How's your fingers? Still stinging?'

Joe lifted his hand from the water, looked at the strips of Elastoplast Amy had wrapped around two of his fingers and thumb earlier. The water had turned the bandages a dark brown.

Joe shook his head. 'Nah.'

'You don't need a fancy fruit knife to slice a peach, Joe, just your teeth.' Amy chomped at the air, but it hardly raised a smile. 'So . . . are you excited about your next riding lesson?'

Joe shrugged.

'Thought you'd be more excited.'

Another shrug.

'Things are always harder first time round, but it gets easier. You'll be riding like a cowboy in no time.'

Another damn shrug. Amy cocked her head. It was her emergency money, her escape money that she'd been hiding in nooks around the house – most of it in a rusted cut tobacco tin that had belonged to her grandfather. She had unrolled the notes, tried to lie them flat on the kitchen bench, and counted her blessings that things had never come to the ending that she'd predicted for herself and her child. The money, she had decided, the money would be for joy. *Fucking. Joy.*

'Joe?' Amy pressed.

Joe shrugged for the umpteenth time and Amy fought to hold her patience.

'Joe?'

'I don't wanna go again.'

'What? Why not?'

'Dunno.'

'I know you love horses. So did I when I was a little girl.'

'I think they're too big. They scare me.'

Amy tossed her head back and laughed. It was loud in the small, enclosed space, and echoed. The sound startled them. The sheer volume of it. Amy made the sound again and listened to it echo off the tiles. She hollered, yelped, and Joe giggled. They'd been used to living in quiet, but in that moment they realised they were no longer fearful of upsetting the bull. They were free to make as much noise as they liked.

Amy encouraged her son to join in. Joe took a deep breath, then made a high-pitched squeal. It too echoed off the walls. Together they began to make a raucous noise that filled the bathroom, building in volume and pitch. The two of them squealed over the top of one another, louder and louder. The elation of the freedom to feel their lungs open.

Joe splashed. He tossed bubbles in the air, blew them from his palms, scooped and flicked them from above the water and watched them float in the air. Amy, caught up in the delight, lunged towards her son to tickle him. Only Joe flinched. He reeled back from his mother's arms. A face smothered with fear.

The reaction both shocked and angered Amy. Scared herself, she stood back from the bathtub, giving her child space. 'Joe? *Joe*. I would never hurt you. I would never touch you like that. Do you hear me? I'd never lay a hand on you in anger. I'm not your father.'

'It's not that.'

Joe sank under the suds. 'I don't wanna horse ride. I *don't. I don't.* Please don't take me back there.'

The look on her son's face before he disappeared under the white plume of froth terrified Amy. The boy had known a lifetime of fear. But this look – *this* – was one she had never seen before.

FORTY-FOUR

It was late by the time Giles dropped Liam Edison off at his accommodation in Scone. She helped him with his bags, but when he invited her in for a nightcap, she felt a flash of awkwardness due to her previous night's behaviour and declined.

It was almost eleven pm when Giles walked into the pub. There were only two patrons left at the bar, and Giles spotted Carol down the other end of the pub filling a metal bucket with hot water. She watched her add a splash of disinfectant and inhale the eucalyptus steam, then dip the mop in the bucket, before dragging the fraying shag over the floor and around the edges of the poker machines. Giles was about to call out; instead, she made her way across the room.

The floorboards creaked and Carol snapped, 'I just bloody mopped that!' But when she spun around and saw Giles, her two pocked mandarin cheeks turned to pomegranates, orange to red, smooth and glossy. 'Well, stuff me! I haven't seen you in twenty years, and now I see you twice in one week.' Her voice was softer, kinder. 'What are you doing here?'

'Two things,' said Giles.

'Yep. First?'

'Just wanted to grab a bottle or a six-pack.' Giles tipped her head, looking guilty for wanting service when Carol was trying to close for the night.

'Chilled?'

'Yeah. To drink now.'

'Not with me, I hope. Because I'm dead knackered, love, and just wanna go to bed myself.'

Giles smiled. 'Nah. Not to drink with you.'

Carol leaned on her mop, exhaled loudly through her nose, her face blank. 'Aside from the booze, what's the second? Because I'm bloody tired, girl. Twelve hours of serving and bitching is long enough for an old chook like me. Save yourself – and me – from pussyfooting around. Straight to the point – what do you want, Rebecca?'

'Oliver Lavine.'

'*Jesus Christ!*'

Carol shook her head, picking up the bucket, which looked heavy. She lugged it out into the main bar area where the two old cockies, grey-faced, skin weather-worn, with long stark white beards and darkened fingernails proof of decades of labour, were still sitting on bar stools having a natter.

'Is that why you, and the burly detective, were here the other night having a steak? Because of that skeleton you found out near Mount Wingen?'

Giles scoffed. 'I can't have a steak with my partner in a pub?'

'You can. You've just never had one in mine. Never popped in to buy a bottle of something either. Only, this week I'm your new favourite restaurant and bottle-o. What do you wanna know?'

Giles dropped her head. Breathed in the eucalyptus from the bucket. They were both buggered, and Carol was right, it was easier and quicker just to get to the point. 'The Cooper family. You know them?'

'Yup. Everyone knows the Coopers. Knows not to piss them off. But the family is more growl than bite. They run a couple of head of Hereford cattle. Old man's tough as nails, no bullshit – two sons are arseholes. One's up Queensland now, other works in the mine. Why?'

Giles rocked her head side to side but didn't answer.

'Oh, police shit, and you're hoping I'm a snitch,' Carol continued. 'But I can't give you much about them. Once I've handed over a beer, I switch off my ears.'

Carol grabbed a sponge and submerged it into the bucket. The hot water turned her hand pink. As she washed down the chairs, Giles heard the bar stools screech, and heavy boots making their way across the wooden floorboards.

'We're gonna choof off now, Carol,' called a voice. 'Thanks for the beer.'

'Night, loves.' Carol squeezed out the sponge and started mopping up drink spills on the tabletops.

'Cheers, Carol. Empties are in the rack,' called another voice.

'Aww, you're a doll,' she called back.

Giles wondered whether they actually had finished their beers that looked like burned cream in a glass, or if they'd caught a bit of the conversation and decided it was time they should skedaddle. She waited a few seconds till she was sure they were alone and the pub was quiet, then asked, 'That's all you're giving me on the Coopers?'

'Pfft! That's all I got. When you're a bar bitch, you learn to keep a few secrets.' Carol tapped the tip of her nose with her pointer finger and gave a wink. 'But honestly, honey, the Cooper family don't share much, and I've never gone out of my way to get to know them.'

Giles nodded. 'What about Oliver Lavine? Do you remember much about him?'

'Shit. We all remember Oliver.'

'You do?' Giles frowned. 'That's weird. Because not once, in all my life, have I ever heard the name Oliver Lavine mentioned.'

Carol's face darkened. 'We might not have spoken about him, but that doesn't mean people stopped thinking about him. That . . . tragedy . . . it shook the core of this little town, Rebecca. You weren't here to understand or witness its impact. Every kid, every mother . . .' Carol jabbed and pointed her finger at Giles, 'Every cop was disturbed and bloody scared. Your father included.'

'I know it's late, but can you give me anything more?'

Carol's lip twitched. 'I saw the kid around. Just about every kid his age has played rugby league for either the Devils or the Cats. Half the games on a Saturday and Sunday are played out on the oval just up the road.'

'And Oliver played?'

'Yep.'

'You're sure?'

'Yep. I'd see him in here after a game. When the footy matches were over, the teams always came back here for some tucker, and the parents would have a wine or beer. It's just the way our little town rolls. The way we like things here.' Carol couldn't help herself. 'Football is what this town loves. Not like Sydney. Not off bloody yacht sailing at Drummoyne or rowing down the bloody Lane Cove River.'

Giles sucked in her lips and smirked. 'Hmm. Can you remember what Oliver was like?'

'Small. Useless. Always walking off the field because he strained something, sprained something, or hurt something. Nice kid. Shit player.'

'I heard he was timid.'

'Timid is a nicer way of saying it. Spent most of the games on the bench. He was littler than the others. Not gutsy. No glory. Should have been over on the netball courts with the girls.'

Giles held up her hand. 'Okay. Okay. I get the picture, Carol. Thanks.'

'Right.' Carol turned back towards the bar. 'So, you wanna try something from my candy vending machine?' She flicked her hand towards the fridge, at a display of coloured alcoholic fizzy drinks lined up. 'I've got yellow shit, pink shit, purple shit or blue shit.'

'I'll skip the coloured confectionery. Case of beer will be fine.'

As Carol turned to leave, Giles asked one last question. 'And Bernard Nestor? Know him?'

Carol froze. When she turned back around, any sign of amusement in her face was gone. 'What about him?'

Giles stuttered. It was a mash-up of guttural sounds. She wasn't sure what to say next.

Carol saved her. 'Bernard Nestor brought out the worst in this town. Look, everyone knows you've found human remains out at Wingen. It's all over the bloody news and radio. Front page of the local paper. It's all everyone's talking about in the pub. But eighteen years ago, the town was in trauma over what happened to Oliver, and people started pointing the finger, and turned on the man. It wasn't heroic of us, it was ugly. Bernard Nestor just looks like a paedo. Ugly and scary as fuck. Lived on his own. Worked with children. Perfect fit to the mould of a dirty old man. Just glancing at him seemed to tick all the boxes. Rumours surfaced and some people took action.'

'Action? Like what?'

'Just made life bloody hard for him. But after three years, no charges were laid. And people started to feel ashamed of their behaviour. Cops were here breaking up brawls over Nestor. Friendships split over opinions. The loss of Oliver was a dreadful time for this town. It's why we don't talk about it. It stirs up old memories of the kind of people we never wanted to be. That shame still sits as thick as cream in a pail of fresh milk. But no-one's forgotten, Rebecca.'

The humming of the cool fridges made Giles feel tired. She nodded. It was time to leave Carol be and let her get on with closing. 'Thanks for your candour.'

'No worries. I'll grab you that six-pack of beer.'

'Or a bottle – something more . . . mature.'

'Hmm.' Carol looked Giles up and down. 'Rebecca, a girl as pretty and smart as you shouldn't be drinking alone. You got someone to go home and drink this with?'

Giles shrugged. But the lack of a smile gave away her answer.

Outside on the footpath, Giles pulled out her phone. It rang for a while and just when she was about to hang up, Turner's groggy voice answered.

'Did I wake you?'

'Nah.'

Bullshit.

'What's up?'

Giles knew Turner had read every sheet of paper stored in the case box; meticulously checked through each piece of evidence submitted almost twenty years earlier. She asked, 'Oliver Lavine's file. Was there anything on his football coach? That he may have been a possible suspect?'

She was running on the theory that if Oliver got into a car with someone he knew, the football coach would be a good place to start. She heard Turner murmur before answering. She wasn't sure if it was an amused grunt or a tired groan.

'His alibi checked out,' answered Turner. 'He was on the list, then scratched off. Not a suspect.'

'What was his alibi?'

'Cataract surgery. Was getting his eyes lasered at the time Oliver disappeared.'

'Uh-huh.' Giles twisted her lip. It was worth a shot. 'Thanks, Turner. Nighty-night-night.'

'Nigh–'

Giles hung up and pocketed her phone.

DAY 6

FORTY-FIVE

'Can I get you a drink?' Giles asked. 'Water, tea? We have a Nespresso machine. I know people don't think that's impressive, but believe me, all of us here at the station love it. Can I make you a latte? Cappuccino? Macchiato?' Giles refrained from adding, *Muffin? Banana bread to go?*

Bob Bradbury looked uncomfortable with the offer, almost suspicious. Giles wanted to tell him, *It's not a trick question.*

'Nah. Ta. I'm good.'

Before the offer of a beverage, Giles had watched Bob read over the statement he'd made some eighteen years earlier. It was like opening a time capsule. Memories fade over a passage of time, though – the brain shrinks, and memory strength wears away. The vividness of the past event slowly declines. Yet, recollections can come back if a person feels they're in a safe space to process them, and Giles was doing everything she could to give Bob that space.

As his eyes had followed each line, Bob had squirmed in his seat, shrinking with each sentence, so that by the time he'd finished, he looked like he'd shrivelled and shortened. Giles wondered if eighteen years was too long ago, and the trauma of losing a friend was long buried, suppressed. On the other hand, maybe if the experience had enough meaning, recollecting what happened that day would be as fresh as if it had happened yesterday.

When Bob was done reading, he'd handed Giles back the piece of paper and she'd slipped it into the file, before moving it to the side of the table. Now she was ready to start the interview, making sure it was as relaxed and as chatty as possible. Except, every time she moved or took a breath to speak, Bob would flinch. He seemed distracted. Fidgety. Nervous. To Giles, this was a good sign.

'Are you sure I can't get you something, Bob? Soft drink, perhaps?'

'Nah. Ta.'

Bob dropped his head, pressed his thumbnail into the groove along the edge of the table, and Giles stole a moment to look him over. His sharp features. Toned body. She knew if she caught his glance in public, she'd instinctively warm to him and inwardly smile. But now, observing the man slumped in the chair, she could see a weakness in him. Damage.

Bob cleared his throat. 'I'm here because of what the cops found the other day, aren't I?'

'What do you think they found?'

'I heard bones. Bones were uncovered out near Mount Wingen. It was on the radio. Everyone's talking about it at work. Is that true?'

'Yes. That's correct.'

'Is it Oliver?'

'I can't comment, but off the record, we haven't confirmed yet who the remains belong to.' *There*, thought Giles. *An honest answer, and now he thinks we're sharing.*

Only Bob didn't look any more at ease. 'Do *you* think it's Oliver?'

Giles gave a small shrug. The non-verbal reply wouldn't be recorded on the tape, and the subtle shrug of one shoulder would be missed on camera. 'I know the day Oliver went missing was some time ago, and memories fade, but after reading your statement, do you think there might be anything else you can remember – or something you'd like to add?'

'Nup.'

'Okay. Could I just clarify a few things?'

'Like?'

'Paul Cooper's behaviour up on the mountain.'

'What about it?'

'The dares. Pranks.'

Bob gave a thin smile. 'Monkeyshines, that's what my dad used to say, tomfooleries. But they were more like wind-ups. More a torment, a torture, than fooling around to get a laugh. Paul was like that.'

'Like what? Can you elaborate on what the dynamics were like with Paul?'

'Dynamics?' Bob looked confused.

'Mood of the day. The interaction that took place.' When Bob still looked baffled, Giles switched course. 'How did you and Paul become friends?'

'Don't know, really.' Bob dropped his head and picked at the table again. 'Paul's older brother was in senior year, and we were in middle high school. Paul hung out mostly with his brother and his mates. With the older boys. But then Lucas Cooper ended up leaving before the end of the first term. I think he was encouraged to. He was disruptive. A bit of an arsehole. Don't think he had the smarts for it either. Only, the older boys didn't want Paul hanging around with them anymore.'

'Paul was left friendless? And you filled the gap?'

'Sort of. Everyone was scared of Paul and fucking scared shitless of Lucas. They could be mean, those two, when together. So, I guess looking back, Paul had no-one to hang out with anymore, so he started talking to me. I didn't make that connection at the time – I just thought that if the scariest fucker in school wanted to be my friend, then there'd be protection in that.'

'Was there?'

'Not really. In primary school Phil and I used to get picked on a lot. A *lot*. I hated it. But in high school, being friends with Paul Cooper just turned me into a bully too.'

'Who did you pick on?'

'Anyone. Just anyone for kicks and laughs. I did it so Paul wouldn't pick on me. I'm not proud of it. It's dumb, I know. But I was just a kid.'

'Are you still friends with Paul now?'

'Nup. Can't stand the prick.'

'What did you do to the kids you picked on? Beat them up?'

'*What?* Nah. We didn't do shit like that. We just pranked them. Hid their schoolbag. Took stuff that wasn't ours. Not expensive things – we took things like pens and lunches. Teased them and said awful shit to see their reaction. I feel sick thinking back on it. The worst we did was throw dried-out lumps of clay.'

'Clay?'

'Yup. Not really hurting anyone, but when they hit their target the result would be spectacular. *Boof*, a huge dust ball. A mini explosion of dirt.'

'Huh. So, on the mountain when you went hiking that day, were you all getting along?'

'Sort of. Not really. Bell was there. It was the first time she'd hung out with us, aside from school and weekends at footy games. It started out okay. Phil was cracking jokes on the way up – Bell was laughing. I was a bit shy around Bell at first, but Phil was making her laugh, and everything was going good. We were excited about reaching the top. Getting to the lookout.'

'And you made it to the top.'

'Yeah.'

'So when did things start going wrong?'

Bob shrugged. 'I dunno. I think Paul wasn't coping with the lack of attention. Phil was running out of jokes, so when we reached the top, we looked at the smoke, the view, ate lunch, then everything kinda went quiet. Like we were all thinking, *What now?*'

Giles tilted her head, encouraging Bob to continue. She wanted to show him she was listening, not interrogating. *Keep going, Bob, what happened next?* When Bob didn't continue, she gave him a gentle nudge. 'After you ate your sandwiches, what then?'

'Paul came up with the idea. He started with his dumb dares, but really it was to make me look like a fuckwit. He knew I liked Bell.'

'What were the dares?'

Bob shrugged. 'Just encouraging us to do stuff that we didn't want to.'

'Like touch the base of a tree that had a goanna up it?'

'You know about that?'

Giles nodded. 'Was Phillip given a dare?'

'Yeah. He had to taste the goanna vomit.'

Giles tried not to recoil at the image. 'Did he?'

The pause was long, then Bob nodded, his voice soft, 'Yeah.'

'Did Paul do any dares? Did you encourage *him* to do something he didn't want to?'

Bob shook his head.

'What about Bell, or Oliver?'

Bob dropped his chin. Swallowed hard. 'He . . . he encouraged Oliver and Bell to do something. But he only did it to rile me up. And it was after that everything went to shit.'

Giles stayed still and silent. *Come on, Bob, keep going. Fill in the gap for me.* Giles could almost feel the missing piece of the puzzle falling into place. All Bob had to do was let it drop.

Bob kept his head down, pressing his thumbnail into the groove of the table. As he spoke, he couldn't reach Giles's eyes. 'He dared Oliver to pull down his pants, and for Bell to touch . . .' Bob swallowed, twitched his shoulder like he was shaking off the memory. 'We all froze. Too scared to object. It was strange. It was like all of us wanted to laugh – make it into a big joke – but Paul wasn't joking, he wasn't laughing. It wasn't a dare. It was more of a threat. And I wanted to step in and say "No". But I think I was too scared because I had no idea what would happen if I did.' Bob fleetingly looked up at Giles. 'I was fucking scared of Paul. I'd never stood up to him before.'

'And what about Bell?'

'She looked fucking terrified. I think she realised – it dawned on her – that she was alone on a mountain with four boys, and now she was expected to touch one of their dicks.'

Bob pressed his nail harder into the groove. 'After, I felt sick like I was a bloody coward. I should have stopped it. I should have spoken up. And Oliver didn't wanna do it. There was this look on his face begging me for help. And I didn't help. Then he pulled down his pants. Only Bell never touched a thing. She laughed. Pretended it was the funniest joke, like the four of us were hilarious, and Oliver just stood, semi-naked . . . pants around his thighs . . . and I hated him for it. I hated him for what he just did.

'I should have hated Paul, but I hated Oliver. Oliver looked humiliated. And Paul turned on him, saying, "Why would you actually go through with it? It was a fucking joke, dickhead. You're a pervo. What's wrong with you?" And Oliver just quickly pulled up his pants. But I saw red. I was so angry with myself for making Bell get out of the situation herself. And Oliver didn't laugh. His eyes swelled with tears. And then it all just kicked off.'

'Kicked off?' *Keep going, Bob, keep going.*

'All of a sudden, we turned on Oliver for doing such a dumb thing. Like it was actually his idea, not Paul's. Oliver started sobbing, and then next thing he stormed off back down the mountain. I watched him run off, but because I felt like I needed to get my dignity back, or I'd lose Bell's respect, I picked up a chunk of clay and threw it at Oliver's head. Because Paul Cooper and I threw clay rocks all the time.'

Bob stopped. He sucked in the air through quivering breaths. His jaw was juddering. Giles didn't want to stop the momentum and offer him a tissue. She pressed gently, 'Then what happened?'

'Nothing. I think I hurt him. He wrapped his arms around his head, and then he just started bolting down the path, took off back down the hill. After a few minutes or so, Paul rolled his eyes and went after him. I think to apologise. It was the first time I saw him with any remorse. The first time Paul actually looked guilty for making another person feel like shit.'

'And Paul chased after Oliver?'

'Yes.'

'Did you see Paul after he followed Oliver?'

'Nup.'

'Did you see Oliver again, after the incident?'

'Nup.'

Bob still hadn't made eye contact with Giles, and she felt like there was something still there. Some small part of the story he was holding back.

'And Bell? It was just you and Phillip and Belinda left?'

'Yeah.'

'What was Bell doing?'

Bob looked up, his eyes red and watery. 'When I threw the clay at Oliver, it hit him right in the head, and I screamed, "Fuckin' bullseye! Dead bang on!" Then I looked at Bell, almost for applause.

To see if she thought I was a hero for protecting her, but her face was stiff. Stuck mid-laugh. And she knew, she fucking knew then, that it was me. I was the cunt that used to toss lumps of clay at her after school. It was me.' Bob wiped his nose with the back of his hand. Swallowed hard, fighting back tears.

'But the two of you are in a relationship?'

'Yeah. In that millisecond, on that mountain, I could see she was torn between accusing me of being her bully or forgiving me. I saw it. I saw it all over her face. The realisation, the disgust. Her making the connection. The transition between shock and disbelief. From sadness and then . . . to forgiveness. And she smiled.' As Bob spoke, his jaw shuddered. 'And I knew right then, I'll never let anyone harm this girl again.'

The silence hung in the air, and neither Giles nor Bob said a word. The images of the event rolled over in Giles's mind.

After a moment, Bob sighed. 'After that day, none of us spoke to Paul Cooper again. Phillip, Bell and I became inseparable. I love her, detective. I know I was only in the ninth grade, but I'll never forgive myself – not for being the bully I was, or for the shitty things I did and didn't do. And believe me, detective, I do love her. Bell's my life.'

Giles gave a small nod. 'One last question, Bob. When you picked up the clay, were you on top of the mountain? Near where the smoke smoulders?'

Bob blinked. 'Yeah.'

Giles dropped her head. Now she couldn't meet Bob's eyes.

Bray was hunched over his computer, chin rolled into his chest, looking at the screen through his dark eyebrows. He had a frown on his face, his forehead puckered, and his hands clutched the mouse like he was choking it in a stranglehold.

Giles fought back the buzzing in her body. She lightly pinched the cotton material at his elbow and spun him around in his office chair so that she had his full focus. She spoke slowly, almost in a whisper. 'I know what happened to Oliver Lavine.'

Bray stayed silent. Still frowning.

'I said, I think I know how Oliver was killed.'

'Are you talking about Oliver, or the skull? Because we still don't know that those two things are related.'

'Okay.' Giles started again. 'If the skull *is* Oliver Lavine, then I think I know how the trauma damage was inflicted.'

Bray's eyebrows slowly unknitted. 'Uh-huh, I'm listening.'

Giles took a deep breath to stay poised. 'Bob said at school he and Paul used to throw clumps of clay at kids.'

'How does throwing clay at school relate?'

'The clay on Burning Mountain had been cooked. The clay out there is like bricks. Cooked by the heat of the coal seam in the mountain. Bob might have picked up a lump of dirt, thinking it would disintegrate on impact, except he was literally tossing a brick at Oliver Lavine's head. And I think when Bob threw that mass of clay at Oliver, he cracked his skull. And this would have been the swelling in the brain, the fluid. I think this is what killed Oliver Lavine.'

Bray scratched at his chin. Silent again. He looked Giles up and down. 'So, what happened to Oliver then? He didn't just dissolve into the ground. Disintegrate on impact.'

'No. Oliver stomped off and went down the mountain, crying. During that time his brain would be filling with fluid and pressure. And the person to leave the mountain next, and follow Oliver down the path, was Paul Cooper. At the bottom, waiting in his car, was Lucas Cooper. What if Oliver collapsed at the end of the track, and Paul, being partially responsible, convinced his brother to put him in the trunk of the car, drive out to a secluded spot, and bury him. And that's why Mrs Lavine never saw Lucas Cooper's car when she drove out to collect her son.'

Bray's eyes stayed locked in on Giles. She could hear the murmuring of the air-conditioning. Distant clicking on a keyboard. Hear her own breath drawing in and out. It was just a theory, but Christ almighty it was the closest they'd got.

Finally, Bray swallowed and spoke. 'The skeletal remains are at the morgue, ready for us to take a look. We don't have confirmation it's Oliver.'

'But if it *is* Oliver, if we can find solid evidence to back up the theory, we might be able to close an eighteen-year-old case, and finally allow Mrs Lavine to bring her son home to bury.'

'Perhaps.' Bray leaned back in his chair. 'Do you think Bob suspects the incident up on the mountain might have been the cause of Oliver's death?'

'Maybe. Only, if he thought that, then why would he tell me he threw the rock?'

'What if he wasn't the one who threw it? What if he's planting the seed to take the fall?'

A few metres from the police station, further up the road on William Street, Bob climbed inside his car, which was parked near a vacant lot. The slamming of his door scared away the grass parrots in the empty field, and he fleetingly felt as spooked as the birds.

He flicked Bell a text: *Done. Off to work now.* He stared at the phone, waiting for it to ring. He was sure she'd want a step-by-step recount of the interview. Instead, his phone pinged: *Good.*

Bob exhaled slowly to calm his thumping heart, then lit up a Winfield and tossed the pack on the dash. He sucked back on the ciggy, limbs twitching, hands trembling. As he puffed the smoke through the gap in the window, he looked down at the cigarette shaking between his fingers, studying his hand. Swollen knuckles. One hand fatter than the other. The skin so taut that he thought it would split. It worried him seeing how inflamed it was. He promised himself that, when all the shit was over, he'd get it checked out.

Bob took another drag and picked at the rotting rubber seal around the window. The crumbling foam felt grimy and blackened his fingers. He briefly wished he might have a little money left over from the robbery for his car. But the ring was the goal.

Focus on the ring first.

As he blew smoke from his mouth and nostrils, filling the cabin of his car in a grey haze, he searched the abandoned lot for a king parrot. Bell and her bloody birds. She would be laughing if she knew, saying, *It's the weebill, Bob. They're there, right in front of your goddamn nose, but nobody notices them. Any old bastard can spot the bright and colourful, hon, but it's the weebill, tiny, almost invisible – finding one of them, well, that's the magic.*

Aside from Bell's love of birdfeeders, it was her fascination with the weebill that made Bob wonder if that was why she was the only one to notice Oliver. The boy who was in front of everyone's faces, yet nobody seemed to see him.

Bob sucked back on his smoke before flicking it through the gap in the window. He bent down, scooped up his work bag and rummaged for a water bottle. In the hot car he guzzled, water dripping down his chin and soaking into his shirt.

There was a mouthful of water spinning in the bottom of the bottle. Bob was about to swallow it; instead, he pulled on the collar of his work shirt and tipped the water down his chest, feeling instant relief.

He had to get moving. Back to the building site. But his story rolled around and around in his head. *That bitch wasn't born yesterday.* Would the cop believe his story? Most of it was true. His love for Bell was true. Bell's moment of terror and Oliver's moment of disgrace was true. Nearly all of it was true. Up to the very last moment. But would the cop buy it right up to the end?

Bob clutched his chest. He needed to calm down. He thought, *What did Dad used to say?* And the sound of his father's voice echoed: *Even a broken clock is right twice a day.*

FORTY-SIX

At the morgue, Kelsey and Liam had finished at the gravesite and were now ready for Bray and Giles to examine the skeletal remains laid out in anatomical position. The room, aside from being cool, was quiet and sterile. Giles walked slowly around the stainless-steel table. The bones had soaked in the colours of almost twenty years being in the earth, organically stained in shades of brown and mossy green. She paused at the foot of the gurney, glanced briefly up at Liam. 'Looks smaller than I imagined.'

'Hair, fat, muscle, skin, organs, clothing, all layers that enlarge us,' said Edison, watching Giles walk a second loop of the table. When she stilled, he asked, 'Did the mother ever ask for a coronial inquest?'

'Nope. No point, really. I think she may've already known it would end up an open finding.'

'Lack of evidence?' asked Kelsey.

'Not even *lack*. None.'

Bray stepped in. 'I think Mrs Lavine was afraid the police would cease looking until further evidence was obtained. No mother wants their missing child's case to be shelved and forgotten. By leaving Oliver on the missing persons register, it kept his case open and ongoing.'

Liam stepped away from the table to give both detectives the room and space needed. 'It's all there. DNA swabs from the remains were sent off to the lab a few days ago. We got the ball rolling on that as quick as we could.'

Giles and Bray nodded a thanks.

'Oh, and the media has been around,' said Liam. 'Phone's been buzzing. Front door knocked on a few times. The community and press are starting to connect their own dots and have also come up with the name Oliver Lavine.'

Kelsey added, 'Of course, we've not given the press a statement, but the aficionados are coming out of the woodwork. True crime enthusiasts, podcasters – *murderinos*.'

Bray scratched at his stubby chin again. He still hadn't shaved, and the stubble was clearly annoying him. 'That's what the town needs, woke do-gooders trying to solve a case before the cops. Eighteen years ago, the police urged anyone, even with the smallest, seemingly irrelevant information, to come forward. Nothing. Now, we might get swamped with tip-offs and leads from people who were not even close to the place, let alone in the area on the day, thinking they have something that might bust open this case.'

'But you have the friends' witness accounts?' asked Kelsey.

'Yes.' Bray flicked his eyes at Giles. 'But at the time, that led to nothing.'

'Then there was Bernard Nestor who was in the area. Again, nothing came from it,' added Giles. 'But as far as information from the community and the townspeople at the time, the police got zip.'

'Nothing?' asked Kelsey.

'Not a single person had anything to offer. Which was strange. Not even information that would waste time. Absolutely nothing in the days that followed Oliver's disappearance. The town went silent. And now, eighteen years later, a dog comes forward.' Giles gestured to the skull, squinted at it, squirmed a little at the thought of it hanging in the animal's mouth. 'Almost twenty years of silence, and then a victim comes to the surface because a dog thinks it got lucky and found a bone.'

Bray grinned at the idea. Edison dropped his head and said, 'We searched the grounds, examined it for further evidence. Sometimes on sites we find bullets, personal belongings, jewellery, but this was clean.'

'Clean, or cleaned?'

'I can't really tell. I've worked on sites that have been immaculately cleaned. This gravesite seemed like somewhere in between. It could have been tidied up, making sure there was no evidence left behind, or there may have been nothing much on a fifteen-year-old to leave behind to find.'

Kelsey interrupted Edison, 'I found you guys a sliver of paint.' There was a slight huff in her voice.

Edison patted Kelsey's shoulder. 'Yep. You sure did.' He turned back to Bray and Giles. 'Oliver went missing in April, only we didn't find any fossilised leaves, seasonal debris, so we can't determine if the victim was buried in autumn. I know you want this to be Oliver, but I guess what we're trying to say is, you won't know for sure until the DNA results come back. And that may be a few weeks.'

Giles nodded. 'And the cause of death, skull fracture causing head trauma. Are you sure about that?'

'Yes.' Liam's voice was firm.

From her pocket Giles pulled out a solid pink rock that had been collected from Burning Mountain. 'Do you think this could potentially inflict the same kind of fracture? That this could be the murder weapon, a rock just like it?'

Liam stepped forward and took the cooked clay stone from Giles. He tossed it up and down, gauging the weight of it, then rolled it around in the palm of his hand. After a moment he looked up and smiled. 'Possible. Very possible.'

Outside by the car, Bray stood tossing his keys in his hands up and down, looking like he was weighing up his thoughts. His head cocked to one side.

'He's a smart man, Edison,' said Bray.

Giles glanced over her shoulder back at Liam, who was standing on the steps of the morgue. She waved goodbye, and Edison returned it with a nod.

The corner of Bray's mouth twitched.

Giles had followed Bray's gaze, saw the change of expression on his face, then frowned at him. 'The answer's no.'

'To what?'

'To what you're thinking.'

Bray scoffed. 'I'm not thinking anything.'

'Well, when you do think it – the answer's *no*.'

FORTY-SEVEN

Since arriving back at the job, Bob felt as if the sounds of the machines were pounding his body. The cement truck spinning around in his head, the *ka-choo, ka-choo, ka-choo* of the nail gun thumping at his brain, and the grinding of the band saw going up his spine. It was like all the tools on the job were working him over. Pulsating in his sore hand.

Bob looked up at the scaffolding wrapped around the building, then back down at his throbbing palm. The swelling made his skin taut and itchy. The skin was torn, and pus freely oozed from the infected wound. He'd already taken the morning off to talk to the detective. He couldn't go home because of a bloody blister, that would be absurd – especially for a bloke who worked on a building site. Besides, he needed Wednesday arvo off, and he needed a good excuse. If he called in another sickie, it could end up costing him his job.

Up on the scaffolding, the tradies had been moving at half pace, but Bob's mind had been going a hundred miles an hour, so by lunchtime his head was thudding.

He'd recapped what he'd said to the detective, over and over, picked it to the bones. Had he given her enough to get her off his back, or too much and she'd be returning for more?

Bob's stomach squirmed. *Fricken hell. Why now? Why this week?*

Eighteen years, it had been. Why did it all have to blow up in his face the week he was trying to bloody mug someone?

Christ. It would be easier to call the whole thing off.

Bob kept thinking up excuses to tell Dill. For a start, the cops were buzzing around. But he feared Dill would see more into it, and realise he was just chickenshit. The only reason he could find that sounded believable was that he was a coward. Fear had won out.

He was gutless alright. He'd never done a brave thing in his life.

As Bob walked away from the tuck truck, his mood was shifting. The heat of the day was starting to get to him, along with the pain in his hand and the idea of ambushing the little man in the alleyway. The sun cooked his exposed shoulders, and sweat dripped down his spine, as he stuffed half a sausage roll in his mouth. He squeezed the dry pastry down his throat, and looked over at the boss.

The site manager was standing under the shade of a banksia, and Bob knew if he wanted the day off, he had better hurry up and ask for it.

He dropped his head, felt the heat move to his neck. *Geez, just ask him. You can rob a man of his takings, but you can't ask your boss for the time off to do it?*

Bob cleared his throat. 'Do you reckon I could have Wednesday arvo off, and maybe Thursday mornin'?'

The boss stopped chewing and looked up. The icing on his doughnut was already melting, pink and sticky. The boss sucked it from his teeth, made a smacking sound with his tongue.

The cement mixers were off, and the tools were silent while the crew searched for shade and something to sit on. A few of them were listening in to his conversation, and Bob gritted his teeth, ready for one of them to butt in and mess up the moment. He shifted his weight. 'Bell's got a job interview. Head office is in Sydney. I said I'll drive her down. For support and that . . .' The words trailed away.

Bob wasn't sure if the boss was buying his story, but he was sure he had 'what-a-load-of-bullshit' written all over his face.

The supervisor shook his head, looked down at the lumps of dried concrete and cut bricks, and Bob felt his chest sink. Yet there would also be relief in a refusal. It would mean he could tell Dill he couldn't get time off work and call an end to the whole damn thing. The idea of it sounded stupid now, more ridiculous than Bell getting a job.

The boss looked back at Bob. 'Yeah, alright. Tell Bell I wish her luck.'

FORTY-EIGHT

Jacob Colton sat in the shade under the expansive grapevine, away from the other patrons and their furry friends. He looked uncomfortable as he dabbed his finger in raindrops drying on the wooden table. A storm had blown through Nundle; lots of noise, claps of thunder, not much water in the rain gauge, but enough to make the humid air sticky, muggy and uncomfortable to sit in. Giles looked over at Jacob sitting in the corner of the beer garden, and guessed being a local and seen with a strange woman would raise all sorts of questions after she left, and none Jacob wanted to answer.

Giles ordered and paid for lunch – she owed Jacob at least a meal for his time – and then grabbed a couple of beers at the bar.

She had changed before heading out to Nundle. At home she had dressed in jeans, a beige cotton button-up top, and sneakers. She'd kept her attire simple because she wanted to slide into the background as much as she could, except her long legs, dark hair and eyes kept grabbing the attention of the barman, and the three old cockies and their two dogs.

'I can't blow up my life because the only thing you have is an interest in the case,' Jacob was stressing. 'You have nothing new, other than a doll.'

'We both have a doll.'

'So what? Bernard Nestor gave kids dumb dolls that he made from hay and his horses' hair. You can't send someone to jail for that.'

Giles wanted to stress, *Grooming, Jacob, it's called grooming*, but she didn't need the meeting to go pear-shaped before she'd even begun. She had to ease into the conversation.

'I just wondered if you remembered anything more,' said Giles. 'Because I did. I went back to the place and walked around, and things came back to me. Things at the time I thought were nothing, but in retrospect –'

'I have a wife. I've never told her a thing about that old geezer. I don't want to now. It near broke my mother when I said something to her nearly twenty years ago.'

'But you did tell her. Jacob, you had the courage to speak up back then.'

'Did I?'

'*Yes*. You did.'

'I only did it out of spite.'

Giles froze. *Had Jacob lied?* 'Spite?'

'Yeah. The prick stole my school blazer. I don't know why he took it, but he did. And my mother at the time cracked the shits. Not at Nestor, at *me*. She thought I was bullshitting when I told her I saw him take it. I mean, why would he?'

Because he was a bloody paedophile, Jacob!

Jacob took a gulp of his beer, curled up his fist and quietly burped into it, then continued, 'Mum said I must have left my blazer in the school playground or on the bus, and if I didn't find it, then no more riding lessons. I bloody loved horses, still do. So I thought if I told Nestor to give me my jacket or I won't be back for riding lessons, he'd return it. But when I got there, his dog had just died, and he was in the midst of burying it. In the shade of the peach tree, the dog lay limp in the grass, like it was sleeping, only the ants were already crawling over its eyes. I think the dog's toys, maybe its blanket and other stuff, were in a black plastic garbage bag. I felt sad watching Nestor toss it into the pit. I stepped forward to tell him I was sorry for his loss. Except, when he saw me, he grabbed me, latched onto me ... and I'd never been so fucking scared in my life.'

Giles knew that exact feeling. It was like it was bubbling up all over again. Her anxiety was rising, and she was worried it would show, so she slipped her hands between her thighs and nodded slowly, partly to say, *I understand*, but also for Jacob to continue.

'The bumping and touching I ignored because I loved his horse. *Loved* it. At first with Nestor, it was pats on the back, the arm, the buttock. You know, "Good job," or "Well done" ...'

The barmaid came out of the hotel and moved between the wooden tables collecting a few empties, and Jacob paused. He watched her and when they met each other's gaze they nodded g'day. He picked up his story the moment she returned inside. 'Then after a few weeks, it progressed to holding my thigh, helping me up on the horse – I didn't need help – and then a brush, a ...'

'It's okay, I read the report, Jacob. You don't need to –'

'That day his dog died, detective, I'm telling you, when he grabbed me, I thought he was about to drag me away. It was in his eyes, it was like looking into, I-I don't know how to explain it. Dark and soulless. It was like I saw my own ending. I yanked away so fucking hard and ran, *ran*, and I never wanted to go back. Ever. I didn't give a shit about the jacket. Mum going nuts over it was nothing compared to how she reacted when I told her about the touching. It near destroyed her. Near destroyed my family. My mother was furious the cops weren't doing anything about it. It was like she forgot about me, and her focus was on getting back at Nestor. I saw what people did to him. My mother incited it, fuelled it. I felt like everything that happened after was all because of a stupid jacket.'

'But it wasn't about a jacket, Jacob. It was about keeping you and others safe.'

'Yeah . . . well . . . you cops did nothing in the end, and my family –'

The story paused again as a plate of rainbow trout, and another with a pie floater and creamy mash potatoes, peas and gravy, arrived at the table. Only now, Giles had lost her appetite and Jacob didn't even make a move to start eating. They stared down at their meals, neither picking up the cutlery nor reaching for the salt and pepper shakers.

Jacob looked up and swallowed, his mouth sounded dry. 'Sorry. I know your father did his best. I know that. I'm not ungrateful. I just don't want to experience it all again.'

Giles raised a brow, acknowledging the apology for the swipe at her father. She squeezed lemon over her fish. 'The courts and law have progressed,' she said. 'People's thinking has progressed. You're an adult, not a child anymore. It's not a minor telling their story – you can't get tripped up on the stand.' She stopped and looked at him. 'Tell your story, Jacob.'

'To who? My kids or wife certainly won't want to hear it. Like I said, you don't have shit, and I'm not turning my life upside down. I have mates, friends, family. I can't have the town look at me differently. This is where I work. My children go to school . . . I just . . . can't.'

'You'll have my support, and my team's. Jacob?'

'Nah. You're not hearing me. I can't be dragging it back up. It was ugly all those years ago. And the moment when it all seemed to settle down, the incident with Oliver Lavine happened, and it enflamed Mum's hatred. Spurred her on. To be honest, I lost my mother to Bernard Nestor. Her tenderness was gone, and, sometimes, living at home became insufferable. She no longer treated me like her son, she treated me like I was damaged. It fucked up the whole dynamics in my family. All because of a goddamn fucking jacket and a few pats on the bum.'

Giles knew she had come to a dead end. She handed Jacob her card. 'If you change your mind, or think of anything, will you ring me?'

Jacob Colton lifted his beer, sculling the rest of it, wiped his mouth and said, 'Thanks for the meal, detective.'

'How'd you go with Colton?' Benjamin's voice crackled through the phone.

Back down the New England Highway, the sky across Murrurundi had opened up. Giles could see the rain falling in the distance and more thunder clouds rolling in.

'Not great,' answered Giles. 'He has nothing new. Doesn't want to get involved with it again. A bloody dead end, really.'

'Ah, well,' said Benjamin. 'You gave it another shot, love. I'm still proud of you, Rebecca. It's the most anyone's done since the case went cold.'

Giles could barely hear her father through the bluetooth. Her thumb hit the volume to maximum on the steering wheel, but it didn't seem to help. 'Where are you? It sounds like you're under water.'

'Nurses stuck me on an oxygen tank today. Just having a little struggle with my breathing . . . that's all. Don't bloody stress.'

'Okay . . .'

'Rebecca, I may have fibbed a little. Just a tinge.'

Giles gripped the steering wheel. Counted to three. All she could answer with was 'Hmm?'

'It wasn't a fox, or the bloody dog, it was Bernard Nestor who killed your hen.'

'*What?*'

'Neighbour said she saw him do it. Refused to make a statement. Said he had a long wooden dowelling rod . . . with a boning knife taped to the end. Like a spear. Cornered your chook in the bush. Stabbed it under the camellia tree.'

Giles felt sick. She could almost hear her hen squawking her name.

'Said she'd say nothing more about it. Didn't want to be the next person he jabbed.'

Giles felt the heat in her cheeks. *Did Bernard Nestor kill her hen so he could lure her into his chicken coop by offering one of his?* 'That was my pet hen, Dad! Couldn't you have done *something*?'

'We didn't all have bloody iPhones back then that we could just whip out and start filming, you know. Hearsay. That's all I had. No official report filed.' Benjamin sounded raspy, breathless. 'But I fixed it, Rebecca. I sorted it out in my own way.'

'How? How did you fix it?' When no answer came, Giles raised her voice. It was loud and harsh. 'What did you do? Dad! *What did you do?*'

'After . . . I baited his dog. Tossed it a steak laced with brodifacoum . . . rat bait.'

'You *what*?' The bleakness of the sky closed in on her. Images of Jacob Colton flashed, of him turning up to Bernard Nestor's home and finding him distressed and burying his dog, then the image of Jacob in the clutches of the old man. Giles could feel the fear of the child all those years ago, recalled the way she'd felt standing outside Nestor's chicken coop. A rush of adrenaline surged through her body and she nearly veered off the road. She had to concentrate as the highway before her blurred.

'Rebecca, don't get mad at –'

'I'm fucking furious, Dad! I can't believe you would *do* such a thing. So . . . you . . . couldn't get at Bernard Nestor, so you got to his dog? Is that it?'

'I wasn't trying to square up.'

'Bullshit!'

There was silence, and when Benjamin spoke again his voice sounded miles away, like he was talking down a drainpipe. 'That damn dog was blooming dangerous – *dangerous, you hear? . . .* I thought it wouldn't be long before the mongrel thing started pecking off all the damn cats and chooks in town, take a bite out of some kid's leg, get into –'

'Miss Giles?' A female voice now. Crisp and clear on the phone.

'Yes?'

'I think that's enough excitement for your father today.' One of the nurses from Merton Court had taken the phone off Benjamin. She could hear his muffled voice in the background, yelling, *Alright, all-bloody-right.*

'Rebecca. He's not had a good morning.'

'Is he okay?' Giles toned down her anger. 'Should I come in?'

The phone hit a black spot and dropped out as the rains met her along the highway. The windscreen began to fog, so she flicked on the wipers and air-con to demist the window. Giles knew if she showed up at Merton Court, Benjamin would only have a sook, or have another crack at her.

She instinctively looked for a traffic cam, but along the New England Highway from Murulla into Wingen, it was hills, cows, windmills and homesteads. She pulled her phone from the cradle, switched it off, then pressed down hard on the accelerator.

As she sped along, she clenched her teeth so hard, her jaw started to ache. She couldn't help wondering if her father had sent her off to boarding school because he was afraid of Nestor's retaliation for the death of his dog.

FORTY-NINE

Giles knocked on Bernard Nestor's front door several times. When he didn't answer, she figured he either wasn't home, or he had no intention of opening the door to her. She crept down the side of the house to the back paddock, and made her way through the orchard, weaving between trees, ducking under the slender branches.

Most of the leaves on the peach trees were vibrant green, yet on some branches, they had begun to yellow and drop. Giles could almost taste the flesh of the fuzzy fruit on her tongue, and it made her want to retch. She swallowed hard, forcing the feeling back down her throat.

Giles moved on, towards Nestor's old decaying chicken coop. Her lips thinned at the thought of all the times as a young girl she had climbed through the boundary fence and ambled through the grove, stealing fruit, and lying in the grass by the windmill and playing with the milkweeds.

Christ. Giles dropped her head and cupped her face in her hands. All those years ago, never knowing she had teetered on the edge of a life-changing experience. *That bastard.* She seethed, then kicked the coop door open and entered.

At the back, where it was closed in by three wooden-planked walls, she stomped towards the old brittle and rusted nesting beds. Her memory of the torn pages of pictures she had seen as a child was foggy. Still, she flipped over a metal drum, and, on her hands and knees, searched through the compost of paper, desperate to find an image that would make a judge and jury's skin crawl. But the paper had disintegrated and decomposed. If Nestor had used the illegal material for his hens' nesting beds, the evidence had long ago decayed.

Back out in the sunshine, Giles needed a moment to breathe. In the open paddock it was fresh and clean and earthy. She snorted, trying to rid her nostrils of the pungent smell of poultry dust. With the back of her hand, she wiped her nose.

Her hip started to vibrate, and it took a moment to register the phone call. She fumbled in her pocket. Bray's name popped up on the screen.

'The rib fracture,' said Bray.

'What about it?'

'Edison said the rib was a perimortem injury, inflicted or occurred before death. The area of the rib bone is porous, new, "woven bone", in the stages of healing. So, from the woven bone, he thinks the fracture would have occurred about two, maybe three weeks before passing. I just got off the phone with the old Cats coach. He coached for the under-sixteen footy team twenty years ago.'

'And?'

'He remembers Oliver. Can't remember him ever hurting himself on the field, but he said Oliver turned up to a match once complaining about a sore stomach. Sat on the bench for the whole game. Couldn't say exactly when. But . . . could be something.'

'Could be.' Giles perked up. 'Do you think the Cooper boys roughed Oliver up for fun, and, on the day at the mountain, it got out of hand?'

'They were bullies. They had that reputation.'

'Yeah. Sticks and stones may break my bones. We know they threw stones. Cooper and Bradbury.'

'Uh-huh. And Edison's been throwing stones all afternoon as well.'

'Really? At what?'

'Carcases. He popped into the local butcher. Came back to the lab with some animal heads.'

'Eh? Bit icky.' Giles squirmed.

'The two of you have more in common than you think. His experiments are not official. But he couldn't let the idea go until he tested the theory himself.'

'What animals?'

'A pig and goat. He said a pig's brain is smaller than a human's. The skull is forty per cent thicker. He ended up cracking the stone before the skull, but when he tried the same experiment on the goat, he thinks the damage is reasonably consistent with the cause of death. It's not an official scientific experiment. He performed it out of curiosity. But the idea of a clay stone – well, brick stone – causing the trauma holds weight. It stacks up, Giles.'

'Huh.' Giles twisted her lips. 'So, Bob Bradbury tossing the stone possibly inflicted the trauma. Now we just have to hunt down Lucas Cooper. And bring him and Paul back into the station. Get them to spill what happened in that gap from when Oliver was struck with the rock and stormed off down the hill. It's the last bit at the end, Bray. How did Oliver get from the bottom of Burning Mountain to Mount Wingen?'

'I don't want to bring in the Cooper boys until we get Edison's full report. Plus, we still need to wait for the DNA result.' Bray had a habit of reminding Giles not to jump too far ahead of herself, and it irked her a little.

'Righto, *righto*. DNA and report first.'

'What's that noise?'

Giles paused, lifted her chin to the sky. Around her the sound of buzzing was thick in the air, but it wasn't cicadas or crickets. 'Beehive?'

'Flies?'

Giles looked around for fruit flies, wasps, or bees. The drone grew louder as she made her way towards the side of the house and Nestor's machinery shed. A swarm of blowflies were bumping against the inside of the shed's window.

'It's coming from inside the barn.'

'What barn?'

'Bernard Nestor's. His work shed.'

'What the hell are you doing there?'

'I-I . . .'

'*Giles*, I said, what are you doing there?'

'I . . .' Giles sucked in the bottom of her lip before answering, 'Curiosity?'

'What?'

'Kicked my ball over the fence, just came to retrieve it. That a better answer?'

'Jesus, Giles . . .'

Giles wasn't listening to Bray's caution. She was at the shed now and slowly opening the corrugated door. The air inside was stale and thick with the smell of rotting fruit, hay, diesel, and other agricultural and organic smells that she couldn't find the names for. But there was also a strong coppery odour, and she had an inkling what it was.

Inside, it was dark, but it didn't take long for her eyes to adjust. When they did, she immediately dropped to the floor and crouched. At first, it looked like dozens of fat spiders were hanging from the roof, dangling down on webs. Then she realised that small pioneer dolls were hung at the end of string, attached to the beams in the ceiling. Dolls of different shapes and colours, no bigger than her palm. They swayed in the breeze.

Bray's voice barked again over the phone. '*Giles*, you're trespassing. You don't have a bloody warrant. Get the fuck out of there.'

Around her face the flies were droning, swarms of them, and that smell, like metal but more familiar to her. The metallic smell of blood. Giles's hand reached to her side, and she touched her Glock 23 lightly. Reassured knowing her gun was there.

'Hello?' She looked about, called out again, 'Hello? It's the police. Is anyone here? I need you to show yourself.'

She could hear the murmuring of Bray's voice through her phone, but not the words. As she inched slowly around a pile of hessian sacks and fuel drums, on the ground, sprawled on the cement floor of the shed, was Bernard Nestor in a pool of thick black dried blood.

Giles instantly lifted her phone back to her ear. 'Call an ambulance.'

'What's going on?'

She dropped to her knees and ripped open Nestor's shirt. Across his chest were puncture wounds. Giles listened for a breath, then grabbed his wrist for a pulse.

'Bray, call an ambulance. I think Bernard Nestor's been stabbed. And I think he's still alive.'

FIFTY

Back at the police station, Giles sat hunched over her desk, head in her hands, massaging her skull. She only stopped pressing her fingertips into her forehead when Bray squeezed past her chair and sat on the edge of the table.

'Here, made you a cup of sweet tea. Drink it.'

Giles took the mug and sipped. She could smell the soap on her hands from her scrubbing, but Nestor's blood was on her shirt cuffs, and lapel.

'Latest update is, Nestor's been transported to John Hunter Hospital. He's currently in surgery.' Bray rested his palm on Giles's shoulder. It was meant for comfort, but his hand was heavy and only seemed to add weight to her burden. 'Still hard to tell if the stab wounds are self-inflicted or by a third party. If he stabbed himself, there's a stronger chance the wound is a non-lethal abdominal injury, and he'll be okay. If it was assault-induced, that could affect the clinical outcome. The hospital will call with a revise of his situation, when . . . or if . . . he comes out of surgery. If the old prick makes it, he'll be in ICU, so we won't be able to interview him for a while.'

Giles didn't respond. She sat still with the mug of tea cupped in her hands.

'You okay?'

'Did I cause this?' Giles mumbled.

'How?' Bray gave her shoulder another gentle squeeze.

'Dunno.' She lifted her head and looked up at Bray. 'By looking into Oliver Lavine before getting confirmation. Stirring up the town and asking Oliver's old friends to come into the station. I'll have egg on my face if the results come back with the wrong genetic information. The media will come at me, at us. So will the town. And all this.' She pushed the file by Bray's side away from them. 'All this will have been a waste of time, and we could have put our resources towards looking at other crimes.'

'What's that got to do with Bernard Nestor's stabbing?'

'Come on, Bray, there are people in town – a few actually – that know my father was hellbent on locking up Nestor. Plus, Jacob Colton's mother made sure everyone knew what he did to her son. Nestor was the person of interest at the time of Oliver's disappearance.'

'Do you think some vigilantes stepped in?'

'The whole district knows a skull was found. That bones have been removed. We've ripped up an old ghost. Retold the horror story.'

'We can't be responsible for the reactions of the town, Giles. You know that. No-one from the station has mentioned Oliver Lavine to the press or the public.'

'But we have, by bringing in the witnesses from eighteen years ago. By jumping the gun and putting the idea out there that it could be Oliver, we may have inadvertently triggered someone.'

'That someone being Jacob Colton?'

'Colton was the one who put forward the first complaint about Nestor.'

'No. His mother did.'

'I'm scared, Bray. What if they're the remains of someone else, and I've given Mrs Lavine false hope, and stirred up trauma in Bob and Bell, made the town relive the tragedy, fired up a vigilante, when I never needed to.'

'But if it *is* Oliver, then we've got a headstart. Plus, we're a step closer to understanding what happened the day he disappeared.'

'Are we?'

Bray was the first to notice Turner loitering by the door. 'Can I help you with something, detective?'

'Sir, Evidence Recovery Unit has completed the sweep of Nestor's shed and house. They've bagged evidence, photographed, and recorded the scene. Not a lot to collect, aside from those creepy straw dolls. No weapon found yet, which may mean it wasn't self-inflicted. ERU photographed a lot of blood. And Detective Senior Constable Callahan found a phone number scribbled on a notepad in Nestor's kitchen. I've just run the number in the system.'

'And?'

Giles turned in her chair, noticed the reddening in Turner's neck. He cleared his throat. 'The number belongs to Amy Louise Thicket.'

DAY 7

FIFTY-ONE

If Giles didn't know better, a person could be fooled into thinking the house was abandoned and no longer liveable, as though it had been condemned and left to rot, but it had been Bernard Nestor's home for the last thirty years.

During this time, the changing seasons had stripped back the paint on the traditional weatherboard home, exposing grey crumbling wood. On the west side of the house, a laundry extension had been tacked on with concrete blocks, laid crooked. Nestor's house had been built with the same amount of thought and precision as a child would build a house of cards – and with a flick of a finger, it would probably collapse as easily.

Giles had been woken that morning a little after seven am by the buzzing of her phone. She had ignored it the first time it rang, but the second time round, she'd reluctantly reached for it. On the other end of the call was Jacob Colton, telling her he'd remembered something.

That 'something' had her springing out of bed and now she was standing by the corrugated shed with the police tape still draped and blowing in the wind like a coiled party streamer left after the event. With Nestor in hospital, Giles was free to observe without creeping around the property. She stood tall with her hands on her hips and gazed at the farm, the decrepit house, orchard, windmill, and the old hutch that once kept Nestor's chickens.

The structure was on a tilt. Lopsided from the wind's determination to knock it over. Giles took comfort that the place was crumbling in on itself.

While Nestor had become a recluse as the years went by, in the last twelve months he'd returned to his love of keeping horses. Giles wondered why, after nearly two decades, he'd decided to get back into the business of offering riding lessons.

Something caught Giles's eye, and she spotted Bray trudging through the adjoining paddock. She grinned as she watched him rethink climbing through the barbed-wire fence, and instead he walked the long way around and came down the gravel drive. It was hard to read his expression with his sunglasses on.

Close to the peach tree, she had laid a large tarpaulin and anchored each corner with small boulders she'd collected from the creek. Beside the plastic tarp was a shovel, pickaxe, trowels, some brushes, latex gloves and even a pair of protective goggles. Items she had pulled from her garden shed and boot of her car.

'You're prepared, I'll give you that,' said Bray.

'Like a girl scout.'

'Hmm.' Bray folded his arms across his chest, rolled back and forth on his heels. 'Think you may have learnt a few things from Kelsey and Liam?'

'Maybe. Let's see, hey?'

Bray lifted his sunglasses and propped them up on his head. He looked over at the peach tree and then down at his steel-capped work boots. He had come prepared to dig, but maybe not completely prepared if they found something.

'You know, whatever is under the peach tree – *if* something is under the tree – it's been there for almost twenty years. I just don't want you to pin all your hopes on finding something.'

'Jacob Colton said, on that day when he arrived, Bernard Nestor was burying his dog under a peach tree, and . . . some other stuff as well . . . *other* stuff, Bray.'

Bray sucked in his cheek. 'Righto.'

'They had drained and searched the old well twenty years ago when they were searching for Oliver and found nothing, but if Jacob's right, and Nestor was disposing of the materials that would send him to jail, then it was the orchard, under the peach trees, where they should have been looking. Jacob's adamant it wasn't just a dog he caught Nestor trying to bury.'

'If nothing is down there, then we haven't wasted valuable resources on a bum steer. But if there is something, the moment we find it,' Bray warned, 'we stop digging and call in the ERU.'

'Deal.'

'Right. Here, pass me the spade. I'll dig.'

Giles beat him to it. 'No, I'll dig. This is my hunch. I'll take whatever comes of it.' She snatched up the shovel from under the tree, stepped on the edge of the blade and scooped up a pile of dirt before dumping it onto the tarp. Bray kneeled at the tarp's edge, picking through the dirt, and began looking for skeletal dog bones.

After a while, when they had turned up nothing, Giles stepped around to the other side of the peach tree to start on a fresh patch of dirt. While the grass made the ground look even, under Giles's feet she felt the terrain dip where the soil had sunk. She knew that, as a body buried beneath the surface began to decompose, the soil above would slump further into the grave. The soil would become loose and softer, less compressed, its density different to the surrounding compacted soil. Giles knew it was a clear indicator of disturbed earth. She stomped on the ground. 'I think I've found where the dog was buried. Hand me the pickaxe.'

Bray took a moment to move. She knew that expression on his face. The look when you know you're about to stumble across evil.

Pickaxe in hand, Giles began to dig again, unearthing a few small boulders, until she hit something other than soil and clay. She had felt the tip of the axe slice through a softer substance. She dropped the tool, grabbed and snapped on her latex gloves, and started sorting through the dirt. First, she plucked out a small grey fragment of bone. She had found the dog. Then she tugged on a piece of black plastic poking out of the dirt.

Bray joined her. With the trowel, he carefully scooped away the soil to unveil a plastic garbage bag. 'Geez. Thank goodness for non-biodegradable plastic.'

With care he lifted the bag onto the tarpaulin, untied the loose knot and slowly upended its contents. They watched the wickedness come tumbling out. Materials and magazines with deliberately posed pictures of children, children's trinkets – and Jacob Colton's old school blazer.

It took Detective Sergeant Bray a moment to speak, and when he did, there was both shock and relief in his voice. 'That's a criminal law section 91H right there. Giles, it looks like you've got yourself a crime scene.'

Giles fumbled in her back pocket, pulled out her phone, and on the screen was the last photo she had taken of her father. Benjamin Giles tossing cheese to a waiting magpie.

She tapped the call button, and when Benjamin answered all she said was, 'Dad, I think we've got him.'

FIFTY-TWO

When Phillip O'Dell's mother saw his skinny legs disappear through the manhole in the roof of the house, she grabbed the kitchen broom and thumped the tip into the gyprock.

'Whatcha bloody doin' up there, Ginger Nut?'

'Nuffin!'

'You'll fall through the bloomin' ceiling.'

'You'll poke a hole in the fricken ceiling. Stop your thumpin'.'

Phil picked his way across the wooden beams. Aside from the dank smell, leaf litter and animal droppings, the roof cavity was sparsely populated with homewares and stored items. Mrs O'Dell didn't own much, and she owned even less that needed to be stored in a roof.

Dill carefully balanced his way across the timber planks, mindful of the accumulated leaf litter and bird waste. Tucked in the corner, he found his father's old shotgun in a zipped-up leather bag. The leather was tarnished with mould, pale green and powdery. Still, Phil smiled. Beside the bag was a cardboard box with '*Winchester. Brass shot shells*' scrawled on it. He felt ready to help his best mate out.

FIFTY-THREE

The ERU had arrived for the second time and taken over the site at Bernard Nestor's home. Bray had stayed, taking charge of the new crime scene, co-ordinating the teams, and sent Giles back to the station to begin writing up the report. When she arrived, she had expected Falkov to want a full update. Instead, he barked, 'You can team up with Turner and MacCrum. We've spent all night going through the CCTV footage. Traced steps. Bernard Nestor is out of surgery, but we still can't interview him, or update him on the progress of the crime committed against him.'

Giles blinked. Her head was swimming as it dawned on her, Nestor was currently a victim of a crime and a perpetrator of a crime. She had just stepped off Nestor's property hellbent on firing up the prosecution's team to convict him for multiple child offences. Now she was wearing a different hat; seeking justice for the attack made upon him.

Turner knocked on the front door while MacCrum and Giles stood behind him.

Giles's fingertips felt light and tingly. She balled her hands and cracked her knuckles. Tilted her head side to side to ease out the tension in her shoulders and neck, then let the expression on her face fall to neutral. When she looked over at Turner, she saw him squeeze his eyes tightly shut, and when he opened them again, he had the same impersonal countenance. Both were detaching. Separating themselves from the duty they had come to perform.

There was a long silence before movement could be heard inside. Then, the sound of a barrel bolt sliding back.

Amy Thicket appeared, her hair swept up in a ponytail and a bandana tied with a knotted bow. She would have almost looked sweet if it weren't that Giles could see it was to hide the yellowing bruise from the car accident. Covering the graze where her head had hit the gear shift of the Honda.

'Yes?'

Turner flipped his badge. 'Mrs Thicket, I'm Detective Constable Turner from the Muswellbrook Police Station. May we come in?'

Amy stepped aside.

As they walked down the hall to the kitchen, Giles noticed packing boxes filled with items wrapped in newspaper, ready to be taped and labelled. The house smelled like wet towels and dust. She wanted to throw open a window. It was like the walls of the house knew only how to hold in trepidation and the cold.

'You're moving?' Turner looked about.

'Fresh start. Clean slate. New life. All that.'

Giles felt the pressure in her throat at Amy's answer. She hung back. Stayed silent.

Turner touched the back of the kitchen chair lightly. 'May I sit down, Mrs Thicket?'

Amy nodded, pulled out a chair for herself, and sat with Turner at the dining table. MacCrum and Giles stayed standing by the wall. Giles felt Amy had sensed they were there for more than just a follow-up to her accident.

On the table were scissors and a stack of newspapers. Turner moved them to the other end of the table, then filled the empty spot with his hands, cupping them. He nodded at Amy, indicating he was about to start his questions. Her eyes seemed to dull.

'Amy Thicket, you are not obliged to say anything unless you wish to do so –'

'I know the caution, detective.'

Turner nodded, but he proceeded with the full caution as the woman eyed the three detectives. 'Amy, did you take your son, Joe, for a riding lesson out at Denman on the seventeenth?'

'Um, yes.'

In the silence, the fish tank bubbled away. There was a radio on in another room; a melancholy tune, an old song from the seventies. Slow in tempo, repeating the word: *sorry*.

'Can you tell me who your son had a lesson with?'

'Um, I think the man's name was Lester.'

'Nestor?' suggested Turner. 'Do you mean Nestor?'

'Yeah, maybe. I only saw the man briefly . . . dropped Joe off and p-picked him up after. Later. After the lesson. Was lucky to say a dozen words to the man.'

Amy was already stuttering. Was she searching for plugs to cover the holes in her story?

Turner pressed on. 'I have footage of you taking the bus to Denman in the morning, returning to Muswellbrook around midday.'

'Uh-huh. So?'

'Did you catch the bus again? Return to Denman later in the evening?'

'Nope, nah, I don't think so.'

Turner gave her a moment to rethink. When she didn't, he said, 'We have CCTV footage of you on Brook Street.' Turner waited for a response. When he didn't get one, he continued, 'An image of you stepping onto the bus. Footage from the bus itself.'

'Me? Are you sure it was me? Could have been anyone. Someone that looks like me.'

Turner's face was neutral, his voice monotone. 'I can prove it was you, Amy. Footage *and* witnesses.'

'Oh. I think Joe left his drink bottle. I think I went back for it.' Amy looked up to the roof as if she was thinking. It was a poorly performed act. 'Hmm, sorry, the accident has left me a little confused . . . foggy, you know.'

'So, do you remember two bus rides to Denman and back on the seventeenth?'

Amy's lips moved into a smile, but not her eyes. 'You saying I'm lying about being a little mixed up after my accident?'

'No. Not at all.'

'Hmm.' Amy twisted her lips. 'I might have, maybe. Is that all?'

'No, Mrs Thicket. We will need you to come down to the station. Thing is, we have reasonable grounds to believe you committed an offence on your return to Nestor's property.'

Amy chewed her thumbnail, her eyes darting between them. 'What offence would that be, officer?'

'I'm arresting you for the suspicion of attempted murder of Mr Bernard Nestor on the seventeenth of February.'

'Attempted murder?'

'Bernard Nestor survived his attack. I'll need you to come down to the station, Amy. Let's talk about what we think happened.'

Amy stood up from the table, her face hard. 'You have no idea what happened with that man.' Then she leaned her thin frame against the kitchen sink, silently listening to Turner formally explain her rights again.

Giles looked over the bare kitchen shelves. The items had already been wrapped in paper and packed in boxes. On the bench were salt and pepper shakers; on the stovetop sat an empty orange and blue floral enamel pot, left out from packing.

When Turner had finished, he asked, 'Do you understand?'

Amy nodded, turned her back to the officers, scooping an item up from the kitchen sink, and when she turned back towards the detectives, she held a knife, the blade long and curved.

Turner sprang up from his chair. All three officers stepped backwards in unison.

Their words overlapped: 'Whoa-whoa now –' 'Amy.' 'Release the weapon.' 'Put down the knife.'

Hands went to hips where their Glocks rested. Giles wanted to warn Amy that holding a knife at police officers never ended well.

'Drop the knife, Amy,' Turner said in a calm but forceful manner.

'Is this what you're looking for?' Amy jabbed the knife out towards him; it trembled loosely in her palm. 'I'm handing it over to you. Go on, take it.'

There was movement under the table, scurrying.

Giles lunged forward, pulled the chair out from the end of the table. '*Shit*, the kid's under there.'

Joe Thicket scrambled across the floor away from Giles, then appeared at the other side of the dining table. He raced towards his mother and Amy dropped the knife. It clanged on the ground and Turner kicked it away as Joe forcefully wrapped his arms around her. She scooped him up and buried her face in his neck as he began to cry. Turner stepped forward to prise the pair apart, but MacCrum caught the tail of his jacket and pulled him back, shaking his head to leave them for a moment.

Giles pulled a latex glove from her pocket and retrieved the knife. She knew it was the weapon used on Bernard Nestor. Amy was now murmuring in her son's ear and the boy's sobs sounded wretched in the small kitchen. His hands were locked around his mother's neck, clinging tight. Two of his fingers and thumb were wrapped in gauze the colour of rust. Giles dropped her head and looked away, feeling more like a voyeur in the moment than a cop.

She thought of the lonely boy who would end up sitting in a bedroom he didn't recognise; with family he wasn't familiar with. She thought of the days that were before him, filled with empty uncertainty.

The only positive thing that would come out of Amy Thicket's arrest was her statement, her motivation for sticking a knife into Bernard Nestor.

DAY 8

FIFTY-FOUR

Giles rolled over, wriggling to disentangle her body from the bed-cover, then kicked the blanket off the edge.

She'd woken with a humming in her ears, a dull thump in her head, and a dry mouth. What did she expect drinking a six-pack of giggle juice before bed? As she slid her fingers under the pillow and reached for her phone, her hand already had the wobbles as she tapped at the screen. Giles dropped the phone on top of the pillow, then lay back with her eyes closed and the phone beside her ear.

It took three rings for Benjamin to pick up. 'Hello, love.'

'Hey, Dad.'

'I heard. Falkov. Filled me in.'

Giles twisted and sucked in her lips, holding back the sob building in her throat.

'Ah, sweetheart. You don't always get the outcome you want. You know that, Rebecca. That's policing. It can be a shitty state of affairs.'

Giles wiped away the dampness from her cheeks with the back of her hand. She kept her eyes shut and listened to her father's voice.

'If it'll make you feel any better – and it probably won't – family services have support for kinship carers. The kid's got a grandmother –'

'I was a day late, Dad. I thought I got him, but I was one day too fucking late.'

'No, Rebecca. I was twenty years too late.'

FIFTY-FIVE

On the back step, Joe Thicket sat hugging his knees to his chest, listening to the musical warble of a magpie. He searched for the bird in the tea tree, spotting a fledgling instead at the base of the gnarled trunk. The bird's feathers were grey and fluffy. It pecked at the papery bark, then started again with its high-pitched call, a chirrup on repeat, only silenced when an adult magpie flapped to the ground and put food in its mouth.

Joe swallowed. His own stomach felt empty. Beside him was a plate of milk arrowroot biscuits smeared with butter and strawberry jam. If he didn't start to eat soon, the ants would be drawn to the sticky jam, and the butter would begin to melt.

From the plate, Joe picked up a biscuit and snapped off a corner.

Snap, thought Joe. *Snap-snap-snap.*

The image of Nestor's eyes flashed, like his father's, dark and cold. Then the shiver he always felt when the uncertainty of what was about to happen next blanketed him. Except in Nestor's shed, while learning how to peel a peach, it had been different. For once, before anything could happen – *snap, snap, snap.*

Joe swallowed, crushed the biscuit in his hand and tossed it to the noisy magpie. He wiped the tacky conserve from his palm across his shorts before selecting another for himself, but as he bit into it, the smell of the elastoplast around his fingers made his stomach jerk. His tongue, the roof of his mouth, and the back of his throat felt just like the fuzzy peel of a peach.

Joe struggled to swallow down the dry biscuit.

As the baby magpie began to warble again, another vision flashed of the long curving fruit knife in his hand. Joe dropped his head, looked down at his hand, at the bandages that covered the wounds where the slippery blade had sliced into his fingers.

He thought of the dips and bumps in the back of his father's head; the indent, the bad depression that always made his father *snap*. He closed his eyes and could hear his mother's voice in his head, hush-hushing him, and then came the image of the police taking her away.

FIFTY-SIX

At morning tea, Bob skipped the tuck truck. He wasn't in the mood for a flirty exchange or a dried-out pastry. Instead, he stayed up on the scaffolding, drank his water, using the tea break to motivate some vigour, hype himself up for the job ahead.

He was as nervous as a long-tailed cat in a room full of rocking chairs, but he'd prove to Bell that he and Dill weren't a pair of boofheads. Nicking a bag of cash wasn't bloody rocket science, and Bell could simmer down on her scepticism.

His phone pinged and he whipped it out of his pocket so fast that it nearly toppled out of his hand and over the scaffolding railing. Dill had messaged: *Il do any thin t keep me best mate in town let z get bell that ring*

Bob fumbled with his phone, sent a thumbs-up. That was it. The mugging was on. Dill was doing it to keep Bob in town, and Bob was doing it to stop Bell from leaving.

He felt a surge of nerves and excitement flood through his chest, and lashed out, trying to rid his body of its tense and zingy energy by kicking the brickwork with his steel-capped boot.

'Oi! You can't knock the fucker down, Bob. Taken us nearly a month to put it up.'

Bob forced a smile. 'Green ant in me boot.'

'Better than down your daks.'

The tradie moved on, and Bob lit up another smoke. He would smoke like a chimney until the time ticked by and eventually it caught up to him. Right on two o'clock, he wiped the sweat from his hands down his fluoro orange and navy-blue polo shirt, picked up his work bag and swung it over his shoulder.

'It's kick-off time,' he murmured to himself.

Bob whistled up to his work mates. Gave a nod of farewell to the sorry bastards he was leaving behind to slog it out in the sun, sweating in the heat and fighting a barrage of flies while they picked up the slack. On trusses, moved and now erected on the opposite side of the building, they were already working at half pace. A few ignored him, a few others gave him the middle-finger wave.

'Hey, Bob.'

Bob jerked at his name. He looked up at the scaffolding and squinted into the sun.

'Tell Belinda our dicks are crossed for her.'

Bob nodded. Gnawed the inside of his cheek and tried to fight the smirk. 'Uh-huh, will do.' Then he sniffed at the heat and moved on, stepping over discarded pallets and offcuts of bricks, unaware the boss was still watching him.

'And bring sunscreen with you next time.'

'Huh?' Bob felt his work bag slide off his shoulder.

'Sunscreen,' repeated the boss. He shook his head, muttered, 'Sunscreen and a hat, you silly bastard.'

The boss returned to work and Bob scratched his fingernails deep into his scalp and flinched. He looked at his exposed shoulders. They were red and blazing from the day's burning sun. On top of that, his infected hand was puffing up like a balloon.

~

A few blocks away from the building site – and the fish and chip shop – the Torana was parked crooked by the kerb under the jacaranda tree. Already, the tree's tubular purple flowers littered the roof and bonnet of the car. Each time the wind blew, the flowers sprinkled the vehicle and nearby lawns like confetti.

In the side mirror Bob caught a glimpse of movement. He craned his neck to see Dill crossing the street, duffel bag in hand as he made his way up along the gutter. Dill reached the passenger door, then thumped on the window before hopping in.

'G'day.'

'Dill.'

Dill's smile widened. He started to laugh, and Bob joined in. It felt good. It helped release the tension.

'*Flamin' hell*. What are we doing, Bob?'

'Getting that ring, Dill. Because I'm stopping here. In this town.'

Dill nodded. 'Atta boy.' Still smiling, he asked, 'Okay, so we're sticking to the same plan?'

'Yes. *Yes!* Snatch and grab,' said Bob. 'Then just bloody run. Simple. Keep it simple. Why does everyone need something elaborate?'

'Everyone?' Dill's fingers drummed on the cracked dashboard.

Bob looked away. He still hadn't let on to Dill that Bell was now part of the secret. He swallowed. 'I'm just saying, it's the same plan as any other robbery. You take it and run. That's it.'

'Yeah, well, I've never been a part of any other robbery before, Bob.'

Uneasy, Bob twitched in his seat. 'Fuck it. Let's just get going.'

Dill pulled the plastic red nets from his pocket and tossed one to Bob. He smirked, 'No different to wearing a fishnet stocking over your head. Come on, Bob, put it on.'

It took three deep breaths for Bob to settle his nerves, then he slid the red netting over his face. It scratched his cheeks and the tip of his nose. He flicked down the sun visor and looked at himself in the mirror. It had distorted his features. It had done its job, and he could tell that Dill was pleased.

FIFTY-SEVEN

Before the team briefing, Bray tilted his head, motioning for Giles to join him for a moment in the conference room. She stepped inside, leaned up against the wall, then cocked an eyebrow when Bray pulled out a seat and told her to sit. On the table in front of her he plonked down his laptop. He sat beside her.

'Giles, this team brief is regarding Bob Bradbury's statement, and our strategy for the Cooper boys.' Bray tipped his forehead towards the crazy board. 'Bernard Nestor's still up there on our suspects list, but I don't want you to derail the meeting by discussing yesterday's discovery. Understand?'

Giles stiffened a little in her seat, however she let Bray continue.

'So, I'm just bringing you up to date. Then, you and I can deliberate after. Alone. Okay?'

She nodded, albeit reluctantly.

Bray tried to smile, and perhaps it was his way of thanking her for not countering his request. 'Bernard Nestor's home has now been combed a second time. The ERU's emailed the photographs of the contents found under the peach tree.' He lifted his chin at the computer. 'While all that other shit has been exposed, I want you to know, at first glance nothing found seems to be related to

Oliver Lavine. I know your father's focus was Nestor, but, Giles, no backpack was found, and none of the shovels collected from the shed has a lick of red paint that can be matched to the fragment found at the gravesite.'

'You look surprised,' said Giles.

'I am a little,' said Bray. 'I know, eighteen years ago, that's the direction the investigation was pointing. However, I can't help feeling if Nestor was involved in the disappearance of Oliver, he would have kept a token. A memento.'

'Didn't need to. He made his own mementos. Those bloody horsehair dolls.'

'Christ, Giles. There were more than a dozen of them hanging from the rafters. You think that's how many kids he . . .'

Bray trailed off, but Giles rethought the idea. 'Maybe they're dolls of kids he thought about. Fantasised. Not necessarily acted upon.'

On the table sat a bag of Minties. Bray had tossed them there for the team to share at the brief. Giles now reached for one, peeled off the wrapper and stuffed the lolly into her mouth. It was soft and chewy, and stuck to the back of her teeth. She mumbled out of the side of her mouth, 'Nestor's not stupid. He wouldn't have kept articles in the open that could incriminate him. Hence why he's tried to dispose of them, and the other items. Like Jacob's school jacket. Maybe we need to dig up every peach tree on the property?'

Bray shook his head. 'Forensics used the GPR. This is a time-sensitive case, I only have limited resources, and the GPR eliminates the need and time for digging. The radar didn't find anything in the ground. So, all we have is the one location. The one Jacob Colton told us about.' Bray rotated his laptop for Giles to see the attachment of images. 'It's everything forensics unearthed. Aside from the sordid material, there are some things I can't make heads or tails of. But they've been put in the ground for a reason. I think they're trophies from possible victims or potential victims. There's a bookmark, a classroom geometry kit with a compass, a trading card. Things I believe once belonged to a child he knew or came into contact with.'

'Or pinched?' said Giles, as she started to click through each image in the file.

'I'm wondering if we should show the slides to Mrs Lavine. She might recognise something that once belonged to Oliver?'

Giles nodded, thinking of the items in Janet Lavine's display cabinet as she continued to click through the photographs. Then, she hesitated on one of the slides. As she zoomed in on the photo, the mint in her mouth started to taste sickly.

'What's that?' Giles dabbed her finger at the screen. At a snapshot of a small empty glass jam-jar, with a dead insect inside.

Bray leaned in and read the side note. 'Coleoptera. Exoskeleton. The outside skeleton of an invertebrate.' He simplified, 'A milkweed beetle.'

FIFTY-EIGHT

Dill angled up against the sandstone wall of the alleyway, tucking himself in the corner with one shoulder nestled hard against the pale blue bin. His knees were bent, keeping his head lower than the height of the dumpster. In his right hand he held the shotgun. Menacing and confronting to look at, he was only carrying it to show the fishmonger they meant business.

Opposite, Bob stood in an alcove intently watching the entry of the alley, shifting his weight from foot to foot. He could feel the day's heat captured in the wood of the locked door, warm against his back. The smell was rank. Bob looked down at the cigarette butts that littered the ground, none of them belonging to him. There was also the smell of urine in the air, and he wondered if he was standing where someone had recently taken a piss.

Dill's distorted face pressed in red checkers was staring back at him. Bob looked at Dill's flattened nose, squashed cheeks, and eyelids forced into a squint. In his hand was the gun. The image of Dill was unsettling, and Bob suspected he looked just as frightening.

As Bob took a deep breath, he heard footsteps entering the laneway. He lifted his shoulders and gave a sharp nod to Dill, which was quickly returned. They were ready.

Silent and still, they listened to the fishmonger amble down the laneway, the crunching of stones underfoot, then a pause in front of the dumpster.

Bob pressed himself up against the door, waiting for the fish-monger to toss one of the bags into the skip. The hairs prickled on the back of his neck. His numb palm twitched. His breath was slow and soundless. When he couldn't hear any movement, he inched his head forward to peek. The small man's movements were slow. He was willowy, bow-legged, his inky black hair thinning at the sides into a widow's peak. Bob had never seen the shopkeeper this close, and the frailness of the golden tanned man wasn't lost on him. He watched the fishmonger tilt his head to the side. Bob stared at the rim of the man's ear as it curved, noticed the sleekness of his neck, tanned and lean. The fishmonger sucked back on his ciga-rette, then blew the smoke from his nostrils. The pause lingered and Bob could feel his body surge with anticipation. He pressed himself back against the door, sucked in his gut. He strained to listen for the sound of the lid of the steel bin. Nothing.

Come on, come on. Just drop the bloody bag in the rubbish and move on. Move on.

The stillness made Bob uneasy. Something didn't feel right. Then came the sound of a shoe stomping out the cigarette.

Ah, cigarette butts all belong to him. A man of routine.

Then again, nothing. No sound of advancing.

Come on, come on. Move.

Bob frowned, and wondered if the only bag the fishmonger had was the money, and the little bloke was just stopping for a smoko. Impatient, Bob was the first to move. As he stepped out of hiding and into the alleyway, he was surprised by his confidence and calmness. He looked down at the fishmonger, gave a small shrug and politely said, 'Sorry, mate. Need you to hand over the garbage bag.'

Dill appeared from behind the dumpster. What looked like bile and spit were stuck between the red plastic netting and his lips. His nerves had churned in his guts and the foulness of the task had made its way to his mouth. Dill's eyebrows were now pressed up high behind the netting. He moved quickly and swung the wooden stock of the gun across the back of the little man's skull, and the fishmonger went down.

Bob flinched. 'Jesus!'

'Grab the bag,' hissed Dill.

But Bob couldn't move. 'Whatcha do that for?'

'Whatcha havin' a conversation for? You said snatch and grab, not have a fuckin' chat about it.'

Bob looked down at the man sprawled out at his feet, recoiling. 'Ah, Dill.'

'Don't say my name!'

'He was handing me the bag. You didn't have to whack him.'

Dill shuffled closer. 'Nah, he wasn't. You said grab and run. *Grab* and *run*. I've just made it easier.' He pressed the tip of his foot into the shoulder of the little man and looked surprised by the stillness.

'Jesus!' Bob snapped. 'Is he dead?'

'Calm down.'

'Calm down? It wasn't in the plan, Dill. And don't tell me to fuckin' calm down. I'm not calm. I'm anything but *calm*!' Bob clenched his fists. Jolted his arms up and down. 'Ah, fuck, Dill!'

'Stop *saying* my name.' Dill's face was now pressed lopsided. A warped expression of surprise and anger was pasted crooked behind the red netting. Dill took another tentative step forward, bending down to take the fishmonger's pulse.

'Don't *touch* him,' snapped Bob, and he slapped Dill's hand away, pushing him to the side. 'You'll leave bloody fingerprints.

DNA and shit.' Frustrated, he crouched down beside the man and could see the light regular beat of a heart in the kink of his neck. He watched the *thump . . . thump . . . thump* in the jugular vein pulsating and could see the man was still breathing. Bob looked up at Dill, his shoulders slumped, and the word 'manslaughter' dissolved from his mind.

Dill grinned. 'Bugger had me scared for a sec.'

Bob scowled at Dill, snatched up the black plastic bag and yelled, 'Run!'

'What?'

'I said, *Run.*'

Back in the Torana, Bob struggled with the key in the ignition. Frustrated, he instantly reached for another Winfield from the pack on the dash. He had trouble getting the cigarette in his mouth before realising he was still wearing the mesh bag on his head. He yanked off the netting. It scratched the back of his ears and left the imprint of checkers on his forehead, cheeks, and the tip of his nose. The engine roared to life and Bob ground the gears as he struggled to find first.

'How much do you think is in the bag?' asked Dill.

'Dunno.' Bob's hand shook. His arm was twitching. There was an ache in his upper left shoulder, and the throbbing in his palm was excruciating. 'We'll count it once we get to Burning Mountain. We've gotta get out of here.'

Dill pulled off his netting and flashed yellow teeth as Bob swung out from the kerb. 'We did it, Bob. We actually bloody did it.'

'Yeah,' said Bob. But the adrenaline was fading, and regret was quickly flooding in.

He instinctively did a U-turn, which led them in the wrong direction back down the road, forcing the car to loop out onto the main drag of town. *Ah, geez.* Bob realised his mistake, but it was a habit. He was as habitual as the bloody fishmonger, and now he was cruising his heap-of-shit of a car – that everyone in town knew was his – down the main street, when he needed people to think he was on his way to Sydney with Bell.

Dill recognised the error. 'Stay calm, mate.'

Bob sucked on his cheek. '*Quit* telling me to be calm.'

There was a school nearby, and Bob eased off the accelerator though every instinct told him to floor it. He slowed through the forty-kilometre zone, and only relaxed when he was out on the highway, heading away from town doing a hundred and ten kilometres.

A flock of galahs took to the grey gums, spooked by the rumbling of the approaching Torana. In the branches, their pink heads bobbed as they squawked. The car cruised between the trees, rolling further along in the nature reserve before parking at the barbecue area at the bottom of Burning Mountain.

Bob pulled up at the picnic benches and killed the engine. He needed a moment to catch his breath, settle himself. Or pinch himself. The plan, as simple as it was, had worked. The black plastic bag lay on the floor between Dill's feet. The sight of it made Bob smile.

'Gee whiz.' He held up his hand for a celebratory high five, and Dill slapped it. Bob instantly curled inwards from the pain. 'Ah, shit.' He turned his hand over. It was wet and sticky.

'What's that smell?'

'My damn hand.' The discharge was a yellowy green. Red streaks under the skin had spread out from the site of the wound. It was large, inflamed and throbbed. 'Blister got infected.'

Dill wiped the gooey fluid off his palm onto the car seat. 'I don't think it should smell like that, Bob.'

'Don't worry about my hand.' Bob pointed to the bag. 'Hope it's worth it.'

'Uh-huh,' said Dill. 'Bag didn't feel light. Might be a bit of money in there.'

'Be nice if it was double the size.' Bob felt no shame at his rising greed. He had struggled enough in life. This felt less like reckless grasping and more like relief. Safe and secure, instead of floundering and failing. This would keep Bell in Muswellbrook.

The galahs in the tree canopy squawked, and the flock took to the sky again as another vehicle rumbled along the dirt road.

Bob lifted his chin. In the rear-view mirror, he caught the reflection of light. Movement. He swung around to look out the back window and the headlights of a Contessa gold SS Torana flashed him. Only one bastard in town owned a car like that.

The driver's door swung open. The sun reflected off the glossy paint, blinding Bob for a moment. He blinked, refocused, and saw Paul Cooper emerge.

'Ah, shit.'

Dill spun around and banged heads with Bob. 'What does *he* want?'

'Dunno. Kick the bag under the seat and just stay –'

'Calm?'

Paul ambled up to the car and, as he reached the driver's window, he rested his palms on the roof and leaned inside the cabin. 'How's it going, Bob?'

'Yeah. Good. You?'

Paul didn't answer.

Bob shifted in his seat, squeezed the cheeks of his bum together and his body rose up an inch. 'What are you doing all the way out here?'

Paul licked his lips, forced a smile. 'Could ask you the same.'

'You're not here because of Oliver, are you?' Bob tilted his head.

'Oliver?' Paul snorted. He looked over the roof of the car towards the trail that led up the mountain, then dipped his head back down. He stared at Bob. 'Huh, fancy that, the place where it all started . . . and maybe where it ends too.'

'You want somethin', Paul?'

'Yeah, Bob. I do. I want the money you stole.'

'*What?* What money?'

'Come on, Bob, don't be a dickhead. You and I know, I wouldn't come back here because of Oliver. What made you pick this place, anyway? Bit gruesome, if you ask me.'

It was Bob's turn for bile to rise in his chest – he could almost taste it on his breath. He had only picked the spot because Bell had mentioned Oliver at the pub. The location was still undecided when he told Dill the details of his plan in the toilets. If it weren't for Bell chatting with the detective that day, he wouldn't have even thought of Burning Mountain. But now, in hindsight, he realised it was a bloody omen.

Paul leaned in closer. 'This is how it'll work, mate. You give me the money. Sort of like paying me to keep quiet. Understand?'

'Quiet?' Bob gave a thin smile. 'I had nothing to do with Oliver disappearing. I told the detective that.'

'Not Oliver, you boofhead. This has nothing to do with Oliver. Stuff him. This is about me not telling that dick-throb of a cop you just mugged the fish and chip guy.'

Bob's mouth began to dry. His chest pain returned, and his fingers were twitching and shaking more than ever.

'Did you hear me, Bob?'

Bob swallowed down the lump building in his throat and whispered, 'Fuck you, Paul.'

'No. Fuck. You.'

Paul reached for something in his back pocket, and the next second he was swinging a wrench. There was a loud bang, and Bob ducked his head simply out of instinct. The front corner of the windscreen splintered. Another bang, then another, and tiny star chips with spidery cracks appeared across the windscreen.

'Christ! Stop. Geez. Just stop it, you whacker! Not my bloody car, okay. Alright. I'll give you the bloody money. Just. Stop!'

Paul walked around the front of the vehicle, and Bob was worried he'd strike at it again with the iron bar. At the passenger window, Paul's abs strained in the tight t-shirt as he swung the tool in his hand, bringing it down on the roof and then the bonnet of the vehicle. Dill flinched at the sound, pressing himself back into his seat, silent and scared shitless.

Bob leaned over the top of Dill and saw Paul smiling back down at him. 'Look at me car. It's cactus now! Whatcha do that for? What's wrong with you, Cooper? Have you gotta couple of kangaroos loose in the top paddock?' Bob pointed to his brain and tapped his finger hard against his head. 'You're nuts. Seriously, you'd have to be the most selfish prick I've ever known. You know that? The meanest, self-centred, craziest cunt on earth!'

'Pfft!' Paul laughed. 'You done?'

'Nah, I'm bloody not!'

'Put a sock in it, Bob, and pass us the bag.'

Bob swallowed down his words, restrained himself, afraid that Paul would hit Dill instead of his car. He bent over Dill's legs and grabbed the bag off the floor. He knew Dill wanted to protest, but when it came down to it neither of them had the balls.

Paul snatched the garbage bag from Bob's hand and raised it in the air. 'Cheers, mate.'

Bob was about to say, *No worries*, but he closed his mouth and huffed loudly through his nostrils.

'I'm not a total prick, Bob. Look, I'll open it and count the money. Let you at least see how much you got. I'll do that for you. Those cash-in-hand orders from the RSL raffles would be in here. What else? Ten per cent off for cash orders. Love a bargain dinner, Bob. Don't you?'

Paul dropped the lug wrench to the ground. He put the garbage bag between his legs and loosened the knot. Inside the bag was a second one. 'It's like fucking pass-the-parcel.' Paul grew impatient with the knot. The smell of fish overtook the aroma of eucalyptus and dust in the air. He ripped the side of the plastic, and the contents spilled. Green peeled prawn shells and fish heads poured out onto the ground.

Bob blinked at dozens of black pearly eyes. He dropped his head. He'd robbed the fishmonger for a bag of bloody prawn heads and fish guts.

'Y-you took the wrong bag, Bob,' Dill stuttered.

'There was only one fricken bag, Dill.'

The sight of the discarded scraps and offal infuriated Paul at first, the prospect of thousands of dollars having disappeared. But when he looked back at Bob's stricken face, he laughed, and this made Bob rage. The humiliation of it. Once again, he was a laughing stock to Paul Cooper.

The pain in his body couldn't be contained inside the car. He swung open the driver's door and leaped out. His swollen hand clutched for Paul's throat while his uninjured hand jabbed at the man's face. Only it wasn't enough to lessen his rage.

Paul's words were gurgled, his arms flailing, missing their landing as Bob squeezed his throat tighter for good measure, then pushed the prick down into the thick tufts of grass.

'Me fucking nose, yah cunt.' Paul snorted, blowing a stream of blood from his nostrils as he lay sprawled on the ground.

Bob spat at his feet, then spun around and went back to the car for the shotgun. He wanted to scare Paul, have power over him once and for all. All the years of torment had bubbled up to the surface. Bob pulled out the weapon and, before Paul could jump to his feet in retaliation, he pointed the gun at Paul's chest – a warning, a threat, and a promise all in one. 'You'll not say a fucking word!'

Dill had also scrambled out of the car now and was yelling, 'No, Bob. No!'

Bob looked briefly over his shoulder, and Paul took his chance, snatching up the wrench. He tossed it at Bob's face, and it bounced off the bridge of his nose, splitting the skin. Now they were even. Warm blood oozed down his lips and chin. He swung the gun in revenge, and with the wooden stock end, he rammed it into Paul's face, fast and hard.

A shot rang out.

Bob instantly dropped the weapon. It had been loaded the entire time.

Paul whimpered, hands up to his face. Bob looked down at his chest and felt a flood of relief that neither of them had been hit.

Then he turned around. Dill lay on his back, staring up at the storm clouds rolling in from the south.

In the front corner of the store, Belinda Marrone rummaged through the op-shop's silverware, looking at the selection of forks and spoons. She contemplated making cutlery windchimes to sell at the markets, along with her birdfeeders. The idea was there, but enthusiasm for the effort definitely wasn't.

When nobody was looking, she filched a cheap pair of sunglasses. The asking price was all of three dollars, but the thrill of slipping them into her reusable hemp sack was worth more.

Bell adjusted the bag on her shoulder, patted down her dress that looked like crinkled cheesecloth, and peered out through the store window. A semi-trailer roared down Bridge Street and she could almost smell the diesel. The noise startled a crested pigeon on the footpath. She watched as it bobbed its head, turning in circles. She didn't credit these birds with much intelligence.

Sucking on her top lip, she thought, *Bob and Dill should be done in the laneway. Gone by now.* Then checked the clock on her phone. *So, where's the cops?*

Bell wondered if the two boys had chickened out. *Surely the fishmonger would have raised the alarm by now? Cops should be combing the area.*

The thought of Bob and Dill backing out of the plan riled her. On a hunch, on her gut feeling that – like everything else in Bob's life – the plan had gone arse up, she needed to see for herself if they were still sitting in the Torana, thinking up excuses for not going through with the task.

Heading down the alley, she slipped on the stolen sunglasses. Then pulled up abruptly. There, lying on the ground by the dumpster, was the fishmonger. Bell hesitated, quickly looked back over her shoulder to see if she was alone.

What do I do? What do I do?

Her hand slid into her bag for her phone, then she thought against it. The last thing she wanted was to be a witness. Talk to the cops again. She was too connected to the crime. But the guy on the ground? *Christ, what do I do?*

Bell saw a hamburger wrapper, its corners lifting in the subtle breeze. She stepped over the little man and snatched it from the ground. She curled the wrapper around her fingertips, searching for a pulse. Through the greasy paper, she felt a faint throb. She tipped her head, her ear inching closer to the man's mouth, and could hear and feel his breath on her lobe. With her head low to the ground, under the dumpster, in the shadow, she spotted something. A small black plastic garbage bag. She stretched her hand, reaching, spanning her fingers, then snatched it up and shoved it in her hemp sack.

Bell sprang back up onto her feet, making a quick exit. As she headed towards home, she felt the universe smiling down on her, and could see herself catapulting free into the cosmos.

'What have you done to me leg?'

'You said the shotty wasn't loaded.' Bob was on his knees, ripping at the tear in the back of Dill's jeans to take a better look. Blood oozed from the cavity and raw muscle above Dill's heel. Bob could see where the spread of pellets had also hit Dill's thigh and buttocks, but the main cluster had chomped up his calf. 'Your leg's minced. I think it's shattered bone.' Bob shook his head. 'I don't know but . . . But it's bad, Dill. Real bad.'

'Nah.' Dill groaned, forcing a shallow laugh. 'Just a bullet nick.' He was shivering, and Bob pulled his shirt off and tied it tight around Dill's calf.

'You're a rubbish shot. Missed Cooper and got me.'

'I'll get you back to town.'

'Nah. Leave me here – I'll call an ambo.' Dill gritted his teeth, rested his head down in the grass, and whispered between puffs of air as he fought back the pain. 'New plan, Bob. You piss off, then I'll call for an ambulance. I'll tell the cops Paul and I did the robbery.'

'Huh? What?' said Paul. He was keeping his distance – Bob still had the gun. 'What are you saying?'

Bob spun back at him. 'Shut the fuck up. I've got one more bullet in this.'

Paul's tongue flicked against a broken tooth.

'It's just Paul's word against mine,' said Dill. 'Who're they gonna believe?' He grabbed onto Bob's arm. 'Mate. This will absolve you of responsibility.'

'But you'll take the fall.'

'Yeah, and Paul will take the fall for shooting me. Just leave the gun. Get in your car. Fuck off, Bob. I gotta call this ambulance.' Dill's face was pale like a full moon. His lip and forehead were wet with sweat. 'Go. Before the cops get here.'

Bob dropped his head and moaned with the shame of it. Dusty mucus mixed with blood ran from his nose as he choked, 'Ah, geez, Dill.' He rested his quivering chin on his mate's shoulder, wrapped his arms around his neck, and held him close.

Dill peeled Bob's arms away. 'Piss off now, Bob.'

Bob nodded, then without thinking grabbed the shotgun.

From the back seat of his Torana, he snatched up the Winchester box, tearing it open and filling his pockets with brass shells, before thumbing one of the shells into the loading flap of the weapon. He aimed at the red SS badge on the front grille of Cooper's car and fired. The booming sound ricocheted down the valley and the birds in the trees squawked before taking flight. Paul Cooper also added to the noise, a guttural sound. The agony of it only spurred Bob on to fire another shot. The second went through the windscreen.

'Payback, Coops.' Bob laughed, but the thrill was fleeting – he had to get going. Dill needed that ambulance. As Bob returned to his car, he briefly looked over his shoulder one last time at Paul, who was now curled up in a ball, with his face cupped in his hands, then at Dill, still in the grass, flat on his back.

Red dust spun under the Torana's wheels as he sped off, the shotgun by his side.

FIFTY-NINE

The Crimes Unit Team had gathered and sat around the conference table. Bray dumped a pile of pink and white rocks collected a few days earlier from Burning Mountain. The unit reached for, and examined, the rocks.

'Coup injury?' Callahan finally asked. He sat hunched over the meeting table, rolling one of the rocks between his fingers.

'People have been killed from a single punch,' said MacCrum.

'I guess,' Callahan mused. 'But wouldn't Oliver have been dizzy? Concussed?'

'Yeah,' said Bray. 'And disorientated. The cooked clay is equivalent to tossing a solid brick at a person's head. The hit would have cause brain swelling, and the skull doesn't expand. So, without surgery, the squeeze would have created internal pressure that may have crushed Oliver's brain.'

Giles's mouth felt dry. She chimed in, 'We believe Bob Bradbury inflicted the injury at the top of the mountain, close to the lookout. It was there he threw the rock. Then, I think . . .' She swallowed and spoke with caution. 'At the bottom of Burning Mountain, Oliver may have collapsed. Or had an altercation with Lucas Cooper, then collapsed. The Cooper boys were bullies. Maybe Oliver got a little roughed up, and Lucas believed he was the cause of death.'

'Oliver had a reputation of being . . . fragile,' Bray added. 'Slight in build. Both Cooper boys would have towered over him in height and brawn.'

'What would they have had an altercation over?' asked Turner.

Bray sighed. 'Impulsiveness. Anger issues. Status. It could have been over nothing, really. Maybe Oliver just pushed a button.'

'Or Lucas pushed a button, and Oliver, not being in the right frame of mind – dizzy and disorientated – chose to retaliate.' Giles leaned over the table and picked up a larger rock from the centre. She cupped it in her palm; it felt as big and round as a baseball. 'Lucas was known for conflict and aggression. It's what got him kicked out of school.'

Bray nodded. 'And we know that fighting is an antecedent behaviour. We also know that occasionally it leads to homicide amongst adolescents.'

The team murmured, but no-one said anything.

After a moment, Turner held up a rock to the team. 'That means this is the weapon, and Bob inflicted the critical injury.'

'Yes.' Giles agreed. 'I believe Bob was the cause of the fatal injury. Unbeknown to Lucas or Paul, who perhaps thought they were to blame.'

'Then panicked. And hid the body over near the campground?' Turner asked.

The room fell silent again. Giles looked over at the crazy board. Under 'Persons of interest' were the names Bob Bradbury – the first link in the sequence of events – then Bernard Nestor, Paul Cooper and Lucas Cooper. The team just had to work out who was responsible for putting Oliver Lavine in the grave at Mount Wingen. Who was the last link? With Nestor in the hospital and the team's focus now on the Cooper brothers, Giles was growing more impatient to have the DNA results back from the lab.

'I don't know,' said MacCrum. 'Did the Cooper boys just happen to have a shovel handy? I mean, Nestor having one in his horse float seems more plausible. And Amy Thicket's allegation points the finger closer. What if Oliver tried to flag down a car for help? And he happened to flag the wrong bloody one?'

'Then we'll have to find that out, won't we?' said Bray. 'Nestor's name stays up on the board. But don't underestimate those brothers. I watched back Giles's interview with Paul Cooper. The kid's more than a bully.'

Giles felt her neck warm and the team's eyes fall on her. She kept her gaze on the crazy board, not wanting to read the expression on their faces. Bray knew Paul Cooper had rattled her.

'Okay,' said Bray. 'Let's get our heads around these two brothers. Remember, it's the web, not the spider, that catches the fly.'

The team had no solid evidence. The purpose of interviewing Paul and Lucas Cooper was to extract further information. Build a case. And maybe, if Giles's theory was correct, they'd get lucky and land a possible confession if one of them cracked. Paul Cooper had been willing to participate the first time round. But Giles was worried Lucas may advise his younger brother that it was against his best interest to participate in a second police interview. And she predicted the only person Paul would listen to, and possibly be afraid of, would be his older brother.

'It's the gap,' said Giles, pointing up to the timeline on the crazy board. 'The moment when Oliver descended the mountain, to when Phil, Bob and Bell reached the bottom.'

'That's if we believe their statements,' interrupted Callahan. 'Maybe the gap is from when Oliver descended to when Mrs Lavine arrived.'

'Hmm,' said Bray. 'Then where does that place the Coopers?'

Giles shrugged. 'The quicker we get them into the station, split them into separate rooms, the higher our chances of gaining a solid lead. Squeeze this gap a little tighter.'

Bray nodded. 'Or at least a better understanding of what took place between Oliver travelling from here . . .' He tapped where the lookout was on the map. 'To here.' His finger landed on the picnic area at the bottom of the mountain. 'Somewhere in this space is the answer.'

The team stared up at the board, slightly distracted by a sudden commotion outside the room. Callahan leaned back on his chair, trying to see what the disruption was, when Falkov entered.

'Meeting's suspended,' Falkov announced, his voice serious and face stolid. 'A call's come in that there's been an assault downtown, two offenders, possible robbery.'

'Don't we have uniforms on duty for that?' Bray looked confused as to why the incident had to break up his planning meeting.

'We do. But straight after, a second call's come in for police and an ambulance to attend an incident at Burning Mountain.' The mention of the mountain piqued everyone's interest. Falkov held up his hand – there was more. 'One injured and one dead.'

Giles rose up from her chair. 'Do we have names for the victims at Burning Mountain?'

'Paul Cooper and Phillip O'Dell.'

Heads turned; eyes darted from one detective to another. A sombre mood swept over the room.

Giles asked, 'Which one is injured?'

Falkov didn't answer; he was already assigning teams. 'Bray, Callahan, you two head off to Muswellbrook hospital. See if you can get an ID from the victim of who his attackers were. Let's see if it was the same two calling for help out at Burning Mountain.'

Falkov turned to Turner and MacCrum. 'You two get to the scene. Uniforms and ambulance from Scone are already at the location. Report back the situation. I want to know exactly what went on out there.'

Giles was about to protest being left behind when Falkov dabbed his finger into her shoulder. 'You're with me,' he barked.

SIXTY

A storm was coming. The air was rank with an earthy-musty smell.

It was a long walk from where Bob had dumped his car near the Hunter River. He was doing his best to salvage the plan. He decided he'd say his car had been nicked, and he and Bell had been stuck at home for the evening. It gave him an alibi, and covered both his whereabouts and why he never made it to Sydney.

The gun was a problem.

He couldn't leave the shotty in the car – and it was too bloody late to turn around and drop the damn thing back at Burning Mountain. He hoped the D's thought Paul had disposed of it. Tossed it in the dam, or up in a bloody tree.

Ah, crikey.

With the dank air and events behind him, Bob was feeling hot and sticky. Flustered. The pain across his palm was intense, and the waft of foul odour made him gag each time he swung his hand by his side. He was unable to control his body. The rapid pounding in his chest. The whooshing rhythmic thumping in his ears. Bob felt as though his body was about to collapse and shred itself free of him.

He squeezed his eyes shut and hissed, *'Fuck. Fuck.'* Then bowed his head and trudged forward, sucking each breath through his teeth.

The air whistled and his throat felt raw as he moved down the middle of Swiftlet Street to number eleven.

Bob willed himself up the steps, pushing forward, then hooked his finger through a hole in the flyscreen mesh and pulled the door open.

The lounge-room and kitchen were empty. Just the lamp on. There was noise, a shuffling in the bedroom. Bob took another step and stared down the hallway at the door slightly ajar, catching glimpses of Bell moving around inside.

'Bell?'

A moment of stillness and silence.

'. . . Yeah?'

She appeared, slipping through the entryway, closing the door behind her. Hands on hips. Head cocked. Cheeks and forehead shining under the exposed lightbulb that hung from the ceiling, warm and yellow. Bob watched her inch forward, then turn and lean her back against the wall. One pale leg, exposed from the side split in her cotton skirt, lifted as she pressed the heel of her foot against the opposite wall, now blocking access to the room.

'What are you hiding?'

'What?' Bell's eyes moved from Bob's shirtless torso to the shotgun dangling at his side, then back at his broken and bloody nose. 'What the hell happened?' Her stare was fixed, waiting for an explanation. Bob had no idea where to start.

'It's . . . it's all gone to shit, Bell.'

'Hmm.' She twitched her glossy cheek. 'I knew it would, Bob. I braced myself for it . . . nah, I think I was prepared for it.'

Bob frowned, glaring at her. 'You think I'm bad luck?'

'I do, Bob. I think when you were a baby, your mother rocked you back and forth in your pram under a ladder.' Bell's voice was more pity than sarcasm, as though she actually believed the stupidity of her statement. She sighed, 'I don't think I even want to know what happened.'

'It wasn't my fault, Bell. The prick only had one bag, and Paul turned up –'

'Stop, Bob. Just stop.'

'Stop what?'

'Just. Stop.'

His anger faded, and suspicion took its place. 'What's in the bedroom, Bell?'

'Nothin'.'

Exhausted and too tired for games, Bob stomped down the hall. He flicked her leg off the wall and pushed through the bedroom door. On the bed was an open suitcase, filled with a mound of clothes. A small pile of toiletries and organic hand creams yet to be packed sat on top of a hemp bag. 'What's this?'

Bell had a hand on the back of his jeans, trying to turn him away. It was weak and powerless, lacking any conviction to get his attention.

Bob asked again, 'What is *this*, Bell?'

'It's the town, Bob. It's Oliver and the police. It's Paul, and you, and Dill. It's all of it, Bob, and I just want to get away from it.'

'The cops don't know anything. I told them that I threw a rock at Oliver. I told them I threw a stone and it hit his head.'

'But you didn't, Bob.'

'But that's what I told the cop. And she fucking believed me.'

'But you *didn't*, Bob.'

'I didn't *kill* him, Bell.'

Bob turned back to the bed. With his free hand he grabbed the handle of the suitcase and upended the clothes on the floor. He flicked the hand creams and toiletries off the hemp bag. They hit the wall and the side table, scattering around the room. Then he emptied the bag too. Only he stopped when he saw the pile of notes flutter onto the bedspread.

'Where did you get this?'

Silence.

'*Where* did you get *this?*'

'Th-the dumpster.'

'Eh?'

'I found it under the dumpster.'

'What?'

'I was watching. From across the road. When nothing happened, I went back to the alley. I saw the bloke on the ground. I knew something went wrong, Bob. But the bag. It was . . . it was just under the . . .' Bell shrugged, her words fading away. Bob didn't look relieved, nor believing. 'It was there, Bob. It was *there*. You just missed seeing it.'

'And now you're stealing it from me?'

'You stole it *for* me.'

'First Paul and now you? What's got into you, Bell?'

'I told you, I want to start clean. Fresh. I thought it was this town. Paul. Oliver. Then the skull that they found. The bloody police. But it's you, Bob, you're the one that's holding me back.'

'Me?' Bob waved his arm about. 'I'm holding you back. Are you for real?' The barrel of the gun swung, circling the room. 'Are you joking?'

'I'm leaving, Bob.' Bell stuffed the notes back into the bag. 'Listen to me. My past, that day up there on the mountain, the hold that Paul Cooper has over us, it's never gonna go away, it's never gonna end. That's why I need to leave.' She swung the hemp bag up over her shoulder, spun on her heels and left the room.

'You're not leaving, Bell!' Bob followed her down the hall. 'Stop, Bell. Just *stop!*'

Bell looked back over her shoulder. 'I'm telling you, Bob, I don't want to be around when the cops return.'

'They're not coming for me. Trust me. I told them it was an accident, that's all. I was just a kid,' Bob stressed. 'A kid that threw a stone.'

'You're a monster that smashed Oliver's skull.'

'I'm not a monster.'

'Then a coward,' hissed Bell. 'A coward who throws stones at *girls*.' She looked ugly as she hissed, repeating his words from all those years ago, 'Fucking bullseye! Dead bang on!'

Bob blinked. His eardrum began to ache as the smell of metallic sulphur suddenly soured the air. The pain in his arm spread to his chest as the last sounds he heard looped in his head.

Boom – thud. Boom – thud. Boom – thud. Again and again. *Boom – thud.*

He dropped the gun the moment he fully registered where the *boom* came from, and his eyes fell to where he heard the thud.

SIXTY-ONE

Falkov and Giles were twenty minutes out of Muswellbrook on the A15 when a call came in.

Giles eased off the accelerator as Falkov barked orders down the phone: *Deploy the tactical team. Pull the uniform officers back. I don't want them tearing down the street – their bloody presence might escalate the situation. Tac team only.*

Falkov cupped his hand over the phone and yelled at Giles, 'Pull over, detective.' Giles hit the brakes and swung the car to the side of the New England Highway. She waited for her next instructions as Falkov went back to yelling commands down the phone: *Get Bray and Callahan back from the hospital and into vests. The options available to the tactical police must be run by me first, understand? We'll need approval from the assistant commissioner. Call back in five with a status update. And every bloody foreseeable possible incident or outcome.*

Falkov ended the call, turned on the siren and said, 'Perform a U-turn. Back to town. Gunfire has been reported on Swiftlet Street.'

Giles arced back onto the highway, heading towards Muswellbrook, fearing the worst. 'Do we have a locale, an address on Swiftlet Street?'

'Yeah, number eleven. Shots believed to have come from the home of Bob Bradbury and Belinda Marrone.'

The smell that didn't belong lingered. Bob gasped for air. Struggled to get it down his throat. He felt claustrophobic in the small stuffy lounge-room. He squeezed his chest with his big fingers, trying to hold his heart still. But there was that smell again.

That fucking smell.

His nose felt doughy, like putty hanging from his face, but it wasn't smashed enough to stop it from picking up the coppery scent of blood, along with the acrid scent of spent gunpowder.

He couldn't look at the ground as he moved past the splash of scarlet on the wall. His jaw quivered, and teeth chattered. His face was starting to cave in at the sight of the hemp bag and banknotes strewn across the floor.

'Huh, geez. I'm so sorry, Bell. I'm so bloody sorry . . . I didn't mean . . . I'm sorry.'

Bob kicked away the gun, bent down, scooped up the notes and shoved them back into the bag.

Joe Thicket had heard a crack of thunder and wondered why there was no flash of light to follow. He knew a storm was coming. He could smell it in the air.

He sat on the edge of the bed in his empty room, looking at the boxes that had swallowed up his belongings. In the lounge-room, his grandmother, a woman he hardly remembered, sat reading over documents and a family handbook given to her by the welfare worker on how to deal with kids whose parent had been incarcerated, along with a list of counselling services. His grandmother had tried to connect by giving him tinned peaches and vanilla ice-cream after dinner. He hadn't told his grandmother about the horse ride, or the peach tree, and he figured his mother hadn't either.

The old lady looked sad when she served up dessert and, after he gagged at the dining table, distressed when Joe kneeled over the toilet bowl and vomited his dinner. She'd run a face washer under warm water, and as she wiped away the puke from his lips, she'd explained to him what her home looked like and spoke of her pets. Two budgies. One green and the other blue, which would sit on his shoulder once they got used to him. The thought of it made Joe's shoulder tickle, and he wasn't sure how he felt about birds flying freely around the house. He only answered, 'Please don't feed me peaches.'

Joe was deep in thought when the bedroom window banged and for a split second he imagined a bird had flown into it. He looked up, startled when he saw his neighbour. The man who drove the loud car. The man he'd heard yelling for the first time in the late hours of the night.

The pane rattled again as his neighbour tapped on the glass.

'Hey, mate.' His voice sounded muffled behind the pane. 'Open the window.'

Joe shook his head. Sharp and quick. But he couldn't look away.

'Hey.' The neighbour lifted a hemp bag up for Joe to see. 'I've got something for you. For you and your mum.'

Joe's ears pricked up. He looked back at his bedroom door, and when his grandmother didn't appear, he slipped off the bed and went to the window.

'That's it, mate.' The neighbour pointed to the swivel lock. 'Open up.'

Joe paused to consider him a moment. He scanned the man's dark eyes. The stubble around his chin. The split nose and blood that had dried across his cheek and in streaks down his neck and bare chest. Joe wanted to ask if he was hurt – did he need help? Only he was too timid to open his mouth. Still, he didn't walk away. He was curious about what was in the bag.

The neighbour spoke again. 'Kid, I need you to open the window. Quick, mate, just a crack. Let me give you the bag. For you and your mum. I think you both need it. Because I won't be needing it now and I want you to have it.'

Joe looked at the bag swinging in his neighbour's hand. He didn't want to tell him that he didn't have a mother anymore. Didn't want to say that he only had a grandmother now, and blue and green birds. Soon he'd be going to a different school, living in a different house. And at the same time, he wanted to tell the man everything.

The neighbour looked impatient. He rapped on the windowsill again. 'Mate, hurry up. I don't have time.'

Joe twisted the lock, slid open the window. The neighbour pushed the bag through the gap and it fell to the floor.

'I want you to stick it under your bed, okay, mate? In the morning, give it to your mum. But tell her not to say a word. Not to anyone, alright? It's yours now. Take care, kid.'

In the distance, there was the sound of a siren, which made the neighbour look even more angst ridden. There was a sense of urgency in his movements and voice. 'Promise me. Not a word.'

Joe looked at his neighbour, then at the darkening sky building behind him. The storm clouds were rolling in. He knew he could make a promise under the blackening sky. He nodded, quick and fast. And with that, the neighbour was gone.

The screaming of sirens had multiplied, growing louder. Then there was the slamming of doors and a banging on his own front door.

Ignoring the commotion, he kneeled on the floor. His small fingers untied the knot. He peeled open the bag and peered inside

at the stack of banknotes. It was more money than he'd ever seen.
He imagined caramel milkshakes with his grandmother, strawberry
bombs, and new school shoes.

'Joe? Joe, honey.'

Joe flung open one of the packing boxes and stuffed the bag
inside.

'In here, Gran.'

He closed the lid quickly at the sound of his grandmother's feet
stomping down the hall. He wouldn't open the box again until he
arrived at his new home. The feeling of trepidation dissolved and,
somehow, Joe felt everything would be alright. He was ten now.
Two digits. Brave and strong. Unlike with his dad, with Nestor he
had learned how to fight back.

SIXTY-TWO

Bob Bradbury was barricaded inside his property. The residents within the exclusion area of Swiftlet Street had been ordered to remain inside and lock their doors. The first arriving officers had made it clear to the residents to stay low and not to come out until told.

The tactical team had arrived and set up. The situation was presumed a hostage crisis, but Bob was unwilling to put Belinda Marrone on the phone or give details of her status – only stating that she was inside the house.

Giles pulled up behind Bray and Callahan's vehicle, and the moment Falkov climbed out of the car he was already in full swing assigning orders. 'I don't want this to turn into hours of an intense stand-off. Let's defuse the situation as quickly as possible. Assess and negotiate the safety of Belinda Marrone first, then we might be able to coerce a surrender.'

Giles felt disorientated. The scene looked terrifying. She only moved when Callahan tossed her a light-armoured vest.

'Ballistics protection, put it on. We have confirmation Bob Bradbury is currently armed with a loaded weapon.'

'Confirmation. How?'

'He told us. Tactical team has him on the other end of the phone line.'

'Tac team, bloody hell, this place looks like a war zone.' Giles flicked her hand at the rescue vehicles and police cars. 'I'm surprised you didn't call in all nine BearCats and a tank while you were at it.'

Callahan scratched at his chin, then grimaced into a shrug. 'Giles, this is more than a domestic. Tac team thinks it's armed robbery, possible homicide, and now a hostage situation. All at the hands of Bob Bradbury.'

'Geez, how did this happen?'

'Dunno. But put your bloody vest on.'

At the back of the Sonata, Giles shook off her suit jacket and tossed it into the boot of the car. She was halfway strapping on the bulletproof protection when Bray's hand latched onto the back of her vest and he spun her around.

'They've got Bob on the other end of the phone. Says he's not talking to anyone but you, Giles.'

'What?'

'You're the only person he trusts.'

Giles glanced at Falkov for direction. His face looked ashen. 'Sir?'

Falkov nodded. 'You follow the instructions of the Tac team, detective. Don't go off script.'

'Yes, sir.'

The tactical team appeared ominous in full blacks and kitted up. At the back of the police rescue vehicle, Giles was quickly briefed on the situation. When they passed her the phone, her hand was shaking, and she knew both the Tac and her own team saw it. She unmuted the call, swallowed and spoke slowly. 'Bob. It's Detective Senior Constable Rebecca Giles.'

Bob's voice came back over the speaker, fast and stuttering. 'Detective Giles, I-I . . . is it really you? Can I . . . can I trust that it's you?' The fear and confusion were clear in his voice. 'I don't want the cops to come in, okay? Okay?'

Giles knew she had to calm Bob down. The image of him, the glimpse of weakness she'd observed when he sat in the interview room, came flooding back. Bob wasn't the type of guy to do something malicious, but in his state of panic he could certainly do something stupid. Giles had to focus on each step at a time. Step one was calming him down, step two was not letting him know the Tac team was already moving in on his home.

'Bob, I know you're scared, but together we can work through this and bring you and Belinda out of the house safely. Nobody is going to get hurt today. The officers out here don't want to hurt you, and I know that you don't want to hurt me.' When no reply came, she asked, 'Can you hear me, Bob?'

His voice crackled on the other end of the phone. 'Yeah, yeah, I can hear you.'

'Bob. I need you to check on the welfare of Belinda. Can you tell me if she's okay?'

'She's not.'

'Bob, can you tell me what the problem is?'

'I can't.'

Giles took a breath. Tried again, gentler. 'Bob. I need you to see if Belinda requires medical assistance. Is she okay?'

'I said, she's not.'

'Can you see if she's breathing?'

Silence.

'Bob. Please.'

'No. I can't.' The line crackled, then she heard the words: 'She's dead.'

~

At the base of Burning Mountain, Turner and MacCrum had arrived to find – aside from a paddy wagon, two patrol cars, a Torana with its radiator blown out and an ambulance – Paul Cooper on his back amongst the brush wiregrass with a shattered nose and tooth, and who they presumed to be Phillip O'Dell on the dusty road under a white sheet.

By the picnic table, MacCrum paced back and forth as he relayed to Bray the layout of the crime scene. 'Got a snake in the grass and the other's a victim of Dick Van Dyke. Bullet missed the dick, hit the vein, bled out and died.' MacCrum grinned. 'Dick. Vein. Died.'

Turner held out his hand, motioning for the phone, and MacCrum handed it over. 'Medics are saying rapid blood loss, bled to death,' said Turner, clarifying the situation. 'Still unclear what exactly triggered the behaviour.'

'Are you saying Bob shot his best mate?'

'My witness is Paul Cooper.' Turner threw up a hand, even though Bray couldn't see it. 'We tested him for gunpowder residue. Not a shade of orange. Negative. Can't find the weapon. Still searching. So, I guess maybe his story could have some credit.'

'Yeah, about as much credit as his Mastercard,' MacCrum quipped over his shoulder.

Turner ignored him. Still pacing in the dust, he asked Bray, 'And your end?'

'We've got Bob sealed up in his house, allegedly with a shotty. So, I'm guessing that's probably the gun that did it.'

Turner looked back at MacCrum, who was pointing to a black plastic garbage bag. 'Oh,' said Turner. 'And we found a bag of prawn shells –'

'Prawns?'

'Nah, shells. Prawn shells, fish scales, guts and fins, rubbish. Fish scrap.'

'Photograph and bag it. It's evidence. It'll connect them to the robbery.'

'You saying these guys robbed the fishmonger and then had a shootout over *seafood waste*?'

'I dunno what to think. Paul Cooper can give his version. I'll make sure Bob Bradbury comes out of the house in one piece, so he can tell his side of the story. Then somehow we'll reconstruct what *actually* happened.'

Falkov's face was set. 'I don't want the situation to escalate. I want a quick resolution – a peaceful resolution. Continue with the negotiation. Bob Bradbury is an armed offender, but he's not active. He's not waving the gun at officers, making threats. Keep him on the phone, talk him down, let him know that you're listening, and let's see if he'll surrender. I need him to voluntarily hand himself over.'

Giles nodded, but Bray stepped forward, adding, 'I want to apprehend and handcuff him, Giles, but make sure he's fully aware that if he steps out that door with a pointed gun, we will shoot.'

Again, Giles nodded, repeating the command. 'Disarm, isolate and resolve.'

It had been almost two hours since the first officers had arrived on the scene, and Giles felt like little progress had been made. The weight of the situation was sitting on her shoulders, and she was worried the pressure of it was starting to show. Time was running out. If she were to talk Bob out of the house calmly, she needed to start making more headway, but Bob was talking in circles, and the longer he was cooped up inside, the more agitated he would become. *Fuck. Fuck.*

The tactical team had moved in around the perimeter of the house, setting themselves into position. The distant storm was building and moving closer, and soon the flashes of lightning could be confused with flashes of gunshots, and cracks of thunder mistaken for a crack from a weapon.

'I'll get him to come out, sir. Don't kick the door in and start with the flashbangs or bullets yet. Please.' She tapped the screen, and the phone rang.

'Yeah?' said Bob. 'That you, detective?'

'Bob, I need you to listen carefully –'

'Nah. Nah. Those pricks are gonna come in shooting.'

'Bob, calm down. It's okay –'

'Pig's arse, it is.'

'Bob. Take a breath and listen to me.'

'Nah, you listen to me, detective. This wasn't the way it was meant to happen. It's not the way it was meant to be.' Bob's words came out in a flurry. 'I admit I mugged the fishmonger, okay, okay, but I didn't mean to shoot Dill or Bell. It was an accident, detective, a bloody accident. Like that day on Burning Mountain.'

Giles felt her spine stiffen. She needed Bob safely out of the house. He was her key witness to the case she had been obsessed with. He had the answer to Oliver Lavine's disappearance. Giles felt her tactic shift, from gentle to firm. *Stuff it, I'm getting him out my way.* 'Bob. We can talk about that day once we get you out safely.'

'Nah. I need you to know what happened now. Before those dogs come in shooting at me.'

'Nobody's coming in shooting, Bob.'

'*Bullshit.*'

There was a pause, and Giles was scrambling for a different approach – her firmness was scaring him. 'Bob, trust me. I promise, nobody is getting hurt. You have my oath.'

When Bob spoke again it was a little calmer. 'Bullshit, but thanks for trying.' He continued with an urgency. 'Detective,

I want you to know, on the mountain, when Oliver pulled down his daks, and Bell was stuck not knowing what to do, I was fair dinkum pissed off. I wasn't lying when I told you I picked up that rock, only I intended to hit Cooper with it. I wanted so badly to smash it down hard on his fucking skull that I scared myself. I hated him in that moment, so much I wanted to kill him. But when I swung my hand around, I chickened out. I froze up. I don't know what got into me. I took it out on Oliver – I hit him instead. Because he was weaker than Paul. Because Oliver didn't scare me. I've never swung a punch in my life, detective. I've never hit someone before or since that day. And I've felt like a fucking coward ever since.'

Giles could hear the snot and tears. The desperation for her to understand.

'I did it for Bell. To protect Bell – her reputation. I couldn't tell the cops back then that I smashed Oliver's head with a rock. Understand? So, I just told you I threw the rock instead.'

Giles imagined it. She could see the moment play out on the mountain and her body tensed, fighting back the empathy for a bunch of kids stuck in a moment of calamity.

Bob's voice groaned on the line. 'And . . . and . . . I robbed the shopkeeper to buy a girl a ring that she never wanted.' The sob that followed was clear. Shameless. Unhidden.

The stillness of the team around her didn't go unnoticed. Giles swallowed, trying to fight the tightness in her throat. 'Bob, I promise, if you surrender, we can talk some more about this. First, you need to help me get you out safely.'

'Are you coming to the door? I'll only come out if it's you at the door.'

Bray and Falkov shook their heads in unison. The Tac team leader flicked his fingers at his throat and shook his head too.

'Bob, if I'm at the door and you come out with a gun, I'll be forced to take action.'

'I'm not going to shoot you, detective. I just want you to know it was all a mistake.'

Joe Thicket's window had prime position to witness the events taking place in his neighbour's front yard. It didn't take long for him to understand what was happening. He had seen it with his mother. It had the same eerie feeling as the stand-off in the kitchen. And he had saved his mother then. He had stopped the police from pulling their weapons from their holsters.

This neighbour of his had given him money. He had been the only person in his small world who wanted to help. He had been a friend, and Joe didn't have any friends.

The boy was still feeling brave and bold. And he was sure he could do it again. As he started to climb through his bedroom window, he was certain he could save this new friend. He could stop the police from hurting him.

They kitted up, checked weapons, and went over final commands and instructions. Then Giles and two Tacs moved into place.

A large drop of rain hit Giles's cheek and startled her. The first drops were starting to fall, and the heavy deluge was on its way.

The three officers inched slowly towards the front door. Weapons were drawn and pointed. Midway down the path they stopped and waited for the door to open.

Giles was breathing heavily, like a bull snorting. The front door cracked ajar, and inside all she could see was darkness. Slowly a pale hand pressed against the screen door and pushed it open.

The hinges squeaked and then through the front door stepped Bob Bradbury.

As he filled the doorway, Giles held her breath. He had one hand around the barrel of the gun, but the other hand was resting on the butt, his fingers nowhere near the trigger.

Though the gun was pointing towards her and her fellow officers, Giles could tell by the way Bob held the shotgun that he had *no* intention of using it.

Bob was hoping to be shot.

That second, Giles caught sight of Joe Thicket climbing up onto the veranda at the side of the house, and the image of the Tac team littering the front door with bullets and Joe caught in the crossfire flashed in her mind.

There are a thousand milliseconds in a second. Four hundred milliseconds to blink. A bullet can travel more than three hundred metres in a thousand milliseconds. The thought of moving out of the way of the projectile would hardly form in the mind before the lead and copper had entered the body.

In that same second, Giles re-aimed her Glock, moving from Bob's chest – the centre of the mass – to his thigh, and pulled the trigger. The words 'Hold your fire! Lower your weapon!' were still tumbling out of her mouth as Bob crumpled.

Giles leaped up the stairs onto the veranda and hooked Joe Thicket up into her arms, and the two of them tumbled off the edge of the porch to the ground below. There was yelling, thuds and thumps. There were footsteps and banging. But thankfully there were no more shots.

On the lawn she had Joe squashed up in her arms. She could feel his feathery hair under her chin, the scratchy feeling of his small, plastered fingers around her neck. Within seconds an officer dressed in full black tactical gear had pulled the boy from her arms and was rushing him away from the scene to a safe location. Everything was moving quick: people, orders, officers. Giles rolled up onto her feet, light-headed, and, when she looked back at the house, the Tac team had Bob disarmed. Callahan was also on the ground, with his knees in Bob's back, restraining him.

Giles pushed her way through the commotion and rain that was now teeming down. She reached Bob's side as Callahan rolled him over. The medics jostled to move in, dumping bags, and went into action. With the weapon removed, and the officers in place, they responded swiftly, cutting the trousers to reveal the wound. Their priority was to stop blood loss. As they worked away, Giles noticed Bob's palm and the pus oozing. She could almost smell the rot.

'He needs medical assistance to his leg *and* hand,' said Giles. But her voice was carried into the rain, and nobody responded.

One ambulance officer was calling a code three as Bob, groaning and in agony, was lifted onto a trolley, and they rushed him back towards the emergency vehicle.

Giles grabbed the arm of one of the ambos. 'His palm.'

The medic turned Bob's hand over and grumbled, 'Jesus, this could be a code two. I'm surprised he hasn't gone into septic shock.'

Bob swallowed, and through his blocked and bloody nose, he groaned, 'You should have let them shoot me, detective.'

'No.' Giles jumped into the back of the van beside the patient as they loaded him inside. 'There's been enough death today.'

Bob, almost delirious, sobbed, 'I killed Oliver, didn't I? I heard the sound of it connecting. But he never fell. He took off down the mountain. I don't know what happened to him – honestly I don't, detective. He just vanished. But it was because I whacked him with the rock.'

'Bob, let's look at your hand and leg first. Get you to hospital.'

The confession came fast and thick in a slur of words. 'I know I hurt him. When I struck him with the rock, his cap fell off, and when he scooped down to pick it up, he tumbled forward. I watched him zigzagging down the trail. I know how hard the blow was. I saw him lift his cap, wipe his head with his forearm, and I saw the blood around his ear.'

'Cap?'

The ambulance officer pulled a bag valve mask over Bob's face, while the other officer was pushing her out of the van. 'We've got to move, detective.'

'Just one more second,' snapped Giles. 'Cap,' she repeated. 'What cap?'

'Eh?'

'*What* cap?'

Bob's voice was muffled under the mask, but still clear. 'His favourite. The Cats.'

Giles held up a finger at the ambulance officer; she wanted just a few seconds more. 'You never said anything about a cap when you were first interviewed. And you never said anything about him wearing a cap when you spoke to me.'

The ambulance officer pushed Giles back out of the van and into the rain. 'Detective, you're hindering now, he'll go into cardiac arrest if you keep bloody questioning him.'

Giles yelled through the closing doors, 'Bob! Are you absolutely sure Oliver was wearing a cap?'

'Yeah.' Bob was resolute. 'Uh-huh.'

She snatched the side of the door before it shut and called inside, 'And it was *you* who struck him with the rock.'

'Yeah.'

DAY 10

SIXTY-THREE

The two Sonatas were parked across the road from the post-war red-brick home. All eyes were on the house.

Giles watched a myna bird flutter around the tilted window-sill, pecking at the glass, chasing insects. The ugly mustard curtains were drawn. The front door was locked. No car in the drive, and nobody was answering the landline.

In the front vehicle sat Bray and Callahan. In the car behind were Giles and Edison. Giles wondered if Edison had realised detective work required patience – and a lot of sitting, driving, waiting, and watching. He squirmed in his seat, restless.

'After a while, you learn to control those ants in your pants,' Giles said in jest.

'Oh, I'm just hot. That's all.'

'Not bored?' she asked. 'We've got a Tamagotchi and a Game Boy in the glovebox.'

'Shit, hey? Really?'

'No.'

Edison grinned.

Giles felt her cheek dimple and turned back towards the house. 'I just hope Mrs Lavine doesn't see us and decide to do a runner. It's been a while since I've been in a police pursuit.'

Edison perked up. 'You think she'd bolt?'

Giles looked over at Edison and, though he looked fatigued, there was a gleam of excitement in his eyes. She crinkled her nose at him. 'She already did bolt – to Crookwell.'

Edison's brow twitched and Giles wasn't sure if it was in agreement; or was it a twitch of indecisiveness? She sat back, quashing the small talk, feeling the pressure of being right about her hypothesis.

The team had been waiting for almost an hour for Janet Lavine to return home. The silence was only broken again when Bray called to check in, making sure no-one had fallen asleep after the five-hour drive in scorching heat. Truth was, they were all getting a little bored and restless.

Giles put Bray on loudspeaker, and after they assured him they were fine, he said, 'Good. Then after this, I'll shout you all a dog's eye.'

'If I'm right about this, Bray,' Giles quipped back, 'I expect more than a meat pie for lunch.'

'Long way to come if you're –' Callahan stopped mid-sentence as Janet Lavine turned in to the street in her beat-up Toyota Camry. He added quickly before ending the call, 'Looks like we're closer to having lunch.'

Janet pulled into the drive and the boot popped. Unaware that she was being watched, she climbed out of her car and began lifting grocery bags, sliding the handles onto her arms. Giles could see celery poking out the top of a bag.

She looked down at her bodycam. Switched the BWV on. Once she was back at the station, she'd sort the recording from the body worn video: yellow DVD copy to headquarters, white audio to storage, and blue copy for them.

Giles knew the recording may be relied upon and used as evidence. That is, if her supposition was correct. She swallowed.

Callahan was right. *Long bloody way to come, just to end up filming yourself with egg on your face.*

She fidgeted with the BWV and commenced recording.

'Would you like me to put the kettle on?' Janet asked.

'No. That won't be necessary. Thank you.'

'I take it the DNA results are back?'

Giles shook her head. 'No. Not yet.'

'But you've found something? Or you wouldn't be here.'

Giles pulled a piece of paper from her pocket and handed it to Oliver's mother. The warrant was only to search the property. She had no grounds to make an arrest – yet. And should an arrest be made, Mrs Lavine would need to agree to participate in an interview.

Falkov had been firm. *If an arrest is made: two officers; dedicated police interview room; electronically recorded; video and audio; clear cautioning; don't get your hopes up – she'll probably stay silent until a lawyer arrives.*

'Mrs Lavine, can we sit at the table for a moment?'

Janet looked at Bray by Giles's side, then at Callahan and Edison standing in the hallway. 'Lot of officers for a few questions.'

'That paper is a warrant to search your property.' In the stillness and quiet of the room, Giles's voice sounded out of place. No matter how gently she spoke, she couldn't find the right tone. 'That means you can't decline our officers searching your home.'

'Why would you search my home in Crookwell? Oliver went missing in the Hunter Valley. That's nearly four hundred kilometres away.'

'Do you have a garden shed out back, Mrs Lavine?'

There was a subtle colour change in the woman's face.

~

In the spare room at the back of the home, Bray drew the curtains and Callahan closed the door. Edison had removed the cap from the display cabinet in the lounge-room and was setting up his testing kit on the spare bed.

'If Giles is right about this,' said Callahan, 'then Janet Lavine didn't pack up and move to Crookwell because she thought the case went cold. She moved because she realised she'd gotten away with it.'

'True,' agreed Bray. 'She thought she was in the clear.'

Callahan folded his arms and leaned up against the door. 'Okay, so, if Oliver wore a cap on that day, like Bob said, and this is the same cap stored in her cabinet, then Janet Lavine was the first to arrive at Burning Mountain, not the last.'

'And the last to see Oliver alive,' added Edison.

'Yup,' said Bray. 'Giles thinks Bob never mentioned the cap when he was a kid, because he never wanted the cops to know about the incident between Oliver and Bell, or about him hitting Oliver with a rock. Better to not mention the cap and risk that part of the story slipping out or draw attention to Oliver's head injury.'

'You think, after the first three years, Janet knew the cap wasn't mentioned during the investigation?' asked Callahan.

'Must have,' said Bray. 'The witnesses all gave a description of what Oliver was wearing that day, and there was no cap mentioned in any of the statements. Janet didn't say anything, nor did Bob or the others.'

'What if Janet picked the cap up off the ground when she arrived, but never saw Oliver?' asked Edison.

'Then why not mention it?' asked Bray. 'Why hide it?'

'Didn't want to give it up to the cops?' suggested Edison. 'Wanted to keep it as a reminder? It *was* in the cabinet with the other keepsakes.'

Bray only grunted at the suggestion. 'Yet, if it was covered in blood, and she was responsible, then that's enough incentive not to hand it over.'

'So then she washed the blood off, and kept it as a remembrance,' said Edison.

Bray nodded. 'Possibly.'

'Christ, I hope Giles is right.' Callahan thumped his back against the door. 'It's a long bloody way to come on a hunch, and lots of hurdles to jump through to get a warrant.'

Bray didn't respond. But it was obvious he was thinking the same. He tilted his head towards the bed.

Edison looked down at the cap. In latex gloves, he carefully picked it up and turned the item over. 'If this *is* the cap Oliver was wearing on the day he went missing . . .'

'Then Janet needs to explain how it came to be in her possession?' Bray finished. 'And if there are traces of blood . . . it could match the trauma to the skull.'

Edison lifted the luminol spray and pointed the nozzle at the material. 'This method will pinpoint the location of even the smallest trace of blood. So, fingers crossed for however you wish the result to fall.'

The luminol reagent was squirted. A moment later, it not only showed a positive reaction, but a splatter pattern.

'Undeniable.' Edison looked at Bray. 'Was that the result you were hoping for?'

Bray let out a soft groan. 'Of all the possibilities we'd put up on the crazy board, I felt this would be the most abhorrent.'

The questioned stain was transferred onto a moistened cotton swab and Edison added a drop of testing reductant. Almost immediately it developed in colour.

'I'd say that is a positive identification of blood. Now we just need to determine the origin of it. We have both DNA samples. Now we need to see if all three match back at the lab.'

'Use the other evidence bag. I want to see Mrs Lavine's face when she sees what we have.'

Edison slipped the cap into a clear evidence bag as instructed, and began packing away his equipment. He looked back at Bray. 'Are you going to give Giles the nod?'

Bray stared down at the equipment bag for a moment. He sighed before answering, 'You and I both bloody know that's the cap Oliver wore the day he vanished. However, Janet could have a reasonable explanation. Her lawyer could argue this is a different hat, and blood from a previous accident.'

'So we still can't be sure this is the cap Oliver was actually wearing on the day?' asked Callahan. 'And the actual cap could have been disposed of by now, anyway.'

'And what if he happened to own two caps?' added Edison.

'And had two separate head injuries?' scoffed Bray.

Callahan shrugged. 'It's not me you have to convince. It's the jury.'

'Yeah. That's why I need that bloody shovel. A shovel with matching red paint to build a solid case,' Bray snapped. 'Let's go out back. Have a poke around in the garden shed.'

There is always a moment of smoothing. *Smoothing* . . . that's what Giles called it. When a person on the cusp of getting caught continues to play the game of normal-innocent-civilian. The 'I'm just an ordinary, nice guy . . . this is just a mix up' moment. Janet Lavine was playing that role.

She unreservedly chatted to Giles, understanding that she didn't have to say or do anything she didn't want to. She had waved off the explanation and caution. But it was that murky time in between. The conversation in which it might appear that anything said was 'off the record' but could be used against the accused later down the track. Only seasoned criminals knew it was best not to say anything to officers.

As Janet talked candidly about the day at Burning Mountain, Giles watched the hallway in her peripheral vision – waiting for Edison and Bray to return with an answer – and declined a second offering of tea. Janet was not under arrest, not until Bray had given her confirmation. Giles stroked her arm gently, trying to resist the urge to brush the crumbs off the tablecloth. The waiting was making her tense.

'Banana sandwiches,' said Janet. 'Mashed banana with a sprinkle of raw sugar on fresh white bread. That was the last meal I made Oliver. He loved banana sandwiches.'

Giles only nodded.

'Can't stand bananas now. Not even the smell.' Janet fiddled with the cuffs of her shirt. After a moment she added, 'It was quite the trek up that trail to get to the lookout. I guess I was slower than most hikers. That's why it took so long for me to call the police. I wish I had done it sooner. It may have changed things. But I didn't know until I reached the top that Oliver was gone.'

Giles sat silent. No probing. Just listening. No questions. Short comments (but loaded).

Janet Lavine went on. 'The trail and the lookout at the top are still vivid. Beautiful. I try to think of that when I think of Oliver.'

'Hmm. It is beautiful,' said Giles. 'It's a pity there are no benches to rest on during the walk up. Sit and take in the scenery.'

'Yes,' agreed Janet. 'It would be nice to sit on a bench and look out at the view. Stunning.'

'Hmm . . .' Giles swallowed. 'You never walked up the mountain, did you, Mrs Lavine?'

'Eh? Yes. *Yes.* I searched everywhere for my son.'

'Did you?'

'*Yes.*'

'There *are* bench seats along the trail, Mrs Lavine. You would know that . . . if you walked the trail.'

Janet went quiet. When she saw Bray and Edison entering the room behind her, holding her son's football cap sealed in a plastic bag, she stuttered, 'You, you can't take that.'

'We have a warrant,' Bray reminded her.

'But it's mine. You can't take it. It was my Oliver's.'

Callahan came down the hallway, and as Bray and Edison parted to let him through, he held a large brown paper evidence bag. One hand – still gloved in latex – lifted a child's backpack from the crime bag for Janet to see.

'Mrs Lavine, can you identify this for me?'

Janet groaned. The sound of her throat gurgling, straining, made Giles think for a moment the woman might throw up on the kitchen floor. When Giles looked back at Bray, he gave her a nod, and if she didn't know any better, she could have sworn his eyes were smiling.

Giles watched Janet begin to dissolve in the armchair.

'Mrs Lavine.' Giles stood. She now had the power to arrest under suspicion of murder. But Janet was already crumbling. The cracks of eighteen years were starting to widen.

'Mrs Lavine.' Giles inched closer to the table. 'I'm placing you under arrest for the –'

She was cut off by a guttural sound. Janet's eyes were wild. 'I *loved* that boy. I truly loved him.'

'Mrs Lavine –' Giles started, but Mrs Lavine slapped the table.

'You can't have that hat.'

'Mrs Lavine, I need you –'

'Do you think I hurt my child?' asked Janet.

'Did you?'

'I-I might have hit him.'

'Did you hit Oliver the day he disappeared?'

'A slap, that's all. Just a slap.'

The team was silent, which seemed to only encourage Janet to continue. 'I-I was the first to arrive that day. I was early, not late. I parked the car and waited for the kids to come down the mountain. But then I saw Oliver alone, crying, and I sank in my seat. He cried about bloody everything. Poor grades at school, no talent on the sporting field. He was always complaining that the other kids picked on him. I would tell him all the bloody time to harden up. Life was tough. But he was soft. And when he came down the mountain bawling, I thought, *Here we bloody go again, with the sooking and the whinging and the goddamn whining.*'

'How many times?' Giles asked. 'How hard did you hit him?'

Through her teeth Janet spat, 'I'd had enough of it. Enough of the relentless moaning.'

'Did you hit him often?'

'Only occasionally.'

Janet rolled into herself, wrapped her arms around her waist, head down, and Giles could see the tears fall onto her lap. She would have had no idea that her slap had nothing to do with her son's death. The incident with the rock on top of the mountain was the cause. Oliver's brain would have swelled and that would have eventually killed him. But Janet, who had hit her son so many times, believed she'd finally gone too far.

Janet wiped her tears with the corner of the tablecloth. 'When he got in the car . . . before he could start complaining, I slapped him.

I slapped him harshly and told him to snap out of it. To grow up. Just stop with the bloody bellyaching. I just couldn't listen to it anymore. I couldn't understand why my boy couldn't play with children, go on a bloody hike without falling apart, and always complaining about being picked on. So I hit him. I hit him . . . and his head hit the side window, and he was still – and he never woke up.'

'And the National Park where we found him?'

'I panicked.'

'Panicked?' Giles carefully nudged.

'I drove away from Burning Mountain. Not knowing where to go, I turned up the road in the opposite direction to home. I didn't want anyone to see me and Oliver in the car together. Then I saw the empty camping area, and kept on driving a little further. I found a nice quiet spot. A peaceful spot. And I buried him.'

'With?'

'A shovel.'

'From where?'

'My boot.'

'Why did you have a shovel in your boot, Mrs Lavine?'

'Doubletails. Wrinklewort. Black-eyed Susan.' Janet lifted her head, looking up at the officers. 'I was searching for native plants. But all I could find for my garden were yellow buttons.'

Outside in the sunshine, Giles stood alone on the sandstone path that trailed along the garden bed. She was knackered. Her body ached and she felt weary, wishing she could pull her skin up like a cocoon, snuggle inside herself and close her eyes. She let out a long deep breath to settle the buzzing of her body.

Earlier, after turning the house upside down, Callahan had been disappointed he wasn't able to find the shovel. He'd perked up when he found Oliver's backpack inside an old suitcase squashed into the corner of the shelving of the garage. And was even more bloody delighted when its contents were the same items listed that Oliver had carried on that fateful day – right down to the treats that had never been eaten, only minus the banana sandwiches.

With the evidence collected, Bray and Callahan had already left with Mrs Lavine to Crookwell Police Station, for her to be charged and formally interviewed. Bray had suggested Giles take a breather. Re-centre herself, and when she felt ready, she could meet up with them later. Edison was waiting for her beside the Sonata, respectfully giving her space.

She shuffled backwards on the path, distancing herself, trying to step away from the emotions that were simmering. She desperately tried to shut down her thoughts of Oliver, Janet, Bob, Phil, Paul and Belinda. Of Amy and Joe Thicket. Of Trent Thicket's corpse littered with metal. Of Bernard Nestor and bloody pioneer dolls. Of dead dogs and chickens. And of Jacob Colton and his mother who only wanted justice.

Giles's hands were trembling, and she tucked them under her arms and breathed in deep the floral scent of the garden. It was over. She could finally ring her father and tell him the case had found its ugly end.

As she turned away from the home, she watched the insects hover and zip amongst the white calla lilies, needing the moment to find her poise and allow the sun to fade the ugliness of the day. As she scanned the blossoming hydrangeas, the lavender and agapanthus crammed together, in the English garden-themed flowers she spotted a native plant. She felt her stomach jerk. A jolt of recognition. *Yellow buttons.* Golden like the sunshine.

Giles closed her eyes and pictured them where they had grown at Mount Wingen. She imagined Janet Lavine planting the flowers in the soft and porous soil above her son.

Reparation in buttons of yellow.

DAY 12

SIXTY-FOUR

After squabbling over what tunes should be played on the jukebox, a mix of eighties classics and country won out. Bray had fed the money into the machine. It fired up, and the leadlight tubes rotated, casting a swirl of neon colours on the roof and walls as the music began to play.

At the bar, Carol was filling schooner glasses and Inspector Falkov was giving her instructions regarding the tab.

'Blimey, Walter, I know how to run a bloody bar tab,' Carol huffed. 'I'll give you a wink and a nod when you're close to your cut-off.'

'Yeah, I know.' Falkov slid the first tray of beers off the bar and made his way through the pool room towards the thirsty table.

At the back of the pub, Carol had sectioned off a private table for the team. The banter was relaxed, the mood light. And with enough distance between the team and other patrons, none of them had to worry about anyone listening in.

It was customary for the Crimes Unit to celebrate the closure of a case. It gave a sense of finality and was considered good for camaraderie. The team had been hypervigilant since the discovery of the skull. While they were now engaging in jokes, song and robust conversations, Giles knew by morning they would all be detached, and exhaustion would set in.

Bob Bradbury was recovering in hospital, and Giles had heard that an inquest was underway as to how the bullet was lodged in his thigh. The story of her playing Quick Draw McGraw with her Glock 23 was doing the rounds in the force. Some had named it the matrix shot, while others said it was just a spray-and-pray shot – that landed with luck. However, Falkov had stressed that she was not to worry, and that she might get a nomination for an award when it was all over. Giles had assured him she was happy with just a beer.

The team milled around the table drinking, eating buffalo wings and brisket sliders. Giles could feel the music's beat under her feet, and tried to ease into conversations, but she was struggling with an uneasy feeling, a niggling she found impossible to ignore. Perhaps it was seeing her father at the end of the table. He'd been invited to the celebration because Falkov felt that the officer who'd started the case twenty years earlier deserved a beer or two as well.

Giles had noticed her father hadn't touched the schooner glass. His tremoring hands sat in his lap, fingers tucked between his thighs. She sidled up beside him wondering if he'd not reached for his beer because he feared he'd knock it over or drop it in his lap.

'All good?' Giles asked.

'Yup.' There was a smile on his face. Nostalgia and pride.

She swapped her near-empty schooner for his full glass, then winked. 'Cheers.' She nudged her shoulder against his. 'Do you miss this?'

'Yeah. I do.' Benjamin nodded. 'But this is your team now, Rebecca.'

Her eyes glazed over the men around the table. 'Shame their singing isn't on par with their policing skills,' she said with a smile, then excused herself to help Carol carry over another round of beers.

At the bar Carol grinned at her. 'Glory me! You scrub up alright in a dress.'

Giles felt her cheeks warm. She tilted her head. 'Ta.' Her dress was floral and flowy. Her hair was loose down her back. A touch of make-up, and plenty of perfume. 'Nice to get out of pants and a suit every now and again.'

'Hmm.' Carol smirked. 'Lot of fine-looking men you work with there, Rebecca. If you're searching for a bloke, ever thought about setting your eye on one of them?'

'Nah.' Giles glanced back at the table. 'I don't need a bloke, Carol. I've a whole team of them. Those are the best blokes I could ever wish for.'

'Kudos, girl,' smiled Carol. 'Well, when you lot get sick of sinking beers with the gents, just know I've got a fridge chock-a-block full of colourful sweet shit – on the house.'

Giles screwed up her face, and as she returned to the table with a fresh tray of beers, Falkov stood and tapped his glass with a teaspoon. The team quietened down.

'I'm not going to make a long and boring speech –'

A few cheers from the table.

'The diligence of the investigation has been outstanding. I raise a toast to you all.' Falkov lifted his glass, and the team followed. 'Tonight, I have both good and bad news. But I don't want to kill the mood too quickly, so I'll start with the good news. I just want everyone to know that we were unable to find the shovel. Pity, because it would have been great for forensics to chemically test the sliver of paint found at the gravesite against a shovel; however, nothing was found in Mrs Lavine's shed or home.

'On the bright side, we did find Oliver's backpack, which Paul Cooper has since confirmed was with Oliver on the day. Forensics have said the blood on the cap matches the blood drops on the backpack's straps. Forensics also believe the blood splatter is consist-ent with droplets falling from the boy's temple. Still waiting for the final report.'

There was applause and fist bumps on the table.

Falkov waited for the noise to settle, then continued, 'I know Janet Lavine has confessed, but anything can happen in a court. So, the good news,' Falkov's face looked serious, but not worried, 'the DNA results have come back.'

Giles swallowed. She fleetingly glanced at Bray, who now looked deadly serious.

All eyes were on Falkov. 'The probability of parentage, that Mrs Janet Lavine is a match to the skeletal remains found out at Mount Wingen and is biologically related to the child is . . .' Falkov paused and smiled. 'Ninety-nine point nine nine. They're a match.'

Giles dropped her head as she let out a sharp sob and was instantly grateful that the choke of emotion was drowned by whooping cheers.

'And the bad?' asked Bray. He stood at the back of the table, beer in hand, shirt tight across his torso. His dark brows furrowed. His question silenced the group.

Falkov looked at the beer in his hand and lowered it. 'Bernard Nestor succumbed to his injuries. He passed away at eleven-fifteen this morning.'

DAY 13

SIXTY-FIVE

They had met at the bottom of Burning Mountain in the dark, walked the trail in the fading star- and moonlight, and reached the top in time for the sunrise. At the lookout, Bray and Giles stilled, gazing over the pinkie-white ash and rising smoke below. The first blush of the day was rosy in colour, yet the air was still cool from the drop in temperature overnight.

The hike was Bray's suggestion. *Closure*. Giles had accepted the offer, hoping it would lift the unsettled feeling she still had, her lack of satisfaction at closing the case.

The morning sun now washed them in gold, and Giles's thoughts shifted from Oliver Lavine, a boy whose life span and allotment of misery and suffering she was unable to change, to Joe Thicket.

At the edge of the lookout, Giles frowned. She bent down and scooped up a long curving twig from the ground. When she stood back up, she pressed the tip of the stick into Bray's stomach and let her hand slide down the length of the branch until her thumb and knuckles reached his abdomen. Through his shirt, Giles could feel the warmth of his body. She searched his face.

'You okay?' he asked.

Giles thought of the band-aids wrapped around the fingers of Joe Thicket's right hand. How there was no hand guard on a fruit knife. She thought of all the years the boy had endured with his father, and how they must have taken their toll on him. She knew he had just turned ten – he was not a little child anymore. If her theory was correct, he *could* be prosecuted . . .

'Giles?'

She wondered briefly if Amy didn't return to Nestor's to kill him, but went back to fetch the knife. Then before the idea could fully form and take root, she thought, *Maybe you can have the outcome you wanted.*

'Yeah,' she said, 'I'm fine.' She dropped the twig to the ground and looked out over the sweeping landscape.

'Sure?' asked Bray.

Giles nodded again. 'Yep.'

Her mind drifted to the sacrifices parents make. Of her father sending her off to boarding school to protect her from a predator. She also thought of the things parents do *to* their child. She knew Janet Lavine and Amy Thicket were two very different parents.

'Yeah,' Giles slowly nodded. 'I'm fine, Bray. Thanks.'

A tiny creamy pale weebill, almost colourless with touches of green and brown, landed on the rail beside them. It made a sweet musical call before flying off. They watched it take to the sky, losing sight of it against the pitch of blue, then Marcus Bray and Rebecca Giles turned and made the long and silent walk back down the track of Burning Mountain.

While the sun behind them was now fully ablaze, the trail on their return seemed darker.

ACKNOWLEDGEMENTS

The path of a writer is not necessarily a solo or lonely journey. It's an adventure. When getting out from behind the desk it often leads to surprise twists and directions in an author's personal life that leaves an enriched, deeply rewarding and unexpected experience. Meeting readers, fellow authors, attending festivals, taking field trips, exploring new places and diving into research. None of which I could have predicted when I started this novel on page one. I feel fortunate for the experience.

Thank you to Durham University. I have now proudly hung my Forensic Archaeology and Anthropology Certificate on my wall, yet still take full responsibility for any errors.

To my Penguin Noir mates, Candice Fox, Amanda Hampson, Margaret Hickey, Kerryn Mayne and Benjamin Stevenson. Thank you for your support, encouragement, wisdom and warm welcome to the crime clan. I am honoured to be in your presence and am in awe of you all.

To my work colleagues, thanks for cheering me on. Big high fives to Pat Griffiths, Renee Nieass, Matthew Shanahan, Jo Wheatley, Sofie Batchelor, Brendon Rose, Jodie Spencer, Louise Gohl, Wayne Hackett, Jodie Clough, Tanya Taylor, Dave London, Paige Dowd,

Liz McKenzie, Jenni Beaumont-Hunt, Melissa Ryan, Angela Cherry, and the honey pot – Cassandra Chan.

To Sally Southan for the big eight-legged warm hug and to Jacqueline McCarthy for your beaming smile every time you asked, 'when's the next one out?'.

To my pals who make me laugh until my guts hurt! Joy Bourke, Natasha Vedda, Debbie Girle-Wainkauf, Angela Jean, Julie Judd and Julie Poddock. And my Novocastrian mates, Trudie Lee Tulloh, Leisa Hardman, Billie-Jo Nicholson, Marc (no show) Hayes and Adam Sulter. You make drinking a cocktail an epic event.

Thank you to Melissa Finnerty, Nandini Bhola, Madi Phoenix, Billy Robertson and Natalie Doyle for your sincere pleasure in my work. The joy on your face is the reason.

To my family, as always. I love you.

Thanks, Uncle Ned, who so eloquently shared his military story of the clover leaf and C4. And my brother, Craig, who so ineloquently shared his mining story of flocculant.

Thanks, Dad, for coming along on the road trip to Crookwell and hiking with me to the top of Burning Mountain. You always plot an exploration of the countryside that rivals any navigation system route. My 4x4 and I are grateful for the dusty adventure.

To my editor, Beverley Cousins. You are the best. Thank you for just everything – everything! I will never truly be able to find the perfect word to thank you – because you'll make me find one better xx.

A mammoth thanks to Patrick Mangan for your keen eye for detail; my characters and I are deeply grateful. And – to the amazing team at Penguin Books. You guys really are the dream team! My sincere thanks and gratitude.

A huge thank you to Hunter Writers Centre and Lighthouse Arts for your hospitality and weeklong residency at your amazing location. My stay at the Nobbys-Whibayganba headland site was an incredible and productive experience. The studio space was both refreshing and inspiring, and my work all the richer for the experience.

Thank you to Jason of the NSW Police Force's State Crime Command for once again giving your generous time and patience. And Mel for your uplifting cheer. Again, any mistakes made are mine (because I'm an over-excited-boofhead-with-a-pen).

Oh – and to my son, Ethan. I love you. Thank you for cooking and feeding me while I was busy working. And yes, even when my face is stuck at the computer screen, I'm still listening xx.

Finally, to the town of Muswellbrook and the Upper Hunter Valley for allowing Detective Rebecca Giles to make a mess of things. I promise she won't get it right in the next book either. We are sincerely grateful for your endless country hospitality. All characters and events in this book are fictitious, with a little creative licence in setting – but the sentiment is real.

Last. To Mum. I miss you.

Darcy Tindale is a dramatic arts teacher, actor, author, theatresports player and director. She has appeared in television commercials, film and on stage. She has written comedy for radio, stage, media personalities, comedians and theatre restaurants. Her short stories, plays and poems have been published in anthologies, journals and magazines. Darcy lives in Sydney and has a BA in Creative Writing. Her first novel, *The Fall Between,* was shortlisted for the Davitt Award and Ned Kelly Crime Writing Award for best debut novel. *Burning Mountain* is her second novel in the Detective Rebecca Giles series.